ALL THAT GLITTERS . . .

As a last resort, or perhaps to wipe the smile of satisfaction off Kit's face, Liberty lunged into her bag and brought out the green cloisonné turtle at last. She set it down on the table between them and watched the colour recede from Kit's cheeks. She didn't know what she'd expected to see registered on Kit's face at this moment. Delight that the long-awaited moment had come? The shock of recognition? But what she saw was utter and complete mortification. Slowly Kit began to work her chair away from the table, away from the turtle.

'Get that thing out of my sight!'

Liberty blundered onward. 'There are men who want you dead. Your mother gave me this turtle as some kind of a sign to prove to you that I'm telling you the truth.'

'Stay out of it, Liberty!'

Golden Triple Time

ZOE GARRISON

SPHERE BOOKS LIMITED

First published in Great Britain by
Sidgwick & Jackson Ltd 1985 by arrangement
with Sphere Books Ltd
Copyright © 1985 by Zoe Garrison
Published by Sphere Books Ltd 1986
27 Wright's Lane, London W8 5SW
Reprinted 1986

Set in Plantin

Printed and bound in Great Britain by
Cox & Wyman Ltd, Reading

To our boys – and to each other

With special thanks to Helen and Edite,
for helping us to get the lumps out –
and to Patty, Gogo, and Jane, for loving it even
when it was lumpy.

ZWAR
1938

Forty-five minutes after the New York toast, he jogged up the moonlit path to the house on his father's compound. She opened the door and pulled him inside.

His mouth fell open. Her naked body beckoned to him beneath shifting layers of silk.

'No one saw me.' His eyes lingered on the dark tips of her breasts. Her black hair shone reddish. She was almost as dark as the native Arab women.

'Good,' she smiled. She placed her hands alongside his face. 'You poor boy. Come sit down.'

A large hammered-brass hookah stood before banked cushions. It was loaded and ready to be lit. He gawked at it. 'Mother never lets me smoke hashish. She says it makes you sterile.'

'Your mother's been in the desert too long.' She sat him down. 'Here.' She snaked the hose between his lips and lit the pipe with a taper from a small iron stove. 'Just suck in and breathe out. It will calm you. You're too nervous now to take instruction.'

He did as he was told, breathing deeply. As the hookah bubbled, funny tastes mingled in his mouth, now tar, now perfume. He looked at her and shrugged.

'Don't worry. Soon you'll feel it.'

After what seemed the longest time, she leaned to rest a cool hand on his shoulder. She held a bowl of water and a sponge.

'But I had a bath!' All the same, he didn't struggle as she took off his shoes, pulled off his trousers and socks, yanked his shirt over his head.

'Did anybody ever tell you you're strong for a woman?'

She began to sponge him with aloe-scented water, and as she did, she told him a story.

'When I was a young girl about your age, living in Paris, your father let me take dancing lessons from the most celebrated master in all of Europe. He was very strict with me. He used to berate me so fiercely!

1

But I bore it in silence – I knew that as soon as the class was over and the other students had left, he would make it all up to me.

'First, he would have me take off my shift and my tights. Only when I was naked could he determine whether I was doing the positions properly, or so he said. He would put me through the barre routine all over again: the pliés, the rondes de jambes, and then I was to rest my leg on the barre. He came up behind me then, and, never taking his eyes off me in the mirror, directed me to turn my leg yet farther out until my body was totally open to the mirror, and to both of our eyes. He would take me from behind, and all the while I was to remain perfectly still in position, while he moved in and out of me. He was the dancer now. Just as the pleasure was so great I thought I would explode, he would begin to strum me with his hand and to whisper in my ear, asking me how it felt to be made love to by him. As he fixed my eyes in the mirror with his, he forced me to tell him how he made me feel with his every thrust, until I'd flush scarlet, and cry out my pleasure to my own reflection.'

Before he knew it, he had expended his own pleasure. He apologised.

'Nonsense,' she said, sponging off his belly. 'I intended that to happen.'

He lay back gratefully on the pillow while she resuscitated him with yet another hoseful of hashish. Then she left him.

A few minutes later she returned, holding a peach. He stared at the two halves she held out to him, baffled.

'Thank you very much,' he said, 'I'm not really very –'

'Of course you're not. That's not the point. Now, bite into it.' She stuffed one half into his mouth and held it there. He practically choked.

'Eat it!' she commanded. 'And don't forget to breathe while you eat or you'll smother.'

He felt the juices dripping down his chin and reached a hand up to wipe them away. She slapped him.

'Don't worry about being messy. Just eat and feel your tongue at work. Concentrate!'

She seemed suddenly enormous to him as she moved over his head and straddled him. Then he realised where she had buried the other half of the peach. 'Finish it,' she called out from somewhere above him, and he took hold of her legs and began to eat the second half, until the peach was all gone and more than peach juice ran down his chin. He was sucking, licking, feeling her body lurch and shudder above him, borne on by forces more powerful than either of them. She shuddered again, and he felt her legs give way. He lowered her onto the cushions beneath him as she regained her senses and began to talk to him.

2

'It can happen again, if you flick your tongue, my golden-haired boy, and don't stop, whatever you do. Oh, please don't stop. You mustn't stop.' He went on until he felt that his tongue would stiffen and fall out by the roots, and then he took over with his chin, as she instructed him in a high, faraway voice. *'Gently, my boy, gently. Always remember to use the beard to give pleasure, not to burn.'* And then, when his neck got stiff, he nuzzled her with his nose, until his tongue was rested enough to take over the main labour once again. And all the while, his fingers never gave up their exploration of the inside of her body, groping their way along those mysterious walls. And where the walls quaked, there his fingers would linger until she bucked beneath him with a force that threw him off. Then he'd re-establish his grip on her slippery body, and she would assure him he'd learned his lesson very, very well.

Then suddenly it was as if he had become the teacher and she was now the meek student. He took her in his arms and carried her over to the carpet bed and, lying down, he lowered her onto himself. She wrapped her legs around him and held on while he moved her body on and off him as if she were a doll and he some great boy desperate to satisfy himself. As dawn lightened the billowing silks, he left her sprawled out on the cushions.

He followed her around like a puppy for the next two weeks. The last thing he wanted was to go back to school in America.

'There's going to be a war. Father says I may not be returning here until it's over. It could take years!'

'That's just as well. America's the place for you.'

'But I want to stay here. My place is with you now.' He dug the toe of his shoe into the sand and kicked clouds of it towards the water. The sun on the Persian Gulf almost blinded him. He felt tears at the back of his eyes.

She laughed, tousling his hair. *'You are a fine young man. You'll find girls in America.'*

'I don't want American girls. I want you.'

'You say that now. But in time, you'll realise that I'm right.'

On the day he was to leave, he came to her. *'Will you write to me?'*

'Only if you write to tell me about your American girlfriends.'

'Just wait. When I'm rich, I'll come back and build you a palace for your sculpture.'

'I don't need a palace!' she laughed. *'I need peace and quiet . . .*

which I shall have as soon as you're out of my hair. Now, go or you'll miss your boat.'

He looked so pitiful standing there in his school blazer, holding his tennis racket, that her heart softened. She went to her jewellery box and brought back a small green cloisonné turtle with sapphire eyes.

'Your eyes are the same colour. Keep it to remember me by.'

The war held off and he was permitted to come home for the summer break. But the carpets, pillows, and silks had all been swept aside. She sat in a pair of men's trousers, sketching a naked Arab boy who squatted on a dusky wooden platform. A pair of men's suspenders crisscrossed above her small, round belly. She was with child!

He knelt eagerly beside her, looking up into her stern face, willing her to remember that night.

'I was counting on the war to keep you away from here.' She kept her eyes on the Arab boy and her hand on the stub of charcoal, scraping away at the coarse grey paper.

'How could I stay away from you? From both of you?'

She shut her eyes and stopped sketching. 'There is no kind way to put this. The child has nothing to do with you.'

'I don't understand.'

'What's to understand?' She turned blazing eyes upon him. 'The child is not yours. Now, leave me to my work!'

He fled the guesthouse. Later, he overheard his parents talking.

'They say the father is the boy who models for her. The emir's son. The emir is most unhappy.'

So was his father, to judge by his voice.

'Then turn her out! Send her back to Paris – there such behaviour is common enough.' His mother's voice was harsh.

'You're asking me the impossible! She's my sister, my only blood aside from my son . . . she's my sister' – his voice broke – 'even if she is a whore!'

He could not stand to listen to any more. They were lying. He ran back to her. The Arab boy was just getting into his clothes.

'Why bother to dress, you stinking bastard! Where do you think you're going?' he yelled.

The emir's son tried to leave, but each time the other boy blocked him.

'Are you afraid to stay and fight me?'

Throwing down his shirt, the Arab boy drew a knife. The two began to circle each other.

She shouted, 'Take your childish brawling out of here, away from my work! Out of my sight, both of you!'

Eyeing each other warily, they backed into the courtyard.

She pinned the charcoal sketch onto a board, then followed them outside.

The servants stood around them in a circle, egging them on as they rolled and wrestled in a sweaty patch of sand. They were so coated with sand she could tell them apart only by the colour of their eyes. One of them was wounded; his blood dripped onto the sand, turning it pink. Finally the white boy's father charged over from the house with a riding crop and pulled them apart, taking his son away.

The emir's people came to claim the wounded boy. They muttered in Arabic as they hoisted him onto a litter, but she scarcely heard them. All she could hear was the white boy's curse:

'I hope it's born with two heads, you filthy whore!' He ran back and flung the cloisonné turtle at her feet.

It took her a week to get back to work. On the day she learned that the emir's son had died of wounds sustained in the fight, the emir called her to him.

'Madame,' the emir commanded. 'When you first came here, I was intrigued by you. Even though you were European, I offered your brother fifty camels in payment for you. He told me I would not want such a devil among my wives. Is this how Allah punished me for desiring you?' His dark eyes fell sadly on her. 'Tell me where the young white devil is.'

He repeated the command in Arabic. The grey-bearded men who sat around him bobbed their heads and sucked on their hookahs. The guards standing behind her placed their hands on the hilts of their knives.

'It was an accident!' she cried.

'My boy is dead!' he bellowed. 'Murdered! How dare you call it an accident. Harlot!'

'Kill me instead!' The offer was on her lips before she knew it.

He smiled slowly. 'Kill you instead? Why should I do that? You may carry my dead son's seed.' He stroked his beard, nodding at her belly. 'What would you do to persuade me to spare him? They say you are a woman who uses her hands. Will you lose one to spare him?'

She spat at him.

'Very well, then.' He frowned. 'My men will find him, whether you help me or not.' He nodded and his men sprang to search her lodgings.

'Wait!' she called out.

He held up his arm; the men froze.

'What if I were to cut off a breast instead?'

He frowned, considering. Then he began to smile. With a flip of his hand, his men surrounded her. One pinned her arms behind her, another stipped her to the waist. A third drew his knife.

She stared at the knife. 'You must promise to spare his life if I make this sacrifice.'

'I promise.'

'Then I will do it myself. Give me the knife.'

The man who held the knife stared at her.

'Give it to her!' the emir shouted.

It was curved and luminous, like the crescent moon. She drew a deep breath, placed the knife beneath the fold of her right breast, and drew it across her chest towards her throat. She was thankful for its sharpness, for its coolness on her flesh before the burning set in. The baby inside her stopped moving. She swooned.

They jerked her head back by the hair. Her white shirt, which they had tied around her chest, was bright with blood.

'I promised that he would be spared. And so he will be. But this' – he pointed to the gory shirt – 'this is not nearly enough to appease me. I will have my vengeance. My children will mark his children and kill them, one by one. And should you ever reveal my plan to him – or to anyone else – I will kill you both.' He turned his back. 'Now, get out of my sight. Go back to your harlot's nest, and may Allah forgive me for showing you such mercy.'

She dragged herself back to the guesthouse, where she bound her breast, and waited for the baby to fall dead from her body.

Four months later, she bore a beautiful, healthy daughter. She named it after herself, for the child would never have a father.

NEW YORK CITY
October 1983

1

Kit Ransome climbed out of the belly of the overnight plane and walked up the carpeted ramp towards the gate. As she passed into the terminal and looked around for her driver, a barrage of flashbulbs exploded in her face, blinding her.

A lone, stubby little man with a motor-back Nikon, wearing plaids the colour of baseball-park mustard and a tie two inches too short, faced her. Jackie O might have Ron Galella, but Kit Ransome had Arnold Blatsky, first-string reporter for a particularly grisly little tabloid.

She suppressed a shudder.

He smiled at her, tongue snaking through the gap in his teeth. Kit Ransome, late, had arrived nevertheless. FEM STUDIO CHIEF HITS GOTHAM TO POWWOW WITH GREAT WHITE FATHER.

'Welcome to the Big Apple, Miss Ransome. Let me help you with –'

She shoved him away with her garment bag and made for the exit, but he beetled along behind her.

'They say you and your lover-boy are going into permanent golden time on *Last Chance*. Any truth to that?'

Kit cursed her high heels, her tight skirt. She'd give anything to be able to break into a run and lose this creep.

'They say *Last Chance* is the biggest tearjerker since *I'll Cry Tomorrow*. A real box of Kleenex. Any truth to that?'

A porter appeared out of nowhere, wheeling his cart towards them. Kit raised her briefcase to signal him. Blatsky grabbed Kit's garment bag. Kit tugged it back. The porter spun his cart and caught Blatsky directly across the shins. He staggered backwards against the wall, swearing.

Tipping his cap, the man turned to Kit. 'Can I help you, ma'am?'

'You already have.' Kit smiled, surrendering her bags to him. Leaving his cart by the still-agonized Blatsky, the porter led her through a side door marked 'Private: Airport Employees Only', down a long, steep concrete incline and out onto the lower ramp of Kennedy Airport.

Kit spied the white limousine standing several doors down.

'There's my car,' she told the man.

The porter nodded. Putting down her bags, he placed his fingers between his teeth and whistled. Kit protected her ears.

'Sorry, ma'am,' the man apologised, 'but your little friend's gonna recover any minute now. And when he does...'

The Mercedes backed up and her boss's personal driver hopped out, apologising for being late. Kit slid gratefully onto the soft white leather seat.

'Good morning, Devin. Thanks for coming.'

Devin Lowe, a sandy-haired young man from the New York production office, kissed her on the cheek and squeezed her hand. 'You poor thing,' he said. 'Circling all that time?'

'No,' she sighed. 'We sat on the runway at LAX for two hours.'

Devin tapped her knee. 'Don't look now, but you've got company.'

Kit turned and found the porter's face pressed to the window glass. He stood back, swept off his cap, and laid it over his heart.

'Want me to get rid of him?' Devin asked.

'No, that's all right. He rescued me from Blatsky.' She rolled down the window and reached into her purse for a ten-dollar bill.

He waved it away. 'My pleasure, Miss Ransome. I just wanted you to know that you were always my favourite. Hollywood made a big mistake when they let you go. You should have got an Oscar for *Enchanted Sloop*.'

Looking at him, Kit could just picture him in one of the second-string houses where *Sloop* played on its first run twenty-two years ago. He would have been a young man then. She smiled. 'Oh, I don't know. I think they've made bigger mistakes in their day.'

'May I have your autograph, Miss Ransome?'

His hand trembled as he accepted the slip of paper.

As the car sped up the ramp, Devin said, 'I saw it, but I don't believe it.'

Kit looked hard at the young man. Of course he'd have trouble believing she'd ever been anything other than what she was now – a studio executive. He had probably been all of six years old when Kit made her last picture.

'I haven't seen it with my own eyes, mind you, but they say your VP Distribution has a picture of you on the wall of his office,' said Devin. 'One of the old Centurion Pictures Pinups.'

Kit smiled tightly. 'There's Randy Sheridan for you. God, but I'd love to get my hands on those prints. I'd make a giant bonfire and burn every last one of them. Shall we get on with it, Dev? This meeting won't be easy. I've made some notes. Here, why don't you read them first? Then we'll organise your assault.'

As he studied the canary-coloured index cards, Kit reached for the phone and found that her palms, which had remained dry on the flight from LA, were sweating now. A female voice answered the direct line to Archer Ransome's office.

'Hi,' said Kit.

'Oh, hi!' said Susie, Archer's secretary. 'We wondered where you were!'

'We were on the runway for nearly two hours.'

'I figured as much. Listen, don't worry. I'm counting on the meeting running over. Something's up with Rush.'

Something was always up with Rush Alexander: Archer's partner and closest friend. She only hoped Rush's meeting wouldn't bump hers.

'Okay, see you in an hour.' Kit hung up.

Kit imagined the metal suitcase riding in the boot behind her, holding the cans of film. Two cans of film: thirty minutes. Rough cut, black and white. The fruits of only the first two months of shooting; yet, right now, they meant everything. In her mind she saw the typed labels on the cans, 'Arm-wrestling scene, *Last Chance*'. She sighed and leaned back, trying to remain calm. Everybody in the industry was saying this might be Kit's last chance too.

She remembered the headline in last Friday's *Daily Variety*, '"LAST CHANCE" FACING EUTHANASIA OR GOLDEN TIME?'

Golden time – triple overtime – that phenomenon that occurred when a movie fell behind schedule, that giddy, hyper-real zone you entered when everybody from the leading lady's hairdresser to the leading man's double worked all day long and half the night to finish the movie. It was the studio's worst fiscal nightmare, and Kit was heading for it with her eyes wide open. She was in town to beg for the gold she'd need to finish *Last Chance* – two and a half million dollars. The only problem was that she dreaded dealing with her cousin. Six months ago, when she decided to make Herman Miller's best-seller into a feature movie, Archer Ransome had been cool, sceptical. Now she had to convince him not to sell out for the insurance money just because the ingénue, Monette Novak, had died on the set. *Last Chance* had to be completed at Horizon: damn Archer Ransome and his SEC difficulties.

Devin put his hand on hers. 'Kit, this is pretty powerful stuff. I agree with you one hundred percent, but do you think our director friend is gonna take it from me? From you, it's one thing, but from me...?'

'You're representing Horizon, Devin, don't worry. Be gentle and tactful: we are respectfully suggesting that he'll have a better picture if he makes the following changes.'

'And if he doesn't make them?'

Kit looked out the window. 'Then we'll drop the project.'

'Universal's more than willing to pick it up.'

'Fine,' Kit said mildly. 'Universal's welcome to it as it stands now. I wouldn't be a bit surprised if they were to shoot it as is. And their accountants, believe me, will be crying into their red ink. Now, Devin, shall we take it from the top?'

Devin made ready to jot down some notes.

While she talked, she got out her compact to look for the damage done by the overnight flight. Was it still true, she wondered, what they said about her? That at forty-five she still looked like the twenty-five-year-old starlet over whom the *Hollywood Reporter* had oozed: '... fabulously feline ... upturned velvety nose ... slow-blinking green eyes ... a perfect symmetry of features ... like some species of swimming cat'?

The swimming cat was out of the water now, high and dry behind a big desk: the head of a motion-picture studio. But the cat image had followed her.

'Cat Woman', they called her. 'Kitty Cat' even in the business columns. 'Lapping up brandy with Paul Newman at the Polo Lounge last night was none other than the Cat, looking as if they'd just shared a canary.'

'Point number five?' Devin prodded her gently.

She made sure her black hair was still tight in its bun and snapped the compact shut. 'Point number five: the suspense has to be introduced earlier than halfway through the second act, or the audience will be snoring.'

Devin paused. 'You really want me to say "snoring"?'

She smiled tolerantly. 'Of course not, Devin. Just say that the suspense is so excellent it ought to be sustained over a longer period of time.'

Devin nodded, looking dismayed. 'You're so good at being subtle, Kit. I don't do a very good subtle. Either I'm pushy or I'm defensive. I'm really afraid of rubbing Watkins the wrong way. He's sitting on three Oscars, for crying out loud. And two out of three were my favourite movies in high school.'

'Don't worry.' She patted his wrist. 'His last four movies didn't make three cents at the box office. He'll listen to us. He may not agree, but he'll listen. He'll take our little laundry list away with him and think about it, and come back with a list of his own.'

'It's like a labour negotiation,' said Devin.

'Precisely,' said Kit. 'We're management, and they're labour, however high-priced. Don't ever forget that.'

'I still wish you were going to be there.'

'I can't. I have to talk to Archer. Before I do anything, I have to show him the *Last Chance* footage.'

Devin looked sympathetic. '*I* think *I* have it bad, right?'

'I am not looking forward to this meeting. Hah! What am I saying! I'm not looking forward to this entire trip! Once I get *this* out of my way, *if* I get it out of my way and he doesn't just shut us down, I get to go look for the Lacy replacement.'

The Lacy Replacement. It sounded like a Robert Ludlum novel.

'It won't be easy,' Devin said.

Kit was getting tired of hearing that Monette Novak couldn't be replaced.

'You'd think Ransome'd give you a break,' said Devin. 'You being his cousin and all.'

'Family,' said Kit, staring at the strobing lights of the Midtown Tunnel, 'has never meant very much to Archer Ransome.'

A week and a half of rain and mudslides had paralysed LA the day Archer Ransome came, the day Ransome Enterprises acquired Horizon Pictures. He showed up on the lot, unheralded, going from wardrobe building to directors' bungalows to commissary. He shook hands with every script boy and girl, every extra, every wardrobe mistress, and every assistant director he came across. By the time he walked into Kit's office, the studio was abuzz with talk of the good times that lay ahead now. But Kit was ready for him.

'It appears, cousin, you have charmed the collective pants off the lot.'

He closed the door behind him, unsmiling. 'I have only a couple of hours before I move on to the Far East. I wanted you to hear it from me first. There'll be some immediate changes made here.'

Kit pushed herself back from her desk. 'Immediate changes?' she echoed coldly.

He began to pace the perimeter of her airy office, hardly noticing, as he passed the one wall of tinted windows, the spectacular view of the entire lot.

'This studio, Kit, has been dripping red for five years running. It will shoot back into the black next year.'

'Cousin,' she said softly, 'when I came here from Warner Brothers six months ago to take this job, it was precisely to embrace the challenge of turning the studio around. It was my impression that I'd be given the time and the backup to do it.'

'Impressions can be misleading, Kit, and management changes. If it's security you want, you're in the wrong business.'

'I'm in the *right* business, cousin,' she shot back. She went on more gently. 'All I want is an opportunity, Archer, to realise my plan. My plan – surely you've read my plan?' Kit hesitated and smiled, not very warmly. 'My plan calls for two and a half years.'

She watched as he examined the framed posters on her walls, her favourite old movies – *The Red Shoes, Double Indemnity, Jules et Jim, The Letter*.

When he spoke, it was as if she'd never opened her mouth. 'We will turn a profit next year. Towards that end, I am terminating forty percent of middle and upper management. I've decided to bring in Crawford from BK/Eagle Studio. At this very minute, he's drafting a trim but tough team –'

'Isn't that redundant? Bringing in Crawford when I'm already here? Besides, Crawford and I don't mesh.'

'That's just it, Kit. You won't be here.'

His words knocked the wind out of her. 'I have a contract.'

'Surely, Kit, you don't think I'd let paper stand in my way.'

'Surely, Archer, you don't want to turn over an already shaky studio to the man who just invested thirty-six million dollars in a totally uncommercial property?'

Kit took a sip of cold coffee, savouring her first small gain over her cousin.

'The word is out,' she went on. 'It will be in the trades tomorrow. But I'll be happy to give a sneak preview right now.'

Ransome sat down on the other side of her desk.

'It seems that Mr Crawford had stars in his eyes when he signed a certain actor hot off his Academy Award-winning Viet Chic flick. And, of course, as everyone knows, when you sign the little soldier, you sign his wife as producer. Of course, everyone also knows she couldn't produce a muffler commercial, much less a feature-length movie. Well, not only was Mr Crawford too busy to visit the set in Wyoming, he assigned some greenhorn production exec – you know the type, a reader one day, and the next...' She paused pointedly. 'You do know the type, Archer? Or maybe you don't.

'Anyway, this greenhorn, instead of keeping his eye on the bottom line, was keeping his eye on the bottom of the DP – that's director of photography, Archer. You might as well start picking up the lingo right now. Just last week the head of Sales dropped by and sat right where you're sitting now and told me that the exhibitors were saying that BK would need the National Guard to make people watch that western.'

Archer said, 'So? The man made a mistake.'

'The man made a big, expensive mistake, Archer.'

'You know as well as I do, Kit, that this business is a crapshoot.'

Now she had him.

'All right, Archer, then let's gamble. Give me two years. If Horizon continues to lose money, I'll quit. I will have worked for you for free. If, on the other hand, it makes money, I stay, and I get a percentage of the profits.'

The next Friday, seventy-three employees of Horizon Pictures found pink slips on their desks, along with their invitations to the annual studio Christmas party. The line in the *Hollywood Reporter* ran: 'MACHINE-GUN KITTY MASSACRES HORIZON.'

Kit walked through the solarium to Susie Shultebrandt's mahogany-panelled office.

'Hello, Kit. You look like you could use some coffee,' Susie said. 'Sit down, Mr Ransome's on the phone.'

Sipping coffee, Kit stared at the lithograph of a seashell on the wall behind Susie's desk, and a memory suddenly overwhelmed her. She remembered lying in the cool sand at the foot of her beach stairs, staring up at the stars, Brendan's breath hot between her bare legs as he whispered: 'You're beautiful ... like the inside of a seashell'.

The white door to Ransome's office slid open, bringing her back to the present. Kit went in. Even though she had seen her cousin hundreds of times, as he came towards her she was struck by how vital, how dashingly handsome he was. All at once she felt dull, drained, exhausted.

'Hello, Kit.'

'Archer.' She went to embrace him with both arms, but he put a hand on her shoulder and, kissing her on both cheeks, sat her down on the couch. Sitting down next to her, he lit up the ever-present black cigarette, inhaling as Kit faced his incredible clear blue eyes.

'You look marvellous, Kit,' he said quietly. 'Still swimming?'

Kit concentrated on the rim of her cup as she spoke. 'Every day. I try to take fifty minutes in the morning before work, but since *Last Chance* ... Lately, I've been going up the coast, and more and more, I wind up swimming evenings, at sunset. It's energising, really.'

He was silent. She went on. 'I've got some of my best ideas swimming. There's a sort of magic that takes over my mind.'

'Speaking of magic,' he broke in, 'I hope you're not far off where *Last Chance* is concerned.'

Kit recoiled. 'I'm not,' she said curtly.

'I certainly hope not, Kit. Should you be so confident? What about that weak third act?'

She narrowed her eyes at him. 'It was a great book, and it will be a great movie.'

'That doesn't answer my question.'

'The third act isn't weak, Archer, and I think it will play well.'

Archer looked doubtful. 'The way it's written now, the violence – which was really a very important part of the book – has been minimised. It's lost its drama. Talking heads, Kit. Twenty minutes of talking heads.'

'Actually it plays in ten minutes, and close-ups don't necessarily minimise drama. I think ...' She corrected herself: 'I *know* the public has had it with graphic violence for the time being. This isn't *The Godfather*, and Jay Scott isn't Francis Ford Coppola.'

'I only wish he were.'

14

Kit eyed him in disappointment. 'Really, Archer, that's not fair.'

'Kit, Kit, Kit.' Archer shook his head sadly. 'Asking for fair . . .' He dragged deeply on his cigarette. 'What I am suggesting is that since you've had to suspend production anyway to recast the Lacy role –'

'So that's why you brought me here!' Kit rose from the couch. 'You didn't call me here to run this dog-and-pony show with the footage. You couldn't care less about the footage. You want a sacrifice, don't you? You want me to fire Scottie. Well, I won't do it. He's brilliant. You should see how he works with the actors. It's electrifying! You can see it in the footage. No,' she said, bristling, her eyes closing to slits, 'Jay Scott stays.'

Archer stared up at her for so long that Kit blushed.

'Sit down, Kit. No one said anything about firing Mr Scott. I wouldn't dream of suggesting that you fire your director.'

Kit sank back down on the couch, still wary.

'Especially when you have all those other problems to grapple with. There's the recasting, for one. That poor girl overdosing right on the set.'

Kit winced.

'I've been reading the clippings, Kit. I can't remember when I've read quite so many production horror stories.' He paused, tapping another black cigarette against his thumbnail.

Kit watched while he lit it with his ivory lighter and took the first deep drag that usually signalled a fresh assault. 'It would be all right,' he continued, 'if things were shaky and they were writing about a six-million-dollar movie. That would be one thing. But they're not, Kit. You know how much money this movie is costing us. Can you honestly say that you're protecting our investment?'

'I can't be responsible for what the press writes.'

'You *are* responsible,' he cut in. 'You're responsible for everything connected with the making of this picture. And all other Horizon pictures. The investment, Kit, think of the investment!'

She shook her head at him. 'I thought you'd be the last person to talk that way. Movies aren't toothpaste, regardless of what your numbers people might tell you.'

Archer ignored her. 'I think you made your biggest error of judgment up front, if you'll forgive me saying so. Against everyone's better judgment, against your own staff's better judgment,' he added meaningfully, 'you cast a has-been actor in the lead.'

'Now, wait just a minute.' Again Kit began to rise. Archer put his hand on her arm to hold her down.

'Face it, Kit, everyone knows Brendan Marsh is washed up.'

'Just because the man can't always judge a script doesn't mean he's forgotten how to act! Think about it, Archer,' she reasoned. 'If people hadn't given Brando a chance, *The Godfather* would have been a different movie – *a lesser one*.'

Ransome persisted. 'The industry never lost all respect for Brando.'

'Come on, Archer,' Kit spat out, 'what's all this "industry" talk all of a sudden? Do you know what the "industry" is? A bunch of people who go to free screenings and throw mental popcorn at the screen. Then after their expense-account dinners, they sit around the coke dish and trash the craft.' Kit finished on her feet.

Archer looked up at her and said patiently, 'I'm concerned, Kit, that you are spending an inordinate amount of your time on *Last Chance*. The studio can't run itself, you know.'

Kit walked over to a bowl of hothouse peonies and fingered their soft petals. 'The way you talk, it sounds as if every other project – investment – were falling apart at the expense of *Last Chance*, and that's simply not true.'

She looked up and widened her eyes at him. 'In fact, we've just had a tremendously successful sneak preview of *Phoenix Waltz* in San Diego. And we're going to sneak it again in Toronto Thursday night. *Straight Flush* has been screening well, and we're going to have some good quotes to open with Thursday. And,' she said, returning to the couch, saving the best for last, 'I was able to set up the Redford project that Warner's has been trying to put together for months.'

'You're having an affair with Brendan Marsh,' he said.

Kit stared at him. She didn't know what to say. She only knew that she couldn't discuss it here, now, with Archer.

'You're having an affair,' he went on mercilessly, 'that's had more coverage than all your features put together. You're having an affair with the man who has closed more bars on Sunset than . . . He's a notorious lush, Kit, and a womaniser.'

'He doesn't drink any more and he's as harmless as a baby,' Kit's voice quavered.

'They say he's showed up on the set drunk.'

'That's not true!' Kit lashed out. Then, more calmly, 'How dare you believe that? And besides,' she pressed on, 'Brendan's drinking is not what's at issue here, is it? What's at issue here is that because I'm a woman I'm somehow not supposed to act the way men do in my position. That's it, isn't it?'

'You're having a public affair.' He jabbed the air with his black cigarette. 'That's unprofessional, Kit, and *that* is the issue.'

She wasn't surprised he hadn't heard yet. Kit guessed it hadn't hit the East Coast gossip columns yet. How had the LA columnists put it? 'KITTY AND TOMCAT CALL IT QUITS IN ALLEY SCRAP'.

Actually, they'd called it quits in August, almost two months ago. But the press had been too high on their romance to believe it was over. Then they had got distracted by Monette Novak's death and the threat to *Last Chance*. Now they were coming back to pick at the old bones. Funny, until she saw it in cold print, she hadn't really believed it herself. She couldn't take her eyes off the white carpet. She was thinking: If I don't look up, I won't cry.

'I might as well tell you now.' Her voice was tight, unrecognisable. Would she lose control? She forced herself to sound normal. 'It'll be in the papers tonight, no doubt. It's over. It's finished. Brendan Marsh and I aren't seeing each other any more. Now, are you satisfied?'

As soon as the words were out, Kit felt released from the threat of tears. She lifted her eyes from the carpet and met Ransome's steady gaze. 'I've brought you the footage of *Last Chance*. Shall we go downstairs and take a look at it?'

Ransome's screening room bore the unmistakable stamp of his taste. Twelve black suede Barcalounges were scattered before a fifty-foot screen. The black suede walls seemed to recede as the lights dimmed. She pushed the intercom on the arm of her chair and asked Frank, the projectionist, to start.

'I'll control the volume from here, Frank, thanks.'

After a moment of white light, Brendan Marsh's unshaved fifty-six-year-old face filled the screen. Kit's throat contracted involuntarily. She stopped thinking about the stony-faced man who sat beside her. In the scene, Brendan had been crying. How dear, how familiar that face was to her. Was she still impartial enough to judge the film? To see when a retake was necessary? To argue a medium shot was better than an extreme close-up?

The camera revealed Brendan and a young boy of about seventeen. The angle was wildly skewed, almost Hitchcockian.

The effect was disorienting, but pleasant: pure movie.

The setting was the interior of a suburban house. Althea Talbot, who had done the sets for nearly fifty films, had really outdone herself here. With a slew of carefully chosen props, the set evoked the tired, well-worn ambience of an American family room: bullfight posters, old skis, soda cans, macaroni mosaics yellowing on the wall, basketballs with the air let out. The camera began a slow zoom towards the boy, who was slowly and deliberately unbuttoning and rolling up the sleeves of his checked flannel shirt. He smoothed his hair back behind an ear.

Smoothing his hair back? What was that doing in there? She'd inspected every frame of this footage, or so she thought. But, yes, now she remembered: they had decided to keep that slightly effeminate, all too real gesture of a scared boy squaring off, for the first time, against his father.

Before Kit knew it, she was no longer the picky technician, no longer the anxious studio executive. She was a woman watching a movie. She was a woman watching the man she had fallen desperately, incredibly in love with.

It had been, in a funny kind of way, like they say in the movies, love at first sight.

Kit had never worked with Brendan Marsh. Yet from the moment she had read *Last Chance*, she had wanted him for the part of Judd Hines.

As she waited to be let in the door of a modest borderline Beverly Hills ranch house, Kit reread in her mind the telex Archer had sent from India: 'Grave doubts Marsh is our man. Insist on test'.

Kit smiled. Archer had to be kidding. Everybody knew that the indignity of a screen test had ceased after everyone from Lana Turner to Bette Davis had to audition for Scarlett O'Hara. Either Archer didn't know that or he didn't care.

Jay Scott set up the meeting. A graduate of USC's film school, he had cut his creative teeth on breath-mint commercials. Then he learned the lesson of a few retakes and no exceeding the budget on some unusually distinguished made-for-TV movies. Jay's senior dissertation, under his own direction, became the sixth biggest grosser of all time and, at the ripe old age of twenty-six, Jay Scott found himself besieged by ambitious studio execs who figured the kid had the Midas touch and they better get him before he burned out at twenty-nine.

Kit didn't have to woo Scott. *He* pursued *her*. He begged her to let him direct *Last Chance*.

'Scottie's in the den with Mr Marsh!' whispered the breathless young thing who finally answered Kit's eighth ring.

The den was dark, except for the light from a small reading lamp next to a wing chair in one corner opposite the sliding doors to the patio. Before Kit could accustom her eyes to the gloom, dapper Jay Scott jumped out of the shadows.

'The lady has arrived!' he cried, with a clap of his hands. 'You look cool as ever, Kit. Just out of the sea, no doubt? Did I tell you, Brendan, she's still a swimmer? Only person I know who swims in May.'

Kit went to kiss his cheek and to whisper something in his ear, but he pulled her over to meet Marsh.

Marsh was in the wing chair, reading. He put aside a *Last Chance* script, swept off his glasses, and rose to meet Kit.

'Why, you look more beautiful than you did in *Sloop*. How many years ago did you make that picture? Twenty?'

Kit blushed and took his hand. 'Please! I try not to count.'

'Nonsense,' he said. 'You ought to be proud to count. Look at you! You're a beautiful woman. If anything, more beautiful now.' His blue eyes looked her over, and he smiled. She felt light-hearted, suddenly – breathless.

Marsh was dressed in a white cotton shirt, an off-white linen jacket, and pressed blue jeans. Kit noticed the hair on his chest was silver against his tanned chest. The tight-fitting jeans clothed the body of a man who seemed much younger, and his eyes were the warmest blue she had ever seen.

'I'm a great admirer of your work,' Kit said. She sounded nervous and young. For the first time in ten years she found herself imagining what it would be like to make love with a man.

'Nice of you to say that – not that you have to – but since you have, tell me which of my films was it that won you over?'

'Well, as a matter of fact,' said Kit, 'it was *Sparring Partner*. You see, I grew up on a small island in the Persian Gulf where there were no movie houses, only oil rigs. Now and then they brought in films for the drillers.' Kit paused. The eyes never left her face. 'It was a terrible print, and it kept breaking, but I was young, and ...

the first time I saw you on screen, I thought you were the most handsome man I had ever seen. I wanted you for my own father.' Kit went on quickly. 'Speaking of fathers, what about Judd, the father in *Last Chance*?' She slid from the arm to the seat of the chair, still warm from Brendan's body.

Scott broke in, 'Kit, Brendan was just telling me before you came that he thinks Judd is the best-drawn older male character since Willy Loman in *Death of a Salesman*. Isn't that right, Brendan?'

Never taking her eyes off Brendan, she asked, 'Does that mean you'll do it? I assume Scottie's told you that I want him to direct. It isn't every established star who will consent to letting a kid call the shots.'

'Kid,' Scott snorted. 'I like that. I invite the lady to meet you –'

'I think we're going a bit too fast here,' Brendan said quietly. 'Surely we're not so Godalmighty New Hollywood that we can't sit down and discuss the story first. How do you know we have the same idea for Judd? I mean, don't kid me, you've seen what I can do with an entire movie just by being, shall we say, *loose* in my interpretation of character.'

'Oh,' said Kit knowingly, 'sort of like the Mexican mercenary you turned into a transsexual halfway through *Prairie Song*?'

'Pretty bloody outrageous, don't you agree?'

'No,' Kit said evenly. 'I thought that business of yours was a little campy, but it happened to be the only interesting thing in that movie. It had a horrible script and no direction. But what I really think was going on was that you were trying to make some fun for yourself while you completed your contractual obligation to MGM.'

'Pretty astute. Don't you think so, Scottie?'

'Astute?' Scott was in the process of slipping out of the room. 'Oh, yes, Brendan, she's very astute. Astute *and* cute. Listen, kids, I'm going to have to leave you alone for a couple of minutes and go snuggle with my date. I'm sure you'll get along just fine without me.'

'Scottie, dear! Do you mind flipping on the light before you leave? It's too dark in here.'

Scott switched on the overhead light, blew them a kiss, and closed the door quietly.

'You're just about the farthest thing from cute I've ever laid eyes on,' said Brendan.

'My, Mr Butler,' said Kit, fanning herself with her hand, 'how you *do* go on.'

Brendan laughed shortly and gestured towards a row of glasses and a decanter set on a ring-scarred table. 'Brandy?'

'I'd love some.'

Kit watched him pour them each a glass. There was something comfortable and bearlike about his back.

He got the script and hefted an enormous wing chair in front of her so that they sat knee to knee.

'You told Scott you like Judd,' Kit said. 'I happen to have a problem with Judd. In fact, I've been thinking of having Herman fly out to supervise some revisions. I just don't think Judd is going to come across on the screen as a hero.'

He eyed her suspiciously. 'You mean the audience will stop loving him as soon as they realise he's out to screw his son's girlfriend?'

'That's part of it. In the book Judd *wasn't* an anti-hero. In the book, he's a victim of violence. But in the film ... No actor could pull it off sympathetically as the script is now.'

Kit sipped her brandy and waited.

'Let me see if I have this right,' Brendan began sarcastically. 'You think *Last Chance* will be a better movie, and Judd a more *lovable* hero, if only he what? Doesn't murder his son in the end?'

Kit sighed. 'I'm not saying we should change the end. I'm simply curious as to how you plan to make the audience sympathise with you, the murderer, instead of with Lacy or the dead boy. How are you going to make people believe lines like, "My poor pathetic son, my own blood. Don't you know that the ravages of time don't eat away –"?'

Brendan took to his feet, bearing down on her so that she stared into the buttons of his shirt. 'The line reads, "My son, my own dumb blood. Do you really think that time can diminish *me*?"'

On the last word Marsh grabbed his groin.

Kit smiled wryly. 'I see you've got *that* part down, all right, but business like that, however good, won't solve the problems.'

'All right, my fine lady. I can see there's only one way to prove to you ...' He jerked her roughly to her feet. 'Stand there.' He pulled her over and planted her a few feet from him by the mantelpiece. 'You're my son. Now, don't move!'

Kit didn't dare. He walked out onto the patio. She heard him out there pacing, mumbling, breathing heavily.

21

The man who came back a few seconds later was not the same man. Gone was the trim athletic profile: a paunch hung down over his belt. Gone was the neat appearance: his shirt-tails dragged outside his low-slung trousers. Gone was the composure: a thick glaze of sweat covered his face and his hair was swept back wildly. He looked as if he had been howling at the moon.

Two hours later, Kit left Scott's house, carrying a videotape of Brendan Marsh's impromptu interpretation of the role of Judd Hines. Scott had not, after all, left their company to go and snuggle with his date. He had gone to stand on the other side of a two-way mirror, the mirror that hung above the den mantelpiece, to operate a hand-held Sony and secretly tape Brendan's performance. Late that night, Archer received her telex: 'Screen test coming by pouch. Marsh *is* Judd Hines'.

As the screen went blank, the lights of the screening room slowly came up. Kit was stunned to see Archer disappear up the spiral staircase. 'Damn him!'

Susie Shultebrandt knelt beside her and laid a cool hand on her arm. 'It's not you, honey. He had a really important meeting to take. He wanted me to thank you for the screening and to let you know that he'll give you his decision on *Last Chance* as soon as he can. Kit? Kit, honey, here, take a Kleenex. It's jet lag ... happens to me all the time. You've got yourself a whopping case of jet lag, that's all.'

Kit took the Kleenex and blew her nose. 'It's not jet lag, Susie. It's *Last Chance*. It's a tearjerker, haven't you heard? A real box of Kleenex.'

2

Madelon Weeks, features editor for *Flash* magazine, squeezed her tweedy thighs into the chair across the table from her former star reporter, Liberty Adams. A big-boned oil widow in her late fifties, Madelon smelled of Joy, lived at the Plaza, and had breakfast every morning in the Edwardian Room. It didn't surprise Liberty that Madelon treated its waiters like so many personal servants. She lifted a ring-heavy hand and summoned the nearest one.

'Coffee, Thomas, *please*. Tell Gordon to *double-drip* for the Old Girl and her little *guest*.'

'No coffee for the little guest, please, Mad.'

Liberty had been up half the night speeding on espresso – all for the Old Girl. Any more coffee and she'd spin right through the floor.

'Very well. Tea for the *little* one, then, Thomas.'

Madelon turned her big powdered face upon Liberty. 'Liberty, *angel*, how *are* you? So *good* of you to come out so early for the Old Girl. You look *adorable*! I always said you had a positive *flair* for *underdressing*. Now, where's my Norman Mailer story?'

Liberty held her breath and handed over the thirty-two pages of overdue assignment. Madelon turned the draft facedown beside her plate without looking at it.

'Are you *surrendering* or *submitting*?'

Liberty blushed and stared at the sheets of paper. 'I thought I'd *submit* something a little different.'

Madelon frowned. She lifted an edge of the paper with a poppy-red talon. 'I don't pay you to be different, angel. I pay you to do what you always do best – draw and quarter the Beautiful People. Elegantly. *Bloodlessly*.' She lifted the cup which Thomas had just set down before her and sipped delicately.

Blood, Liberty thought, swallowing hard. Not that she could blame Madelon; after all, Liberty had got the Old Girl used to the taste. Liberty had started out in the business with Madelon, first as a college guest editor at *Mademoiselle*, and then after graduation, as

23

her secretary at *Flash*. Seven years ago, she had transformed *Flash*'s rather bland 'People in the News' section into 'Stocks & Trades', one of the hottest gossip-cum-interview columns in the country. The logo beside her byline had been a pilgrim's pillory and stocks, and before a whole nation of readers, she asked the Beautiful People questions everyone else was too polite to ask.

Yet nine months ago Liberty had suddenly tired of it all and had quit to free-lance. Hoping to turn her career around, she began to discover it wasn't easy to escape her reputation – or her old *Flash* habits.

She was patient with Madelon. 'Everyone's mean to Norman. Readers expect meanness. I think you'll find that what I did is unexpected. And the unexpected is almost as titillating as the brutal, Maddy.'

'Oh, *dear*, I wish you were still *mine*. Then you wouldn't be running off *half-cocked* like this. Take it from me, angel: a pop reporter coming on *heavy* makes for *very crappy copy*.' She tapped Liberty's story sternly. 'Is that what I have here?'

'You don't have Norman's balls dangling from every metaphor, Mad, but it's still very sexy reading. Relax. Order your eggs Florentine and relax.'

Madelon's big shoulders came down an inch or so. 'Speaking of *sex*, angel, you don't look as if you're *getting* any lately.' She snapped her fingers for Thomas, and ordered eggs Florentine for two.

'So...' She leaned forward and lit a Gitane. 'Give me *dish*.'

'Dish, Maddy? I've got none. People don't talk to me the way they used to in the old "S&T" days.'

'People *always* talk to you. It's those *angelic* little-girl looks. That's why you're so *good*. Now, give me the latest dish about Kit Ransome and that *hunk* Brendan Marsh.'

Liberty shrugged. 'All I know is what I read in the papers.'

'But you're doing that *Metropolitan* piece on Kit Ransome, yes?'

'Yes, but she's playing hard to get. I've been calling the woman for three weeks and so far she's granted me zip.'

'That's outrageous, angel!' Madelon slapped the table and her rings rang. 'How long have you been working *up* this thing? You're *due* next week, no? Libby, it isn't *like* you to let things *slide*.'

'Stop overreacting, Maddy. You know Kit Ransome doesn't talk to reporters.'

'To Stocks & Trades, angel, no, but to *Metropolitan*? If *Franny*

24

Coppola can do it for *The New Yorker*, Kit Ransome can do it for *Metropolitan*. Take it from the Old Girl.'

Liberty shrugged glumly.

'Tell me ...' Madelon leaned forward again. 'You *did* get to that *mother* of hers, no? I happen to *know* it was that schlep of yours to God-knows-where that kept me from getting *Norman* here on time.'

'I got back from the Middle East three weeks ago.'

'Well, don't just sit there with your *big* violet eyes all *gaga*. What was she *like*? She's a real living legend, no? Is it true that she has only one tit? They say she sliced it off herself, like a real Amazon. If you ask me, that's going a bit far.'

Liberty shrugged. 'She's given me one hell of a story, that is all I can tell you. The best story I've ever hit upon, in fact. *The* best.'

Madelon's eyes bulged. 'The best? That's all you're going to tell me?'

'Look, Mad, it's not that I don't trust you. It's just that it's a work in progress –'

'Dish in progress, you mean.'

'Dish in the oven.' Liberty smiled.

'Imagine, dishing Kitsia Ransome!'

Liberty threw up her arms in disgust. 'Dish doesn't enter into it, Mad.'

'Darling, dish *always* enters into it.'

'She's a serious artist, Mad. She's seventy-two years old. She doesn't give a shit what anybody thinks of her. And by the way, she pronounces it Keat-sia.'

'Keat-sia, *teat*-sia. So, give me some dish on Ronni. I hear he's on the wagon again, yes ...?'

Two hours and two undigested eggs Florentine later, Liberty was heading down Fifth Avenue towards her next appointment. The corporate headquarters for Ransome Enterprises rose in a sleek copper wedge eighty-three storeys above her. It was hard not to be impressed. She was about to interview the man who had *built* all this – Archer James Ransome. She wondered now if she might be a tad underdressed. Catching her reflection in the building's polished façade, she found a small woman with a haze of auburn hair – flaming but not raging – tripping along in red spike-heeled boots, lavender suede jeans, and matching jacket. Not *too* underdressed.

Two men in expensive business suits stood arguing by the entrance. One just missed being handsome; the other was shorter and heavier, with the large head and jaw of a bull terrier. They paused long enough to check her out as she plunged through the revolving doors. She looked down, avoiding their eyes, and they resumed their dispute. She stopped at the lobby news-stand to buy the latest issue of *Flash*, with her cover story on an upcoming movie called *Domino*. She asked the man if he stocked Camel Regulars.

'Sorry, Red, I'm out.' He looked her up and down. 'And with tits like those, I'd take care of my lungs.'

Liberty smiled sweetly. 'Watch your mouth or I'll rip your lips off.' She bought a pack of Life-Savers and walked over to the lifts. A spotless sheet of Plexiglas separated her from the last set of doors: the executive lifts. Footsteps sounded behind her. She swung around and saw the two men who had been arguing outside. Both were smiling amicably now. The lift doors hissed open and Liberty stepped in just as Not Quite Handsome snapped long white fingers and said, 'I forgot to get something! You go up, Tony. I'll see you later.'

Liberty glanced impatiently at her watch. It was 10:03. She was already three minutes late for her appointment upstairs in the penthouse.

The stocky man stepped in just as Liberty pressed P.

He leered openly at her as the doors closed. Liberty did her best to ignore him. The trouble with being small was that men thought they owned you outright. She concentrated on the lit X above their heads marking the express from floors one to fifty.

Somewhere between fifty-eight and fifty-nine the light failed. Liberty heard a loud *tock*, like two wooden blocks being smacked together. Suddenly, noiselessly, airlessly, the small white carpeted box began to fall. Then it jerked to a stop.

'Damn!' Liberty slammed the heel of her hand into the console, hitting the red button marked 'Emergency'. A voice, maddeningly calm, came over the small white speaker above the console and asked, 'What's the problem?'

'The problem?' Liberty shouted. 'We're falling, that's the problem! Something snapped!'

The voice droned on. 'The lifts in this building are in perfect working order. We have a foolproof system of safety brakes. If the first set fails . . .'

26

Liberty's eyes widened as the man across from her clutched at his chest. His breath came in the rapid little wheezes of a much more delicate creature.

'. . . the second set will cut in.'

'Hey,' she said to her companion. 'Take it easy. You heard him. If the first set . . .' The words died on her lips as she saw his eyes bulge, his face turn vivid violet. His head seemed to be squeezing out of the neck of his blue Oxford shirt, like a blob of something thick coming out of a tube. He jerked spastically at his tie.

'Shit!' The lift started to drop again. She lunged over and tore open the neck of his shirt, falling with him to the floor. As his weight crushed her, an even more terrible weight began to bear down on them and Liberty felt both ears pop. Suddenly it stopped again. The doors opened, and for an instant Liberty saw safety. She jumped up and stuck her arm out. The doors closed, crushing it. They opened. She pulled her arm back. They slammed closed again.

'For Chrissakes, help us!' she screamed at the speaker. 'This man is having a heart attack!'

The voice on the speaker didn't respond. She heard a ringing somewhere far off, then another *tock* overhead. The lift scraped against the side of the shaft.

'Please!' Liberty begged. 'Help us!'

The plunge continued, only faster now.

The voice was silent. She imagined its owner springing away from his post like a ballplayer leaving base, rushing down all those stairs to the basement to catch them before they hit.

The man in her arms stiffened, then closed his eyes and sagged against her.

The fall seemed endless. Liberty prayed silently, a jumble of every prayer she'd ever been taught.

Then the lift bounced like a yo-yo at the end of its string. The doors slid open on a wall of solid brick. Tears stung Liberty's eyes. This was worse than the fall; this was torture. They fell another six feet and bounced again. Liberty screamed. Below the brick wall a gap of about one foot widened to two, three, then four feet, until she saw the blessed white marble of the lobby. 'Oh, thank God!' Liberty breathed.

She looked down at the man in her lap. His heavy head lolled against her thigh, cutting off its circulation. She wondered whether he was dead. She was afraid to touch him.

'Get an ambulance!' she called down to the people below. Heads bobbed up into the gap and disappeared.

'Whatever you do, don't jump!' someone shouted up to them.

The lift began to shudder as if about to resume its fall to the basement. She eased the man's head gently to the floor and leapt out of the gap, falling six feet to the floor. People swarmed over her.

She got her breath back. 'He's still in there. I think he's had a heart attack. Hurry!' She heard an approaching ambulance. 'I hope he's not dead,' she said in a small voice.

'Don't worry, he ain't dead, but ain't none too happy, neither.'

The owner of the voice was a good-looking black man with an Afro-like topiary, dressed in a white jumpsuit with 'RE' embroidered on one pocket and 'Melvin' on the other. He smiled at her in frank admiration.

'Yo, Littlebit!' He grinned. 'Welcome to earth. You damn near flew out of that thing!'

Liberty elbowed her way over to the medics. 'How is he?'

The medic groping for a pulse didn't answer, as the other two men bearing the stretcher headed for the side door.

She followed them outside as they hustled him into a private ambulance. He definitely looked dead. 'And I don't even know his name,' she said aloud to herself as the ambulance took off the wrong way up Fifth Avenue.

'The dude's name is Tony Alvarro.'

Liberty spun around. It was Melvin again. 'He's one of the VP's.'

'VP? For Ransome? Which VP?' The reporter in her lunged for the story. 'Never mind. I'm late.' She dashed back into the building.

The lift doors hissed open on the eighty-third floor and Liberty stepped out. She took a deep breath and closed her eyes. The blood still beat in her ears, the memory of the fall pressing at her ribs. She felt weak and small.

She appeared to be in the midst of a mini rain forest. Green carpet lay beneath her feet as thick as moss. Thick, lush shrubbery grew everywhere. Trees taller than telephone poles brushed up against the glass ceiling. Liberty could make out the blue October sky. She breathed deeply: cedar chips. She heard running water and looked around to find a waterfall trickling over boulders, heavy and substantial, as if they'd just been hauled up from Central Park. A person might hide out here unobserved for days on end. The moist air carried the sound of voices calling her name.

'Miss Adams? Miss Adams.'

She took a deep breath, squared her shoulders, and smiled bravely.

A pale blonde of medium height in a yellow shirtwaist dress ran through the trees and came to a breathless halt before Liberty. She had an exquisite white forehead, polished as a Fabergé egg, and serious eyes behind flesh-coloured horn-rims.

'Miss Adams? I'm Sasha. We've been holding a telephone call for you. Would you come this way, please?'

'Okay.' Liberty drew herself up and followed the blonde through the forest. Behind a glass wall the sound of computers clicking and telephones ringing obliterated the illusion of the great outdoors. It looked like a nurse's station. Intensive care.

Sasha propelled Liberty past a raft of printout-strewn desks, over to a blinking telephone console.

Liberty sat and paused before taking the call. 'Could somebody get me a pack of Camels and a cup of tea with lemon?' *And a Valium.*

She picked up the phone. It was her assistant, Peg.

'Oh, thank God it's you. Listen.' Peg gulped and caught her breath. 'It's been crazy here. Morty Rich has called five times in the last hour. *Five times*! He said if you don't retract what you wrote about *Domino*, he's going to sue.'

He would have been suing a corpse if that second set of brakes hadn't worked. 'He must have had a rough night down on the waterfront.'

'This isn't funny, Libby. He means business. The man is crazy. You wouldn't believe what he called me. And what he called *you*! I promised you'd get back to him before lunch.'

'It *is* funny, Peg, but skip it,' said Liberty. She took the tea and the Camels from the redhead with the complexion of a boiled lobster.

Peg was silent. Sulking?

'Okay, since I have you on the phone,' Liberty went on, 'do me a favour. Move my twelve-o'clock Tea Room reservation up to twelve-thirty and call Victoria at *Metropolitan* and ask her if she wouldn't mind making it a half hour later. I want to give myself a little more breathing room. Get me a line on a Tony Alvarro. He works for Archer Ransome.'

'Tony Alvarro? What's the angle?'

'Call it a hunch, Quasimodo. Any luck with Kit Ransome?'

'Zilch, per usual,' Peg said dully.

'Did you try the life-and-death angle like I told you?'

'I tried it, but her secretary wasn't buying it. "Very funny", I think she said.'

'Did you tell her it wasn't a joke?'

'It *is* a joke, Lib. I call that woman a dozen times a day. That's three business weeks ... let's see, that makes about three hundred calls I've made to this woman. And still no dice.'

Liberty sighed patiently. 'Punch up the Alvarro poop. Consider it a priority. I want everything by the time I go home tonight. Keep at Kit Ransome, Peg. We can't give up on her! And, Peg...' Liberty's voice softened. 'Relax. These people aren't important. They only *think* they're important. By the way, what *did* Morty call us?'

Liberty hung up chuckling as the redhead bustled over to her and said, 'Mr Ransome is ready to see you now.'

'Give me another second, will you? I've got a small fire that needs dousing.' The redhead blushed and sputtered. Obviously people didn't do this to her boss. 'Really,' Liberty reassured her, 'I'll just be another second.'

She dialled Morty Rich's office. These calls weren't pleasant, but they came with the work.

Morty's voice oozed control. 'Let me read you this –'

'I *know* what I wrote, Morty.'

'Do you know how much damage you've done to this film? And it doesn't even open for another two months!'

Liberty held the receiver away from her ear, waiting until he wound himself down. Then she spoke to him as though he were a mental patient whose Thorazine was wearing off and not the vice-president of publicity for a major motion picture company.

She swivelled and bumped into somebody's leg. Her eyes travelled up the willowy length of a tall black woman in a smoky Dior suit. With brown hair pulled back in a classic braid, this had to be the famous tigress at the Ransome gate: Susie Shultebrandt.

She whispered coolly, 'Mr Ransome is asking for you, Miss Adams.'

Liberty held up two fingers, then swivelled back to Morty. She could just see him, pink-faced in a salmon gabardine suit, sitting in his office, all glass and Bill Blass overlooking the park, doodling on his personal stationery. You could tell a lot about a person from his stationery. Morty's – hot pink and glossy with 'Morty' printed in purple caps across the top and 'Rich' a lavender whisper at the bottom – said it all.

'Liberty, you broke bread with his wife and kid,' Morty was saying.

'I sniffed cocaine off the top of his valet's head, Morty. A bald dwarf for a valet – no wonder this man can't make movies. He's snorted his brains up his arse!' They loved it when she talked dirty: the convent girl who swore like a coke slut.

'Tell me, Liberty, is your mother proud of what you do for a living?'

'I wouldn't know, Morty. I'm an orphan.' Click.

That always got them – that she was an orphan. It was a real conversation killer.

Liberty sighed and got up to follow the woman in the Dior suit. They headed down a long coral-coloured hall, passing through a brown womb of an office, then out into a vast white-carpeted space that was mostly glass except for two smooth white marble walls. The woman led her to the centre of the room and vanished.

Liberty blinked at the brightness. Never had she been in a room so purely white. It was as if she'd been thrust out into a snowy day without goggles.

Archer Ransome sat behind an antique marble-topped table talking on the telephone, completely ignoring her. Was he punishing her for keeping him waiting? Liberty walked over to the windows, looking out on the hazy green and grey expanse of upper New York. You should have to scale a mountain to get to a vista like this, not just slide up in a lift, however treacherous. Liberty turned her back on the view and looked for a place to set up.

Taking out her pad, she sat on the white wool couch and made some notes: 'White on white on white. White bowls and crystal vases of white flowers on white enamel tables and white marble pedestals. A most unbusinesslike atmosphere here – peonies, narcissi, and gardenias? He must have his flowers flown in from some part of the world where it's springtime.'

She looked up from her notes to find Ransome staring straight at her, still talking into the receiver. He was even better-looking than his head shot. Hair the colour of burnished pewter. Slow-toasted rich man's tan. Deep Mediterranean-blue eyes fringed with long black lashes. His lips curled naturally at the corners, giving his face a look of urbane good humour even when he wasn't smiling. She wondered fleetingly whether she'd wind up sleeping with him. If she did, it wouldn't be the worst thing she'd have to do to complete an assignment.

Returning the receiver to the high-tech console beside his desk, Ransome rose. 'At last!'

As he walked over to her, his right leg swung in a shallow arc away from his body. There hadn't been any mention of a limp in research – but then again, research on him had been scant. The only place he turned up with any regularity was on the Ten Best Dressed list. With his light blue wool Armani suit, the oyster-white silk shirt, the yellow-gold cufflinks, and a widish tie with an exotic floral pattern, he had her vote, too.

He bowed over her hand and drew up an armchair next to her. It gave off an expensive hiss as he settled himself.

'I see your hair is as fiery as your pen, Miss Adams. Or is it your word processor?' He smiled at her and she smiled back: the smallish chip in his front tooth was decidedly sexy. Maybe he wasn't into cosmetic dentistry. You never knew: some of these magnates were as vain about their looks as they were about their bottom lines.

He went on in a lightly mocking way. 'I'm glad you were able to make it. Finally.'

'No thanks to your lift.' She smiled sweetly.

'My lift, Miss Adams?'

'Your lift, Mr Ransome.' She extended her arms. 'You find me fresh from a most invigorating free-fall. If that second set of brakes hadn't kicked in, I'd be a lot shorter than I am right now.'

His eyebrow arched. 'Strange. I was under the impression that the lifts in this building ran exceptionally smoothly.'

'Tell that to the man who had a heart attack on the way down with me.'

He frowned. 'A man had a heart attack?'

'That's what I said.'

His face hardened perceptibly. 'You seem rather collected for a young woman who's just had a heart attack on her hands.'

She shouldn't have brought it up. 'It must be the shock.'

'Miss Adams, I think it's only fair to remind you that I don't like being interviewed. In fact, I'm not a fan of your kind of writing.'

Hostility out of the blue still surprised her. 'I didn't think you were,' she managed.

'I don't approve of the kind of gossipmongering you're paid to do. I have to say, however, that I'm relieved to find you so young and pretty. It doesn't make you seem quite so...'

'Threatening?'

He smiled coolly. 'One can at least attribute your cockiness to youth. I'd advise you to quit while you're young.'

They were certainly off to a wonderful start.

'I'm just curious, Miss Adams,' he went on. 'How did my aunt and her daughter react to your writing this piece? Frankly, I'm surprised either of them consented to an interview with *Flash*.'

Liberty closed her eyes. Be nice, she told herself, even if he isn't. 'Didn't your secretary brief you, sir? The piece I'm writing isn't for *Flash*, it's for *Metropolitan*. It's a profile.'

He knew perfectly well it was for *Metropolitan*. Otherwise, she would never have got past that nurse's station.

'Still, that they consented to let you write it at all puzzles me. Kit abhors journalists.'

'It was your Aunt Kitsia's idea. I get the feeling Kit isn't thrilled with it.'

He started visibly. 'Kitsia's idea, you say?' His blue eyes deepened a shade. 'I find that difficult to believe.' For a moment he was lost in thought. 'Then again,' he came back brightly, 'it wouldn't be the first strange thing she's done.' Suddenly he seemed eager to continue. 'Shall we get on with it?'

'I appreciate your seeing me. I can understand how you might be a little up in arms lately, press-wise.'

He shrugged, but she could sense his irritation. They both knew what she had hit upon: his stonewalling of the story that had broken two weeks ago in *The Wall Street Journal*. Ransome had been putting reporters off for thirty years now, but this story was a little hard to shake off. A man named Greenhause, a higher-up in the Securities and Exchange Commission, had admitted taking bribes from big business over the years. He cited Ransome Enterprises the most heavily.

'Miss Adams.'

Liberty's head jerked up from her notes.

'You seem to be doing more insinuating than asking.' He smiled and his dark lashes came down like a hand patting a bored yawn.

'Ah, yes, *questions*. I do have a list prepared, Mr Ransome.' She reached over and turned on her tape, giving it a spin forward to make sure it was clean.

He winced at the sound and sat up a little taller. 'I assume I don't need to remind you of the guidelines I've set forth as far as this interview is concerned. I'm to provide background only, and absolutely no quotes.'

'Trust me.' She smiled blandly. 'No SEC. Not a word.'

Ransome took an ivory cigarette case off the arm of his chair. He was not the kind of man who let a cigarette pack break the line of his suit. He offered her one: filterless, probably Egyptian.

'No, thanks.' She waved them away and took out one of her own, which he removed from her fingers. With disarmingly old-world flourish he lit both cigarettes in his mouth and handed her hers. They each settled back into private clouds of smoke.

'I've got a good question for you. Describe your aunt to me in a word.'

He hesitated. 'Will you accept a sentence instead?'

'A sentence will do.'

'My aunt is one of the few truly original minds I have ever known. There's your word: original.'

'Do you two get along?'

'Come now, Miss Adams. You've met her. You know one doesn't *get* along with my aunt. One simply *goes* along, trying to keep up. By the way, how did you find her? Was she well?'

'She's well, all right.' Liberty noted the ease with which he was turning the interview around. 'She's the wellest seventy-two-year-old lady I've ever met. I found her to be remarkably lucid, cranky, evasive, full of shit...'

'She's a character. I find it difficult to imagine my aunt actually entertaining a journalist on Zwar. My aunt is eccentric, Lord knows. Perhaps she felt she was in charge there. But can she control you now that you're back?'

'Obviously, she feels she can. Or she doesn't care. "Eccentric" is another good word for her. So is "forthcoming".' She watched him closely.

'Really? I hope you don't intend to publish this interview in an ... eh, unexpurgated form?'

Liberty tapped her teeth with her pen. Was he blushing? Amazing! 'I'm thinking about it, Mr Ransome.' She shrugged and went on. 'I gather from what you've said that you and your aunt are now on speaking terms.'

'My aunt and I have never *not* spoken.'

'Oh, yeah? That's not what I hear.'

'I'd be interested to hear just what you have heard.'

'Don't worry. It's all up here.' She tapped her temple with her pen, then suddenly realised she'd got the pen tangled in her hair. The harder she tried to untangle it, the more stuck it became.

He leaned over and began to help her unwind her hair from the clip. 'If your memory's as tangled as your hair, I'd say I have nothing to worry about.' He freed the pen at last and handed it back to her.

'Very funny.' She shook her curls free. 'You've certainly got a light touch, Mr Ransome.'

'Don't you think "Archer" will serve from now on?'

'Don't I think "Archer" will serve *what* from now on?'

'Very witty, Miss Adams.'

'Call me Liberty, Archer. Tell me, what sort of person is your cousin Kit? All I know is what I read in the movie magazines way back when I was a kid in grade school.'

'My cousin hasn't had an easy life.'

'Forty-five years old and looking better than when she was a twenty-five-year-old starlet? Head of one of the Big Seven movie studios? Earning high six figures? Having an affair with an extremely magnetic leading man? I don't think she's suffering all that much. Although I suppose it can't be easy being the daughter of one of the world's leading female sculptors.'

'She'd take exception to your use of "female", don't you think?' He grinned. 'But she *is* a sculptor in every sense of the word. She chips away at people as if they were works in progress. Have you yielded to her yet?'

Liberty recalled Kitsia's voice grating against her naked flesh. *'Stay put and don't fidget. Yours is just another body.'*

'Thanks. That makes me feel great.'

'You have the instinctive recoil of a woman used to undressing in the dark.'

Liberty stared down at her concave self. *It was as if her body were trying to fold itself in half.*

'Open up!' the old woman cried.

Liberty came back to Archer. 'I don't know. She did get me to pose for her. It was so hot, clothes were a curse anyway. I don't know how she survives there.'

'She's even changed her metabolism to fit the climate, Liberty. You move around a place like Zwar on high speed, you overheat rather rapidly.'

'You sound like the voice of experience.' She watched his face carefully. His tongue traced the chip in his front tooth as he mused.

'What was she like, Archer?' You're one of the few people alive who knew her then.'

He seemed to relax quickly into his memories – Liberty was a little surprised at *how* quickly.

'They were orphaned, my father and Kitsia, in Paris. My father was more interested in kingdom-building than in raising his ten-year-old sister. He'd leave her in Paris in the care of women friends while he went to the Near East. Eventually he moved to Zwar, leaving Kitsia to Paris . . . or was it the other way around? He used to bring me to Paris every spring to visit. I still find it remarkable that my father was willing to forsake Paris for that dusty rock in the Persian Gulf.'

'I don't know.' Liberty shrugged. 'It has a certain medieval *je ne sais quoi*. That was some funeral they had for the emir. The only thing missing was Omar Sharif. I found the Zwarians, as a whole, to be an exotic combination of flashy and shifty.' She watched him carefully.

'That's why my associate, Rush, is so well suited to handling them. I think he identifies with their style; I don't care for it myself. My father certainly got on well with them. I don't think he'd have minded seeing the emir and his boys take over his compound. I had no need for it.'

'I was told Ransome Enterprises sold it to them for a hefty sum. But getting back to Paris and Kitsia . . .'

'Ah, yes. I much prefer that . . . My aunt was every boy's dream.'

'And what is every boy's dream, Archer?'

'Every mother's nightmare, of course.'

Liberty raised an eyebrow. 'This is beginning to sound like hot stuff.'

'And you're beginning to sound suspiciously like a *Flash* reporter, Liberty Adams.'

'Once a smut-hound, always a smut-hound. Come on, Archer, tell me about it.'

He smiled, abstracted. 'My aunt figured prominently in the tattles in those days. Too prominently, my mother felt. After letting me spend the first seven springs of my life in Paris with Kitsia, she laid down the law and wouldn't let me see her any more.'

'Any scandal prompt this decision?'

Ransome stared back at her.

36

She forged ahead. 'Surely some particular incident must have caused her to deprive you of your yearly treat. I mean, Zwar is swell, but for a kid never to get a break from it...'

He leaned back again. 'I must have been seven when my mother learned that Kitsia had been travelling all over the continent as the paid companion of a Middle European prince who had been blind since birth. She took him to the casinos and gambled for him while he sat beside her with his hand on the head of a silver cane. She won him a substantial sum of money, they say. Later, it was revealed that he was neither blind nor a prince, but a carnival hypnotist. There was quite a scandal when it got out that they had been practising their act on the card room dealers, hypnotising them into folding their winning hands.'

'Then your mother must have been really scandalised when Kitsia gave birth to a bastard in her very guesthouse. Any idea who Kit's father might be?'

She had hoped to catch him off guard, to no avail. '"Illegitimate" is a better word. Not to use one at all is more gracious. Mother was appalled. And, no, I have never bothered to speculate who Kit's father might be... Besides, I wasn't there at the time. You see, I'd stopped going home when I was fifteen.'

'Oh really?' Liberty cocked her head. 'Why was that?'

'The war,' he said smoothly.

'Ah, yes.' Liberty nodded. 'The war. Did you return to Zwar after 1945?'

'As a matter of fact, no. My parents died in an auto accident after the war. I used to see Kit whenever Kitsia brought her to the States.'

'Is that a fact? Still, it's strange that you never went back to Zwar. Yet you developed the mining business your father left you into a multimillion-dollar operation. And you've also positioned one of your notorious casinos there. How do you manage all of that? By remote control?'

He smiled blandly. 'In a manner of speaking. My partner, Rush Alexander, takes care of them perfectly. He's in charge of the entire Middle East. So there's no reason for me to involve myself personally.'

'How convenient. Your acquisition of Horizon Pictures throws you and your cousin together, doesn't it? Was that deliberate on your part?'

'No. An associate had been scouting for leisure-time acquisitions for quite some time. He tells me he settled on Horizon before Kit was appointed its head.'

'Since she still is its head, I'm assuming all's well between you kissing cousins.' She hit this last phrase deliberately hard, and watched his expression. It remained noncommittal.

'We're satisfied.'

'Satisfied that she's being painted in the press as a bedroom executive? Satisfied that her recent movies have opened to less than spectacular business? Satisfied that she gets reviewed more than her movies? I would think that as her cousin you'd find such coverage particularly insulting. I know she's only your flesh and blood, but she does head up one of your subsidiaries. And surely news such as she's generated in the past few weeks does your company no good at all.'

'Miss Adams' – he seemed disappointed – 'consider the source of this news.'

'The LA *Times*. *Time* magazine. The Washington *Post*. I'd say they're substantial sources.'

His glance flickered. 'It's a colourful business, Miss Adams.'

'I thought it was "Liberty", Archer. It's a colourful business, yes, but generally not that colourful. And you're hurting enough as it is with this SEC thing. If you made a move to clean up on another front, it might serve as a confidence booster, help shore up your Dow Jones.'

The intercom buzzed. He leaned over the table between them and spoke into it, then excused himself to take the call at his desk. Liberty, restless, got up and wandered around, sniffing absently at the flowers, looking in vain for evidence of the flesh and blood man in this pristine showplace. A blood-red Rothko rose up in an alcove to the right of his desk. She wondered why he'd hidden this one gory spot of colour. As she backed up, a railing caught her midway down her back. It was at least a fifty-foot drop into blackness. She looked down a spindly spiral staircase and then took a couple of steps into a carpeted cavern. Down here the walls were black, the ceiling was black, the furniture and floors were black. Only the fifty-foot screen built into one wall was white. His private screening room. She turned around and came back up. He was still on the phone. He looked worried. If only he'd get off the phone so she could get on with it! A mass of pink marble shimmering in the sunlight standing in one corner of the room caught her eye. It seemed to be lit from within. She walked over and peered at it. Where the natural veins of the stone came together, they formed a deep, dark pink star. Swallowing hard, she reached out.

'Do you recognise it?'

She pulled her hand back, blushing.

She found her voice. 'I'd know it anywhere. It's an original Kitsia Ransome. Part of the Jewel Series, isn't it?' She began to giggle. 'Sorry.' She got herself in hand. 'I was just remembering the name she originally wanted to give the series. The name Guggenheim board absolutely refused to let her call it in the sixties. "The Cunt Series".'

'You see, my aunt doesn't *always* get her way.'

'She told me she really didn't care what they called it so long as they took it.'

'She wouldn't be so easy now,' he said. Then, after a thoughtful silence, 'You know, Liberty, I've just learned that the gentleman in the lift who had the heart attack was our head of finance, Anthony Alvarro.' He kept his eyes on the statue.

'Oh,' said Liberty lamely.

'He's in intensive care at Mount Sinai,' he went on. 'They're not at all sure he'll pull through.'

She made a mental note of it. 'I feel terrible.' She recalled the weight of his great grey head on her lap.

'You sound as if you were to blame. Shall we?' He steered her back to the couch, his limp suddenly more pronounced.

'I was asking you who runs Horizon Pictures.'

'Were you?' he asked. 'Why, Kit does, I'm sure.'

'Are you? That's not what they've been saying. They say that Paramount has its mountain, MGM has its lion, BK has its eagle, and Horizon has its' – she paused – 'Kitty Cat. I hear she's just a figurehead and you really make all the major decisions.'

'All my businesses interest me. Liberty, you're waxing *Flash* again. What do you actually know of the woman?'

'What do I know? Let me see.' She began to count coyly on her fingers. 'I know her hobbies are swimming and collecting old movie posters. She has long skinny feet and she has her long skinny shoes custom-made. She has a house on a cliff in the Pacific Palisades which she calls Clara, a pun, I gather, on Tara. She's a gourmet cook, and, let me see, what have I left out?' Liberty made a fist. 'That's the point. I've left out a great deal. Because she hasn't let me near her.'

'Can you blame her? She'd had' – he hesitated deliberately – 'bad luck with the press.'

'Luck has nothing to do with it!' Liberty snapped. 'The press is just people responding to impressions. A woman like Kit Ransome – a slow, steady rise from starlet to studio chief – gives a strange impression to the press. Enigmatic. Shadowy. Is she bitchy or just shy? In any case, I'd like the opportunity to find out for myself, but at the rate I'm going . . .'

'I have complete confidence in your ability, Liberty.'

'You wouldn't if you knew what I've been through trying to run her down.'

'Be patient, Liberty.'

'Argh.' She wrung her hands. 'My palms are beginning to itch.'

'Your palms itch, Liberty?'

'When I feel like punching somebody. Patience? I've called the woman personally every day for the last three weeks. My assistant tries a dozen times a day. We've tried everything. Perhaps you could put a good word in for me?'

He laughed. 'Surely a woman of your delightfully diminutive stature can't go through life picking fights.'

'Are you kidding? That's exactly what I can do. Who would punch a five-foot, ninety-five pound redhead –'

'With eyes the colour of irises and such kissable lips?'

Liberty gawked at him and coloured to her ears.

'Have I embarrassed you, Liberty?'

She fought for composure. 'Tell me, is there room for only one tycoon at Ransome Enterprises?'

As if on cue, a panel in the marble wall slid open and a tall, dark man appeared. In his blue pin-striped suit, he looked the essence of a corporate businessman. As he strolled towards them, she realised with a start who this was. This was Not Quite Handsome from down in the lobby. Before the Fall.

He didn't even look at her, so there was no telling whether he recognised her. 'There's room for only one tycoon around here,' he said, grinning, 'And we all know who he is – eh, Mr Ransome?' He stood behind Archer's chair and his eyes skimmed over Liberty. She was a racy book: he was very interested.

Archer's face lit up boyishly. 'That's for sure. One tycoon and one buffoon.' Then darkened. 'Did you hear about Alvarro?'

'I heard.' He let a piece of paper drift down into Archer's lap and waited until Archer read it and began to laugh. The other man grinned crookedly, holding the back of Archer's chair. Had someone called 'playtime' without her noticing?

Not Quite Handsome wiped the corner of his eyes on his handkerchief, tucked it neatly back into his breast pocket, and came over to sit beside Liberty. He offered her a long white hand.

'You are by far the most delightful-looking creature I've seen on this couch in a long, long time. I'm Rush Alexander.'

Rush Alexander! She hadn't recognised him; he photographed ten times better than he looked.

'Control yourself, Rush,' Archer said indulgently. 'The lady's here on business. She's with a magazine.'

Rush looked at Liberty with new eyes. 'Well, Magazine Lady, do you mind if I interrupt this important meeting long enough to borrow old Arch here? Time and tide await no man, particularly when we're ten minutes from the closing bell at the London Currency Exchange.'

Without waiting for an answer, he guided Archer to the far side of the room. Liberty could just barely make out their conversation.

'It seems, Arch, that Casa Verde is planning to provide a libretto for the Potomac Opera Society.'

'Yes, but I'd prefer to discuss this matter when I've had time to study the score.'

'Time is running out, Maestro. The first act will be performed on Friday, and unless some enforced rehearsal time is called, it's going to a mighty rusty performance. The tenor, Ebenezer, may accept some vocal training, but I can't be sure until I've tried.'

Liberty was trying very hard not to laugh. Grown men speaking in code. Still, here was Not Quite Handsome, the man whose reputation with the press was legendary. Ransome might be conservative and reclusive, but Alexander was flamboyant and exhibitionistic. He was gregarious: he made friends wherever he went – on Wall Street, in DC, up in Albany. He had the boys at the *Times* in his pocket and had only just lost the *Journal*. He was the Prince Charming of the media, using print as if it was his own personal PR agency. He steered clear of TV – too frivolous – made no bones about being a son of a bitch. His spies were everywhere, but his methods worked.

They came back to the centre of the room. Rush sat down next to her.

Liberty wondered why he wasn't using his legendary powers to keep this SEC thing quiet. She stopped wondering when she felt his leg pressing against hers. His thighs were twice as long as hers, but not much wider. She knew that if she were to reach over and touch them, they would be rock hard. She could just see those big feet in running shoes. He'd run the Boston Marathon as recently as last spring.

According to *People*, he was your basic jock executive. She remembered the picture of him, in shorts and a tank top, and the caption: 'MEGA EXEC TRAINS TO BE MEGA JOCK'. Apart from a balding head, he didn't look older than forty. He made Archer, by comparison, seem just a bit soft in the gut, definitely nearing sixty and aging.

'Then I gather, Arch, that I can proceed with your blessing?'

'Haven't I always counted on your impresarial skills, old boy?' Archer's smile was lazy, but Liberty could sense a change. He was back at work now, and something was definitely up.

'What would you do without me?' Rush cracked his knuckles.

'Why, do it myself.'

'The floor is yours, Miss Adams.' Rush nudged her with his thigh. 'But first, let me tell you how impressed I am that you actually got old Arch here to come out and play. He doesn't normally come out for the press. Even when they're as pretty as you are.'

'You'll excuse him, Liberty. It's part of his job description to be insolent enough for the two of us.'

'That I know,' said Liberty, looking him over. 'He's the Papa Bear I had to phone for permission to interview Mama Bear. Rush, you're a real brick in my book.'

Rush stared at her appraisingly. 'I thought you were smarter than the average reporter, but you're not. You're just shorter.'

'Edward G. Robinson, *Double Indemnity*, 1944, and fuck you. Where did you get to know movies?'

'My daughter's a fan.'

Liberty nodded. 'The family that studies together . . .'

He squeezed her thigh and turned to Archer. 'This one calls my secretary up last week and says, "I've got to interview *Mrs* Alexander for this piece I'm doing!"'

Liberty cringed to hear herself being mimicked.

'Why don't you tell Arch the whole story.' He squeezed her thigh again.

Liberty swung out of his reach and whipped out her Camels. 'I

42

wanted to schedule the interview for this Friday. She said she'd have to get back to me.'

'And?' He nudged her with his foot.

'And then your secretary told me no dice. It was the maid's day off.'

'And then you said . . .'

Liberty rolled her eyes. 'I said that I'd appreciate her reconsidering because –'

'Because, Arch – are you ready for this? – Friday is her birthday!' He sneered.

Archer was enjoying this as much as Rush was. Right now she didn't much like either one of them.

Archer's tone was patronising. 'I'd say, Liberty, you're not above a little storytelling to get your foot in the door.'

'I admit it,' Liberty allowed. 'Friday was convenient for me.'

'Ah, but is Friday really your birthday?' Rush pursued playfully.

Liberty ignored him and dragged on her cigarette: Friday marked the anniversary of the day she showed up on the doorstep of St Mary's on the River. She might be as much as three weeks older than that. 'So the sisters at the orphanage tell me.' She glared at Rush.

'Isn't that fascinating?' He sneered. 'Another deprived child.'

'Being nice doesn't count much with you, does it?' she said sourly.

'That's because I'm also "not nice" enough for the both of us, right, Arch?'

Ransome nodded.

'Then again,' Rush went on, 'you happen to be just about the nicest lady in print today, aren't you, Liberty Adams?'

'Cut it, Rush,' Archer said quietly.

He grinned. 'She's very pretty, isn't she? In spite of her poison pen.'

'Yes, she is,' Archer said thoughtfully.

'Small, but perfectly formed,' Rush said softly.

'Absolutely,' Archer agreed.

Liberty shifted uneasily. She felt them both looking at her. 'Cut it out, you two.'

Archer laughed. 'Forgive us, Liberty, we have a weakness for the same fine features in women. And you, my dear, are possessed of many of them.'

Liberty wasn't flattered. 'I've heard how your friend here comes on to women reporters, but I didn't expect it from you. Then again, you two buddies are the boys who made it together. I'd like to write a story about you two.'

'Would you? Well, it would make more interesting reading, that's for sure. Who wants to read about that old dyke?'

'Rush,' Archer warned.

'Just joking, Arch. I'm sure this young lady's article will make for stimulating reading.' He winked at Liberty.

She wondered how she could work them into the story. Archer, the good cop, Rush the bad; rich boy, poor boy; sun and shadow. A classic tale, more interesting than most business history.

'You guys work well together, don't you?'

'We've done all right,' Rush drawled. 'Would you care to hear about it?'

Liberty tried to look bored.

'Of course you would,' he answered for her, rising and beginning to pace dramatically. 'Archer James Ransome and Kazimir Borisifnov Alexandriev, room-mates and buddies, Harvard class of forty-six –'

Liberty interrupted in spite of herself. 'Mind telling me where you get "Rush" out of all that?'

He stopped pacing and grinned unpleasantly.

'I was the "Black Russian" to my mates. Archer shortened it.'

'Cute,' Liberty said dryly.

He resumed his pacing. 'Both only sons of only sons, spared the inconvenience of fighting in the Big War, Archer for His Majesty's Royal Air Force, the Russian for his adoptive Uncle Sam, we got ourselves a head start on the rest – isn't that right, Arch?'

Archer stretched out in his chair, chuckled, relaxed now, enjoying the show. Liberty yawned elaborately. Rush continued.

'Our steadfast friends made their first money hawking bonds in the boom years after the war, following a short but sweet stint with the lovable but gruff shipping tycoon Hampton Barclay, may he rest in pieces.' He held an imaginary hat to his chest and looked up. 'The intrepid duo bought out old Ham on his deathbed – mind you, with Archer's money – and founded Ransome Enterprises.' Rush paused, as if expecting applause, then went on. 'And so, boys and girls, was born Ransome Enterprises, a small but cohesive multinational corporation having under its sterling aegis a dozen odd – and I do mean odd – subsidiary companies. Ransome

Enterprises may not have hit the Dow Jones index of the thirty leading companies, but I predict that the mid-eighties will see us go blue-chip.' He leaned towards Liberty. 'Are you getting this down, Miss Adams?'

'Every word.'

'Save your applause. With its worldwide chain of resort casinos, the Trips Group, in Macao, Monte Carlo, Freeport, Rio, Zwar, and with its semi-major motion-picture company, Horizon Pictures, Ransome Enterprises is never without gold and a steady supply of cold cash with which to fuel its more capital-intensive industries – Barclay Oil and Shipping, Ransome Petroproductions, Ruba Cosmetics.'

Liberty drummed her fingers on the arm of the couch.

'I'm getting to the juicy part.' He leaned over the back of the couch and spoke into Liberty's ear. 'Business watchers claim it is hard to tell where the power lies in the Ransome empire, with its chief executive officer, old Ransome himself, or with Alexander, its chief operating officer. Note, Miss Adams,' he said slyly, 'the subtle difference in the two titles. While the company might carry the former's name, some say that a certain Russian runs things.'

'I think Miss Adams is getting restless,' said Ransome, not amused. His face was stony now.

Liberty saw that he'd carried his comedy monologue one step too far. 'No, really, I'm riveted. You're quite the thespian, Mr Alexander. It's just that I thought we had these rules, you see.' She looked meaningfully to Ransome.

'To hell with rules. If you must write this article, why don't you interview me, Liberty Adams? I can give you lots of goodies about the weird sisters.' He had turned suddenly sincere, like a bad little boy trying to be good.

'Weird sisters?' Liberty echoed.

'Rush's nickname for my cousin and aunt. Another puerile little joke. Nothing more.'

'I see,' Liberty said, looking at her watch.

'No you don't,' said Rush, 'but you will once I give you the story.'

'I'd love to hear it, but I'm fresh out of time. I hate to tape and run . . .' She snapped off her machine and put it into her bag along with her pad. 'But I have an *easy* interview to do now.'

'Did you hear that, Archer? I think she's trying to tell you something.'

Actually, it wasn't going to be easy. It wasn't even going to be an interview. It was lunch with her editor from *Metropolitan* to beg for an extension.

Rush was at her ear again. 'Aren't I even tempting you, Miss Libby?'

She craned her neck to look at him. He was draped over one of the chairs now. Propped up lazily on his elbow, he grinned like the Cheshire cat.

'Yeah. Tell me, do I have to telephone your wife to get permission to talk to *you*?'

'No, my sarcastic little darling. Why don't you come for lunch in my office on Friday before you see my wife? I'll have a birthday cake for you, and presents, and everything.'

'I can't wait.' She narrowed her eyes at him and decided it was time to say it. 'I remember you now. You were downstairs in the lobby arguing with Alvarro before we got into the lift that almost killed us. You missed all the fun.'

The grin persisted but his eyes darkened. 'I always miss out on all the fun, Miss Adams. Ask old Arch here.'

Archer had sat up a bit. 'Is that true, Rush? Why didn't you say so?'

Rush didn't say a word. Suddenly they were impatient for her to go. Right now. She got up and put her jacket on. Neither man helped her.

'Well, good day, Archer. Thanks very much for your time.'

Ransome nodded without looking at her. He pushed a button and the *Star Trek* doors opened.

Liberty repeated as if they were both deaf, 'I said, "good day". I'll call you for a follow-up, Archer. You too, Rush.'

She turned around and ducked through the brown womb, zipped past the nurse's station, fought her way through the rain forest, and caught an open lift. She held her breath all the way down to the lobby, and didn't begin to breathe normally until she reached Fifty-seventh Street on her way to the Russian Tea Room. On impulse, she hailed a cab. So what if she was only going two blocks? Just then she caught sight of a creepily familiar figure in front of the Trump Tower. As he waited for the light to change, he was watching her. As she stepped into the taxi, she wondered idly: Could he have thought I was waving to him?

3

Kit held her breath, plunged her face into a basin of icy water, and lifted it, dripping, to the mirror. Under the fluorescent light of the ladies' room, she looked frail, the skeleton surfacing through transparent skin. Her eyes looked crazy. Her lips were chapped, her hands sweaty and cramped. She patted herself dry with a rough brown paper towel and took out her make-up bag. The nervous flush that had freshened her looks this morning had given way to a hollow-eyed pallor by evening. She fixed her make-up, brushed her hair fiercely until her scalp tingled, then tossed her head back, revived. Now she was ready. It might be seven o'clock in the evening here in New York City, but out in LA it was only four in the afternoon, and people were just getting back from siesta.

Back in her office in the penthouse suite of the Ransome Enterprises building, Sasha was talking on the phone. She motioned for Sasha to join her as soon as she was free.

'How was the screening?' Sasha mouthed to her.

Kit stared at her blankly.

Sasha put her hand over the mouthpiece. 'Didn't you just see *Nursery Games*?'

Kit roused herself. 'Twenty-five minutes too long.'

She closed the door behind her, leaning against it. *Last Chance* was all she could think about. Every time the phone rang, she thought it would be Archer.

Placing a finger lightly on the side of her neck, she felt her pulse jerking against it. She sat down with her back to her desk and stared out the window.

Dusk had claimed Manhattan, or so the string of lights down the length of Fifth Avenue told her. She was used to gauging time by the way the sun swung around her office in LA, making a sundial of her desk. Here, she never knew.

Sasha came in and switched on the lights, ready to work.

'Let's go through the calls first. By the way, were you able to get me tickets to *Lord Passion* for tomorrow night?'

'No problem,' said Sasha. 'I called the producer's office. I'm sending a messenger to pick them up.' She paused. 'At nine-thirty, Gerry Braxton called. Said it was urgent. He wants you to postpone the opening of *Straight Flush* until after the New York Film Festival. He told me about eight times he was worried that the festival would take the press's attention off his film. Does that make sense?'

'It makes sense, but I don't agree with him. Make a note: we'll call Sheridan tomorrow and tell him to get back to Braxton that the date is firm.'

Sasha continued. 'Mike Wallace, twice. Once at ten-o-five, and again just before noon. His secretary said he wants to see you for lunch this week. He'd like to do something on *Last Chance* for *Sixty Minutes*.'

'That's all I need,' Kit said sardonically. 'Make a lunch date for Wednesday.'

'You have the budget meeting Wednesday.'

Kit smiled wryly. 'Then you'll just have to cancel for me on Tuesday.'

'Devin dropped by to say the meeting went well. He said Watkins was harmless as a baby.'

'Some baby. Well, we'll see. What else?'

'Sheridan's office called at eleven with the final figure for the opening weekend on *Comin' and Goin'*.'

'Yes? And it was . . .?'

'Just under $3,650,000.'

'In how many theatres?'

'Six hundred.'

'Let's see: that's about six thousand dollars per screen. That's really very good. Better than I had hoped for. I thought we'd do about two-point-five, two-point-eight, tops!'

'It played very big in the South.'

'Did he give you any competitive figures?'

Sasha looked at her blankly.

'Figures for the other companies' weekend openings.'

'Oh! No. I guess not. That's all he gave me.'

'Okay, fine. Remind me when I call him about Braxton to get them.'

Sasha said, 'Before I forget. I've put all the reviews of *Comin' and Goin'* on your desk.'

'Did you read them?'

Sasha nodded. 'I'm afraid they were pretty bad. They seemed to be more interested in Jimmy Greco than the movie.'

'That doesn't surprise me. But you can see, Sasha, how little reviews mean to the success of this kind of movie . . . to almost any kind of a movie nowadays. The great critics just aren't writing. Where are the James Agees?'

Sasha cleared her throat. 'Speaking of critics, Liberty Adams' secretary called.'

Kit rolled her eyes and said, 'Good Lord, not again.'

'She called at ten-thirty, eleven-fifteen, one-thirty, two-forty-five, three-fifteen' – Sasha turned the sheet over – 'three-forty-five, four, four-thirty, and five-fifteen. She sure is persistent.'

'That woman! Well, she can have her secretary call as many times as she likes. And tell me, is it still a matter of life and death, our getting together?'

'As of this evening, yes.'

'Honestly! Oh, well, go on.'

'Ms Ransome, one more thing: Susie Shultebrandt came over here especially to see you this afternoon just after you left to screen *Nursery Games*.' Sasha paused, choosing her words carefully. 'She said that Mr Ransome suggested you spend some time with Liberty Adams.'

'He did? Fine.' Kit smiled sweetly. 'The next time she calls, I'm still too busy to see her.'

'Yes, ma'am.' Sasha paused again. 'I think I should tell you that Ms Adams was in this morning to see Mr Ransome.'

'Thank you for telling me, Sasha. Now, may we please continue?'

Sasha blushed and turned her attention back to the sheet. 'Your LA office called. The Variety Club would like you to be chairperson for their fund-raising drive this year.'

Sasha waited, then repeated, 'The Variety Club –'

'I heard you, Sasha. Next?'

'Ralph English called. He wants to set up an appointment to discuss this novel he's bought that he wants to make into a movie. He says he's had some serious nibbles from Columbia, but he wants you to get first shot.'

'Yes, and I'm sure he's given the exact same line to all the other studio heads. "Serious nibbles"! What's the book?'

'It's that best-selling mystery set in China.'

'*Yellow River*,' Kit said. 'Okay, call Rita at the studio and have her send the coverage –'

'Coverage?'

'Synopsis and reader's comments,' Kit explained patiently. 'So I can read it before I have the meeting. Schedule it for tomorrow just before the Julie Rentz meeting. But remind me to read the coverage first.'

'Right.' Sasha made a note. 'Robert Redford called. He would like you to call him back, but he didn't leave a number.'

'I'll call him from the hotel tonight.'

'Mr Alexander's office called to remind you about the budget meeting.'

'How could I forget?' Kit looked at her watch. 'Before we do anything else this evening, Sasha, try to get me Peter Weir in Sydney. It's fourteen hours ahead in Australia. He should be home.'

'Okay,' said Sasha. 'Let me call from my own desk. It might take some time. This new phone system has been acting up lately.'

Sasha left to put through the call and Kit dialled Jay Scott in California.

'Well, don't just sit there making nicey-nicey, Kit,' he said. 'Tell me what happened. Wait a minute: you don't need to tell me. He loved *Last Chance* and he told you to wrap me up for a three-picture deal before I get too expensive, right? Kit, darling, you're not talking. Oh, Kitty Cat! Tell ole Scottie, how did it go?'

'I know it sounds ridiculous, but I don't know.'

'You're right, Kit, it does sound ridiculous,' he said harshly. Then, more gently, 'Didn't you talk to the man?'

'Yes, but only before he saw it.'

'He hated it. That's why he wouldn't talk after.'

'Oh, Scottie, don't be masochistic!'

'It's true, he hated it. It's clear to me and I'm three thousand miles away.'

'Scottie, dear, you are a million miles away, but I love you.'

'And I love you, Kit. Oh, Kit!' He sighed mournfully. 'Tell me good news. Tell me we're not going to shut down the production. Tell me you're going to find the new Lacy first thing tomorrow morning. Tell me she'll be perfect, a sweet young thing who thinks that heroin is a female hero.'

'We *will* find the new Lacy,' she said gently. 'And she'll be *better* than Novak.'

'Kit!' he keened. 'How can you be so cold? The poor child is dead.'

'The poor child was a young woman, and I realise she's dead. I paid for her funeral.'

'Baby's breath and wild roses.'

'Look, I understand that your flip tone hides real grief, but –'

'And I understand that your Ice Queen exterior hides none whatsoever.'

'Let's not argue!' She checked herself, took a deep breath. 'I *miss* you. I haven't laughed once today.'

'Well, what's to laugh about? *I* think he's being deliberately mean to you, not telling you what he thinks of our picture.'

'Perhaps.'

'I'll bet he's fucking you over,' Scott singsonged.

'And he didn't even kiss me first.'

Kit looked up to see Sasha gesturing madly at the door.

'Listen, something's up here. I'll call you tomorrow. Don't worry, for goodness sake, stop being so gloomy. And, Scottie, if you happen to run into any of my colleagues on the lot, like one Randy Sheridan, I'd appreciate your showing a little discretion.' Kit kissed the receiver and hung up.

Sasha stood in the doorway with her hand over the receiver, 'Ms Ransome, I'm sorry, but this is Frank, the projectionist. He says Mr Alexander is sitting in Mr Ransome's private screening room downstairs. He wants to see the *Last Chance* footage. He wants to know where the print is, and he isn't leaving until he sees it. Frank's got the print, but he thought he should check with you first. Mr Alexander is raising hell.'

'I can imagine,' Kit said dryly. 'Tell Frank to thread up the footage. I'll show it to Mr Alexander myself.'

She found him slouching in Archer's chair, puffing on his pipe.

'Rush, how are you?'

'Fine, Kit, fine.' He unwound his legs and rose to kiss her briefly on the lips. 'You look fantastic.'

'And *you* sound grudging.'

'Do I? I don't *feel* grudging.' He smirked. 'You know I'll love you forever regardless of how poorly you treat me.'

'Rush, please, I'm tired. Do you want to see the footage or not?'

'Why should I? If you know your business – and we all know you do, don't we? – it has to be good, right?'

Kit hesitated. 'You're serious. You've kicked up all this fuss and you don't even want to see it?'

'Now, don't go getting your back up with me, Kitty Cat. You know it's the *business* that turns me on, and not the *art*.' He jerked his thumb backwards. 'Tell him to beat it.'

Kit hesitated again and then punched the intercom. 'Leave it threaded, Frank, but that will be all for tonight, thanks.'

A few seconds later, the screening-room lights went off, leaving them in a dim amber night-light.

'So,' said Kit, avoiding his eyes now that they were alone. 'What's up?'

He brought her chin up to make her meet his eyes. 'I hope you know what you're doing on this one. I truly do.'

She arched a brow. 'What's it to you? I haven't noticed you taking any particular interest in Horizon lately.'

'Archer wants to shut down *Last Chance*, Kitty Cat, did you know that? So does your friend Randy.'

'Randy?'

'Randy Sheridan, vice-president for Horizon Pictures. Know the outfit, Kit?'

'And what about you, Rush? Do you want to shut me down?'

He touched a finger lightly to her nose for a minute, then stood up and left.

At that moment, she didn't know who infuriated her more: Archer or Rush. Almost automatically she pressed the button and switched on the *Last Chance* footage. It seemed that she had spent half of her life in places like this: in the flickering depths of movie business, screening rooms, cutting rooms. Was this thirty-minute reel of celluloid, this scene of two men wrestling, the culmination of an entire career?

Kit Ransome had arrived in Los Angeles in 1958 with an acting contract at Centurion Pictures. She was twenty years old and had done some modelling, a couple of television commercials, and the usual acting in the one year of college she had before dropping out. She had taken the contract on a lark, for Kit by no means considered herself an actress. Centurion's talent scout in New York disagreed.

At first Kit was just another filly in Centurion's stable. And, pretending to be a dumb animal, she let them lead her where they would. They worked with what they had, those wily studio trainers. And what they had was an exotic-looking woman with poor projection and the gorgeous legs of a swimmer. So they put her in beach-wreck movies set in distant locales – Hawaii, Tahiti, Bali – cast her as a native girl (so she wouldn't ever have to open her mouth), dressed her in skimpy tunics (to show off those great gams). The public adored her.

Off screen, the studio held her to the image her fans loved. They dressed her in tunics adapted for street wear and instructed her to keep her mouth shut. It wasn't her poor projection that bothered them, it was the fact that they never knew what she was going to say next. 'Just shut your mouth and let the guys with the cameras do their stuff,' they told her. In those days, Kit was still innocent enough to obey them.

But Kit would learn in time to regret her openness with the camera. Her face was everywhere, from the covers of tabloids to the puff-piece sections of news magazines. It was like being locked in a room with too many mirrors. In time it got worse when the mirrors became trickier, bent, like the distorting glasses of fun houses. Kit would catch sight of a tabloid picture of herself on an actor's arm, an actor she'd never even met. She would recognise the background, the front of a restaurant she frequented with a girlfriend. And she'd remember that night when a cameraman had caught them exiting arm in arm. The girlfriend was gone, cut off at the wrist; grafted in her place was a stranger in a tuxedo, a new star Centurion was touting. It unnerved her, as if this were a picture of an event yet to happen, or happening while she was deep in a trance.

Then they began to quote her. At least she recognised her own face in the pictures, but the Kit they published in words was a frightening stranger. This woman was vain, shallow, and bent on sleeping her way to the top. It amazed Kit that the public continued to embrace this woman. By the fourth year of her contract, Kit's press persona had a momentum all its own; even the studio was powerless to control it. Kit moved about Hollywood like an escaped convict waiting to be locked up. She waited for the day when they would discover that she had no real acting talent, to discover there were plenty of prettier women, to discover that she was a fraud. While Kit plotted her escape, she cut down on her public appearances and kept to herself more and more.

Kit went out of her house only to go to work at the studio or to visit her few friends, or to drive her white convertible Oldsmobile mile after mile along the beach late at night. People at the studio began to complain about her antisocial behaviour and her agent took to calling her twice a day.

'Kit-honey...' Sam Rothman spoke with his mouth so close to the receiver Kit could hear him breathing, swallowing, smoking – and thinking, always thinking. He always called her Kit-honey, like it was a single word. 'Kit-honey... they don't like what you've been doing lately.'

'I know they don't, Sammy. But I can't help it.'

'You have to help it, Kit-honey. You're under contract. They –'

'– own me,' Kit finished for him.

'So you gotta be more cooperative.'

'I do my job. I learn my lines, I'm always on time. I do the best I can and then I go home. I don't even ask them for more money.'

'That's like a secretary saying she can type. For God's sake, Kit-honey, you should know the rules by now.'

Kit sat cross-legged in a rocker in her small bedroom, her embroidery in her lap. She jammed her thumb into a silver thimble, listening for the sound of her nail inside the hollow top.

'Maybe I don't understand the rules, Sammy.' Kit spoke down to her silver thumb.

'Yes, you do. You're smart. You just think there's a way around them. But there's not.'

'Are you sure?'

'Yep. I'm more than sure. I'm a pretty successful man, Kit-honey. I make my money by knowing what people will buy. I gotta know people pretty good if I'm gonna be able to survive. Lots of guys go around saying they know what people want to see. But I go around saying I know what people will *pay* to see. It's all a question of money, Kit-honey. All of it's money. Now, these people I convince, you know, the studio people and the public – they all want a little free of what they're gonna pay to see. A little free. Now, in your case' – Sam Rothman interrupted himself with a cough, swallowed hard and went on – '... in your case, Kit-honey, a little free Kit can be found in the newspapers and magazines and before the TV cameras. If the free Kit is good enough, then they're gonna be happy to pay for the high-priced Kit... then you'll keep working and I'll keep working and Hollywood will keep whirlin'.

It's all money, Kit-honey. That's what business is all about. You gotta step up to it, Kit-honey.'

Step up to it. Kit mulled it over. She wondered where Sammy got his phrase, but he always used it when he was serious, when he expected her to give in, to straighten up. She wondered if it were sports slang or agent's jargon, or maybe gambler's code.

'Just give me some more time.'

'Time, Kit-honey? That's the one thing a pretty young actress like you doesn't have. You go down to the studio tomorrow –'

'It's my day off.'

'So. Good. You autograph some pictures of yourself, offer to answer some fan mail, make nice to the press guys. Give out a little free Kit.'

'Guess what I found at the studio yesterday, Sammy? An original poster of *Double Indemnity*.'

'Yeah? Isn't that the one where Barbara Stanwyck gets someone to kill her husband?'

'Yeah, Sammy, she really stepped up to it. Murder.'

Sam hung up laughing.

Kit held the letter nearer to the fire and read aloud.

'"I find the desert still my greatest friend, my craftiest enemy. The heat has infiltrated my body so that I move slowly. But still the Angels multiply. Rows and rows of torsos surround the cats. They whine up at the statues as if they were asking me to give them heads and legs. I resist. The heart, the cunt, the wings ... they are enough ... for now. Received your letter and all the clippings of you from ... what did you call them ... fanzines? Your question about the press ... and the pressure. Transcend and never trust a journalist. Kitsia Ransome."'

Kit crumpled the letter and stuffed it into her slacks.

'What are the Angels?' Kenly, her actress friend, wanted to know.

'That's what she calls her work, her sculpture, when they're female nudes. All she ever does now, Angels.'

'You shouldn't read me your mother's letters. They're private, Kit.'

'No, they're not, Kenly. Really. She wouldn't mind. She doesn't believe in private and public. It's all the same to her.'

Kenly Smith fitted an unfiltered cigarette into a gold filagreed

55

holder and lit it with a long fireplace match. Absently she stroked her neck with her fingers and watched the fire.

'Everyone keeps some things private. Secret. Even your mama, Kit.'

'I doubt it. Did you hear how she signed this letter? "Kitsia Ransome". Not "love, your mother", or "love, Kitsia", or even just "Kitsia". No, "Kitsia Ransome". It's like she's signing one of her statues.'

'You should go easier on her, Kit.'

'I can't help it. She's so...' Kit hesitated. The music had stopped. Kit waited while Kenly got up and changed the record; watched her glide over to the hi-fi, her pale lavender kimono falling like a fountain down her back. Kenly Smith was forty years old and a big movie star whose career was teetering. She needed a special role to put her back on track – one that would show her public she was still worth seeing, not just as a beautiful screen siren, but as an actress.

'Would you prefer *Turandot* or *La Bohème*?'

Kit shrugged. 'Either's fine.' Kit knew very little about opera. Kenly knew all there was to know.

Kenly had been a star for Centurion for nearly twenty years. She had made them a lot of money. But she and her husband, Moss, lived modestly. He was a successful costume designer. They had no children. Kenly had worked all her life, worked hard at being a star; nothing else really mattered. Nothing could.

'Kit. You should listen to Sam. He's right. If you want to be a star.'

'Oh, Kenly, that's just it. I don't want to be a star.'

'You don't?' Kenly said, sitting back down.

'No. I'm not a very good actress. I'm not even a mediocre actress. I hate the publicity and the press. I'm *embarrassed* by all the attention.' Kit strained towards the fire to thread her needle. She pulled a dark green thread taut through the material, filling in a segment in the design of a cactus plant.

'Now, me, I'm never embarrassed. Fantasy. Pretending. It doesn't embarrass me. And that's what all of this is – pretend!' Kenly extended her arms wide, embracing the aria.

Kit bent over her work. The clicking sound of the needle against her thimble made a racket to her. Kenly seemed to hear only the Puccini.

56

'I guess I should be embarrassed,' Kenly went on, 'about . . . you know . . . but I'm not.'

Kit nodded weakly. Even before they met, Kit had known all about Kenly from the newspapers and magazines and from the gossip.

'A little more wine, Kit?' asked Kenly, filling her own glass.

'No. Thanks.'

Kenly was a beautiful woman. Very blonde, she wore her thick shoulder-length hair parted on the side. She had pale blue eyes with tiny pupils. The studio had once wanted her to wear tinted contact lenses to make her eyes darker, but her pale eyes turned out to be the thing her public liked best about her.

Kenly's cheeks were bitten with acne scars. But Kenly always wore heavy theatrical make-up whenever she went out, and all her photographs were retouched. It was strange, Kit thought, how she could know so many intimate things about Kenly Smith, and the one thing that seemed so obvious, so hard to hide – what she looked like – was actually a secret to her public.

'Kenly, you're a beautiful woman,' Kit said at last.

'Moss says I'm a goddess.' Kenly laughed away the compliment. 'Now, *you* could be anything you want. The problem with you, Kit, is you don't know who you want to be. You only know who you *don't* want to be.'

Kit refitted her embroidery hoop over another segment of the cactus plant. She didn't answer Kenly. When *Turandot* was over, she got up, thanked her for the poster, and got in her car to drive back to her apartment in Topanga Canyon.

In the fifth and final year of her contract, Kit made good her plan to bolt from the stable. She kept her eye on the board, and when an opening in the production department was posted, she went for it with everything she had. And so, in 1963, she retired from the screen and became assistant to the studio's brightest young man. Richard Bickley Crawford, or Bic, as everyone called him.

Her office was a tiny room the size of a supply closet at one end of a long corridor. At the other end was Bic Crawford's large and well-furnished office. Kit did her best to decorate her office, no matter how small. She came in on Saturday and painted the gunmetal-grey walls bone white. She hung her posters of *Double*

Indemnity and *The Letter* on the one clear wall. With Bic Crawford at the other end of that hall, she'd need Stanwyck and Davis to give her strength.

Kit wound up spending most of her time on Bic's court, even though, for the first two years, she was only on the sidelines. How could she be otherwise? She had no real job there, no real job description. She never spoke up at meetings. She did one thing, and that was to write helpful memos to Bic. Since Bic was one of sixteen production executives at Centurion, and didn't intend to stay in the pack for long, he accepted all the help she could give him. Yet in spite of the advice he sometimes took from her, he still didn't trust her enough to let her conduct any business independently for him. Kit understood his reluctance and didn't push him. Men, she figured, moved in their own time, according to their own internal clock. She could bide her time. In the meantime, Kit was content to write her memos to Bic; about the scripts she read, the movies she'd seen, the books or news items that would make good movies, her thoughts on an industry she was only just beginning to learn from this side of the lights.

'Bic, you know, I saw an important movie yesterday.' Kit was standing at his desk, swaying slightly towards the desk and then pushing off with her fingertips.

'Write it up for me, Kitty ... will ya? I'm kinda busy right now.'

'It's important, Bic. You've got that creative meeting after lunch, and I've got some ideas for you,' she said sweetly.

Bic leaned far back in his chair and reached behind him for his Atlas grip. Squeezing it, he directed his attention to her.

Kit sat down in a club chair. She tugged at her navy-blue skirt and flirted a little. He wasn't noticing.

'Okay, shoot.'

'Well,' Kit began, 'yesterday I saw *Dr Strangelove or How I Learned to Stop Worrying and Love the Bomb*, and I realised right then that America is really starting to shift ... to move to –'

'America's *what*?'

'It's beginning to change. You can't imagine how irreverent *Dr Strangelove* is ... it pokes outrageous fun at everything.' Kit began to talk faster. She herself was only just beginning to get it. Maybe because she was a foreigner, she could see America differently. She had to make Bic see it differently too.

'Listen, Bic ... the New York *Times*'s movie critic said ... "there was a feeling which runs all through the film, of depreciation and even contempt for our whole defence establishment..."

'Don't you see, even the press has lost the scent for the moment? It's like we're all suspended in time – no, in space. We're hovering between the old and the new. The press is usually there, putting its foot into the new soil quickest. But not this time. Here the movie has taken the lead and now we're all bound to follow. You'll see the *Times*'s critic will be gone soon. He doesn't get it. Bic, you've got to follow... cross over now.'

'I'm not sure I get it, Kitty.' Bic stood up and began to touch his toes.

'It's simple, really –' Kit began.

He interrupted her. 'You're telling me that everybody's fair game. New means young. We got to make different movies now... movies that will get people like Bosley Crowther and my old man and the head of this fuckin' studio mad.'

Kit nodded.

'It's just like the kind of basketball young guys play today. Everybody says the old basketball was better. It was patterned, skilful... ball players played defence. But these new guys run and jump on natural neighbourhood raw talent. They're young and black and in a hurry to get down court and score.'

'Exactly.'

Bic came round and kissed Kit on the top of her head. 'You're real smart, Kit. I love your brains. I bet I'd love your cunt, too.' He grabbed at her. She pushed him away, but slowly.

Sure enough, the *Times*, *Time*, and *Newsweek* all hired younger critics. Bic Crawford became senior VP Production for Centurion. And Kit Ransome became his story editor and his lover all in the same day.

'Stroke me a memo on it, Kitty Cat, if you think the story's that good. Then we'll see.' Bic walked back and forth in front of her desk as if he were on a treadmill.

'Bic, there's something important we need to talk about.'

'Don't have much time, Kit. Can't we talk about it tonight?'

Kit suffocated. 'Bic, I want to become a production vice-president.' She waited for him to comment. He kept pacing, hands on his hips, and said nothing.

'I've paid my dues for four years...'

He stopped pacing and looked at her. His eyes jumped around as if computing the number of years he had known her. He started pacing again.

Kit's heart began to pound. She knew she was as good as or better than any of the men who worked for Bic. It wasn't her creative ability she doubted; it was her business ability. She had half-expected Bic to come to her and reward her for her good work: reward all the little things she did that went unnoticed, all her behind-the-scenes manoeuvring. She'd helped Bic a lot over the years. Her memos were exciting, concise, manipulative; they convinced people to make a movie. He almost always used them to make his case to his colleagues. She advised him how to go about changing his look, too. Instead of open shirts and gold chains, she put him in expensive Italian suits. She even convinced him to wear clear nail polish.

'As you know, Bic, I make considerably less than any of the men on your staff.' There, she'd said it.

Bic flopped down on her couch and lay lengthwise with his eyes closed. 'Yeah.'

'Yes. And I want a fifty-percent increase.'

'Forget it, Kit! We don't give fifty-percent jumps.'

'I want it . . . the money *and* the title.'

'Uh – hunh. It's one or the other, babycakes. A fifteen-percent rise with the title . . .' – he opened one eye – 'and an office upstairs . . . near me. Or it's the money and no new job.'

Bic stood up and pretended to putt imaginary golf balls onto a green. He smiled up at Kit and ran his tongue over his very white teeth.

'Rita,' Bic called over his shoulder, keeping his eyes on Kit, 'get your boss packed. She's movin' upstairs.'

Several months had passed and Kit was settling into her new job.

'Yes?' Now she held the receiver right against her ear with her shoulder.

'Have you been watching the dailies on *The Red Desire*?' Bic screamed into the phone. 'Have you seen what they're doing?'

'Bic, calm down.'

'Jesus, Kit, at the rate they're going, this movie will go way over budget.'

'I know.' Kit's voice was as calm as a thickly frozen lake. Bic's anger skidded across it. 'Have you read your mail yet?'

'No,' he answered petulantly.

'Well,' Kit went on, leaving out the *if you had*, 'when you have a chance, you'll see I've sent you a memo recommending we replace the director –'

'You mean *fire* him?' he interrupted rudely.

'Yes,' Kit said.

'Then say *fire*!' He slammed down the phone.

Kit replaced the receiver and sat staring at the phone console ... the light grey pushbuttons sat in the middle of the console. Two rows of colourless squares were strung along the top and in one long narrow strip of paper were typed all the production executives' initials and their private intercom numbers.

All the production people were connected in two ways. In the obvious way, one secretary would dial another secretary, and then their bosses would pick up, once contact was made. Then there was the other way – the private intercom system which allowed for quick and secretive communication. One executive just picked up the receiver, dialled two numbers, and another executive's phone buzzed directly in his office. A lot of side deals were made this way. Things were said on this private line which were often denied on the regular lines. It wasn't unusual for people to leave a meeting and a few hours later to find all the decisions from that meeting had come unravelled by the Buzzer Brigade. It took Kit a while to get used to the power of the buzz.

Bic buzzed Kit twenty or thirty times a day. Usually it was with a quick question. What's the start-of-production date on such and such a film? Did you get the second-unit director we wanted? Sometimes it was an ambush: Bic being his brambly self.

'Rita,' Kit spoke into the intercom. 'What are my appointments today?'

'Shall I come in, Miss Ransome, in a moment?'

'Yes. Fine.'

Kit knew this was Rita's code for 'Someone is standing near me'.

Rita was a good secretary. Kit and Rita were the same age, thirty-two, but whereas Kit was beautiful, Rita was cute. She had a round face, brown eyes, and bleached blonde hair that she permed in short curls all over her head. Rita dressed every day as if it were eighty degrees outside – in sandals, cotton skirts, and T-shirts. She changed her nailpolish three times a week.

Where secretarial skills were concerned, Rita was not a hot property. She was a virtuoso performer on the telephone, but beyond that, her typing was mediocre, her shorthand sluggish and often untranscribable, and she filed only on the fifteenth of each month. But Rita had an instinctive understanding of the subtle workings of office politics. She knew where her loyalty lay. With Rita standing guard outside her door, Kit never had to deal with surprises.

And yet, for all her fierce loyalty, Rita treated Kit as if she were a creature from outer space. It wasn't because she was the first woman executive she had ever worked for, it was because Kit had quit being a star to sit behind a desk. In Rita's book, that was just plain crazy. When Rita learned that Kit had grown up in a place called Zwar, she felt vindicated. Kit was different from other people, she *was* strange. Yet, oddly enough, Rita did not think it was strange that Kit slept with her boss. After all, even *normal* women did that.

Rita came in balancing folders in one arm and gently dragging a package behind her.

'*The Red Shoes* poster,' Rita explained. 'It finally came. It took me two years to track this sucker down.'

'Good. Get someone to hang –'

'Maintenance will be here at eleven o'clock while you're at dailies. Let me know where you want it hung. You've got ten minutes before Jim "Don't-call-me-Incredibly-Talented" Robinson gets here.' She closed the door behind her.

Kit met with Jim, met with the ad agency, lunched with a screenwriter, worked like a fiend all day, stopping only occasionally to drink a tall glass of lime juice with a touch of honey.

'Rita . . . come in . . . do I have a three-o'clock with Philip and Josie?'

'Mr Nigel can't make it, but Josie's coming. You have to give BC your casting suggestions by six.' Rita examined her nails carefully.

Kit smiled. The highest compliment Rita could give someone was to refer to him by his initials. 'Okay. Let's try to return a few of these phone calls.'

'*Daily Variety* called. They want someone to confirm or deny the rumour that the director of *Red Desire* has been fired.'

'God, word travels fast. Tell them we don't –'

'– comment on rumours. I already did.' Rita was by the door. Bic buzzed her. Rita left her office.

'Yes?' Kit answered.

'Do we still have the option on *The Parade's Over*?'

'We let it lapse.'

'Why?'

'You said *you* wouldn't go see a movie about two lovers who worked in a carnival,' Kit reminded him.

'I did?'

'Yes.'

'I'm right. I wouldn't.' He hung up.

She wondered why Philip Nigel had decided not to come to the casting meeting. Just yesterday he had seen her at the commissary and had made a big point of scheduling the meeting. Kit ran some red lipstick over her lips. She buzzed Philip.

'Yes?' His voice sounded as if he were expecting someone else. 'Oh, Kit . . . what can I do for you?'

'I just wondered why you've dropped out of my three-o'clock.' Kit brushed a little grey shadow onto her eyelids.

'Just too busy. I've got to get a rough cut of *Too Hot* ready for Crawford. We've got a full-court press on.'

'Hmmm.' Kit dabbed lime-base perfume on her throat. Philip, she thought, had picked up this trick of not attending any meeting that Bic didn't attend. If Bic wasn't there, it couldn't be important.

'Look, Kit, you and Josie can handle this. I'll go along with whatever you suggest.'

'Talk to you later.' Kit hung up. No doubt Philip was confident that Bic would go along with him against Kit and Josie. Otherwise, he'd be waltzing into her office right now with his ever-present sunglasses on, holding one of his orange note cards with six 'gorgeous' names neatly typed.

'Yes, Rita.'

'Miss Ransome . . . Josie's here.'

'Send her in, please.'

Josie Winnerhauwer, Centurion's director of casting, came into Kit's office without paper or folders or so much as a pen. Josie talked and listened, talked and listened. She never took notes. Josie had a good memory, a memory not unlike Bic's except whereas Bic could remember lots of different things, Josie had an idiot savant's memory – for actors and actresses only.

'Don't tell me Mr Sunglasses is too busy?'

Kit nodded.

'Anything we decide is just fine with him.'

Kit nodded again.

'That lazy prick!' Josie put an ashtray on her lap and slipped her shoes off. Without missing a beat, she began her casting monologue. It was always the same: she'd name an actor, rattle off three of his credits, rate him from one to ten as an actor and then rate his 'rightness' for this particular movie part from one to five.

Kit listened with one ear. Rita said you had to be a rocket scientist to follow Josie's intricate rating system, but Kit had the hang of it.

'So, Kit . . . we've got a sixty-three, a twenty-five, and an eighty-two. Which one you figure Crawford'll buy? Fucking Christ, I forgot Alan Dalton. He's only done one movie, but not only has he got a cock eight feet long, but he's a seven . . . four . . . yeah a seventy-four. I'd take that over an eighty-two. Philip will hate him.'

'Well, as long as Philip left it up to "us girls".'

'Done?'

'Done.'

Josie left and Kit dictated the casting memo and then began to read a script. She stopped and glanced at her wristwatch: five forty-five. She was waiting for Bic to buzz her, as she waited every day at this time.

'Yes,' Kit answered. It was Rita's buzz.

'Sunglasses on two for you.'

Kit picked up.

'No sixty-nines, eh, Kit?'

'I don't know what you're talking about, Philip.' Kit kept her eyes on the console.

'Your and Josie's memo – no sixty-nines!' Philip laughed again at his own joke.

'So?'

'I don't think you *ladies*' – he strung the last word out – 'have quite hit on it.'

Bic buzzed her. Her heart leapt. Philip's call, his attempt to cross her and Josie, now seemed very unthreatening.

'Hold on, Philip.' She had trouble keeping the note of triumph out of her voice as she put him on hold and picked up on Bic. 'Yes?'

'You free tonight? I am. Why don't you meet me at home around seven. I've got a couple of steaks we can scorch.' Bic hung up.

Kit released the hold button. 'Look, Phil,' she spoke dismissively, 'I suggest that we wait and hash this out at tomorrow's meeting. That'll give you time to read the script tonight so you'll know what you're talking about.' She depressed the button. *This round, I'll win, Sunglasses!*

Kit woke with a start. Six-oh-five a.m. The sun had crawled under her eyelids. She had been dreaming about Zwar. In her dream there was a huge white screen and Kitsia was arranging her Angels behind it. Making the screen come alive with shadows.

Kit looked at Bic sleeping soundly. He lay flat on his stomach, arms splayed, like an exhausted hunting dog. Sometime in the night Bic had put on his black satin sleep mask. Kit teased him about it, calling him Miss Crawford. 'My Mildred can still *Pierce* you,' he had told her, taking out his cock. It had been a very long night.

Kit swung her legs over the side of the bed and stared down at the Kleenex crumpled all over the floor.

In ten minutes she was dressed, back into the clothes she had worn yesterday and into her old white Oldsmobile driving to her house.

Kit had spent almost every night of the last four years with Bic Crawford. Every afternoon Kit would sit in her office waiting for him to buzz her to let her know if they were on. He *always* buzzed between 5:45 and 5:50. If it was after 5:50 and Bic needed to speak with her, but he didn't want to see her that night, he'd have his secretary place the call.

If they were on, Kit would drive herself over to his house. She chose to keep nothing at his house – no change of clothing, no make-up, nothing. In the morning, she would leave his house on Mullholland Drive and drive to her house in Topanga Canyon, shower, change clothes, and be at the studio by 9:45.

Kit's house was a six-room bungalow tucked between two clumps of sage. She spent very little time there. It had minimal furniture, no plants, and large closets with plenty of hangers. Kit had a maid service, an answering service, and a gardener. It was just like a hotel. Her Oldsmobile felt more like home.

Kit slammed the car door shut. She grabbed her sunglasses off the dash and fitted the tea she had just made into a plastic holder. She backed the car out of his driveway, turned on the radio, punched buttons until some music came on, and settled back. Her left arm, resting on the top of the door, was warmed by the sun. She was on her way back to her normal life, to herself.

It was as if she had been split into two women: Kit Ransome, the studio executive, a woman who had the authority to read policy to producers, the intelligence to make important script decisions, the power to hire and fire directors; Kit Ransome, the mistress of Bic Crawford, a woman stripped of all authority, drained of intelligence, and done out of her power by a lover who was bigger, stronger, and more dominating than she. She gave herself to him at night, and took herself back in the morning.

It was easy. During the day, she simply ceased to think of him as her lover. She'd look across the conference table and see the same Bic they all saw: a big, handsome all-American boy. And if at night he put her through bizarre trials that would now and then make her loathe the sight of him, all she had to do was close her eyes and bring to mind that all-American boy at the conference table and she'd forgive him anew.

In 1972 an international film festival was held in Sri Lanka. Kit convinced Bic to put in an appearance.

'All right, Furry Kitty,' he conceded one night, 'If you want me to rub elbows with the wops and the geeks, I'll come.'

'Can we stop off and visit my mom on the way back? You'll like her.'

'Mom.' What would Kitsia have done if she'd heard herself called that?

Bic had walked up one aisle of Kitsia's studio and down the other, whispering to Kit out of the corner of his mouth. 'I've never seen so many tits and cunts in my entire life. What's with her?'

Kit could tell from the set of her mother's back that Kitsia sensed what was being said about her. Still, Kitsia patiently completed the tour, escorting the two of them out of the studio and off to their luncheon. She would not join them.

Kitsia had no intention of interrupting her work to entertain guests. As a result, Kit spent most of her time 'out on the town' with Bic.

She hardly recognised the town. Nightclubs had sprung up all over in her absence. Cousin Archer had started a gambling casino called Trips, and the casino had attracted other similar businesses. Bic fitted in here as he would in any nightclub environment anywhere on earth, from Vegas to Rio to Macao. Kit found it distasteful, this new, civilised Zwar, and like her mother, blamed it all on Cousin Archer.

'Hell, Kitty Cat, it's not such a weird place after all,' Bic told her.

Everywhere they went they ran into the emir's sons. Akmed and Dhali played baccarat at Trips every night, handsome in their dinner jackets. They often joined Bic and Kit at night, driving them about in their bronze custom Mercedes, and stirring their hundred-dollar-a-bottle champagne with gold swizzle sticks to spin out the bubbles. Bic, impressed by their style, enjoyed these hot desert nights, and it began to seem to Kit that he belonged and she was the outsider.

'How dare she not entertain us!' she said to Bic one night.

He was unperturbed. 'Ease up, Kitty Cat, the lady's obviously a fiend for her work. And who could blame her? Look at these babes.' He patted the rump of the nearest statue. 'I never saw angels with arses like these. And the amazing thing is that the old lady herself is such a skinny-arsed little thing.' Reaching between her legs, he grabbed her from behind, whispering in her ear, 'Tell me, Kit, how does it feel to have a mother who digs cunt more than cock? Does it make you want mine even more?'

Indeed, Kitsia's home and Kitsia's sculpture, and Kitsia's working day after day in that big grey building, proved to be something of an aphrodisiac for the already stimulated Bic. All day long, Bic followed Kit around the house, wanting her. He saw the photographs of her when she was ten years old, sleek as a wet cat, and he wanted to make love to her while he looked at them. 'I want to pretend that I'm fucking that little ten-year-old pussycat. I bet if I'd been around back then, I could have shared you with Akmed, eh?'

Kit blushed furiously to think what Akmed might have told him. Four days before their two-week stay was to end, she was summoned to her mother's studio.

Kitsia was sketching a nude. She spoke as if the naked woman crouching up on the table were not in the room.

'I want you to take that American boy of yours and leave my house immediately.'

Kit winced. The sound of charcoal scratching against the dark green paper, like fingernails over slate, brought tears to her eyes.

'I've had to abandon my big project because of him. I can't concentrate on it. I can't work with him in the next building. I can scarcely *breathe* with the knowledge that you and he are together.'

'What do you mean?' Bic had been nothing but charming in her mother's presence. She'd kept an eye on him, watching for the chink in his behaviour through which Kitsia would pour herself venomously, as only she could. But none presented itself. 'What are you talking about?' she asked. 'He makes me happy.'

Kitsia kept her eyes on the model. 'Happiness isn't important, compared to the things I can think of.'

'Like what, Mother?'

'Like being true to yourself!'

'Oh, please, Mother. I'm harder on myself than you. *I* think I make a special effort.'

'That doesn't mean that you don't have blind spots. What do you think love is but the development of a huge blind spot to the weaknesses in those we love.'

Kit saw it coming.

'I love him, Mother, if that's what you're getting at. And he loves me. Sometimes he's a little aggressive, sometimes things he says come out sounding coarse and cruel. Why, you sound cruel a lot of the time, but you don't really mean it. Bic's no more cruel than you are.'

Kitsia flung the drawing board off her knees and pitched the charcoal after it. She rose to face her daughter. 'Cruel, my dear? He's a *monster*. He cares for no one but himself. He'll eat you alive.'

4

Liberty slid open the gate of her lift. The hall light fell on Paul Newman in the *Hud* poster. In that instant she knew why she was so attracted to Archer Ransome: he was very nearly as handsome.

She stood for a minute without turning on the rest of the lights, not sure she liked the feel of the dark or her loft's close clutter. Tonight, it made her the slightest bit itchy. She'd spent too much time here lately. Three weeks of nonstop writing. Then again, that's what she had quit the column to do: not flirt, not play office politics, not do business lunches and drinks and parties, but write. To put herself at ease, she went around and turned on every single light in the place: in the bathroom, over the couch in the living room, in the kitchen, and finally, the friendly gooseneck in her study. Her desk was built into the dormer and faced uptown. The Empire State Building shone jack-o'-lantern orange tonight. She threw open the window and let in the warm wind, smelling of ocean and monoxide. The wind riffled a fresh sheet of paper in her red Selectric. She shrugged and sat down to work, not bothering to take off her jacket or boots; she picked up where she'd left off early that morning before she left to have breakfast with Maddy.

At eight-thirty Liberty looked up from her typewriter for the first time and realised, as her stomach thundered, that she hadn't eaten since the blinis and caviar at the Tea Room. Victoria had sat there popping those little Beluga balloons with her fork, saying that an extension was out of the question. They were still expecting the draft next week, and Liberty hadn't even got to Kit yet. She was realising, however, that when it came to Kit Ransome, the deadline wasn't the only thing bearing down upon her. She had to get to her – and soon.

Liberty peeled off her trousers and jacket and stripped to her underwear, easing her aching feet into the fuzzy red bunny slippers she kept parked beneath her chair. She wheeled herself over and turned on the phone-answering machine to collect the day's messages. Then she got up and began to tidy the loft.

Like all lofts, it was a single large room, but this one was so tightly packed up underneath the eaves and among the dormers – three windows facing uptown, three windows on the Hudson – that each dormer made of the space within it a natural room. The rooms were just right for Liberty, since, in bunny slippers or spikes, she never cleared more than five-foot-three. The men who came here had to be warned to duck. The kitchen, underneath the skylight in the centre of the floor, provided the only airy, open space. You didn't have to duck here, but it wasn't cosy either. The creeps washed over Liberty once again as she stared up through the dark skylight and imagined, for a moment, that she saw a man's face peering down on her, his nose mashed against the glass. She shook her head and the face disappeared. Last night it had been a weird insect in the bathtub. Another night, asleep, she'd heard a pounding on the fire door, only to wake to the sound of the blood beating in her ears. It was the writing that was doing this to her. Her imagination was on golden time these days, so fertile that *anything* seemed possible, but the cost might be tremendous.

The tape beeped and Liberty jumped.

'Liberty! My irascible vixen! We're at Elaine's and it's not the same without you. Stop tickling those typewriter keys and come tickle me.'

Liberty would know that voice anywhere: Robert Ross – or 'Broadway Bob', as she called him – the high-strung director-choreographer she'd interviewed for a *Flash* Attachment – 'The Happy Hoofer'.

The service beeped and she heard Bob again: 'Sweet Liberty. I want your tiny body in my great big bed this week.'

In the past, the men Liberty slept with had two things in common: they were usually over fifty, and they were the subject of *Flash* Attachment interviews. *Flash* Attachment subjects were generally male: interviews were at Lutèce or in bed. Bob differed from the others; he'd hung in there longer. They were approaching their third anniversary – if you could call it that.

Liberty stood at the open refrigerator and took a swig from a half-full bottle of Pouilly Fuissé, and then a swig from an open bottle of seltzer: a spritzer in a gulp.

Her stomach growled as she foraged for the makings of a sandwich and made herself a real spritzer in a frosted tumbler.

'Liberty, this is your friendly, unobtrusive downstairs neighbour. Descend from your skylight loft when you get a chance and take a look at the new haircut I've just designed. It's made for you. You're looking shaggy, little fox.'

Liberty looked at her reflection in the window next to the refrigerator. She did need a haircut. When the story was filed, she'd get one.

She sniffed the cheddar cheese and examined the tomato for signs of refrigerator odour. She sliced thick black pumpernickel and slathered it with mayonnaise before piling it high with slabs of cheese and tomato. Sitting on a high stool at the cooking island in the centre of her kitchen, Liberty scanned the printout Peg had punched up concerning Anthony Alvarro.

He had been on Archer Ransome's payroll for twenty-five years starting out as Ransome Enterprises' first bookkeeper and working up to vice-president of financial services. In 1980 he'd left Ransome Enterprises in a huff over some territorial dispute with Rush Alexander. Ransome had wooed him back, two years later, from the Midwest, where he'd gone to be president of a petrochemical outfit. According to Peg, Alvarro's secretary had come unstrung when she'd called to flesh out the computer data. From what Peg could tell, the woman was paranoid that Peg was discreetly researching for her boss's obit. Anthony T. Alvarro had plenty of fight in him yet. Why, hadn't he just come back from a special top-secret troubleshooting mission in Zwar?

What sort of mission? Peg had the presence of mind to ask, and was told that just after the emir had died, Alvarro had been sent over to the QT to solidify Ransome Enterprises' position with the new emir. Peg said she could just hear the woman clam up after that. Peg wouldn't print any of that, would she? She'd lose her job, etc, etc. Peg said she'd think about it. Peg was learning.

Beep.

'Only for you, angel, would the Old Girl talk to one of these *machines*. I've read it, my dear, and I have only one thing to say: *Too nice!*' Click.

'No rewrites. Mad, not even for you.'

She pulled out a tin of Italian roast espresso and dumped a handful into the electric grinder. Filling the pot with fresh grounds, she set it over a low flame and started to write while it dripped. The sound of boiling coffee, like airgun pellets on a window, roused her from her work.

A few minutes later, carrying coffee and pad, she retired to her desk, thankful that the message tape was over. She left the machine turned up so that she could hear who was calling. Espresso at her elbow, she sat down and studied the notes on her bulletin board, filling out new cards with the notes taken that day.

'Potamac Opera Society. Casa Verde. Ebenezer. Ebenezer Scrooge?' Archer and Rush's secret code didn't exactly require a decoder ring. Potamac Opera Society was Washington, DC, or someone *from* DC. Casa Verde was Spanish for Greenhause, the SEC guy who was preparing to sing. But Ebenezer threw her for a loop. Dickens and opera? The boys were mixing their metaphors. She was stumped.

Still, she had to admit that Ransome and Alexander were a fascinating team. She took down Hamilton's *Greek Mythology* and looked through the index. Flipping to the right page, she skimmed until she got to the story of the legendary brothers.

'"... who in most accounts were said to live half of their time on earth and half in heaven... Accounts of them are contradictory. Sometimes Pollux alone is held to be divine, and Castor a mortal who won a kind of half-and-half immortality because of his brother's love."'

Castor and Pollux. It fit, all right. She snapped the book shut. Just how strong was their bond?

She wandered over to the vanity unit and sat down, picking up the small green cloisonné turtle with sapphire eyes and turning it over in her hand. How could something so small and so beautiful be such a pain? How had she got herself into this, clinking around in Kitsia Ransome's closet with all those family skeletons? Why had she consented to play the messenger girl, carrying that turtle halfway around the world to deliver it to Kit – when she couldn't even get close to her?

She looked at the hand holding the turtle: it was trembling. Too much coffee, too little sleep. Settling the turtle back down on the vanity unit, she stared straight into the photograph taped to the upper right-hand corner of the mirror. It was a blurred black and white: a snapshot of a young woman, about Liberty's age, with long, rippling hair like the princess in a 1940's book of illustrated fairy tales.

The photograph had fallen out of the second-hand prayer book that she'd been given on her second birthday. When Liberty had shown it to Sister Bertrand, she had explained that it probably belonged to the missal's previous owner. Orphans had to get used to previous owners: they couldn't be proud. But Liberty was proud: she liked to pretend the woman in the photograph was her mother. Not that they looked alike. Liberty didn't look anything like a fairy-princess. 'Fallen Angel' was more like it.

In the pagents at St Mary's, the sisters always cast her as an angel, even though offstage she was the worst behaved of the girls, the biggest tomboy of them all. It was her eyes that made her look so innocent and angelic. The colour of spring violets, they were as large and round as those of the figures in seventeenth-century religious paintings. Her wild red hair and the generous sprinkling of freckles over her nose got her into trouble.

The service clicked on.

'You have reached the machine that answers the telephone for Liberty Adams. Please tell it the nature of your business and we'll take it from there.'

Beep.

She heard a man's laughter. 'I like it, Lib, I really like it. Your mean little machine. You sound like one of Alvin's chipmunks, you know that?'

She swivelled around.

'I'm at the Plaza, Lib. I just happen to be staying in the same suite we had on your eighteenth birthday. Remember? Join me for lunch tomorrow, okay? Say, twelve-thirty? At the Oak Room? For old times' sake.

'Lib,' he went on, 'lots to talk about. Lots of catching up to do.' Silence. 'I mean it, Lib. I really want to see you.'

The machine clicked off.

That voice.

It was a voice that she hadn't heard in eight years, yet she carried a memory of it in her very bones: the charming Virginia drawl, clipped and polished in New England. He had this way of taking it easy as he spoke, as if he had all the time in the world to let you hear the spaces between the words – the things *not* said.

Liberty got up slowly. Standing at the refrigerator, she bent to remove the faded tissue-wrapped bottle of Louis Roederer Cristal '68 from the vegetable bin where it had been sitting for the past eight years. Shredding her clothes as she went, she carried the bottle to the bathroom. She turned on both taps full force, clouding the full-length mirror and her framed print of Monet's water lilies. Opening a bottle of lavender salts, she tossed a handful into the whirlpool beneath the tap.

Next she went to the stereo and dug out a record from the very back of her cabinet. Dusting it off, she put it on the turntable, setting the volume on loud. The Beatles sang 'Here Comes the Sun'.

She returned to the bathroom and, peeling the foil away from the cork, eased it out of the bottle.

Pop! The sound echoed off the tiles. The cork shot into a corner and bounced into the tub. Champagne foamed over her hand. She licked her fingers and filled her glass. Immersing herself in the fragrant water, she reached for the telephone and dialled the Plaza from memory.

'I'd like to leave a message for Senator Pierce, please? No, don't bother to ring his room. Tell him...' She took a deep breath; her heart was knocking at her ribs. 'Tell him Liberty Adams will be happy to meet him for lunch tomorrow in the Oak Room.'

She hung up and raised her glass solemnly to her naked reflection.

It was Sister Bertrand who had been responsible for Liberty's going to Sarah Lawrence. Left to her own devices, Liberty would have settled for Marymount or Manhattanville – or some other Catholic college for nice Catholic girls. But Sister had stood over her as she filled out the interminable application and coached her before her interview. Liberty might have lacked the requisite good grades, but she had the highest test scores of any girl in St Mary's history, plus she had something even more important: spirit.

'You're the garlic in the spaghetti sauce,' Sister Bertrand liked to tell her favourite orphan girl.

The girls at Sarah Lawrence made fun of Liberty for hanging a poster of Paul Newman over her bed next to the poster of John, Paul, George, and Ringo crossing Abbey Road. After all, weren't convent girls supposed to nail crucifixes to their wall, stow rosary beads in their bedside tables, and never wear patent leather or red? In fact, at the convent, Liberty had tacked movie-magazine clippings in place of her crucifix, hidden make-up in her bedside table, and made a point of wearing red, if not patent leather, whenever she went down into Ossining. The local boys made serious sport of 'cherry-popping' St Mary's girls, and Liberty came close, but never yielded.

74

At Sarah Lawrence, her convent background seemed to have the opposite effect on boys – negative. Virginity was now an obstacle she longed to be rid of. Yet dates, at mixers and weekends at Harvard, Yale, and Princeton, simply didn't try to score. The aura of the convent seemed to hang about her like a halo.

By January of her freshman year, the 'ex-con' had given up on dating and taken up a life more solitary than any orphan's. She spent the winter in bed, reading, wondering whether it might not be a good idea for her to become a nun, after all.

When spring came, she was read out, restless to be out in the world. After all, the other girls there would be graduating and going on to help make some good man make good money. Liberty didn't run in those circles; after three more years of scholarship, she'd be on her own.

Sister Bertrand had a friend on the outside, working at *Mademoiselle*, who was willing to choose Liberty as a guest college editor, although she would have preferred a Vassar girl.

The first day on the job, Liberty fell in love with Madelon Weeks. On a typical day, Madelon would hold all calls, bring Liberty into her office, and lecture behind closed doors for hours, until Liberty's head was light and her throat burning from the fumes from Madelon's Gitanes.

'There are private people and public people, Liberty angel. Private people, on the one hand,' she went on, 'are people like Mr Dimitri, my doorman. Now, Mr Dimitri gets his paycheque from the building superintendent. His job is to open the door, ring people in and out, be nice but not nosy, accept deliveries, and keep out the creeps. Now, I don't need to know a thing about what makes Mr Dimitri *tick*, what he believes in, or how he lives his life. Let Studs Terkel do that!

'Public people, on the other hand...' She let the ash on her cigarette drop into the ashtray she held on her lap. 'Movie stars and politicans and sports Adonises ... now, *they* get their paycheques – which are a hell of a lot fatter than yours, mine, and Mr Dimitri's combined – from you and me. And you know something? It's their obligation to show us what makes them tick, to keep us in the know. But you know something, Liberty precious, they aren't too good about doing that. Unless it makes them look awfully *pretty*, they like to keep things *private*. So it is my job – and it's *your* job too, Liberty angel, if you have the *balls* to take it on – to probe, to poke, to badger, to bully, to hound them to hell and back to get them to

75

give out with the goods so that *you* can turn around and tell Mr Dimitri all about it, and so that Mr Dimitri can know where his buck has gone. Now, where were we? Oh, yes . . .'

Liberty was miserable when the term was up, putting an end to her internship with Maddy. She stayed on campus that summer and, determined to follow in Madelon Weeks's footsteps, read from a list she had compiled for her – mostly biographies and profiles heavy with local colour.

One night in mid-June, she was reading Twain's *Innocents Abroad* when Madelon called her.

'What's up, Maddy? You sound like Mrs Toad.'

'I feel like . . . You don't want to *know* what I feel like, *angel*,' Madelon honked over the crackling connection. 'Listen, precious, I've got an interview the day after tomorrow with Eben Pierce. That's right: the congressman from Virginia, twenty-nine years young, a bachelor, and a *dreamboat*. It's in DC. But even if it were across the river in *Hoboken*, precious, I couldn't make it. I've got *strep*. And the doctor absolutely forbids the Old Girl to leave her bed. You know I'm his slave. Much as I'd love to infect the entire House with my germs, I'm going to have to *pass*. I was just about to call one of his chippies to *reschedule* when I thought: Why miss the back-to-school issue? Why not give little Miss Liberty a crack at it?'

Liberty arrived at the office of Eben Pierce two days later with a steno pad, a fist of sharpened pencils, and a stack of three-by-fives full of typed-out questions, notes, and a brainful of newly acquired leftist attitudes to test.

When he finally arrived, two hours late, apologising that his car had got a flat tyre on his way in from Georgetown, Liberty couldn't believe a politician could be so good-looking.

He took one look at her and shook his blond head, grinning. 'Interview *me*? A cute little thing like you? You've got your work cut out for you, kid.'

She did, too. Instead of sitting in Pierce's office and asking her prepared questions one at a time in a nice, orderly fashion, she spent the day dogging his every move around the Capitol.

10:00–12:00 noon: Congressman attends Joint House Committee on Anti-Ballistic Missile Vote – ABM. (Boring parade of Air Force generals and missile experts putting it all on the record one more time. Pierce provides the one bright moment when he interrupts a rambling testimony at one point to quote Everett

Dirksen. 'Yes, General, I understand, but one billion here, and two billion there, pretty soon it adds up to real money.')

1:00-2:00: Luncheon with the DC chapter of the Daughters of the American Revolution ('Dirty Albanian Refugees', Liberty tells the congressman out of the corner of her mouth while munching on watercress sandwiches and crunching radishes that look more like roses than roses.)

2:30-5:00: Closed meeting of House Appropriations Committee.

6:00: Dinner alone with the congressman at Sans Souci. (They discuss her day's observations and six or seven people – mostly women – come by their table to say hello to the congressman. She insists on paying the bill; he resists. They struggle and tear the bill in half. He pays.)

8:00-10:00: George Washington University for panel discussion: Urban Renewal, National Priority? (Meeting degenerates into a discussion of the war. All other guest speakers walk out except His Truly, who toughs it out, and winds up inviting a half-dozen students back to his office to eat Chinese food on the floor.)

'You still with me, kid?' he asked her around midnight as the last of the student radicals straggled out of his office, tamed, docile, shaking his hand. They sat on the floor of the darkened office in a litter of Coke cans, take-out containers, and hot-mustard and duck-sauce pouches. It was the first time, really, they'd been alone all day, since dinner with him at Sans Souci was like being alone on a Hollywood set. He was in his shirt-sleeves, propped against the skirt of the couch, grinning at her.

'What's so funny?' Liberty was slumped on the floor against a chair.

'You're so little and so scrappy. You know, you asked some pretty tough questions today.'

'Oh yeah?' She raised her eyebrow. 'You gave me some pretty tough answers.'

They sat talking until the morning, when he drove her to Dulles Airport himself. She never even checked into the room the magazine had reserved for her at the Shoreham.

When the article appeared two months later in the back-to-school issue, Liberty was quite pleased. She knew it was more than what Madelon would call a 'pussy' piece. It was snappily written and, thanks to some of the first on-the-record quotes concerning the recent spread of college moratoriums to protest the continuation of the war, even newsworthy.

Madelon clipped a note to the two advance copies she sent her: 'Precious: If Mr Dimitri went in for this rag, he'd *eat* it up. Let the Old Girl know when you're ready to leave that finishing school. I'm waiting for you in the *Real World*. M.'

Along with her original notes from the day in Washington, Liberty had saved a few snapshots of Pierce. There was one taken by his secretary, of Liberty and the congressman together. On an impulse, Liberty had it framed and sent it to him, along with a copy of the issue. Her cover note, on her own lilac stationery, read: 'To the Dreamboat Congressman from the Girl Reporter. The girls at Sadie Lou are green with envy. Thanks for everything'.

She regretted it as soon as she sent it, burning with embarrassment whenever she imagined him opening the package and reading that stupid, ingenuous note.

One October Friday night, when the noises of the girls getting ready for their Princeton weekends had faded, leaving only the lone clicking of a typewriter down the hall, Liberty heard the hall phone ring. As usual, she didn't bother to answer it. The typewriter ceased, a door opened, and bare feet padded to the phone. Liberty thought that it must be Bambi's timid footfall. Bambi was the name of an unfortunate girl who weighed 190 pounds. A moment later, Bambi was at Liberty's door, out of breath and red in the face.

'It's some guy for you. I think it's long distance 'cause I can't understand what he said. I think he said his name's DC. Sound like somebody you know?'

'Dumb cunt?' Liberty suggested cheerfully, wondering whose big brother from Princeton DC was, why it was that preppies took such joy in initials, and how fast she could get rid of him. 'Yeah?' She spoke into the receiver with little enthusiasm.

'Hello. I'd like to speak with Liberty Adams.'

'This is she.'

'This is Eben Pierce.'

Liberty slid down the wall slowly.

'It is?' she said stupidly. The graffiti on the wall in front of her nose read: 'Sarah Lawrence girls are horny'.

'Yes, it is.'

'I'm sorry,' said Liberty, clearing her throat. 'The girl who took the call said it was "DC".'

She heard him laugh.

'Isn't that what you called me?'

'What? When?'

'Dreamboat Congressman.'

'Oh, God,' Liberty groaned.

'I was wondering whether you'd mind joining me for a little late dinner tonight.'

'Sure.' She paused. 'Where?'

'A place called the Left Bank. Know it?'

'Yeah, I think so, it's in the Village, right?'

'Wrong. It's on Connecticut Avenue.'

'Connecticut Avenue?' Liberty blurted out. 'That's in Washington, DC!'

'I'm aware of that, Liberty. So am I.'

'But –'

'There's a ticket for you at Eastern's VIP desk. Try to be on the seven-o'clock shuttle. I'll meet you at National at eight. Got a pencil?'

Liberty found a clearing in the forest of graffiti on the wall and jotted down the flight, the airline, his number.

'I gather they'll be expecting me at La Guardia?'

There was a short silence. 'Look, Liberty, I don't do this all the time, if that's what you're thinking.'

'Don't do what?' Liberty asked innocently.

'Call up young girls out of the blue and summon them down for the weekend.'

'Oh, I didn't realise this was a *weekend* invitation.'

'Go pack, brat. See you soon.'

The next morning Liberty found herself alone in his bathroom, terribly conscious that this was the first bachelor's bathroom she had ever used. She opened the medicine chest and cased it with unashamed curiosity. She closed the cabinet door. 'The man has no drugs,' she said aloud to her flushed reflection. She made a face in the mirror, stuck out her tongue. 'Jesus,' she said aloud. 'How cute can I get? Gidget and the Congressman.' She saw in the mirror that his clothes from last night were hanging on a bamboo clothes tree, along with hers. Then she saw something else hanging there. A white silk robe. Really beautiful. There was only one thing the matter with it: it was a woman's robe.

Before she realised what she was doing, she had slipped it on over her naked body. It was huge on her; the woman must be an amazon. No, she thought as she rubbed her cheek against the smooth fabric, just statuesque. Statuesque and beautiful and the first love of Congressman Pierce's life. It smelled good, too: a scent Liberty didn't recognise. No over-the-counter scent, this. Probably custom-mixed. Probably all her clothes were custom-made. Custom-made by top designers. She was an inspiration to them. Worse yet, she probably designed all her own clothes. She was a genius! Liberty rifled the pockets of the robe, in search of further evidence. Aha! Matches. At least she had one fault: she smoked. She has to wear that wonderful perfume to cover up the stench of nicotine. Eben has to hold his nose every time he kisses her. She turned the box over in her hand and read the name on it: 'The Left Bank'. Liberty ran an instant scenario of last night: the headwaiter turning to the bartender, whispering 'I see the congressman has fallen on hard times. He's brought a midget with him tonight.'

Liberty tore off the robe and turned on the shower. She was a moron. God! She began to cry as the water washed over her.

So almost from the start, Liberty's vision of Eben was tinged with a certain fatalism. While she never mentioned the white robe to him, she waited for the day when its tall, serene owner would walk up the marble steps of 211 Franklin Street and claim her man. And, as only a condemned prisoner can savour a last meal or a last cigarette, Liberty enjoyed each time with Eben as if it were her last.

He flew her down to Washington every weekend, and sometimes flew up midweek because he couldn't stand being away from her. He was scrupulous about keeping her name out of the press, although she appeared in the columns regularly as a blind item: 'Petite Coed', 'Mystery Flame'. When his own name appeared, linked with other women's, he shrugged it off as the machinations of his PR people – 'beards' – to keep reporters away from her. She wanted to believe him.

One day, three years after she'd started seeing him, in the spring of 1972, one month before Liberty's college graduation, Eben called her.

'I don't believe you're telling me this.'

'It's a political move, Liberty,' he told her. 'But I wanted you to know first. I wanted you to hear it from me before it hit the papers.'

Liberty was in the hall in the dorm, facing into a corner of the booth.

'She's the daughter of Governor Rutherford, Liberty. We grew up together. Took tennis lessons together.'

'She's a childhood sweetheart. You're telling me you're marrying your childhood sweetheart. And all this time I was just a chippie on the side.'

Tears were burning her eyes and sliding down her cheeks. The collar of her blouse was soaked. Her speech came out in gasps.

'I love you, Liberty. You're more than that to me.'

'I'm an Orphan Chippie, that's even better. "Little Orphan Chippie".'

'Stop it, Liberty. I love *you*.'

'That's why you're marrying her. You love me, but you've got the *political* hots for her. Sure. I understand.'

'Look, I'd be a fool to try to deny that it isn't politics, but maybe we could, you know ...' His voice trailed off.

'We could *what*?'

'Liberty, listen, what I mean is that it doesn't have to *change* our relationship.'

'Oh, my God!' Liberty cried. 'Please go away. Please don't ever call me or see me again.'

She dropped five pounds that first week and wore thin the grooves on the Beatles' *The Long and Winding Road*. Through finals, she carried herself around campus like a convalescent recovering from open heart surgery. With newly dried tears and a fresh batch welling up, she held her face stiffly to the mild spring air. And what a glorious spring it had been. The campus was frothy with azaleas, rhododendrons, lilacs. The girls wore the blossoms in their hair. Liberty strung violets through the holes of her earlobes and sobbed out her sorrow to her don, a fiftyish writer – whose recent book was currently number-two on the New York *Times*'s best-seller list – and teacher of freshman literature. His consolation – in bed – did little to help.

A year after the breakup, almost to the day, Eben called her at *Flash* magazine, where she worked as a researcher-reporter in the movie section. She had come back from lunch to find a message from him, inviting her to dinner.

Clutching the message, she went to talk it over with Madelon.

'I can handle it,' she told Madelon. She felt successful, tough, a woman of the world capable of handling the situation.

'But why put yourself through ...?' Madelon checked herself. '*Hell*, angel, what's life worth if we don't take chances? Besides, he really *is* a dreamboat!'

Liberty left Madelon's office feeling excited, brave, as if 'mistress' were a role out of a fairy tale, a sort of tragic princess. She called him back and told him she'd join him for dinner, went to Bendel's and spent an entire weeks' salary on a dress. Black, naturally.

For a year and a half, he flew her down to Washington Friday nights, and home to New York Sunday evenings. At National Airport she claimed the red MG that waited for her there all week long. Since his town house in Georgetown was now off-limits, she drove twelve miles up the Potomac to a tiny colonial cottage on the river, part of the Pierce family holdings.

She was under strict instructions to keep her hair up in a hat and never to drive with the top of the MG down. The hats she wore to hide her hair became a private joke. Newly liberated from braids, her hair ranged to the small of her back, like a red flag.

'My Little Red Flag', he called her when he took off her hat and watched, fascinated, as her hair spread like fire over her small body. She'd see it in his eyes then: the pyromaniac's fascination. Liberty felt at home in the tiny white rose-covered cottage with its low ceilings and tilting floors. Since Eben spent his days in town with Cornelia or at the office, Liberty was often there alone entire weekends, waiting for him to get away and come to her. All day long, she prepared for him. Mornings, she'd do the marketing at the local shops, where they knew her name. Afterwards, she'd sit on the porch shelling peas or peeling potatoes, glorying in the little V of river sparkling between the aged trunks of the chestnut tree. When the weather was fair, she'd often strip naked, sunning herself as she listened to the bees buzzing in the apples, thinking of how he'd touch her later that night.

Some afternoons, she'd prepare tea for the two of them, and when he didn't arrive in time, she'd have it by herself, sitting in the kitchen, rocking, listening to the clock tick, wondering where he was, what he was doing, waiting for the sound of his car grinding up the gravel of the half-moon driveway. At times like these, the cottage began to seem small and mean. She'd sit in the rocking chair, not getting up to turn on the lights, sometimes not even rocking, as the night fell and her dinner for two went untouched. It would be ten o'clock when she'd take the pots of food, walk down the path to the dock, and toss their contents into the river.

The last time she saw him, it was a Monday, dawn. He had driven her to the airport himself because he needed her MG while the BMW was in the shop. He was in working uniform: blue blazer, pressed khakis, Oxford shirt, Williams tie. She was wearing a dress for him, her Tricia Nixon Special. She would change in the taxi for La Guardia and arrive at *Flash* wearing jeans, a T-shirt, and a crushed-velvet jacket. He had told her she couldn't come down next weekend. Corny was going into the hospital for tests and he had to hand-hold. He'd bitten the cuticle on his thumb, brushed away her tears, and driven all at once. Liberty thought there was no one on earth so harried as the man keeping two women.

'I can't handle tears,' he told her, brushing them away as if they were a physical deformity he didn't have the guts to face.

Liberty arrived at the office still crying. Madelon drew her behind closed doors and gave her a shot of brandy.

'I'm not the crying type,' Liberty managed between sobs.

'I've got news for you, angel, you are now. And if you ask me, your dreamboat has turned into a *nightmare*.'

Liberty stopped crying suddenly. Her life *had* become nightmarish. Thanking Madelon for the brandy and sympathy, she went back to work. He called three days later, as he called every Wednesday, from a telephone in a coffee shop.

'I've been very depressed lately,' he told her.

'So you thought you'd call and cheer me up.' Liberty knew it was a weak joke, but she didn't care.

'This is serious, Liberty. I'm not doing you any good. I'm just being selfish.'

These were not unusual words for the congressman. Liberty usually disagreed vehemently, but tonight she kept silent. And when he said, for the fiftieth time, as much to himself as to her, that theirs was not, could not be, a long-term relationship, that he could never leave his wife, that it would ruin his career, that it would ruin Corny's life, that Corny would kill herself, Liberty interrupted his depressed ramblings.

'Look,' she said. 'This is the hardest thing I ever had to say, so please listen because I won't be able to say it again. I can't take this any more. I am worn clean through. Please don't ever call me or see me again, Eben.'

Madelon told her that one of the best cures for a broken heart was redecorating. Liberty did her one better. She moved out of the East Eighty-second Street high-rise apartment she shared with two other *Flash* researchers and moved downtown to the triangle below Canal, to the top floor of an old granary where the walls were filthy and caked with dust and the floors scarred and rutted. She came home from the office every night, changed into cut-offs and an old T-shirt, and scraped, hammered, and plastered, slowly but steadily reclaiming the space from the industrial wilderness. Late each night, she fell into bed, aching and exhausted, too done in even to think – let alone dream – about Eben Pierce.

On the day she christened the new bathtub, when the loft was finally in shape, she walked up West Street to Houston and asked Howie, the liquor-store owner, for the best, most expensive bottle of champagne he had in stock. He recommended Roederer Cristal, 1968, and Liberty wrote out a cheque for it, cleaning out her bank account. As she stood at her window that night, looking out on the Hudson, tracking the new moon, a hook snagging the white night clouds, she told herself: '*One day. One day, he'll be back*'. And with those words, she went and put the bottle of champagne in the vegetable drawer of the new robin's-egg-blue refrigerator.

5

The telephone woke her up.

'Hello, Liberty.'

'Hello?'

'I hope you won't want to punch me for waking you this early.'

'I've been up for hours.' She yawned into the phone. 'Who is this?'

'It's Archer Ransome.'

She picked up the bedside clock. Twenty minutes after six. Her alarm wasn't set to go off for another two hours. 'You don't mess around with follow-up, do you?'

'I've decided to extend the interview if you're willing.'

'Don't ask me to talk you out of it. What d'you have in mind?'

'Can you be ready for breakfast in a half-hour?'

'Can I? You got it.'

'Be casual, dress warmly, and don't forget that tape recorder.'

Liberty was downstairs waiting for him a half-hour later, dressed in dungarees faded to translucence and a fringed tunic of turquoise calfskin. Her tape recorder and notebook were in the cowhide satchel under her arm.

The white Mercedes limo glided up to the kerb, the door snapped open, and Liberty jumped into the back seat. Ransome was talking on the car phone.

'Hi!' she said.

The driver took off around the corner on Beach and headed towards Church Street.

'I want you to get back in there and talk to them. None of these duelling memos.' Archer stabbed the air beside the white receiver with his black cigarette. 'These people can't write whatever they damned well feel like writing on a hunch and no evidence. Talk to them, do you understand?' He pressed the button on the receiver. 'Hello, Liberty. I'll be with you in a moment.' He spoke three digits into the mouthpiece, then said, 'Good morning, Susie. I want you to get me those numbers in the Bahamas, after all' – he glanced at Liberty absently – 'and I want you to get them without stirring up any fuss. Is my meaning clear? I knew it would be. And thank you, Susie.' Then, three more digits, and he began a third conversation. 'Hello. Tom, I hope I didn't wake you...'

She kept her ears open, helping herself to the glass of fresh orange juice sitting on the car's bar. *The Wall Street Journal* lay creased and opened to page two. Her eyes drifted to the second column headline: 'GREENHAUSE TO TESTIFY IN EXCHANGE FOR IMMUNITY'. No byline. Liberty picked up the paper and read, her heart thudding. 'Senator Eben Pierce, recently appointed chairman of the Select Subcommittee of the Senate Finance Committee to investigate charges against the SEC, met yesterday morning at Ransome Enterprises' headquarters with A.J. Ransome. Both men declined to comment...' She read on: Eben Pierce was in town to investigate the as-yet-unsubstantiated reports concerning the existence of a so-called Ransome Enterprises slush fund earmarked for Greenhause, said to be stockpiled in the Bahamas. Ransome himself had yet to comment on the allegation.

She sank back into the seat. She and Eben must have just missed each other yesterday.

So he hadn't, after all, looked her up for old times' sake. He wanted to pump her about Ransome. She looked over at Ransome: that perfect *Gentleman's Quarterly* profile. Regardless of what the papers said, she didn't buy it for a minute that the elegant man sitting next to her was a white-collar crook. Well, one thing was worth betting on: she wasn't going to help Eben flush him out.

She set the newspaper aside and tried to figure out where he was taking her. They were shooting crosstown, east; working their way downtown, deeper and deeper into the blue-box canyons of the financial district. Liberty was sorry she'd taken his advice to dress casually. She'd be the lone hippie among urban cybernoids. The car swung onto cobblestones and Liberty looked around her. Buildings, startlingly ancient, passed on either side of them, inches from the car's windows. She was about to ask the driver to let her out, when they lost the buildings on one side and gained a high stone wall overgrown with coils of bitter-sweet vine. The car stopped in front of a door.

Ransome hung up at last and leaned over to open the door.'Welcome to the Sculpture Garden, Liberty.' Liberty caught the scent of lime and musk. She beamed at Ransome, grateful to him for rescuing her from high-tech premonitions. It was to be a picnic, after all.

'The Sculpture Garden? I've heard of it, but I've never been invited here.'

'She owns it.'

'She?'

'Why, Kitsia, of course.'

'Of course!' Liberty cried, and clapped him on the shoulder. 'Now, that's what I call ambience! Rush was wrong about you. You are a sport.' She grinned and slid out.

A peephole clicked shut and a dark, delicate man opened the door. He was unmistakably an Arab. She recalled seeing such men on Zwar, on the quay, at the casino.

On the other side of the wall was a Georgian brick box, two storeys high, with freshly painted green shutters. It, too, was wrapped in bittersweet. The Zwarian led them underneath a long, low arbour. The gnarled silver vines of wisteria cut them off from the sky. At last they broke into the open. Kitsia's sculpture lay all about, scattered, like petrified fragments of a single enormous body. Pillars suggested thighs; sundials, breasts; and birdbaths, upturned armpits. She felt Archer's eyes on her as she took it all in. Swiftly he disappeared through a parting in the high hedge, and Liberty dived after him. Just as she caught sight of him again, she realised that the hedge was a maze. Pieces of sculptured stone pierced its walls. She stopped and listened for the *crunch, crunch* of Ransome's shoes on the gravel up ahead, but it was no use; time and again, she wound up with a face full of hedge. Cross and irritated, she fell finally into a clearing.

Here stood a second brick box with green-painted shutters, an exact replica in miniature of the colonial out front. Once the garden house, now it must be the kitchen. Waiters – more Zwarians, from the look of them – moved in and out of the swinging doors, carrying trays. The guests were nowhere to be seen, seated in heavily trellised gazebos. She counted six gazebos standing in a circle. Ransome called to her from the nearest one.

'Like all great artists, Kitsia feels she has to control one's view. I think you'll find the view is better from up here.' He held out a hand to help her up the four steps.

'You're not kidding!' From this height, the maze they'd just passed through formed an intricate undulating design. 'Sculpting trees just like she sculpts stone and iron, eh? Amazing!' Liberty breathed, looking all around her. 'That patch of ground cover over there looks like a quilt. This is great. You know, I've always had a soft spot for gazebos. And gardens. It's like another world! And yet those office buildings seem so close. I feel as if I could climb to the top of that wall and touch them.' She caught his eye a little shyly, and leaned against the railing.

'Who comes here?' she asked.

'Kitsia's people. People in the arts. People in government and high finance. Mavericks, most of them.'

'Tell me, Archer, do you fancy yourself a maverick?'

He shrugged. 'Not really . . . I'm less anchored in a personal life than most men. Or rather, my business life *is* my personal life. If that makes me a maverick, I'm sure I'm not the type my aunt had in mind when she opened this place.'

'Oh, I don't know. She's really no different from you. Isn't *her* business her personal life?'

'Ah, but is art business?'

'You bet your bottom line it is. Big business.'

'You're so confident. I like that. Then again, I suppose I was that sure of things when I was your age.'

'Really? What were you up to when you were my age? I'll make it easy on you. I'm thirty-two.'

'Are you? You look eighteen.'

'Answer the question, please.'

'Someday, Liberty . . . Someday, perhaps I will.'

'I'll settle for that.' She patted him cheerfully. He was wearing a suit of grey nubby silk, pleasing to the touch. His tie matched his eyes. There could be worse reasons for getting out of bed at six-twenty a.m.

'May I ask how the article is progressing?'

'Since yesterday? Swell, Archer, just swell. I'll take that as my cue.'

She took out her tape machine and set it down on the glass-topped table. Switching it on, she noticed he didn't flinch as he had the first time she'd turned it on. He *was* in a good mood. She sat on a curved stone bench that caught the sunlight as it sifted through the trellis. Still, the stone was cool on her thighs. She shivered. He was sitting next to her. She shivered again.

'Allow me,' he said, taking off his jacket. 'I'm afraid you didn't dress quite warmly enough.'

She didn't argue as he draped his jacket around her shoulders.

'Look down,' he said.

'Hunh?'

He tapped the glass-topped table and she sat up and peered through it.

Liberty was looking down into a large illuminated fish tank built into the floor of the gazebo.

'Now, that's what I call a floor show!' she murmured.

Red and black fish darted back and forth through coral canyons. A sheet of Plexiglas kept the guest's feet out of the fish bowl. Suddenly Liberty felt seasick, as if she were in a glass-bottomed boat. She looked up quickly.

'How about some tea, Liberty?'

No sooner said than an Arab sprang up the steps and set down two steaming mugs, filling the air with the aroma of many spices.

'Oh, thanks!' Liberty leaned over and inhaled the steam.

He hooked his thumb into his mug and leaned back against the railing.

'So, Archer. Tell me a Kitsia story.'

'Well, let me see... Have you heard the one about how Kitsia took her leave of Paris?'

Liberty shook her head, glad he needed so little priming.

'Apparently she stopped going to the cafés one day. This was just before the war. She abhorred the talk. The Communists among them lobbied for fighting in Spain. And of course, everyone wanted her to join the Communists.'

'I can understand their wanting her on their side. She's a powerful presence.'

'Her friends went looking for her and eventually found her on the Île St Louis, in the room... How did that poet friend of hers describe it?'

'Let me see...' Liberty squinted to recall. '"In the lacy grey shade of Our Lady... in the bosom of the flower district..." Something with bosom in it, I'm sure.'

'Yes, well, they found her there, all alone, with the double windows thrown open like doors, painting flowers on huge canvases.'

'She was an artist, after all –'

'Yes, but no one knew that yet. Or rather, only *she* knew it. The closest she'd come to art until then was modelling for artists. She used to make fun of the amateurs in berets, pretending to paint along the Seine. And now, it looked as if she were joining them.

Her friends were quite concerned, but they threw up their arms and left her to her dallying. They next heard from Kitsia two years later when they were sent a handpainted invitation to a party at Maxim's. No one was particularly surprised. After all, she was the most colourful and eccentric kept woman in Paris... at least according to the tattlers we – my mother and I – used to read in Zwar. Three hundred people turned out for this party.'

'Were you there?'

He chuckled softly. 'I only read about it afterwards. Believe it or not, there are people in Paris who still talk about it. I wish I had been there, but no, I was at prep school in America then.'

'Poor Archer.' Liberty could just see him, a golden-haired schoolboy languishing behind ivy-covered walls, waiting for life to begin.

'At midnight, two of Diaghilev's dancers lifted her onto their shoulders to toast her guests. She drank to their good health, in war, as in peace, and then excused herself, saying she had to go see a man about a camel.'

'Heck of a toast.'

'Nobody thought much about it at the time. She told them she'd be back before the champagne ran dry, and the dancers carried her off. Well, they said it took a week for the champagne to run dry, but Kitsia was never to return.'

'You mean she threw her own farewell party and left without saying farewell?'

'Yes. She boarded up the big room in the flower district and left all the paintings she'd secretly done in the last two years – there were thirty-six of them – to one of her lovers.'

'Which one?'

'Monsieur Vernière-Plank. An unassuming but industrious Swiss businessman – the man to see if you want to get hold of a rare early Ransome. Or any other Ransome, for that matter. He's been her exclusive dealer for over forty years.'

'Talk about loyal servants.'

'Have you any idea what those flower paintings sell for nowadays? But Kitsia hates them. She thinks people like them for the wrong reason – because they're pretty.'

'That sounds like Kitsia.'

'I have several of the Île St Louis paintings up at my house in Millbrook. I'd love it if you came up to see them sometime soon.'

Liberty blushed.

'Perhaps at that time you'll be kind enough to let me read this article of yours, *before* it's printed?'

So that was what he was up to. 'So finish the story,' she prompted him. 'What's this about a man and a camel?'

'She took the Orient Express to Baghdad, and from there she went to live among the camel drivers of Zwar.'

'And that's when she retired from the world?'

He looked sidelong at her and laughed. 'Those of us in the family didn't get the feeling she was retiring, believe me.'

'Really?'

'She arrived on Zwar with thirteen trunks, and twelve of them were delivered to the emir's harem. They went to his thirty-five wives with Kitsia's Ransome's compliments.'

'A sort of reverse Welcome Wagon, eh? You did say harem, didn't you? As in veils, eunuchs, and Arabian Nights?'

'Precisely. Imagine, if you will, these thoroughly medieval creatures donning Kitsia's Diors and Chanels. After all, Kitsia was one of the most fashionable women in Paris before she gave it all up –'

'And retired. The emir must have been in seventh heaven, with all those fashionable wives.'

He laughed shortly. 'On the contrary. He sent a runner to my father's office wanting to know why it was that his wives had taken to dressing like European whores while my father's own sister was squatting in the bazaar dressed like a twelve-year-old boy, smoking hashish with the locals.'

'She didn't waste any time, did she?'

'And she got right down to work, too. She'd like the way some impossible old Arab looked, and she'd drag him back to the guesthouse and sketch him for hours, sending out for meals, ignoring everything . . . She was off flowers now, you see. Mother was appalled.'

'And what about you?'

He sat there, working his chipped tooth with his tongue. 'What?' He snapped out of the memory.

'Were you appalled too? What did you think about Kitsia?'

She knew exactly where this would lead her. She wanted to hear the story from him. Maybe if she did, it would seem more real to her, instead of something that had come to her in a cloud of hashish twelve thousand miles away in another world.

'Things became rather awkward between us. Actually, Liberty,

91

I prefer to remember my aunt from earlier days.'

'Yes?'

He sat up and stroked his tie. 'In Paris, when I was a much younger boy, when life was less complicated.'

'How was life less complicated for you then, Archer?'

'I remember as a boy thinking that it was always springtime in Paris. We'd arrive at the train station at the beginning of April and my father would drop me into Kitsia's arms and then disappear into Paris for the next six weeks. "Swallowed by the oasis", Kitsia liked to call it. Paris was exactly that for us – an oasis . . .' He trailed off, and she brought him back.

'Were these visits a welcome occasion for your aunt? After all, she did have her . . . eh, business to run.'

'Business went on as usual. It was understood in those days that kept women kept pets. And I was her pet.'

He spun around on the bench and opened his ivory cigarette case. Long wooden matches stood on the table in a tall ceramic striker shaped like a woman's neck. Drawing a match slowly up the length of her throat, he lit a cigarette, then smiled at her through the haze of smoke. Was he smiling at her or his memories?

An Arab quietly appeared and Ransome murmured a single sentence in Arabic. Liberty gathered he was giving the breakfast order.

'Kitsia had a Pierce Arrow,' Ransome went on. 'It was one of the first cars with a rumble seat. While she never rode in it when she was by herself, she would ride back there with me. We'd cruise through the Bois de Boulogne while she fed me Turkish Delight or grapes or pomegranates. I remember one afternoon she let me smear pomegranate seeds into her dress because she liked the colour of the juice on the fresh white linen, or so she said. She always wore white in those days, with a long white cat's-tail boa that she used to run beneath my chin. She used to tickle me, to make me laugh. I loved that rumble seat. I was never so happy.'

His face was so soft that Liberty believed him.

'My father used to be appalled whenever he saw us out riding. My father was an engineer as well as an arms trader, you see, and it was not a car an engineer could admire. It was a useless car, really, with its headlights built into the bumper. But Kitsia didn't care. She loved the way it looked. She also loved the looks of its driver. He was a Punjabi by the name of Mohammed Yakub. Have you ever seen a Punjabi Indian, Liberty? They are a race of giants. He was six-foot-seven. He practically lived in that Pierce Arrow. Unlike other chauffeurs, in their proper black caps and suits, he wore loose-fitting trousers and an embroidered vest of many small mirrors. He drove barefoot and always smelled of saffron.'

'Sounds like you all made quite a showpiece,' Liberty commented quietly.

'Oh, Kitsia was ostentatious, all right. She used to dress me up in little sailor suits, miniature Chinese jackets, lederhosen... From what the pictures tell me, I was quite a striking boy.'

'You're not exactly the Elephant Man now,' she murmured.

The Arab strode up the steps into the gazebo and, working rapidly, set down two straw mats, two silver spoons, two earthenware pots.

Liberty turned around on the bench and bent to sniff at the contents. 'What do we have here?'

'What's the matter, Liberty?' he chided. 'Don't you trust me?'

'It's not you. It's me. I don't trust food in the morning.' *I also resent it for interrupting your story*, she added silently.

'Do you always have trouble eating in the morning?'

'When I'm working, I do.'

'You're very involved in your work, aren't you? You have the look of a nocturnal creature. All eyes and fingers. For such a tiny person, you have very long fingers.' He shook out her napkin and let it fall onto her lap. 'Why don't you try a little.'

'Why is everybody always trying to get me to eat?' But she did as she was told, and it was the best yogurt she'd ever tasted – light and foamy and filled with surprises: mandarin oranges, berries, nuts, spices.

'Do you sleep eight hours each night?' he asked, eating his yogurt in large spoonfuls. 'Most successful people I know – including myself – require less than half that.'

'Not me, but every so often I lapse back into being a night person. I used to be a real night person in school, but not now... I've always felt that sleeping during the day was the first step on the road to decrepitude. When you're an orphan, it's easy to picture yourself winding up in some kind of public institution: a ladies' shelter on the Bowery, maybe,' she said cheerfully, sucking her spoon.

'How did you get into this business anyway?'

'Very tricky, Archer, turning the interview around like this. I've noticed you like to do that.' She grinned. 'But since you ask,

Madelon Weeks gave me a job when I was in college.'

'The notorious Madelon Weeks! That explains a good deal.'

'Notorious or not, she confirmed for me the belief that journalism was a noble calling.'

'Did you always want to be a journalist?'

'I never wanted to be anything else. Except maybe a kept woman.'

He laughed, as if somehow he doubted that.

'There was this nun at St Mary's,' she went on. 'Sister Bertrand... She had this old cigar box under her bed, full of postcards from the Caribbean, Australia, Polynesia. She used to let me come into her room and look at them, so long as I promised not to read them. I loved the scenes of water. That blue, blue water. She told me if I studied hard to be a journalist in college I could see that water one day. If I didn't, all I'd see was the Hudson on the mill side of Ossining. I fell for it. The thing is, though, all that real blue water never looks quite as blue as the postcard variety.'

He dropped his head and began to rub his eyes. When he lifted his head again, he looked suddenly exhausted.

'Are you all right?'

'I'm all right,' he said quietly. 'I didn't realise how much I'd forgotten.'

'That happens. But it's easy to trigger memory. It's my job.'

'Is it?' He looked at her strangely.

'Yes.'

'I'm wondering, Liberty, just what your job is and who you're working for.'

'What are you talking about? I thought we cleared all that up. I'm working –'

'Please, Liberty, do me the favour of not mentioning *Metropolitan* yet another time. We both know that this job runs more deeply than that.'

'I'll admit to you, Archer, I'm really into it. But as far as being on somebody else's payroll, please believe me –'

He touched her shoulders lightly. 'Forgive me, Liberty. That was thoughtless of me; thoughtless of me to suspect you of working for my aunt.'

Liberty's eyes widened and she thumped her chest. 'Me? Working for her? That's the wildest thing I've ever heard.' She felt her face redden, and prayed he wouldn't notice that he'd come remarkably close to the truth. In fact, the turtle was in her cowhide satchel this very minute. She remembered Kitsia's instructions. *Tell no one but Kit: no one else can be trusted, not even Archer!*

She dived into her bag and fumbled with her Camels pack. She was thankful when he relieved her of the chore and lit a Camel for each of them.

'Is my aunt still smoking hashish, or is that a foolish question?'

Liberty nodded vigorously. 'I'm not accustomed to smoking such huge amounts. It was never my drug in college. I'm afraid I nearly lost it there for a while.'

'Kitsia gave my wife hashish when she was carrying our child. When I found out, I nearly killed her.'

Liberty gaped like a fish. *'She what? You what?'*

He went on calmly smoking in silence.

'Did you say you had a wife?'

His voice softened. 'We were married for less than a year before she died. It was over thirty years ago, Liberty. Relax.'

'How can I relax, Archer? Look, I don't skimp on research. And believe me, nowhere in the script does it say you had a wife. What gives?'

'My life isn't a script, Liberty. Nor is it an as-told-to story.' He put out his cigarette and got up. 'I have to go.'

'Hold it a minute!' She pulled off his jacket and handed it back to him. 'I must say, your timing stinks. You're going to drop that bomb and then just leave?'

He smiled and wound a lock of her hair around his finger. 'Feel free to stay here and . . . organise your notes, but it's eight o'clock and I have a busy day ahead of me.' He ran a finger from her forehead to her chin. 'I'm sorry if I was suspicious of you, Liberty, but please bear in mind at all times that my aunt is a meddler and not to be trusted. I had to know whether you were involved.'

She gulped. 'I understand.'

'Take care of yourself, Liberty. Get some sleep. I don't like those circles under your eyes.'

'I don't either – any suggestions?' She winked at him, 'Anyway, thanks for meeting with me.'

'By the way,' he said on the stairs, 'I think when you try Kit again that you'll find her altogether more . . . cooperative.'

'Incredible!' She called for the phone, watching him work his way back through the maze.

'Peg, hi. It's me.'

'Where are you, Lib? You sound far away.'

'I feel far away. Listen, before I give you your whopping assignment for the day, what's up? Anybody want to sue me?'

'Your ticket for LA will be at the TWA desk, prepaid. You're wait-listed for first class.'

Liberty watched the black fish dart behind the rock and a red fish reappear, then a red fish spin around a plant and come back to a black fish. Black fish, red fish, black fish, red fish. Liberty chasing Archer Ransome. Archer chasing Kit Ransome.

'A car will pick you up at LAX,' Peg went on, 'and take you to Morton's, where Jay Scott will meet you for drinks.'

'Great,' Liberty said. 'Anything up with Bic Crawford?'

'His office says he can only see you for dinner tonight. I told him you couldn't . . .'

Liberty groaned. 'This day is gonna last forever. Tell him okay. Morton's at seven forty-five. Do you have the poop on him?'

'All punched up.'

'Any luck with you-know-who?'

'Don't you think I'd be jumping up and down if there were? I'm going to try her West Coast secretary again. This Sasha is sweet, but I get the feeling she couldn't connect the *President* with Kit Ransome.'

Liberty grinned. '*I* have the funny feeling you're going to luck out soon.'

'I'll believe that when it happens. Alvarro's off the critical list, you'll be happy to know, but his doctor says he's still in no shape for questioning. So what's my whopping big assignment?'

'I want you to go see Madelon Weeks in her office today. She always eats at *Flash* on Tuesdays. Tell her I sent you. Ask her to dredge up memories of the good old days when she worked at the *Trib*, penning obits. Ask her if she remembers, oh, about thirty years ago, doing one for the child bride of Archer Ransome.'

'You're kidding. He had a wife?'

'That's what I said. Ask her if she can remember any news – or even gossip – about the woman. There's got to be a good reason why this wife of Ransome's was *expunged* from the public record.'

'Fine, but what'll I tell her if she wants to know why you want to know? I gotta admit, I'm curious myself.'

'Just tell the Old Girl we're trying to complete the public record – for my highbrow article. If Maddy knows anything, Maddy will tell. Tell her I'll call her from the Coast to explain, if you have to.'

'Gee, Lib, it sounds like you're taking your critics to heart.'

'Hunh?'

'Remember the guy in *Time* who said your new stuff read like a cross between Raymond Chandler and Erma Bombeck? You're getting to sound more and more like Chandler...'

'And less like Bombeck?' Liberty rang off and called for a second cup of tea as she pulled her papers out of her cowhide bag. She looked around. Feeling safe enough, she took the turtle out and set him down on the glass-topped table – just for company – as she settled down to read her first draft:

I hear a faint buzzing.

'Anybody home?' My voice ripples back to me on the desert wind as I ring the doorbell for the sixth time.

The buzzing continues. It sounds like a chain saw, but there are no trees here. Only large, oddly shaped rocks that raise one's eyes upward from the flat pan of the desert. I am surrounded by them. It's as if I'm standing in the middle of an ancient ritual site, like Stonehenge. Yet the compound itself is like something out of a science-fiction movie. The structure at whose door I now stand is large and flat, with high, narrow windows like a factory. An enormous plastic bubble sits to one side. A hydroponic garden, perhaps? Behind it, a windmill spins briskly on top of a high tower. Dwarfing all else is an enormous stone box rising up windowless, bleak, the size of an aeroplane hangar. The buzzing seems to be emanating from there. I leave my bags at the door and follow the path that leads along the front of the building. As I take the corner, the buzzing grows louder. The hangar looms, the small door in its side stands open.

I walk over and look in. I half-expect to see alien beings swarming over some gargantuan project. Instead, I see a young boy in olive-drab overalls and watch cap, face mask and goggles, standing high on a scaffold working. He is applying an electric buffer to the belly of a gigantic stone angel. I cough the dust from my throat and work my way towards him through rows of scrap metal, slabs of stone, bales of tin and copper and wire. Tarpaulins are tossed here and there over what I gather are works of art. I come beneath the scaffold and squint upward, shielding my eyes. The sun pours down through long windows high in the vaulted ceiling. Reeling slightly, I realise how tired I am from my journey.

'Is Kitsia Ransome here?' I force my voice above the sound of the buffer.

I clap my hand over my mouth, horrified at my error. This is no boy. For now I see that the brown wrinkled skin on the forearms of the worker vibrates loosely. The face behind the amber goggles is fine and delicate. I am thankful that the buffer seems to have drowned out my gaffe. I cup my mouth and shout, 'Hello, Kitsia Ransome!'

The old woman looks down and turns off the buffer, setting the heavy machine down on the scaffold with surprising ease.

'You!' she exclaims. It is a hoarse, croaky sound. She *sounds* like an old woman.

I can think of nothing to say.

The old woman takes off the goggles, the dusty watch cap. The white hair coiled around her small face is a shocking sight. It's as if she were somebody's granny, dressed up to join the motorcycle gang.

'Well,' the old woman croaks, 'don't just stand there staring! Help me down.'

I looked helplessly at the mass of rope that runs up and down the scaffold. 'Sure. Tell me how.'

'Hah, hah, hah! I can see you're going to be a big help.'

I wince. The old woman's laugh is quick and loud, grating as the bark of a small pedigree dog, and just as intimidating. More testily now, I say, 'Tell me how to help you down and I will.'

'That's a girl. I admire your willingness to learn. See that piece of rope? The one with the end painted red. No, not that one. Is that one painted red? The other one. That one. Right. Now, uncoil it from around that bar. Yes, that metal thing there is the bar. No, wrong direction. Good girl. Now, lean back and use your weight to hold it until you can knot it around that weight there. A square knot will be sufficient. Don't you know how to tie a square knot? That's a girl. See? You knew all the time. Some knots we tie by instinct. Now, hand over hand, easily, hand over hand. Don't drop me now, whatever you do!'

She steps off the scaffold and claps me on the shoulder. It hurts, but I refuse to show it by rubbing my arm. 'Hah! You're no bigger than I am. Well, well.'

Failing to see the humour, I smile just the same. 'No one came to answer the doorbell.'

Her eyebrows rise and her forehead breaks into a filigreed network of wrinkles. 'They must be out the back smoking hashish.'

I smile politely.

'You're wondering what kind of household it is I'm running, aren't you? The help all hashed up. Local custom, my dear, nothing more.'

She puts her arm around me and walks me back through the bales of wire and metal, past huge rolls of canvas and pyramided buckets of clay, to a carpeted denlike nook where the embers still glow in a brick fireplace and two cats bat at each other on their hind legs. They stop when they see me and drop to all fours.

'This is Fati.' She bends over to pat the reddish-brown Abyssinian. 'And this is Nati.' She gestures to the dainty Siamese, who comes up and greets me with an upraised tail.

Kitsia straightens up slowly, holding her lower back betraying her age. 'I suppose you'll be needing a cup of coffee and something to eat before I put you to work.'

My eyes widen yet again. I just spent twenty-four hours in three aeroplanes to get here. A shower, a meal, bed, and then work is what I have in mind, in that order.

'Sit down and I'll order you something from the kitchen. What would you like?'

I shrug, still stunned.

The old woman picks up a telephone and presses an intercom button. It's an incongruous sight in these primitive surroundings.

'What are you up to?' she snaps. 'I don't suppose you care that you left my guest standing on the doorstep? Oh, you found her luggage, did you? Well, put it in the guest room and then fetch her some cold lamb, yes, and a salad. See that you hurry. I haven't fired you yet. No, I'll see to the coffee here. Sit down, I said!'

I sink onto what feels like a bale of hay covered by an oriental rug. Everything is a little dusty. Wistfully I think of bedsheets cool against my skin.

The next thing I know she is slapping my face lightly and rapidly. 'A cup of coffee will have you feeling much more worthwhile.'

Worthwhile. I think this is a strange turn of phrase, but no stranger than the hostess herself. She's hardly what I expected. The old woman squatting in front of the fire seems ageless. It will make for a good, rich profile. A piece of cake. I clear my throat and take my tape recorder out of my bag. 'I hope you don't mind that I'm going to use this. But I'd hate to lose anything.'

'Any *what*?' The old woman's eyes twinkle. 'Afraid of losing something, are you?'

I blush, not quite sure why. 'I'm too tired to take notes. You know, jet lag?'

I hope the old woman will take the hint and sympathise, but sympathy doesn't seem in character. She is busy making our coffee, pouring the beans out of an amber bottle into a coffee mill. Filling the bowl of a copper crucible with the grounds and water, she puts it directly into the coals. Then Kitsia turns upon me, seizes my hand, and drags me away from the fire, back into the studio. She yanks a tarpaulin off to reveal a mass of metal and wire.

'I just finished this a while ago and I want to know what you think.'

I stare at the sculpture, conscious of the old woman's eyes on my face.

'Well?' the old woman asks.

'I'm not sure,' I answer.

Impatiently the old woman draws me over to a sketch tacked to a sheet of Masonite. 'Then look at this.'

I look at the drawing for a while, while Kitsia looks at me. It's like an oral exam. I manage to concentrate and eventually begin to understand what I'm looking at.

'Well?'

'It looks like a woman's thighs and crotch.'

'Pah!' Kitsia practically spits. 'What do you think this is? A game? "Name the picture"? Yes, it is a woman's thighs and crotch, but *no*, that is not the point.' She forces me to look at the sculpture again and I realise now that the drawing is a preliminary sketch for the sculpture.

'I think I like the drawing better,' I say finally.

'Hah! That's because you don't know how to look at sculpture. Don't feel badly. Most people don't. Come here.'

She pulls me closer, directing my eyes to a certain juncture of wire and copper. 'Look right there.'

I look; then, I get it. 'I understand! They're both depicting the same thing. Only the sculpture is so much more *alive* – more dimensional – than the drawing!'

Kitsia is triumphant. 'That's very good!'

'But that's only when I look at it from here,' I add, taking two steps to the right. 'I don't get it from here. You should put an X here so that people will know where to stand when they look at it.'

Kitsia looks at me as if I'm an utter moron. 'Viewers have to discover for themselves where to stand.' The hard eyes are still upon me.

I pick this moment to ask, 'Miss Ransome, why did you choose me to write this profile?'

She looks away. 'Because I can use some youthful help around this place. Because most of my arms and legs have run away to the casino. Which reminds me: I need you over here. I think the primer's dried by now.'

She has none of the slowness of an old woman, and I have to run to keep up as I follow her to another work area, where canvas has been stretched over a frame shaped like a three-dimensional harp. The old lady has a staple gun and follows my fingers as I stretch the canvas even tighter along the frame shooting staples inches from my fingers. I jump each time a staple is released, wondering how I'll be able to write this profile with stapled fingers.

'Gun-shy, eh?' Kitsia asks with a twinkle in her eye.

She alternates between scolding and commending me for the extra tension I am adding to the canvas.

Now and then, I manage a question. 'Did your daughter Kit used to help you out in the studio?'

'My daughter was a child when she lived on this island, and quite useless to me in the studio. Her way of responding to a simple command was to burst into tears.'

'Your daughter broke down once at a press conference, didn't she?'

Creases radiate from the corner of her eyes. 'That was years ago ... when she was most unhappy.'

'Is she happy now?'

No answer. Back to work. Finally the job is done; I nearly collapse with relief.

'What now, Oh Master?' I ask.

The old woman laughs and slaps my back, nearly sending me face first into a pile of rags. 'All right, my little friend, you deserve a rest.'

She steers me back to the den and sits me down, smiling mysteriously. Opening a carved box on the hearth, she takes out the biggest hunk of hashish I've ever seen. I watch, speechless, as she tosses it into the same grinder she'd used for the coffee. Was the coffee I drank a while ago full of hashish? Am I high right now?

I remember leaning towards Kitsia and taking the tip of the

101

hookah's hose into my mouth, sucking deeply. I remember the old woman's black eyes never leaving my face.

'Yes,' the old woman says, nodding. 'I had to ask you here. I see that now: you are my only hope.'

One of the cats lands in my lap; I jump.

'I don't understand.' I stroke the cat, puzzled. 'How am I your only hope?'

'You'll see. Soon. You'll simply have to. You're the only one who can save her life.'

'Save whose life?' I exclaim. The cat jumps out of my lap and the old woman shoves the hookah back into my mouth.

'Whose life?' I repeat, leaning towards her. I smell the hashish on her breath now.

'Why, the life of my daughter, Kit Ransome. There's so little time, I'm afraid.' The old woman takes the hose back and fixes me with onyx-hard eyes. 'Pay close attention. For it all rests on you now.'

Late in the winter of 1940, she wired a friend,

Dear Posy:

Unable to work since daughter's birth. War has closed Europe to me. Farther East I will not go. America my only hope; you my only patron. Six weeks all I ask.

Kitsia

Dear Kitsia:

Entrenched in rigorous academic experiment. To open door to volatile creatrix and unmanageable two-year-old would disrupt all control.

Posy

Dear Posy:

Volatile creatrix will garretise self. Unmanageable two-year-old has nurse. Control will prevail.

Kitsia

Dear Kitsia:

Would that I could simply set it all aside!

Posy

Dear Posy:
   Fuck it all. Vernière-Plank shipping African-violets watercolour from Genève. Least I can do in return.

Kitsia

Dear Kitsia:
   Come. Wire $ needs.

Posy

What is she hiding from me? Kitsia wondered. Still, she was pleased at the prospect of being off this island, back among old friends. It was not the seclusion that bothered her, but the dead period: no work coming out; no work being sold – despite Vernière-Plank's insistence that she was on the verge of being recognised.

Kitsia went out to the market place to the souk for one last visit. It had been the only place she had been able to work during this dead period. She went to the teashop and, picking her way down the cluttered aisle, entered the back room, where the greybeards sat in a circle around the hookah. Retired to the cushion and the hose, they accepted her, the woman who dressed like a man. Their dark rheumy eyes betrayed no interest in the Great Whore, as the emir had taken to calling her.

Back on the street, she chose a table among the shopping stalls, laying her drawing pad flat on the table. The only woman in public – and a white one at that – she tried to be as inconspicuous as she could, sketching what she saw.

She remembered Paris, and the view from her windows of the flower stalls in the lacy grey shadow of Our Lady. A great sadness rose inside her: she would never be returning there. Time to put it behind her, to concentrate her hopes on America.

Her brother, complaining bitterly that the war had made travel nearly impossible for civilians, had used all his influence to get his sister and her bastard off the island. Though the child was charming, every time his wife saw her she backed off in search of smelling salts. And the emir claimed the girl had the eyes of his murdered son.

One day late in May, mother and daughter boarded an arms boat bound for Cairo via the Suez Canal, and from Cairo to Lisbon, where the clipper flew them to Havana. Tropical storms caused them to turn back three times to Havana airport, but finally they touched American soil. *The train ride from Miami to New York was an adventure for the child. She bounced on the seat and pressed her nose to the glass. They arrived in New York on the crest of a heat wave that had transformed the formal grey metropolis into a tropical zone. After a week, they proceeded up the coast to Boston, where the ferry carried them to Provincetown, to Posy's house in the dunes: Sandcastle. Kitsia collapsed onto the living-room settee and lit up a black cigarette.*

'Phew!' *Posy fanned the air with her hand and reached into the drawer of the Queen Anne desk for an ashtray. She put it beneath the cigarette as if it were dripping cyanide.* 'That things reeks. Whatever is it?'

Kitsia exhaled. 'Egyptian blue tobacco mixed with hashish.'

Posy clutched her breast. 'I hope you're jesting. Surely that substance will ruin your mind.'

'Not working is the only thing that ruins my mind. I'm here to do something about that. And to look at a fresh stretch of ocean.' *She gazed out the mullioned windows at the iron-grey, white-flecked Atlantic.*

'Tell me, is it the child that prevents you from working, or the circumstances of her birth?'

Kitsia shrugged. 'Both, I suppose. But I've decided to wean her. She's old enough to gain some independence from me. I had hoped this last nurse would fulfil the rightful function – fetching her from her crib when she is hungry and bringing her to my breast is all they've been good for up until now.'

Posy interrupted. 'She doesn't resemble her father, I must say.'

The two women stared silently at the child, who kept trying to stand upon the slippery hooked rug, repeatedly sliding to her rump and laughing uproariously. She had crisp black hair of an almost Indian straightness, bright green eyes, and cheeks as ruddy as Lady Apples – good enough to eat.

'Protective colouring,' *Kitsia replied dryly.*

'I know you haven't asked me for my thoughts, my dear, but I don't understand how you can remain on that island . . . after all that's happened. Surely it isn't the artistic Eden you imagined it to be when you first set out there.'

Kitsia stared moodily at the wild roses trapped by the wind against the mullioned glass. 'I sometimes wonder myself. T.E. Lawrence says that the desert is clean.'

'Ha!' *Posy burst out.* 'Paris is a filthy hole. Yet you loved it.'

'Yes, and now it's filthy with the Boche. But no, I would have left

Paris anyway, war or no war. I'm not being funny when I say that the desert is clean. It's unblemished by any human impression. There is nothing to influence the eye. Nothing but this.' She thumped her skull. 'And the light! The light is sifted through millions of grains of sand. It glitters, Posy. But enough. Tell me about this experiment of yours.'

Posy, who had been looking out the window as if expecting someone, said, 'Your timing has always been extraordinary, Kitsia. Here she is now!'

The doors blew open and a tangy salt breeze invaded the living room, along with the most extraordinary creature Kitsia had ever seen.

She had a boyish grace that turned suddenly feminine as she saw there was company. Pulling herself up like a princess, she clutched her skirts and proceeded into the room as if balancing books on her head.

She had to be fifteen, to judge from her size, and yet there was something distinctly childish about her. Perhaps it was the cut of her periwinkle-blue dress, oddly old-fashioned with a high neck and lace trimming at the cuffs. Yet for all the formality of the costume, her hem was damp from the surf and she smelled of seaweed.

The girl stared at Kitsia, openly curious. *'Are you the one they call the Lady? The artist Posy knew in Paris?'*

Kitsia nodded, staring back. Her dark blue eyes were immense, faintly protruding. Her hair was the colour of oak leaves in autumn, shiny brownish-red. Kitsia felt that if she were to reach up beneath the tangled mass of curls she might discover a softness there where the bones of the skull had not knitted together: the infant's fontanel.

The girl thrust out a hand still cool from the surf and said, *'I'm honoured to meet you, ma'am.'*

Posy said, *'You've forgotten something, haven't you?'*

The girl's hand flew to her mouth. Her eyes darted about the room as if searching for something.

Posy motioned to her feet, which were bare and sandy.

The girl looked down, then raised her hand like a student volunteering in class. *'I've forgotten to wipe my feet!'*

Posy nodded solemnly. *'Don't you think you should go out and come in again? Formal introductions will wait.'* Posy's tone was that of a teacher of the retarded: patient, loving, yet resigned to resistance – and a certain failure.

The girl went out and dusted off her feet. When she came back in, she closed the doors carefully and turned around. Straightening her skirt at last, she released a shower of seashells and sand onto the rug and a timid: *'I forgot about those too, I guess.'*

Posy cried out and lunged for the fireplace broom, squatting on the rug like a parlour maid. The girl busied herself trying to save her treasures.

'They go back to the beach where they came from!' Posy said firmly.

'Oh, no, Posy!' The girl picked them out of the dustpan. 'I brought one especially for you. You wouldn't throw out a present from me, would you?'

Posy sat back on her haunches, grudgingly charmed. 'Very well. Show me my present.'

The girl pawed through the seashells.

'It's like a flower: a tulip. See?' *She held it up to the light; an exquisite hue of pink.*

Posy took it. 'It's very pretty. I'll put it on the sideboard with the rest of my treasures.'

'No, you won't,' *the girl said matter-of-factly, taking it back.* 'But I offered it anyway. A flower from the sea.' *She seemed pleased with herself.*

'Flower!' *Kitsia's baby toddled out into the open room behind the settee where she had been trying to capture the slippery tail of Posy's Burmese cat.* 'Ooooo!' *she cried, seeing a shell and grabbing it away from the girl. She peered inside it, and her mouth formed a perfect O of wonder.* 'Flower!' *she repeated.*

Kitsia nodded, dragging on her cigarette.

'How lucky you are!'

'Hah!' *Posy laughed.* 'I hardly think so.'

'Posy said you've lost your nurse. I'll be happy to help you with her. While you're here,' *she added shyly.*

'Who are you?' *Kitsia asked. She wanted to hear it from the girl herself, but Posy spoke for her.*

'I found this child in the street two years ago, half-starved, unschooled. Now, as you can see, she is dazzlingly healthy, literate, and occasionally – when she puts her mind to it – accomplished at piano and needlework. Next autumn she'll be admitted to the best girls' school in Boston.'

'Ah!' *Kitsia nodded. Posy wasn't exaggerating. This was an experiment of the highest order. Posy had plucked this child from her slum environment and transplanted her among upper-class Boston intellectuals. She wondered if the girl would be able to survive it in the long run.*

'She's weak in the sciences but excellent in languages.'

'In the image of her mistress,' *Kitsia said blandly.*

The girl was playing on the rug with Kitsia's baby, oblivious of being discussed as if she weren't there. Kitsia tried to include her in the conversation.

'You have a marvellous way with children.'

'I have eight foster brothers and sisters,' she said proudly. Glancing at Posy, she added in a low voice, 'Had.'

In the days that followed, Kitsia watched the girl furtively, as a man watches a wild animal in close quarters, careful not to betray too much interest lest the creature bolt. Kitsia observed in her a total lack of the vanity which characterises the common teenage girl. She passed mirrors blindly, sometimes wildly, as if refusing to be trapped.

'I come from the South End,' the girl told her. 'My mother died having me, and her best friend took me in. I grew up knowing I'd killed my mother. "Mother Killer". That's what she used to call me. "Do you know what the Mother Killer did today?" she'd report to her husband when he came home from the docks. "She left the pot on the fire and it burned clear through. Now we don't have a pot!" It didn't bother me. I worked like the devil around the house. Not that she didn't, too. When there are eight kids no more than a year apart, everybody works hard.

'But he – her husband, that is – started looking at me funny once I got big. He'd pull me off in a corner and kiss me. Then he took to bringing me into the bathroom with him and sitting me on his lap. My foster brothers and I knew all about that – we'd practised, I guess you could call it, on each other. So I knew what was happening to me.

'Posy gets angry with me when I say "make love" when I talk about that man. She says "rape" is the word, but I don't know . . . It was the only time I remember being held. I love to be held. Sometimes I think that's all I need to be happy . . .

'One day his wife told me to get going before he knocked me up good and the baby killed me just like I'd killed my mother, so I did. I couldn't stop crying when I kissed those kids good-bye. I miss them sometimes. I moved into the basement of a South End cafeteria, begging scraps to eat. Then I met Posy. She was driving this big old blue Cadillac, like the politicians drive. At first I thought she might be a politician's wife, but when she took me to her Louisburg Square town house, I realised she wasn't anybody's wife at all . . .

'First she had her maid scrub me and then she took me to a doctor to see if I had fleas or anything.

'She took me to her dressmaker and had all these beautiful dresses made up from patterns she'd kept in a trunk in the attic. They were dresses her grandmother had worn. She's taught me so much.' She trailed off wistfully. It was a hot August day and the attic was like an oven. Sweat poured off her nude body. Kitsia, stripped to the waist, and balancing a board on her lap, sketched.

'How did you lose your breast?' the girl asked.

'Someday I'll tell you. Not now.'

'Someday? Does that mean I'll always know you?'

Kitsia didn't answer. She was listening with only half an ear, as she always did when she worked. Capturing the girl on paper took all her concentration.

There was a look of abandonment on a woman's face, Kitsia thought, in her very limbs, in every inch of her flesh, just before she submitted to climax. It was a look of attenuation – of pain beyond endurance and yet of limitless joy – as if she were being pulled apart by angels. The girl walked through life with such a look on her face.

Amazingly, this wild girl had got Kitsia back in touch with her deepest artistic impulses. She now felt ready to return to Zwar, to work in her studio on the larger pieces. These hundreds of studies would provide the basis.

For the next twenty-one days, she sketched as tirelessly as the girl posed. On days when the weather was bad and the light poor, they took Kitsia's baby for long walks on the beach. The Portuguese boys from the village trailed along behind them, dogging the girl's scent. The girl herself was oblivious of their attentions. Resigned to their presence, Kitsia put them to work, dragging back large objects to the beach in front of Sandcastle, where she erected an enormous sculpture out of driftwood, old tyres, bits of buoys, and torn fishing net. Years after she was gone, it would remain partially standing, gradually being sucked away by spring tides or blown back to the sea in a gale – a slow dismantling of the artist's intended effect.

On the day Kitsia and her daughter were to leave Provincetown, Posy and the girl came to the ferry dock to see them off. It was one of those bell-clear days of which there are only a handful in a year. Kitsia kept her eyes on the horizon, avoiding the girl's eyes, which were bright with tears. When the ferry whistle sounded, Posy pulled the girl towards her car. Kitsia and the baby boarded the ferry. At the last minute, the girl broke loose from Posy and ran up the gangplank to press a small wrapped box into the baby's chubby fist. To Kitsia she whispered, 'Save me, please! Save me!'

As the ferry pulled away, mother and daughter sat on deck and unwrapped the box. Sliding open the matchbox, they discovered *countless perfectly formed miniature seashells.*

'Flowers!' the baby squealed. 'Mine!'

'Yes, they are yours,' Kitsia said.

They waited in the New York hotel whose address she had wired to the girl in Boston, along with the money for the train.

She did save the girl, taking her back with her to Zwar. Once they were settled in, they established a peaceful domestic routine: the girl took care of the baby and sat for Kitsia while the baby napped.

'I'm so happy here. Even the beach is calmer. Not that I'm ungrateful – she's taught me so much. But she wanted me to be perfect and smart and I know I'll never be good enough. She wants to keep me like I'm... You know that row of Tiffany vases? I feel like one of those vases. And I can't stand it. I'd smash myself to bits rather than stay on that sideboard.'

Kitsia returned from the souk one day to find her daughter unattended, crying hysterically, the girl cowering in a corner while Posy tried to coax her out into the open. Posy turned upon Kitsia.

'You thief!'

'Take the baby and leave us,' Kitsia instructed the girl, who obeyed. 'Is she one of your possessions, to be stolen?' she went on. 'She left of her own volition. She's desperate for freedom.'

'You understand nothing about love. You never have and you never will. You're completely selfish.'

'Who's being selfish here? To you, she's nothing but a captive bed warmer. She deserves her own life.'

'Be as bitchy as you like, Kitsia, but you still can't have her.' She held out a piece of paper: a court document appointing Posy the girl's guardian.

Kitsia crumpled the paper. 'That's how much your paper and your courts mean here.'

'Either Cassie comes home with me or I pay a visit to the emir.'

Kitsia watched her carefully. She cursed herself for having once had the need to confide her terrible secret.

'You can't have them both. Choose, Kitsia. Because, so help me God, I'll tell them about Kit.'

'Take the girl.'

Kitsia tried to forget the look of betrayal on the girl's face as Posy dragged her to the boat. Two years later, Posy broke the silence between them with a letter announcing that her ward had been accepted to the freshman class of Radcliffe College.

'Congratulations on the success of your rigorous academic

experiment,' Kitsia wired her. *'What next? A chimpanzee to Wellesley?'*

Then she began to get letters from the girl. Written in a remarkably even, almost calligraphic hand, the girl complained bitterly. *'I've begged her to let me live in Cambridge, near campus, but she won't hear of it. I feel more like a prisoner than ever.'*

Like all prisoners, she began to develop self-destructive habits. When the boys at the college looked at her hungrily, she wrote, she gave herself to them. She liked having men want her. She wondered if they suspected the kind of life she had shared with Posy. Yet she wouldn't sleep with just any man, only with the scholarship boys. They reminded her of the poor boys she had known in the South End.

'It is as if I am trying to get that part of me back,' she wrote, *'like a dog rolling in the dust to erase its master's scent. Posy is my mistress. I need to own myself again!'*

Kitsia's first thought was to bring her back to the island, but she knew that was impossible. She wired money and an introduction to the Royal Academy of Art in London. Vernière-Plank handled the details, so that Kitsia wasn't distracted once again by the girl who existed so vitally now in her work.

To please Kitsia, the girl studied art history. She wrote to tell Kitsia she had never been happier. When she decided to return to the States after completing her studies, Kitsia took a break from her work and crossed the Atlantic with her. She entrusted the girl to Hampton Barclay, an old friend and client. Barclay boarded her at his house and got her a job at a museum. Kitsia instructed him and his wife to eliminate Posy from their guest list. Satisfied, she returned to the island to her work. A postcard awaited her when she arrived.

'Shame on you, Kitsia, for not telling me about him! I have Ham and Ethel to thank for introducing me to the world's most wonderful man.'

A second postcard followed soon after; *'Day by day, I'm falling more in love with him.'*

By the time Kitsia wired to confirm her worst suspicion, it was too late. They had already married: the flawed one and the cursed one.

6

Kit is dreaming she is back at Clara with Brendan. They are sitting out on the crow's nest terrace watching a storm blow up at sea. They have just made love. She sits wrapped in a blue silk robe, and Brendan smiles as the wind shows him her breast.

Then they were indoors and she is serving dinner. She has made a haunch of pork that tastes like wild boar because it has been marinated in red wine and juniper berries, thyme, and sage picked from her cliff. She ladles a rich sauce of celery root and potatoes into a blue ceramic dish. She passes a dish of carrots and dill to Brendan.

Afterwards, Brendan is doing the dishes. Kit is sitting holding a glass of red wine by its thin crystal stem. He is talking to her, but she cannot hear his voice, she can only hear the sea.

He turns away from the sink and dries his hands on an embroidered dish towel.

'Take your clothes off. Hurry.'

He is in her now. Her orgasm is so sharp, she cries out.

The phone rang. Kit picked it up.

'Good morning, Miss Ransome. This is your wake-up call. It's ten o'clock.'

Kit let the receiver fall back into the cradle. She wanted to go back to sleep.

Kit got up and went into the shower. Her dream was disturbing. She felt she had found Brendan again. She let herself enjoy the memory of his company. Each day, it was becoming easier to remember him. Not like two months ago, just after they broke up, when his face had been blasted from her thoughts. Now even his voice came back to her.

'Kit, turn that damn machine off!'

'Just a few more minutes, Brendan. I'm almost through.'

It was Sunday morning – time to check on the weekend's openings.

111

Brendan was preparing breakfast and Kit was studying the city-by-city grosses that she punched up on the computer's glowing green face.

'That thing will make you sterile!' he yelled at her.

'Brendan, I bet we do six million this weekend. If the small towns hold up today.' Kit spoke facing the machine.

'It'll make you go blind, woman!'

'Look, Brendan. This is important to me.' Kit came over to the table and sat down. She picked at the tiny pancakes filled with apple sauce.

'Is it, Kit?' His question hung in the air until even he was embarrassed. 'Well, I thought we were going to work on Last Chance today.'

'We are, just as soon as I call Archer and let him know how we did.' Kit couldn't bear to drink the glass of milk next to her plate. It looked so beautiful in front of the jar of raspberry preserves near the mound of butter.

'You don't get it yet, do you?' Brendan asked.

'Get what?' Kit reached for the phone.

'I don't think anyone reads a script and know how to fix it better than you. I don't think anyone knows how to direct the director . . .' Brendan's voice trailed off.

Kit covered the mouthpiece with her hand and whispered, 'Thanks . . .'

Kit finished drying and went back into the bedroom to dress. She put away the maroon Halston she had laid out last night and instead put on grey gabardine slacks and a man-tailored white shirt. She went into the living room.

A knock on the door brought a waiter with her breakfast, and Sasha. Sasha looked young and sunny in a pumpkin-coloured shirtwaist dress.

Kit asked if the coverage on *Yellow River* had arrived.

'Yes, and you have to read it first thing. The only time you had free for Ralph English is in about' – she looked at her watch as she poured them both coffee – 'fifty-five minutes.'

Kit stirred her coffee vigorously. 'Okay. Fine. But first I have some memos.'

'No problem.' Sasha cracked the top of her hard-boiled egg with one hand and picked up her pen in the other. 'At college I learned to chew and take shorthand at the same time.'

Kit removed the tray and placed her notes in front of her, a stack of canary-coloured cards filled with dark blue ink.

'This is to Myra Franklin, re *Smarty Pants* –'

'*Smarty Pants* . . .' Sasha paused with her pen in the air.

'Yes, I know. We need a title change. I reread *SP* last night and I have the following recommendations:

'One. Suggest you make second lead, Reggie, Regina. Think sex change would create much-needed triangle between the sister and the brother.

'Two. Second act is too much talking heads. Find a way to open up action and get them all out of that claustrophobic cottage.

'Three. Suggest Alan Pakula direct. Send him the script as is, outlining your plans for a rewrite. Pakula's not a screwball director, but I think he'd lend this some style which is lacking. As is, comedy is *too* broad.

'Get back to me. If you can work out these points, I'd like to green-light this project by first of the year. It's possible!'

Kit turned two of the yellow cards face down and went on.

'The next memo is to Jay Scott. Please make sure you send it right away on the telecopier machine. I want him to get it first thing this morning.'

Sasha nodded.

'This is re music for *Last Chance*. Picking up on our conversation on the way to the airport. You still haven't convinced me that Sondheim is right. He's too subtle, and won't give us a hummable top-ten theme, which we badly need.

'I think we want something very contemporary, ie, Lacy's music. Brendan's Judd needs some feminine counterbalance.

'Think about it. Period. Reach a decision soon. Period.'

The phone rang and Kit answered it before she could catch herself.

'Scottie! I was just memoing you.'

'How sweet, Kit. I've been thinking it over and I've decided I've got to come out there.' His voice was shrill.

'For heaven's sake, Scott.'

'I'm worrying, Kit. I'm sitting here at seven o'clock in the morning and I'm worrying.'

'What are you worrying about now?' Kit settled back into the chair and brought the phone onto her lap.

'I'm worried about the casting. I'm used to making all our

decisions together. It'll be a jinx if you decide alone.'

'Jay Scott, pull yourself together. It's as important for you to be there as it is for me to be here.'

'But what if the perfect Lacy walks into that casting office and you're looking the other way? Doing something else? God knows what you people have got on other burners.'

'"You people", Scottie?'

'You, Kit. *You*! How many projects can you handle at once? You're so busy processing projects –'

'Stop it!' Kit's voice was low. 'Will you please stop and listen to yourself for a minute. You're getting all worked up for nothing.'

'Nothing!' he wailed. 'The picture has stopped shooting, we have no leading lady, and do you want to know what the gossip is, Kit . . . ?'

Kit steeled herself. 'Since when have I wanted to know gossip?'

'Well, Kitty Cat, you better make it your business to know *this* gossip. Everyone says *Last Chance* will *never* start up again. They say Archer Ransome is going to collect the insurance money. They say he needs some quick cash to get out of the SEC thing.'

'Scott, you don't know what you're talking about!' Kit spoke sharply. Her pulse was racing. The insurance alone was nowhere near enough to bail Archer out of his trouble. 'Where did you hear this?'

'It's on today's *Variety*.'

'It isn't true!' Sasha was staring at her. Kit sat back. 'Don't worry. I'll find a new Lacy and everything will be fine.'

'You sound like an executive. Kitty, do you still love me?'

'Of course I love you. You forget that *Last Chance* is my baby, too.'

'I know. I know. I'm a self-centred prick.'

'A *gifted* self-centred prick,' Kit joked. 'Gotta go.'

'Wait, Kit. Don't hang up. I have to tell you about Brendan.'

'Look, Scottie, I don't want to hear anything. Brendan is your problem. You handle him your way.'

'No, Kit, you don't understand –'

'I do understand. Good-bye.' She hung up the phone.

'Is anything wrong?'

'Just an overwrought director in need of assurance.'

'I guess it's true,' said Sasha. 'They need hand-holding.'

'We all need hand-holding, Sasha.' Kit said. 'With the possible exception of our boss. Have you ever asked yourself why that is? Why he doesn't need any reassurance?'

Sasha shook her head. 'I know what you mean. Mr Ransome seems like a Fortune 500 Superman to me. Of course, I don't really know him. Susie keeps him...' Sasha caught herself.

'Well, maybe Rush gives him reassurance. Or maybe it's the old profit-and-loss sheet that keeps him tranquil. Who knows?'

'Well, don't you get reassurance from your own balance sheet? When one of your films makes a fortune, doesn't it make you feel good?'

'The fact is,' she said, after a moment's serious consideration, 'that good movies can make money, but so can bad movies. So, no, I don't feel particularly good when a mediocre film makes money. Take this script.' Kit flipped through it. 'It's not a very good script. It needs to be rewritten front to back. But because Paul Newman wants to do it now – not in six months, now – we don't have time to rewrite it.

'There we have it. We have Newman and the director he likes best in the world *and* we have the outside financing lined up, and even if I say no, there are four other studios in town waiting in line to say yes. So what am I going to do?'

'Make the movie?' Sasha suggested.

'Maybe... We'll see if Mr English can convince me that a well-written script isn't the most important thing.' Kit scooped up her notes like a solitaire player reshuffling. 'Why don't you take this meeting with me, Sasha?'

Sasha smiled, pleased.

'Ralph needs an audience,' Kit went on, 'otherwise he winds up talking to the wall. You'll see what I mean. He's a character,' – Kit paused – 'right out of one of his made-for-TV movies.'

Twenty minutes later, Sasha let Ralph English into Kit's suite. He was a small man with a yellow tan and row upon row of gold chains hanging over a small paunch. He had combed what was left of his hair forward to hide his baldness, but it had come unstuck at some point and now his hair stood up in three wispy cowlicks, giving him a deceptively defenceless look, like a baby quail.

English was five minutes late and apologised all the way over to greet Kit.

'Kit, honey, how do you do it?' He embraced her heartily. He spoke in a loud voice, as if he thought everybody were hard of hearing. 'How does she do it?' He turned to Sasha. 'How does she stay so young?'

Kit smiled and gently disengaged herself from his hug. 'Kit-honey' made her think of dear old Sammy Rothman.

'So tell me how much you loved my script.' He sat down on the couch and spread his arms over the back. Turning to Sasha, he said, 'Read it yet, honey? Ain't it something?'

'She hasn't read it, Ralph. And I have to confess I didn't have a chance to finish it either.'

English jumped up and started to pace the room. 'Kit, honey, what are you trying to do to me?'

'If you prefer, we can postpone the meeting –'

'No, no, no, no,' he said. 'You read the book, right?'

Kit nodded.

'Hell, the script's the book, only better!'

'Naturally,' said Kit dryly. 'You're making me seasick, Ralph. Don't you want to sit down?'

'You know me. I like to boogie while I do business.'

'I liked the book very much. What I thought was most intriguing about it was the sexual relationships of the characters. Frankly, Ralph, they won't be easy to translate into an R-rated movie.'

'We got ways of doing the dirt. You like the sex stuff, eh, Kit, honey?' He grinned roguishly. 'We've got ways of doin' the sex, little lady. You remember some of my made-for-TV movies?'

Kit suppressed a smile. 'How could I forget them?'

'I want to tell you,' he said, waving a paw, thick with rings, at her. 'I have made some of the sexiest made-for-TV's on record. The censors were so busy coming, they forgot to fucking cut it. Sorry, ladies.'

'That's okay, Ralph. We've heard the word "cut" before.'

'Ha! Ha! Ha!' English's laugh sounded like a machine gun. 'You kill me, Kit, honey.'

'I'll tell you what will really kill you, Ralph.' Kit stole a glance at Sasha, who was missing none of this. 'What I did read of the script read like a television movie. Listen, just because it was a good book doesn't mean it isn't really and truly made-for-TV material. Look at *Thorn Birds*!'

'No, no, no, no!' English dropped onto a hassock. He hunched over his knees and spoke to the floor. 'This is strictly a feature. Paul Newman wants to do it.' He paused to let this sink in. 'And I ask you,' he continued, raising his head to look at Sasha, 'is Newman made-for-TV? 'Course not. Newman's a fucking movie star. Excuse me, ladies.'

'Has Newman committed to this project, Ralph?'

'Well, yes and no.'

'Yes and no,' Kit repeated.

'Yes, he's committed and... uh –'

'No,' Kit finished for him, 'he doesn't like the script either.'

'Who's ever heard of a perfect script? We'll have a rewrite done in a coupla weeks. It'll be fine. It'll be great.'

'Ralph, who's going to tell this rewrite person how to rewrite it?'

'Whoever puts up the money, Kit,' English said seriously.

'I see,' said Kit. 'And part of the package is Patti Wainwright... Mrs English,' – Kit turned io inform Sasha – 'as the female lead. Yes?'

'You kidding me, Kit, honey?' English was pacing again. 'The part was made for her.'

'Ralph...' Kit started slowly, choosing her words carefully. 'Patti is a limited actress. Limited experience. And I understand she's, shall we say, difficult. Ralph, Patti's career has thus far consisted of being in a highly rated TV sitcom in which she spoke in cutesy monosyllables.'

'Patti is very talented. And she's not difficult.'

Kit was done being tactful. 'I call an actress who requires the producers to limit the screen time of the other actress on the show to just eight minutes an episode difficult. And I would stay away. I don't like screen hogs, Ralph.'

'I know. I know. I know.' English sat down next to Kit. 'Listen. Nobody knows better than me. Patti's a cunt. So I'll talk to her. I'll take care of it.'

'You'll take care of it?'

'Yeah. That's just TV. Patti's got no respect for TV. But for features, for movies,' – he kissed his fingers – 'she's got all the respect in the world.'

'I'm sure,' Kit said sarcastically.

'So,' he said, slapping his thighs and standing up. 'We got a deal. Right?'

'No, Ralph,' Kit said patiently. 'We don't have a deal. Yet. I'm not prepared at this time –'

'Look,' he broke in, 'I gotta tell you. Some of your people on the Coast are very high on *Yellow River*. Randy Sheridan *loves* it.'

'That may very well be, Ralph.'

'And, Kit, honey, let us not forget that a certain somebody at BK/Eagle told a certain somebody at my ski house in Aspen that he would love to get his hands on a Newman adventure project.'

Kit pushed the script towards English. It never failed. Producers always tried to pressure her by telling her Crawford was interested.

'Look, Ralph. If Bic Crawford told your story editor, Stephanie Hansen, during a tête-à-tête in a ski lift that he wants *Yellow River*, *as is,* that's his business. I don't want it, as is. If you don't make a deal and you do decide to rework the script, I'd love a chance to look at it again...'

'Okay, okay, okay, okay. I hear you.' English turned to Sasha and winked. 'This lady loves me. We speak the same language. Hey, Kit, how come a pretty lady like you stopped acting?' He turned back to Sasha. 'Honey, am I wrong or am I right? Is she beautiful? What a face! Why is it, you can tell me,' – English launched into another direction – 'that nowadays all these pretty girls want to direct and produce? Why does a cute thing like Goldie Hawn want to head up her own production company? I ask you?

'My own wife. I get her parts that any young actress would fuck her ears off for ... Excuse me, ladies. And what does she want to do? She wants to take my money and direct. Can you figure that out?'

'I certainly can't figure *that* out,' Kit interrupted him. 'Ralph,' – she held out her hand – 'I've got to get to the office.'

'That's my cue.' Ralph smiled. 'Oh, oh, oh,' he said, tearing into his elaborately tooled turquoise-inlaid saddlebag. 'I almost forgot.' He handed a fresh script to Kit.

'*Bug-a-boo*?' Kit read the title aloud, suppressing a smile. 'Great title, Ralph.'

'You knew it right away.' He slapped the table and turned to Sasha. 'She knew it like that.' He snapped his fingers. 'I tell you, honey, you're lucky to work for this lady. Kit Ransome is the best. And that's why I'm letting *you* be the first.' He wheeled on Kit. 'This script is ready to shoot. Not a comma out of place. And, oh, Kit honey...' He paused at the door. 'Don't be surprised when you come across the gorilla. Now, I've personally met this gorilla and he's a beautiful human being. Think of the promotions!'

Kit closed the door on him slowly as he said into the crack, 'Remember, Kit, honey. I'm calling you. We're working together.'

Kit held her finger to her lips until she was sure that Ralph had walked away. When they heard the elevator click open and then shut, they burst into laughter.

'Oh, my,' Kit laughed, wiping a tear from the corner of her eye. 'He really *is* funny.'

Sasha shook her head. 'I can't believe he's a producer. I mean, I've seen his name a lot on TV, but that man' – she pointed to the door – 'can't be a producer.'

'Listen, Sasha. That man is not stupid. He may be crass and he may wear too many rings, but he gets things done. That's the hardest thing in this business – getting things done, moving a project forward. Pushing people like me . . .' Kit let her voice trail off. 'Never mind, Sasha. Do me a favour and get all this stuff together while I finish dressing.'

The lift doors opened on the tiny lobby of the Sherry Netherland, and Kit and Sasha were hit by an explosion of flashbulbs.

'What is this?' said Kit, shielding her eyes and instinctively clutching Sasha's arm for support.

'There she is!' Kit heard a screech. The reporters parted. Kit wasn't surprised to see Arnold Blatsky's sweaty face in the crowd.

'I'll tell you what this is.' A small thick-set woman of about fifty-five marched up to Kit and brandished a fist to Kit's chin. 'A lynch mob. Right, boys?'

Kit looked at the reporters. Perhaps their faces would tell her whether she had anything to fear. Some were turning away. Sasha grabbed for her arm.

'May I help you, madam?' Kit ignored the fist and put herself in front of Sasha.

'That's a laugh, right boys? Help me? Help me like you helped my daughter into an early grave?'

'Good God,' Kit said quietly.

'Who is she?' Sasha whispered.

'It's Monette Novak's mother.' Kit took Sasha's arm and tried to ease past the woman. 'Just keep moving and we'll be able to get out of this.'

'Oh, shit!'

'Precisely,' Kit said as they made a break for the revolving door. No sooner did Kit step into it than the woman yanked it in the opposite direction, crushing Kit's toe. Kit cried out in pain.

'I know you were there!' the woman screamed! 'You were one of those sickies who stood there and watched her die.'

Kit remembered it all too well: It had been one of the most powerful scenes in the movie. Lacy was to shoot up drugs while she sat at the kitchen table. Judd was to watch, powerless to stop her. The scene was playing well. Novak was acting better than Kit had ever seen her. The crew knew it too. Everyone knew it. They were transfixed. Her performance was so real. Suddenly Scott yelled 'Cut', but Monette went on, ad-libbing her own final scene.

Four hours later Monette had died at Cedars Sinai Hospital of an overdose of pure heroin. No one realised until it was too late that the syringe she was using was not the dummy from the prop box, but her own works.

Brendan had stared out the window at the hospital parking lot, nearly catatonic. Scott wept uncontrollably. Kit wrapped him up in a blanket and held him as if he were suffering from shock. Strangely, Kit herself had felt nothing.

'You're a murderer!' The woman was shaking Kit. 'You drove her to it. You let her kill herself. You threatened to take the part away from her. She wanted that part!' The woman's voice rose to a scream. 'Oh, God, you killed her!' The woman struggled with her handbag. The crowd fell back when they saw the revolver in her shaking hand. She aimed it at Kit's stomach. 'This is what you have coming to you, murderer.'

Without even thinking, Kit swung her handbag and knocked the revolver out of the woman's hand.

Surprised at first, the woman regrouped and came at Kit as if to strangle her.

Kit pulled back her right arm and landed a punch on Mrs Novak's jaw as twenty cameras moved in to capture the moment. Mrs Novak lay motionless on the pavement. Kit could see the headlines now.

'FEM CHIEF DECKS MAD WOMAN OUTSIDE SHERRY.'

When Kit found her voice, she said to Sasha. 'Get Devin here. Quick!'

7

Question: How do you find Senator Eben Pierce in a crowded room?

Answer: Look for the prettiest woman.

Liberty walked into the Oak Room, a sea of three-piece suits, white shirts, and well-groomed heads poking through cigar smoke. Eben was talking to a preppy blonde draped over his table. Liberty came up behind him and covered his hand, which was resting on the blonde's Ralph Lauren sleeve.

'Pierce!' she said to Eben. It came out sounding more butch than she'd intended it.

He noticed, but kept himself from laughing. 'Adams!' he said. Rising from his chair, he added, 'Claudia, I want you to meet an old friend, Liberty Adams. Liberty' – he put his other hand on her arm – 'I'd like you to meet –'

'Don't tell me,' Liberty said smoothly. 'Another old friend. So nice to meet you... but the senator and I have a scheduled interview and there's a three-forty flight to LA I'd just *hate* to miss.'

Even whistled low and gave her one of his country-boy grins. 'See you around, Claude. Give my best to Player.'

Ah, the names! How could she forget? They tumbled off the tongue like overpriced delicacies: Claude, Player, Corny, Mina, Eben.

She looked at Eben Pierce for the first time in eight years.

The blue blazer was gone; instead he wore a sedate three-piece suit. The lock of blond hair that used to fall constantly in his eyes had been hot-combed into obedience. It even looked as if he'd stopped biting his nails. Of course, she thought, why should he bite his nails now? Everything had turned out for him. The woman he'd married, not for love but ambition, was dead, leaving him with a clear conscience and an improved career. He'd moved up from the House to where he'd always wanted to be: the Senate. He looked august enough, she conceded as he turned to her.

'Lib. Absolutely great to see you. I can't tell you how good it is.'

He came up and gave her a bear hug. Liberty was so surprised that her arms stayed limp at her sides. 'Good to see you, too, Pierce,' she said without much feeling.

He sat across from her, just looking. She noticed the grey at his temples, the wrinkles around his mouth and eyes. The boyish grin had definitely aged. She felt a small twinge to realise that the Eben of her memories was just a boy compared to this man. To the boy, she would have made a smart-arsed rejoinder. To the man, she was polite, acknowledging the compliment.

'You wanted to see me?'

'You don't have to sound so prissy, Lib. We *are* friends, even after eight years of not talking. Can't we bury the past?'

Liberty widened her eyes innocently. 'This is a burial you've invited me to?'

'Very funny, Adams.'

'I try to stay on top,' she said.

He raised an eyebrow and just smiled.

She blushed, but quickly pulled herself together. 'I know this isn't for old times' sake, Pierce. No need for the act. I do *skim* the hard news. I know about your appointment to the SEC investigating committee, and I know what you're up to. You found out I've met Ransome and you want facts. Well, sorry. Can't help. The view I saw of Archer Ransome was so narrow I'm still squinting.'

'That hard to read?' He looked as if he didn't believe her.

'That hard.'

'Well...' He smiled sadly. 'You can't blame a man for trying.'

'No, you can't,' she said – but she could blame him for being so quick to admit it. Ten years ago, a crack like that would have rankled. 'Is this a liquid lunch?' She signalled the waiter. 'I'd like a champagne cocktail. With Dom Perignon, please.'

The waiter looked to Eben, puzzled.

'Is there something wrong with my order?' she asked. 'Are you out of Dom?'

The waiter bowed. 'The senator has already ordered Heinekens and a tray of Liederkranz with crackers.'

Liberty turned to eye Eben blandly. 'The senator has, has he?'

'The senator thought you'd be pleased with his excellent memory.' Eben grinned disarmingly at the waiter and sent him away, turning the grin on Liberty.

'Save it, Senator. I haven't touched a beer in eight years. I banished brew – along with you.'

'Well, it will be a good sign for me when you join me again in an afternoon's brief respite, won't it?' He winked.

'Oh, it will, will it?' She flirted, in spite of herself. Flirting with him was almost instinctive. It felt good after all these years, but if he thought he could fill her up with Dutch beer and pump her about Archer Ransome, he was sadly mistaken. She rolled up her sleeves and rested her arms on the table. She pouted for a minute, wondering whether or not to say it. Then, grudgingly, she said, 'Pierce. It's good to see you.'

'Well, now, Adams. It's good to see you. But I've got to tell you, you're looking smashing.'

Liberty shrugged and dropped her eyes to the table.

The waiter set down the tray and poured Liberty's beer into a frosted glass.

'I guess hard work agrees with me.' Liberty etched the frost on her glass with her fingernail.

'How's that, Lib?' He ducked to find her eyes.

She went on avoiding his look. 'I'm writing this article for *Metropolitan*. It's a profile on Ransome's cousin, the movie exec, and his aunt, the artist. I'm really cooking. I knew it was something big, but I'm finding out that it's bigger than I imagined.'

He waited for her to go on, but she drank instead.

He joined her. Then he said thoughtfully, '*Metropolitan*, eh? Pretty uptown stuff, Lib.'

She was about to make some wisecrack, but catching herself, said, 'I suppose you're right, Pierce. It is pretty uptown stuff.'

'Where are the raw edges I remember so vividly? Ten years ago, you would have sliced me to ribbons for making a comment like that.'

'I've mellowed,' she said.

'Let's drink, then. To our mutual mellowness.'

They clinked glasses and drank.

'To the wrought-iron table we sat at in the kitchen down at the cottage.' Eben raised his glass again.

'Really, Eben . . .' She withheld her glass. 'Drinking to a table?'

'How about toasting the rosebushes, then?'

'That's better,' said Liberty, clinking her glass with his. 'The rosebushes outside the front door where you liked to piss.'

Eben shrugged. 'You have to admit, it was just what they

123

needed. Remember those beehive mugs we used to drink from?'

Liberty remembered them as she remembered every detail about the place: the cesspool that clogged after a heavy rain, the doorways so narrow Eben filled them, the floors pitched so that they conspired against them those silly, tipsy nights they stayed up all night drinking and talking at the kitchen table and stumbling into bed at dawn. She remembered their lumpy colonial bed with the dusty worn velvet canopy. She used to get sneezing fits after they'd kicked up the dust making love. She remembered coming and sneezing and then coming some more, the one climax refuelling the other. She remembered the long Indian shirt, saffron yellow, that she'd worn as a mini-dress, with nothing on underneath. It hung in the closet in their bedroom; she'd never returned to take it back. In her memory, it hung there still, waiting for her to slip it on.

Liberty felt sad and empty, as if her whole life since then had been a waste. This wouldn't do. He was talking about their midnight picnics on the river dock when Liberty broke in wearily, 'Look, doc. This is all very sweet and nostalgic, but...'

'I know, you have a life of your own now; Liberty Adams, Girl Reporter.'

'I have a certain reputation –'

'You have a reputation,' – he smiled smugly – 'for sleeping with dirty old men. With Justice and Liberty for all!' He toasted her.

Liberty looked disgusted.

'I don't hear you denying it.'

'What I do in the privacy of my own home has nothing to do with the kind of articles I write.'

He frowned. 'Of course not.'

'Absolutely not,' he agreed. 'I do have to admit, however, that I'm surprised you haven't found a husband yet.'

'I haven't been looking for one. Besides, why should you be so surprised? Remember what a handful I was?'

He unfolded his hands gently and looked at them. 'I remember what it felt like to have you on my hands,' he said simply. '*All* over my hands.'

'Pierce,' – she blushed – 'you're still talking dirty.'

'Seeing you, Lib, it's hard not to talk dirty.'

'Oh, Eben...' She smiled fondly at him. 'I always did adore that side of you. So much more than the *political* side.'

'All sides of me are political, Lib. Remember what Jefferson said?'

'"Quick, throw another slave on the fire, my feet are cold"?'

'Very funny, Lib.'

'How about... "One more time, Sally dear, this time on all fours"?'

'You're slaying me, kid.'

'I give up.' She yawned. 'What did Jefferson say?'

'I don't think you deserve to hear it, but I'll tell you anyway: "When a man takes on the public trust, he becomes the public's property".'

'My arse,' said Liberty.

'No,' said Eben, popping a piece of cheese into his mouth. 'Mine.'

'Please, Pierce, it's too early in the day for that kind of crap. Save it for your sports-stadium dedication.'

'Why, Liberty, you're familiar with my agenda.'

'Eben, the whole world knows your agenda. But I really didn't come here to flirt with you. I know it's hard for you to believe ...'

'Why *did* you come, Liberty?'

'Morbid curiosity.'

He nodded. 'I know what you mean.'

'I don't know about you, but I think I've about satisfied mine. Take heed: I'm leaving after the next beer.'

'Come on, Lib. I deserve more time than this. Take the four-thirty. I can have my office switch it for you. Stay and talk.'

'What about, Pierce?'

'You know what about. I'd hoped you'd be a little more cooperative.'

'Listen to the district attorney here. I'm not discussing Archer with you; I thought I made that clear. So please end the interrogation right now.'

'Oh, it's *Archer* now, is it?' he teased.

'Please, Pierce, don't even pretend to be jealous. It's too implausible.'

'Let's just say I'm mildly curious. He's a good-looking man, Ransome. And, as I found out, he isn't exactly the most accessible man in the world.'

'Unlike your available old self,' she put in.

'Then again, you've got yourself quite a string of – what did you call them – press *cherries* over the years: Garbo, Ben Hogan, Vesco. You've managed to corner some of the real diehard press-haters. Tell me, Lib.' He leaned towards her. 'Was I the first?'

'You're in love with the press, Pierce. You don't count.'

'I was teasing, Lib. I can see you still hate to be teased.'

'That's right, Eben, I still hate it.' She looked around for the waiter. 'Where's that other beer? *My* agenda beckons, Senator.' She lit up a Camel.

'You shouldn't smoke, Lib. It's bad for you.'

Liberty inhaled deeply and blew smoke into his face.

'So tell me. Are you travelling light?'

'Not much going on beyond the Ransome SEC business,' he said, lowering his voice. 'Local media mostly. Fund-raisers, monkey suits, backslapping, wife-pinching – a little rubber chicken.'

'Sounds to me like you're campaigning,' Liberty said dryly. 'Oh, that's right, you're going to have to get yourself elected next term. If the good senior senator from Virginia hadn't dropped dead on the seventeenth green of Burning Tree Country Club, you'd still be languishing in Congress.'

'This is all very snappy, Lib, but why don't you stick to the glitter and the patter and save the political reporting for those with a broader data base?'

Liberty narrowed her eyes at him. 'Look, Pierce, you can't get to me. I'm not even going to play with you.' She paused, gritting her teeth. 'Don't you ever feel just the tiniest bit full of shit?'

'Sure I do,' he said amiably, straightening his jacket and pulling down his waistcoat, 'Sometimes.'

'The amazing thing is that your average voter had no idea of the kind of shit that stokes a star machine like you. The consultants, policy, and wardrobe. The writers – idea men and joke men. The researchers you send to the Library of Congress to find out your stand on an issue and those who call the Hall of Records for the birthday of some fat cat's greasy fat wife.' How many times had she rehearsed the speech in front of the mirror? Here she was climbing up onto the soapbox for real. 'The cocktail-circuit ladies who introduce you to the Right People. And last but not least, your pollsters. And every year you redesign yourself from bits and pieces that floated up through the polls.'

Liberty was aware her voice was rising, but she let it. *Frankenstein Goes to Washington*, directed by Roman Polanski.

And the amazing thing is, those people out there love it. They actually believe you're spontaneous. But you and I know that you're just live on tape.'

He leaned towards her, grinning. 'You want to repeat that one more time for the good folks in the kitchen? I know my bodyguards heard you loud and clear...'

Liberty looked around at the two sides of beef sitting at the next table, slightly larger than life-size in their cheap suits, white socks, and Mason shoes. They stood out in the Oak Room crowd like linebackers at a Munchkin convention.

'I'm sorry I ever brought it up.' The speech was an eight-year-old remnant of her youth, unutterably embarrassing.

'I understand, Lib. Really I do.'

She was saved by the maître d', who arrived holding a telephone. Pierce watched her take the call, interested.

'Liberty, angel, tell the Old Girl what you're up to.'

'Didn't Peg tell you I'd call you from LA?'

'If this is code for "Fuck off", Angel, I'm not going to do it. Darling, Archie Ransome *did* have a wife. Bill Thompson, who was a legman for Winchell back then, was obsessed with the child. Archie and Cassie Ransome were quite *the* couple for a while there, I remember. You don't forget a woman like Cassie Ransome in a minute. She was the sort of woman who made you want to get a sex change.'

'Why didn't you tell me?'

'Angel, you never asked. Well, something happened – we never knew what – and she died. When Thompson lit out on a crusade to find out what had happened, he was axed.'

'Axed?'

'Like Anne Boleyn, angel. Obviously, Ransome meant business – even back then.'

Liberty thanked her, signing off. She'd have to have Peg get a line on Thompson, find out what he knew.

Eben was staring at her. 'If you could see the look on your face.' He moved closer, covering her hand with his and whispering. 'You've got a face that makes me fall apart.'

Liberty flushed hotly. The phone conversation with Madelon melted from her thoughts. It was no good; she couldn't pretend. 'I have a confession, Eben. I turn on the news constantly to see if you're on. I hate it when you've had a live press conference and I've missed you. I love to see the microphones jockeying for position

127

under that perfect WASP chin of yours.' She reached over and took it into her hand, felt the stubble that was always there from the first hour and a half after shaving. 'You know what I'm thinking of?'

'Well, now...' Eben said slowly. 'I can't even guess.'

'Well, the thing I'm thinking of is long and strong.'

He looked startled.

'No.' Liberty blushed. 'I'm thinking of your tongue.' She withdrew her hand from his and raised her beer glass shakily. 'Let's drink a last toast to your tongue. Lord knows, this is the closest I'll ever get to it again. To Eben Pierce's tongue: the busiest on Capitol Hill.

'And speaking of coming,' she hastened onward, 'whatever happened to that aide of yours, that 'droid from Atlanta who came in on us that afternoon –?'

'What afternoon?'

'Come on, Eben.' She lowered her voice. 'You know what afternoon.'

He leaned back in his chair and loosened his tie. 'You tell *me*, Lib.'

She blushed furiously. 'No.'

He shook his head. 'Same old Libby. Still just a wee bit uptight. You mean, whatever happened to Tom, who walked into my office the afternoon I was going down on you?'

She nodded dumbly and stared at the head on his beer.

'On top of my desk?' he added.

She nodded again.

'I remember you came to my office in the middle of the day to get the keys to the MG because you had accidentally dropped yours down the lift shaft.'

'Oh,' said Liberty. Suddenly she wanted to be alone with the memory. It was rushing over her now: strange, small details, like the colour of her dress that day – lavender with green piping – like her need to buy bobby pins, like the fabric of his corduroy couch beneath her bare legs.

The gooseflesh had tingled so that it almost hurt as he slid down her underwear. His hands buried themselves in her wetness, fondling her, until she couldn't stand it and her legs gave out. He lifted her onto his desk and spread her legs open wide, working his tongue and fingers inside of her until she keened her way through those sudden, long orgasms she was beginning to live for.

'Earth calling Libby.' Eben was clicking his glass with hers. 'What's running through that wild red head of yours? Tell old Eben.'

Liberty came back to the present. 'I was just thinking of what a shit you were to me, old Eben.'

'What do you want?' He held out his arms, defenceless. 'I was twenty-nine years old!'

'Exactly,' said Liberty. 'You should have known better.' Funny how twenty-nine had seemed so old to her then. 'I am speaking relatively, Eben. Relatively speaking, twenty-nine years old was old then. I was nineteen. And I definitely didn't know better.'

'I admit it!' Eben threw up his hands. 'I was a brute. As a member of the US Congress, I conducted myself like a gentleman, but emotionally speaking I was a toddler, a brutal toddler.'

'Emotionally speaking, Eben, you were an arsehole.'

'You're absolutely right,' he agreed.

'You're not gonna get off that easily,' she went on, out of control. 'You knew you were the only man in the world for me. I never went to so much as a lousy mixer after you sent for me that October.'

Tears stung her eyes. Irritated, she grabbed the handkerchief out of his breast pocket and wiped them away.

'You see, Eben, I believe that people who honestly love each other don't marry other people,' she whispered.

'For God's sake, Libby,' he whispered back. 'Corny's dead. Let it be. Besides, you know that neither of us would be where we are today if I had thrown it all to the winds and married you. I wouldn't be a senator. And you certainly wouldn't be anywhere near the successful writer you are today.'

'Oh, absolutely!' Liberty pushed his handkerchief around in the moisture on the table. 'I never knew what ambition was till I met up with you. But I looked at you there, trapped in your political marriage to handsome Cornelia Rutherford, the governor's daughter, and I said to myself: If he can fuck up both of our lives so royally for the sake of his career – if he's that *blindly* ambitious – then, by God, I can be just as ambitious as he is!'

'And by God, you are.'

She looked for the grin, but it wasn't there.

'I can almost understand your marriage, Eben. She brought the money and influence. You brought the beauty and brains. What I can't figure out is why you still wanted me. I mean, I can understand your wanting a mistress. Cornelia didn't come across as the warmest girl in the world. But why me? Why not a competent professional? You knew I wasn't cut out for it, yet you pressed me into service. From then on everything was shit. Shit!'

'Take it easy, Libby.' His voice was low, kind. His hand was on her arm. She flung it off and continued.

'Why didn't you just leave me with my memory of those first years? That part was such a nice, uncomplicated affair.'

'Uncomplicated?' Eben broke in.

'Yep. Because your sadism and my masochism hadn't surfaced yet –'

'Or vice versa?'

'No, Eben. It's not that easy. Our roles were set. If you call dragging me all over Europe on your fact-finding tour – "fuck-finding" is more like it – with your wife, stashing me in pensiones so that you could come there and fuck me during her sickly siestas – if you don't call that sadistic, then you're not only cruel, you're incredibly stupid as well.'

'Libby, Libby. Can't we have a conversation without you whipping out the knives?'

She lit her third Camel.

Eben swatted at the smoke. 'I don't recall having to twist your arm to get you to come to Europe. You could have refused to go. In fact, what you should have done was to slap me in the face for daring to make such a suggestion, and insist that I cancel my trip so that we wouldn't have to lose two weeks of seeing each other. But that's not what you did, is it, Libby? Do you remember what you did do, Libby?' He put a finger beneath her chin and brought her eyes to meet his.

'Yes,' she said meekly. 'I remember what I did. I ran around like a silly fool, collecting guidebooks and buying clothes. Why I even brought you two shirts. And, oh God, I bought you a blue silk dressing gown to wear when you were with me. I carried it in *my* luggage!'

'I loved that robe. Libby, we had some wonderful times in Europe. Remember the day in Florence when Corny was sick and we had all afternoon and evening together? I picked you up in the little Fiat, and we drove up into the hills behind Florence?'

'Fiesole,' Liberty said dreamily.

'Remember the sight of the sun on the trees – like the background in a Da Vinci? We actually cried. The two of us, sitting in that damned car on the shoulder of the road, with tears on our cheeks. And we drove to that taverna and comforted ourselves with coffee and Sambuca.'

Liberty said, 'And the woman insisted that we have three coffee beans in our glass, because she said two was unlucky.'

Eben said, 'And I let you eat my beans...'

Liberty said, 'You said you'd let me eat your beans if I let you eat my cookies.'

'Yeah,' he said. 'And then, after you stopped laughing at me, you said that if somebody were to jump out of the bushes right then and there and pump you full of bullets, it would be fine because you'd die happy.'

'I would have.' She wagged her head. 'Jesus, what a sick thing to say.'

'I thought it was the sweetest thing you ever said.'

Liberty shook her head sadly. 'I thought you were the most handsome, magical man in the world.'

Her head reeled with images of pensione rooms, with their high ceilings, the wine cooling in the bidet, the afternoon light pouring through the shutter, striping his face and bare chest.

'After you'd leave, I wouldn't go out. I didn't want anything to come between me and my memory of your face.'

She realised she was saying these thoughts aloud, but she didn't care. She'd already blown it.

'Then there were the nights when you couldn't come. Whatever reason – cocktails with Cornelia at the ambassador's, or Cornelia sick and needing you near. Those nights I would panic because I couldn't conjure up your face. I couldn't remember what you looked like. You weren't mine then. Gradually I came to see you weren't ever mine.'

'Liberty, please. Don't.'

She pulled her hand away, looking at him hard. 'What did you think I'd be today? What kind of company did you think I'd be? Go pick up where you left off with Claude over there. She's more your type than I ever was. I don't photograph nearly as pretty as she does.'

'Liberty please,' he begged. 'I can't stand to hear you go on this way.'

'Well, you won't any more,' she said almost cheerfully. She looked at her watch and stood. 'Don't bother getting up.'

He put out a hand but didn't rise. 'I thought we could talk. I see now that's not possible.'

At that moment, she felt genuinely sorry for him. 'Oh, all right, Senator, whip out your pad and pen, because I'm going to say it only once.' She took a deep breath, closed her eyes, and began. 'I was in Ransome's office yesterday when Rush Alexander came in, and the two of them started talking in some kind of code that I guess they figured I was too bimbo-brained to understand.' She proceeded to relate to him verbatim all about the Potomac Opera Society and Casa Verde. 'I have to admit that I was a little stumped at first about the Ebenezer part, but I'm not anymore. It's you, dear boy. You're Ebenezer. Good luck with your singing lessons.'

She started to leave, but then she remembered one more thing. 'There's a man in a hospital bed in Mount Sinai. His name is Tony Alvarro. He's Ransome's head financial guy. I was in a lift with him when he had a heart attack. If he doesn't die, he might have some interesting things to say.'

He looked up from his small leather-bound pad. His eyes were moist. 'How can I thank you, Liberty?'

'You don't have to thank me, Pierce. I never could deny you whatever you wanted.'

She walked away from him then, not daring to turn around. Even if the tears running down her cheeks were fifty percent Heineken, she didn't want him to see them.

8

The boys at the Eighty-sixth Precinct turned out to be a bona fide chapter of the Kit Ransome Fan Club. If she hadn't seen her old studio pin-up on the bulletin board next to Morgan Fairchild's and Linda Evans', she wouldn't have believed it. Her refusal to press charges against the woman in the next room, who had just threatened to kill her, baffled them.

'Look, Officer Ballard. She's lost her only daughter. Her daughter was an actress too. The headlines are all she can grab hold of now. I hope you won't be too hard on her. Just do me a favour: When she comes to, please don't give her that gun back.' Kit shuddered. 'Now, if you gentlemen will get me that poster you wanted autographed... I'm afraid I'm expected at a casting session.'

Devin greeted her at the Ransome building's casting office with a cup of milky coffee. 'You poor thing.' He steered her to the nearest chair. Around them milled the eighty-six girls who had answered that day's call for a new Lacy. Kit wondered how she would be able to concentrate on the work at hand, knowing what the headlines had in store for her that night.

As if he had read her thoughts, Devin patted her hand and said, 'Not to worry, Kit. None of this will show up in the papers tonight. At least no names will be named.'

'How can you say that, Devin? There must have been twenty reporters there who witnessed the whole fiasco.'

'Yes, and while you dealt with the boys in blue, I made those guys swear on their press cards to keep all names out of it. For now.'

Kit stared at the young man who was grinning proudly. 'Devin, how in the world...?'

His grin broadened. 'I simply told them that I was a spokesman for Rush Alexander and if they kept this quiet, we would have something five times as juicy for them tomorrow.'

'But Devin – what are you going to give them tomorrow?'

133

'You mean, what is Mr Alexander going to give them? He's a very resourceful guy, Kit.'

'But what if it gets back to Rush that you –?'

He patted her arm. 'No sacrifice is too great, Kit, to keep your name out of the papers. Even if it's just for a day. Let them cool their heels for twenty-four hours. The headlines won't look half so gruesome tomorrow. *If* it makes the headlines at all, the day after.'

Kit's throat tightened. She was at a loss for words. 'I don't know how I can...'

Devin turned away, embarrassed. 'Shall we get down to work?' He said it loud enough for the crowd to hear.

All gum chewing, shuffling, and résumé rustling ceased as Kit rose. Devin followed.

'Ladies,' he said, 'as you were. Miss Ransome and I are just going to walk among you, ask you a few questions. Just be yourselves.'

The girls became lively again, this time artificially so. Kit felt as if she'd joined a crowd of extras.

Devin filled her ear with the steady stream of data.

'The tapes we made of the girls we saw this morning are already on a plane to LA for Scottie to look at. There's not much there, but Scottie will want to see them anyway. They're all Charlie's Angels from what I can see. Pure neoprene plastic. We might as well be in LA for all the flesh and blood we've found here. This afternoon's batch looks a little better.'

They paused in front of a young brunette dressed in a purple leotard and orange leg warmers. She had a dancer's face as well – small and birdlike.

'Too much neck,' Devin whispered to Kit. 'We're not casting *Swan Lake*.'

'Right,' Kit turned to the girl. 'Thanks, we'll call you. Let's go over there, Devin, where we can talk.' Kit pointed to the couch in the corner. They settled there and resumed the review of prospective Lacys. 'Tell me something about the girl on the far right. The one with the pale skin and pink lipstick.'

'Genna Somebody. She had a small part in Scorsese's last movie.' Devin riffled through his papers. '*Morris*. Genna Morris. She's primarily a singer, but she has acted some. Has a certain quality.'

'Yes,' Kit agreed. 'She has an interesting face.' Then she

remembered seeing the girl at a party at Clara. She was one of Brendan's wenches. 'She's all wrong.'

Devin shrugged and made a note. Then ran down the list of remaining girls. Occasionally Kit asked one of them to come over.

Kit had to make herself forget what it felt like to be one of the girls to make it through these interviews. It seemed like yesterday that she was a young actress lining up for calls. How she had hated the casting people then – from the Devins on up to the Kits. When they were kind to her, she had hated them even more. Steeled to the inevitability of rejection, she found kindness more painful than cruelty. Kit made it a point never to be too kind.

She had Devin call over a sleek black-haired girl because she reminded Kit of herself years ago.

'What have you done lately?' Kit's eyes never left the girl's elegant face.

The girl held her chin high and fixed Kit with an amused, bored expression. 'Stock. Last summer. Westport Playhouse. *Seesaw*. Featured dance and understudy for the female lead.'

Kit could imagine her, night after sweltering night, waiting for the big break to play the bitch in black tights.

'Don't you think you're a bit ... sophisticated for Lacy?'

The chin dropped ever so slightly, then lifted itself a touch higher. 'I think I have the range,' she said. But the conviction just wasn't there.

'Thank you for your time,' Kit said coldly, instructing Devin to fetch the next girl. And so it went, one clipped interview after another, until Kit had run through two dozen actresses. Through it all, Kit's approach remained cool. Each girl reacted differently: some were hostile, others hurt, still others foolish and giggly. She waited for the girl who would react in the right way. What the 'right way' was, Kit wouldn't have been able to say – until she saw it. Finally, her patience wore thin.

'Devin, you mean to tell me this is it?'

'No.' Devin spoke quickly. 'There are a couple of others in the next room. Brendan's singled them out and he's reading them right now.'

Kit turned and stared at him. 'What are you talking about?'

'I said Brendan –'

'I heard what you said, Devin. What is he doing here in New York?' she demanded.

'I guess,' Devin proceeded cautiously, 'he thought he could be of some . . . help.'

'You guess? Does Scott know about this?'

Devin stammered. 'Didn't Jay tell you? He said he was going to tell you.'

'Where did you say he was?' Kit's voice was hoarse, low.

'He's in the other room. You want me to get him?'

Kit twisted her earring. Since the breakup, she had never been alone with Brendan without Scott. Why hadn't Scott warned her? She thought back to her phone conversation that morning. Perhaps he had tried.

Devin was fending off one of the girls.

'I have another call. Just tell me how long I have to wait,' the girl whined to Devin.

Kit lashed out at her. 'My dear, consider your wait over. You may leave now. Devin, I've seen enough. I think I'll look in on the reading.'

The young redhead in braids tied with plaid bows looked up nervously when Kit came in. Brendan, straddling a chair opposite her, held his concentration – ever the Method actor. Kit found a chair against the wall, at the back of the room.

The sound of his voice filled the room, settling about her like snow, immobilising her. She closed her eyes and lost all track of time. Suddenly Brendan was standing over her. She rose to her feet and brushed the unexpected tears from her cheeks, offering him neither hand nor cheek.

'Kit,' he said shyly.

'What the hell are you doing here, Brendan?' Her voice was a harsh whisper.

'Trying to help you find Lacy.' He smiled and smoothed his moustache. 'For all the trouble we're having, you'd think we were casting Scarlett O'Hara. I've been thinking maybe we should consider some established young actresses. Maybe we won't be able to find an un –'

'Was this Scott's idea?' Kit cut him off coldly, fixing her eyes on his Adam's apple. 'You shouldn't have come. I was supposed to handle this alone. You should be in LA with Scott looping those scenes. We're behind schedule as it is, but you take it upon yourself to come in to New York at Horizon's expense – I assume – to be a casting expert. I thought I could trust you to act like a professional and do your job and not try to do mine. Of course, I know your professionalism all too well.' Kit moved closer to him, her fists curled in her pockets. 'And Scott! I don't know what's got into him. I'm afraid he's gone into one of his tailspins when all he does is send people on errands and worry if they're going to come back alive.'

Brendan's hands fell onto Kit's shoulders and silenced her. She felt their familiar, warm weight. His blue eyes were concerned. 'My God, Kit, you're trembling all over.' Kit couldn't answer him. The weight on her chest sealed in her voice. 'This isn't good. Sit down, Kit.'

'I'm fine.' She scarcely recognised her own voice. 'I don't want to sit down.'

'Kit, darling, what is it?'

'I'm not your darling. Take your hands off me, please.'

He looked at her sadly and removed his hands. The lighting in the room made the wrinkles on his face cavernously deep. 'It's me, isn't it? Kit, please believe me – all I wanted to do was be with you –'

Kit jerked her head away from his gaze and saw that the three girls standing near the stage were watching them. She despised his sympathy, despised their prying eyes.

'All I seem to do is hurt you,' he went on. 'I know what hurts you. You think I don't understand you.' He grabbed for her again.

'Don't be ridiculous.' Kit pulled away from him like a boxer eluding a blow.

'Maybe I should go away. Goddammit, I *should* go away. I shouldn't be in the same hemisphere with you. I oughta be in goddamn Katmandu.'

'Don't you dare start,' Kit warned. 'Don't start in with that pitiful self-indulgent act of yours. Don't start any act at all. You're not terribly convincing as the spurned . . .' Kit meant to diminish him, but it was she who was shrinking.

'Oh, God, Kit, please don't cry. Sweet Jesus. I never thought we'd be so far away from each other.'

Kit slapped him hard across the face. One of the girls let out a small cry. Brendan held his hand to his reddened cheek. He looked astounded.

Kit ran out of the room, ran through the casting office, past Devin, past the waiting girls, past the secretary, who futilely held out phone messages to her, through the doors, into the lift, and out into the street, where she hailed a cab.

*

137

At home in Pacific Palisades, Kit found her solace in water. She swam every day in the Santa Barbara Channel. Each day after work she would come home and was no sooner through the door than she'd strip off her clothes and put on a bathing suit, seaweed thin, one-piece, usually black. Then she would step into her rubber net sandals and pull on whatever old shirt was lying about. She would stop at the door only long enough to grab her worn sun-bleached hat and to leave her glasses on the table beneath the mirror. Then she would skip down the wooden steps – ten steps followed by a landing, followed by ten steps – and on down to the Pacific Ocean.

First she would swim straight out fifty yards. Then she would swim parallel to the beach northward, tracking the shoreline. *Stroke, stroke, breathe. Stroke, stroke, breathe.* On every upstroke she would spot comforting blurry landmarks. *Stroke, stroke,* past the house with the chalet peak. *Stroke, stroke,* past the beached catamaran with its light blue mast jingling in the breeze. *Stroke, stroke,* past the Cape Cod cottage and its wild patch of bougainvillaea, a fiery pink haze. *Stroke, stroke,* past the glass box occupied by the Arabian playboy and his three wives, and on two and a half miles into the inlet where the public beach began. The beach was only really crowded during the late spring and summer. Then the parking lot was jammed with cars, umbrellas dotting the shore and bathers splashing in the shallows.

Kit was a familiar sight to the lifeguards there, who would wave or whistle at her as she swam by. At these times Kit would feel divinely conscious of her fine, slippery form working the water. It seemed to her as if she ceased breathing through her nose when she swam. Her body drew its strength from the water, not the air.

It was usually sunset when Kit swam. She would paw the red-ribboned water, forcing her body into the current. Putting her face into the water, she'd open her eyes and see the light hanging just below the surface in golden stalactites.

One evening in early spring of last year, she saw it. To her nearsighted eyes it looked like a small red lozenge in the parking lot. It might be a Triumph or an MG. At first she thought it might be a pair of lovers on a regular tryst, since it was off season and the parking lot was theirs. But several days later she saw that it wasn't lovers. It was a single man. He might be a bird-watcher, or a whale-watcher, or a lover of sunsets, or... Every evening, just as she broke into the inlet, she would see him pull into the parking lot at the beach. Whoever he was and whatever he was doing, Kit began to look forward to seeing him each night.

One night, she realised with an odd twinge of pleasure that he was watching her. He sat on the bonnet of his car, legs propped up on the bumper. She didn't feel unsafe, as she sometimes did, as when she was undressing in her own bedroom and suddenly became frightened of the dark, imagining the pale face of a voyeur beyond the window. It felt good to be watched by him; it felt as if he was watching over her. After she'd passed the public beach on her way home and stroked past the marina, she would turn around, and, treading water, see that he'd gone. Then she would feel deserted, even forsaken. The ocean would seem cold and vast beneath her.

That same spring, Kit visited the set of *Last Chance* in the first week of shooting. The unit was in a Victorian house up the coast. She was about to go to say hello to the crew when she saw it parked outside the front gate: the car, the lozenge. One of the grips, a pretty young woman with freckles, braces, and a lumber shirt came bounding out of the house.

Kit stopped her. 'Whose car is that?'

'The junky old Saab? That's one of Brendan's.'

Kit glided into the house as if borne by waves. She entered the Victorian parlour and greeted the cast and crew, hugged Jay Scott, who paraded her around proudly introducing her to every single person there. She and Brendan didn't say much, but there was a look in his eyes that made her smile at him, a smile she hadn't given to a man in a long time.

Later that afternoon, Kit stopped on her way home at all her favourite shops. She bought pine nuts and fresh pasta at the Italian market, Parmesan and a wedge of running Brie at the cheese store. At the baker, she bought two loaves of whole-wheat Italian bread and some thin anisette cookies, and at the tea shop, Hawaiian coffee beans. At home, there was a litre of Chianti, a garden of basil and tomatoes, and a small grove of orange trees where she would pick the dessert.

She ran downstairs to undress. Downstairs in the one big room that was her bedroom, the whitewashed walls danced and shimmered from the reflection of the ocean below.

She pulled her jersey dress over her head and draped it demurely over the nude female sculpture. How her mother would cackle to see her work used as a clothes tree. Kit chose a sea-green bathing suit, picked up a faded black shirt, and stepped into her sandals.

She ran upstairs and caught a glimpse of herself in the mirror by the door. Two green eyes swallowed up by pupils stared back at her.

Kit slipped down to the beach and set out on her swim – *stroke, stroke, breathe* ... When she rounded the inlet and saw that the parking lot was empty – no lozenge – she felt bereft. The swim back was harsh and breathless. She was less a fish and more a dull-hulled boat cutting clumsily through the water. She barely saw the glass box, the bougainvillaea, the catamaran, the cottage, the peak of the Swiss chalet. She swam the fifty yards to shore, exhausted. Emerging from the breakers, she collapsed on the beach, doubled over with cramp.

She applied the towel like a bandage to her thighs and arms. Salt stung the invisible wounds in her flesh. She threw her shirt over her shoulder and stepped into the gritty rubber sandals, unsure she'd be able to make it up the stairs.

He was there, waiting for her, on the second landing, eating a tomato from her garden.

'Damn, these are tasty.'

Kit caught hold of the railing.

He looked vaguely surprised. 'Don't tell me you weren't expecting me.'

'I ... I ... You weren't in the parking lot.' He grinned. She blushed, looking at her feet. 'I didn't think you were coming back.'

He held out his arms to her. His voice was gently mocking. 'Not coming back?' He laughed softly. 'Why, Aphrodite, I'm here to stay.'

Kit sat in her living room with Jay Scott. Brendan had just left to buy Triple Sec for the fruit compote she was making for dessert. They were watching the sun set over the Pacific and drinking tea from thin pink cups.

'Look at the size of that gull!' Scott ducked involuntarily as one flew close to the window. They were both avoiding serious conversation.

Kit stood up and jerked down the windowshade, then sat back down and closed her eyes. She was conscious of the ocean lapping at the rocks below, tame as a lake.

'Damn, it must be something living with Brendan full time!'
Scott began. 'I've noticed he's not drinking half as much as he used
to. And none when he's on the set.'

Kit kept her eyes shut and waited.

He went on. 'He's also stopped most of his weird public trips
since he's moved in with you. His womanising...'

She sighed loudly and stretched out her bare legs.

'Brendan can be wild, Kit. I remember one night, I was in
Sardi's at the upstairs bar when Brendan walked in and jerked Eder
of the *Times* off his bar stool. He started to read him out. Loud and
ugly... in front of everybody... other press guys, tourists. One
guy took out his camera and took a picture of Brendan. Brendan
ignored him. He just kept raising hell about some review Eder had
written. And get this, Kit, he wasn't even in the fucking play. Some
buddy of his had the lead. Brendan and his buddies.'

Kit smiled benignly. 'Brendan is very loyal. I thought you knew
that. What most people don't understand is that he's really quite
gentle. He just has a strong sense of right and wrong. And it's his
big voice. He can't always control it offstage.'

'Face it, Kit, the man's a born ham. He plays to the gallery. I
know he promised to behave –'

'And he *is* behaving, Scott, you just said so yourself. It's the
press that's acting up. They won't leave us alone. They know what
questions will get him riled. One day he's going to throw one of
them through a plate-glass window.'

'Kit, look, I know it's none of my business, but you're a Blue
Suit and you've got to start acting like one again. Blue Suits are
supposed to stay *behind* the scenes. You know those guys in New
York take a dim view of one of their executives carrying on like the
stars she's supposed to control.' Scott paced back and forth. 'It's
just that I'm beginning to see those elegant bones of yours in all
those inelegant tabloids. Brings back the bad old starlet days.'

'Scott, stop. Don't you see, it's not his fault? He doesn't mean to
do it. I know he doesn't! He knows I can't deal with the newspapers
on that level.' She fixed him with a pleading look. 'I don't even read
any more. Imagine! Oh, I read clippings. I have whole magazines
shredded into clippings, minus the items about Brendan and me.'

'Well, I've read them. They don't make you sound very...' He
hesitated. 'What I mean is, Kit, they make you sound like you slept
your way to the top. And Brendan's this... I don't know... this
plaything, this reward you've given yourself for succeeding in a

man's world. This big . . . game . . . trophy.' Scott's voice dwindled and died.

Brendan was standing there, scowling. 'I forgot my keys. I was halfway down the drive when I discovered I didn't have my keys. And I'm not even drinking!'

'They're hanging on the kitchen board,' Kit told him. Scott raised an eyebrow. Kit shrugged.

Brendan came back from the kitchen. 'I'm not coming all this way for my goddamned keys without getting a kiss.' His lips came down hard on hers. 'Here, old buddy.' He tossed the keys to Scott. 'Why don't *you* pick up the fucking Triple Sec. Miss Ransome has some trophy bagging to do.'

It was their first party as a couple: a brunch. Most of her friends had already left; his had stayed to see the sunset.

Brendan was leaning against the sink, pouring lots of water into a glass with a little bourbon. Kit came over and, wrapping her arms around his bearish middle, whispered in his ear, 'I want you.'

Letting his empty hand drop slowly down her back, he squeezed her bottom hard. Kit pushed closer to him until she saw him wink at a friend standing behind her.

'Hell, man,' Brendan continued talking as though Kit were not there. 'You can't expect those pea-brains to know what they're doing. So long as Ted Roland's balls hang in the right leg of his blue jeans during the ninety minutes he's on screen . . .' Brendan disengaged himself from Kit in order to make his point. 'They don't care how the rest of it plays.'

'Brendan, don't!' Kit broke in. 'Don't talk like that. It makes you sound like you don't know anything about movies. It makes you sound paranoid. It's not that simple.'

'It is for me, Kit. Look what the studio did to my buddy. His part in this movie he's doing has been whittled down from six minutes to seventy seconds. The studio is the enemy of real art. Acting for a studio can only be servile – not free – art.' Brendan sipped his drink.

'Hegel, huh?' The friend grinned, pleased to have his tribulations defended so loftily.

Kit started to walk out of the kitchen, but she turned around and said louder than she meant to. 'Then I guess I'm your enemy too, Brendan.'

Kit wandered away and over to a group of young women who were talking near her computer. She counted one king-sized redhead, two medium blondes, and one petite brunette.

'Can I get anybody anything?'

'How can you stand to live with this thing?' said one of the blondes. 'It's so cold and icky.'

Kit patted the machine fondly. 'This cold icky thing enables me to keep tabs on an extremely complex business.'

The redhead shrugged. 'Yeah, but doesn't it just reduce the whole thing to numbers? I mean, don't you feel it puts you out of touch with creativity?' She giggled. 'Brendan thinks it makes you sterile.'

'I hear he calls it your "hubbie",' one of the blondes added.

'Actually, I call it my "hub", by which I mean it is the hub of my business life,' Kit corrected her, angry with Brendan for sharing their secrets with these young women. 'Brendan doesn't like computers very much, I'm afraid.'

'Brendan's into people – women.' The redhead stretched langorously and shook out her hair. She sauntered over to join the men. The two blondes followed, as if the move had been choreographed.

'I don't believe we've met.' The little brunette stuck out her hand. 'It's a nice party.' She swivelled her head around. 'A lot of different people.'

Kit tried to play the gracious hostess, but it was no good. Listening to her delicate wicker crackle beneath the weight of his friends, Kit thought she'd never seen so many strangers so at home in her house. She wasn't sure whom she resented more, the women – girls really – young enough to be her daughters, or the men, who were older, franker, and louder.

'My name's Susanne. I'm a friend of Lily's.'

'Brendan's daughter? That Lily?'

Susanne nodded.

'How do you do? I was under the impression you were one of the . . .' Kit caught herself.

'One of Brendan's "wenches",' Susanne finished for her. 'No Lily and I are real close. When Lily found out she couldn't come tonight, she sent me to spy and report back to her.'

'Spy?' Kit repeated densely. 'Oh, spy . . . on me. Do I pass muster?'

'Absolutely.'

'I certainly hope so.'

'You really have nothing to be jealous about, you know.'

'Whatever are you talking about?'

'All these young things. I see how you've been watching them.'

Laughter broke out across the room. Brendan was demonstrating some sort of headlock on the redhead. 'It's just that he seems so fascinated with their youth...'

'I know what you mean,' the girl agreed. 'Being thirty, I'm beginning to understand. It's like youth were some kind of accomplishment.'

'Yes.'

'Well, don't worry. They're just remnants of his mid-life crisis. He's practically over it, thanks to you. You want to know something, Kit – may I call you Kit? I envy you: this house, that man, your job. If you aren't the happiest woman in the world...'

'Yes...?' Kit raised an eyebrow.

The girl shrugged. 'Well, you *ought* to be, that's all. I have to go now. I'm driving down to San Diego tonight. Don't worry. I'll give Lily a glowing report.'

When the girl left, Kit felt strangely deserted. She went downstairs and stood there in the dark looking out at the blackness, at the winking lights of the buoys. Why wasn't she bursting with happiness? Was she really jealous of the girls upstairs? She pulled out a sweater, draped it over her shoulders, and went upstairs to tell Brendan she needed some fresh air. She found him out front in the garden saying good night to one of the blondes. He was kissing her, with his hand resting familiarly near her breasts. Kit turned and hurried back through the house to the beach stairs.

Halfway down the stairs, they started to shake beneath her and she turned to see him pounding down after her.

'Where are you going?'

'I thought I'd get some fresh air.'

'Are you mad at me for some reason?'

'Of course not. Why should I be mad at you?'

He looked hard at her. 'You've been walking around with a bug up your arse all evening long.'

'I beg your pardon?'

'It's them, isn't it – the girls?'

'Your "wenches", you mean?' She didn't mean to sound so snide.

'So it *is* them! Jesus, Kit, you should have told me you were jealous. A strong woman like you -- a man doesn't expect it. Look, Kit, they're my friends. They happen to be young and beautiful. I like women, Kit. I like to touch them, too. I like to touch men, for that matter.'

She dropped her head. 'I'm sorry, Brendan.'

'Sorry, *hell*!' He left her there and went back up the stairs. She turned around and plunged down to the beach. It was colder down there, and new-moon black. She followed the steepest stretch of the beach around the point where she wouldn't be able to see the lights of Clara, nor hear the noises of the party. She was numb by the time she reached the beached catamaran. She collapsed onto the canvas and fell asleep, listening to the wind jingling the rigging.

She jerked awake, rising to go back. It would be safe now. As she rounded the point, she saw only one light burning. Its distance from the top of the cliff told her it was the bedroom light. She walked towards the light, hopeful, ran up the cliff stairs and through the living room. The mess from the party could wait until tomorrow. She couldn't risk hearing him accuse her of the *fucking sense of order that froze his nuts*.

The vacant bed brought her up short. She looked around wildly. The side of the closet where he kept his things was empty. She sat down on the bed and stared at nothing, anaesthetised. Then she crawled down to the foot of the bed and fell asleep.

He threw something on the floor near her head and she woke up right away. It was a script.

She rubbed her eyes and reached for the script. Then she remembered. She dropped it and pulled back. 'I don't feel much like reading tonight.'

'Is that so?'

'When I didn't see your things in the closet, I thought you'd left.'

'Don't you remember? I moved them into the hall closet upstairs.'

'Oh.'

He rolled her over and looked into her eyes. 'Take off your clothes.'

She lifted her dress over her head. He rolled her back onto her belly and began whispering in her ear, his voice setting the hair on the back of her neck on end. 'I wanted you so much tonight I was going out of my mind. After you left, I broke up the party and went looking for you on the beach. I kept looking for your clothes at the tideline. I had this idea that I'd driven you into the channel.' He laughed. 'I went back up to the house, but I couldn't stand being there without you. I drove down to Scott's. He poured me a bourbon and put me in my reading chair with this script, but I couldn't concentrate. All I could think of was you in that room the night we first met. Scott had to drive me back to Clara. Remind me to pick up the Saab in the morning.' He put his hand between her legs. 'Nobody feels like you, Kit.'

She felt him wedge himself deep inside of her. She gasped.

'I love to fuck you, you know that. You think I love you because you're elegant and uptight. Well, you're wrong. I love you in spite of that. I love you for the softness that manages to creep through that elegant, uptight shell you live in. I love you for your sweet soft self. Your friends are right: I *am* bad for you. You let too much of that softness escape around me. They all worship your bitch hardness. Well, I hate it. It makes my dick go limp. When you're sweet like this, it makes me hard as a rock. Tell me I'm good for you, baby. Tell me.'

She closed her eyes and arched her back, taking him more deeply into herself. 'You are good for me. You are ...' Then they were making love, wordlessly, soundlessly. *Stroke, stroke, breathe.* She had been right to wait for Brendan. He was pulling her down, into the deep water. *Stroke, stroke, breathe ...* pulling her home.

At the River Club, she came to rest at the deep end of the pool and knocked the water out of her ears. 'What did you say?'

'I'm sorry I can't bring the phone to the pool, Miss Ransome.' It was one of the policemen. 'Shall I tell the party you're engaged?'

'Officer Ballard, haven't I already told you you're going to have to stop following me around? I don't like being followed. Who is it on the phone and how in hell did they find me?'

'It's your secretary.'

She pulled herself up the ladder and snatched the towel off the diving board before he could reach it. She wrapped it around her middle and went dripping to the phone.

'Hi. I wouldn't bother you for the world, but Mr Ransome's office called. He says you're to call him this afternoon without fail.'

'Without fail, eh? Well, thank you. Thank you, Sasha, for taking the trouble to track me down.'

'It was no trouble. Devin said you'd probably be there, since your club is closed today.'

Thanking her again, Kit hung up and looked around impatiently for her bag. Officer Ballard clicked his heels together and held up his fingers. 'One thin dime at your service, ma'am. Can I get you a second towel?'

'Yes, Officer Ballard, thank you.' Kit took the dime and dismissed him with a smile as she dialled Archer's office. They put her through immediately.

'I'm glad you could get back to me, Kit.'

'I'm curious, Archer. Is it a good sign or a bad sign that you've taken so long to give me your decision?'

'I'm afraid I've decided not to give you my decision on *Last Chance* until you've given Liberty Adams *her* chance, too.'

'Oh, Archer, really! I thought we both agreed that we'd had enough of the press where ...'

'I think that if you'll let down your guard a bit, you'll find that Liberty Adams isn't so bad.'

'What does that *mean*?'

'She deserves more consideration than you've given her so far, that's what it means.'

'But, Archer –'

'Call her and set a time, Kit. I strongly recommend it.'

Click. Kit shook her head rapidly. Had she heard him correctly?

'He's cracking up!'

'I beg your pardon, ma'am?' He swung the towel towards her.

'Nothing, Officer Ballard. It's my problem, not yours.'

'I understand, ma'am.'

'Will you please drive me to my hotel, Officer Ballard, before you go back to your other duties?'

'Anything you say, ma'am.'

'I think I need a drink.'

Later, in his own defence, he will say that it was a trick of the light, a phantom of one of those grand Technicolor sunsets at Clara that leaves you blind to anything but silhouettes.

He stands on the terrace as it darkens against the pale blue scrim of sky, wearing the robe she gave him even though she isn't home to appreciate his modesty. His erection bobs out of the opening of the robe

147

and he smiles down at it sadly, nursing a grudge against the studio she runs off to day after day. A full glass of freshly squeezed lime juice sits on the parapet. He flings it back and winces as the citrus acid stabs at his glands. Then he sprints, taking the rough wooden steps two at a time, flinging off the robe as he strides towards the ocean. Standing at the water's edge, he raises his voice above the booming of the breakers and rehearses Judd's soliloquy on fathers and sons. The surf surges around his ankles, scrubbing him like sandpaper. He bellows on.

Finally he stops and turns, looks up automatically at the windows of Clara, now tinted crimson with the sun's last rays, and sees her. Her silhouette is etched against the glass. He throws on his robe and starts up the cliff towards her, his erection rising anew.

'Kit! How did you know how much I wanted you?'

He strides across the living room towards her. He draws up short and stares. Her smile seems to make fun of his surprise.

'Don't you know who I am?'

He nods dumbly. It is a good trick; he has to admit it. She is dressed in a shift – black, with buttons down the front like a man's shirt. The body is smaller, harder, more wiry. The hair, slicked back in the same bun, is white, and the voice is entirely different.

'It's been a long time since I've seen such virility. You have an enormous amount of magnetism, don't you?'

Fearlessness. That is the quality she has. Nerve. It seems to flow out of her into him. He grabs her by the wrist and thrusts her hand roughly into the opening of his robe. 'You want to. Go ahead!'

'You're a real man, aren't you?' She squeezes him rhythmically. 'Hard as Kelsey's nuts. Well, let's see how hard you really are.'

He takes her head between his hands, wanting to crush it. Then it dawns upon him: how tame his lust for twenty-one-year-old girls is compared to the desire he now has for this seventy-two-year-old mother of the woman he loves.

He lifts her like a fragile idol and sets her down on the bony white wicker couch, with her back to him, looking out into the sunset. As he wedges himself deep into her, he realises he wants to restore the illusion that she's the daughter, and not the mother. Once he begins, he realises that he is somehow possessing them both, daughter and mother – and it is all that he has ever dreamed of.

9

'So. Give me dish about Brendan and Kit,' Liberty demanded. She sat with Jay Scott at the bar at Morton's, just starting her second margarita.

'Is this how you start all your interviews?' He covered his glass as if she were about to toss a Mickey into it.

She scooped up a handful of peanuts. 'The interview hasn't started. We're just talking. I read about the breakup on the plane coming out. Who dumped whom, and why? I just got word from my secretary that I'm finally going to see the lady tomorrow – for tea, yet. The more I know, the more understanding I can be. Come on, Scottie – your friends do call you Scottie?'

'Yeah,' he said flatly. 'But don't let that stop you. What's to tell? It's like they say in the papers. Only it didn't happen the day before yesterday – more like two months ago.'

'Two months! Why the delayed reaction?'

'Kit's a very private person. And so is Brendan, where this relationship is concerned. *Was* concerned,' he added glumly.

'So what broke them up, Scottie? You haven't said.'

'You're a real dog with a bone, aren't you?' He stared sullenly into the dregs of his margarita. 'If I tell you, will you promise not to quote me? If Kitty Cat ever found out, she'd kill me.'

'I'm talking to you for background, Scottie. Background only.'

He spun his glass around and around. 'The old woman broke them up.'

'The old woman? You mean Kitsia?'

He nodded and gulped.

'What happened? What did she do?'

He shrugged. 'She came to visit last August. Just dropped in out of the blue. Kit wasn't at Clara, she was at the studio. But Brendan was at Clara...'

'And...?'

Scott whistled silently. 'She and Brendan, well... Kit came home early and caught the two of them on the living room couch.'

149

She was wary. 'How come you know so much about all this? You under the couch or something?'

'Not exactly. But I was in the middle, so to speak.' He pushed his empty glass towards the bartender and munched morosely on some more peanuts. 'I got both sides of it – from Kit *and* from Brendan. Mostly from Brendan. Poor Brendan. He never knew what hit him. He said that Kitsia Ransome was the most beautiful woman he'd ever seen – next to Kit, that is. "Powerful", that's what he called her, a "female godhead".'

'You sound as if you've met her.'

'I did.' He threw back the entire margarita. Liberty quickly exchanged glasses with him, eager to have him continue.

'I thought she hadn't been off Zwar in umpteen years.'

He belched delicately and pounded his chest. 'She hadn't. I was at Clara the night she came. I saw her before Brendan did. I had gone over to work with Brendan on a scene from *Last Chance* and to keep him company while Kit worked late. The old woman was in the living room watching Brendan orating down below. She couldn't take her eyes off him. It was like he was this new species she'd just discovered. She has this quality most women don't have. She just doesn't give a shit about what people think. She doesn't care how she looks or how she sounds.'

'There are plenty of women who don't spend half their lives in front of the mirror.' Liberty stared at her own face over the bar, pale in the darkness, her eyes enormous.

'Everybody is hung up on how they look. But Kitsia Ransome has no shame. And all that intelligence . . . all that vision . . .'

'You're a fan of her work?'

'My first major investment was an original Ransome. A very early work. A small woodblock of blue dahlias. Besides, how could someone like Kitsia not be attractive to men like me and Brendan? Especially to Brendan, who's usually attracted to young girls. That poor man. When he came up from swimming and found her there instead of Kit, he was so confused. He looked sort of hypnotised to me – he was squinting like there was too much sunlight in his eyes. I ducked out quietly. He didn't even know I was there.' Scott took a deep breath. 'I guess I shouldn't have left him. He was so defenceless, but I couldn't help it. It was too much for me.' Scott looked around the restaurant and came back to stare at Liberty. 'What kind of article is this you're writing, anyway? The "Stocks & Trades" kind?'

'We'll see,' said Liberty.

'Kit called me up the next day. She was shattered. I never saw the woman so unhinged. Normally, she's so elegant and controlled that you forget that there's this incredibly sensitive soul underneath. "My mother taught me to hate men," she says to me, "and what does she do but fuck the only man I've ever been able to love." She kept saying that over and over again. I felt so sorry for her, so helpless.'

'And how did Brendan take it?'

'Brendan! Jesus, Brendan! At first he acted like a bull struck by lightning. He was completely disoriented. I think he viewed the sex with Kitsia and the tirade from the daughter that followed afterwards as steps in some baffling Amazonial ritual.'

'And he was the sacrifice?' she supplied.

He nodded. 'It took him a few days to realise that he was out of Clara on his arse. Kit was merciless. After a while, they both went into mourning. But the two of them are too stubborn to go back and pick up the pieces.'

'Is that why you've sent Brendan east? To try to get them to pick up the pieces?'

'It was Brendan's idea. He's been... subdued since Monette died. After Kit threw him out, he went from one bed to the next. These "wenches" are just itching to catch him on the rebound. But now all he wants is to finish *Last Chance* and reclaim what's left of his life. I want to finish this film too.' He banged the bar. 'Oh, God, I hope Kit finds us a Lacy. If we can only get back to work again! Concentration is everything, and when something happens to break it...' He fell silent.

Only when he spoke did Scott look like the kid that he was. Dressed in a green corduroy suit with leather-covered buttons and leather elbow patches, he looked very much the graduate student. He vibrated faintly as he spoke.

'Did the role trigger Monette Novak? I mean, she *was* playing a junkie, after all.'

'I would never let one of my actors get that carried away,' Scott said defensively. 'Besides, we all thought she'd kicked drugs months ago. Some romance of hers had fizzled – who knows? Who knows what triggered it?'

'I'm sorry, Scottie.' She patted his arm.

'It's not your fault. I'm just a mess. It's all this Mr In-between business. I'm like a referee now, not a director. Kit and Brendan

151

can't even be in the same room together. They can't even be in the same city, for crying out loud. Kit calls me up from New York today and throws a screaming fit 'cause I sent Brendan out, and Brendan's calling me on the other line saying he's gonna quit. Quit!'

Liberty noted this with a slow nod.

He shrugged gloomily. 'What does it matter? They'll take the insurance, anyway, you'll see.' He ran his forefinger inside the rim of his glass and then sucked on it. 'I'm a little drunk, in case you hadn't noticed.'

'Me too,' Liberty confessed. 'Let's change the subject, okay? What can you tell me about Bic Crawford? I'm meeting him for dinner tonight.'

'You're actually gonna see him at night?' He was round-eyed.

'So what? Is he Dracula or something?'

He shook his head. 'Oh, Lordy. You better order another drink while I go to the little boy's room. You need to be properly prepared for the Bic Bad Wolf.'

Liberty ordered herself a glass of cold milk. Was it only six hours ago that she had had three beers with Eben? She pulled out her Bic Crawford notes and scanned the printout. She re-read a list of the pictures Crawford had released in the eight years he'd headed up BK/Eagle Studios. While the figures were impressive, the movies were not. Crawford had not won success by taking risks. He played to the rabble, to the lowest common denominator. His record to date consisted of tits-and-arse (beach movies), crash-and-burn (action movies), stab-and-slab (horror movies), and, most recently, what was known in the business as 'high concept comedies'. Whatever that meant in real English, in money it meant big yearly grosses for BK's happy stockholders.

'So, Hedda Hopper.' Scott jumped back up onto the bar stool. 'What do you want to know? Hey, are you okay? That stuff looks mighty dangerous.' He pointed to the empty glass of milk on the bar.

'I'm fine,' Liberty said emphatically. 'Milk's the best thing for jet lag. Scottie, tell me about Kit Ransome and Bic Crawford.'

'What about them?'

'People say Kit only got where she is by having certain sexual liaisons.'

'We all use sex to get things,' Scott smiled at her.

'Yes, but isn't it particularly true in Kit's case?' Liberty went on cautiously. 'People say that without Bic Crawford she would have disappeared from sight. When he took her to the other side of the camera at Centurion, she'd had zilch production experience. What do you think he saw in her?'

'A sense of timing.'

'Explain.'

'There are some people who say that movies are just a fashion business. You figure it takes two years to make a movie, so you're essentially gambling on the taste of the movie goers two years down the road. The kind of hunch you need to go on is timing. For Chrissakes, look at the first big moguls – Goldwyn, Mayer – they were all Seventh Avenue shmatta cutters who turned from cotton to celluloid.'

'So you're saying that Bic Crawford found himself a good little fashion consultant in Kit Ransome?'

'Don't make fun, Liberty,' he said, pushing his drink away, half-finished. 'Kit had something – and still has – something that the average commercial studio exec has lost, or never had in the first place. She has innocence. Deep down, there's not an ounce of cynicism in that woman. She loves movies. Most of these folks . . .' He gestured at the crowd behind them, dining at small tables. 'They don't love movies. They'd just as soon be making aerosol deodorant sprays: it's all *product* to them. Merchandise. And it's beginning to show.'

'The proof is in the celluloid?'

'You bet your Bic pen it is. Look at the last five movies Crawford's released at BK/Eagle and look at the five Kit's released at Horizon.'

Liberty didn't need to answer; he'd made his point.

'But meanwhile, back at Paramount. Tell me about Kit Ransome, the young production executive who is having an affair with her boss.'

'You needn't wear your cynicism on your sleeve, my dear. It wasn't easy for a woman in those days.'

'And it's a piece of cake nowadays?' Liberty clenched a Camel in her teeth and lit up.

Scott giggled.

'What's so funny?'

'I gotta tell you a great story, Liberty. About Kit as a young production executive.

'This is the scene: it's 1967 and Crawford has just promoted Kit

153

from his story editor to production VP. The rest of Crawford's VPs are pissed. You see, Crawford ran Centurion like a frat house. Nowadays, he runs BK the same way. The brothers didn't want Kit. It's her first production meeting and she's the last to arrive. They're waiting for her, Bic and the boys. Kit walks in and sees that they've plastered all over the walls – and I mean *all* over – these girlie-magazine pictures. Kit's cool. She takes the meeting. She pretends the wallpaper's fine. Next week. Next production meeting. The boys are waiting to see if she'll show. Kit walks in the door as the meeting's about to begin with her blouse off: naked from the waist up. Now it's their turn to pretend nothing's wrong. Only they're not half as good at it as our Kit.' He slapped his knee and said, 'I'd give *anything* to have been there.'

Liberty frowned. This didn't sound like the elegant woman she had pieced together so far. It sounded more like Kitsia, in fact.

'Speaking of Bic,' Scott went on, 'there he is right now.'

Liberty stared over her shoulder. Bic Crawford was a big man. His shoulders filled the entranceway, his wavy hair swept the top of the doorjamb. He looked like a great ship squeezing through a lock. He was dressed more like the captain of *The Love Boat* than the president of a major motion picture company: blue blazer, red ascot, white shirt, white trousers.

'Are my eyes playing tricks, or what?' she whispered to Scott.

'I know what you mean.' Scott returned to his drink. 'He ought to be wearing a varsity letter on a *very* big sweater, don't you think?'

'Oh, God.'

Liberty turned around and slid Scott's glass towards her, finishing off his margarita in one desperate gulp. 'Oh, God,' she repeated.

He commiserated. 'He's so healthy-looking, it's almost obscene. I don't know how Kit stood it. And the things he did to her...'

'*For* her,' Liberty corrected him, 'while he advanced her career.'

'You have no idea what that man is capable of,' he said solemnly.

Liberty turned and took another quick look. Bic and a blonde were now wedged in at a corner table. His head was huge. He had a baby face, soft and pudgy, with big brown eyes. He was attractive, in a larger-than-life sort of way.

'I don't know' – Liberty turned back to Scott – 'I think I can imagine.'

'Why imagine? You're the brazen reporter. Go over there and

introduce yourself and find out from the whoremaster's mouth.'

'Gimme a break, huh?' said Liberty. 'Dinner's at seven forty-five. I've got fifteen minutes.'

'Well, I hope you've done your homework, my dear. I hear he has a room in his mansion containing the chained-up remains of nosy girl reporters.'

'I know his reputation,' said Liberty. 'Always available to the press. Absolutely charming while you're with him, but you walk away and realise he's snowed you.'

'I hear the board of directors at BK/Eagle leave their monthly meetings feeling much the same way,' he added.

Liberty nodded. 'I wouldn't be surprised.'

'It still amazes me, though,' he said. 'It amazes me that he can get away with it. It's those little-boy looks. You think you're dealing with just another pretty LA face and suddenly he's robbed you of your five best story ideas and got your agent to sign you up for less than you'd normally take for one –'

'And meanwhile,' Liberty broke in, 'he's coming on like *you* put one over on him. But everyone knows that. Tell me something I don't know about the still single Bic Crawford. Give me the real dirt and filth.'

'Liberty!' he said. 'Shame on you for tempting me to betray Kit. It was years ago. The Centurion days.'

Liberty nodded eagerly.

'I don't like you very much right at this moment, Liberty Adams. And I don't like myself much, either. You do this for a living? What does your mother say?'

'Look at it this way: if it all happened years ago, as you say, it's history, not gossip.'

'Really?' He seemed unconvinced. 'Well, I don't consider myself a prude, mind you. Let's face it, who can be, living in a town where any child actress can grow up to crave golden showers?'

'And the town where the premier host serves cocaine on a bald dwarf's head.'

'Ugh!' he said. 'You were at that party? I only heard the grisly postmortem. I hope you didn't actually take any of that coke, Liberty.'

'White Line Madness! I resisted the urge,' Liberty lied.

'Thank God.' He fiddled with her matchbook. 'Because had you accepted that coke, I would have had tremendous problems respecting you, Liberty Adams. And I certainly wouldn't be breaking my long-standing vow to be boring with reporters.'

'You're not boring, Scottie. Just careful. Tell me, why's the hair coming down tonight?'

'I don't know,' he said soberly, removing the pencil from Liberty's hand. 'Don't get me wrong...' He blinked spasmodically and touched Liberty's hand on the bar. 'I love Kit. I could *kill* her for getting involved with Brendan in the first place. But then, to throw him out! To refuse to speak to him. Brendan's falling apart at the seams. He's insanely in love with Kit.'

Liberty ordered him another drink.

'Scottie. Let's return to Hollywood history. You were telling me about *Bic* and Kit.'

'Well,' he sighed hugely. 'I wasn't under the bed, mind you, but I do know a woman who was at the Polo Lounge for breakfast the day Bic and Kit broke up.'

'You mean they broke up in public?'

'Doesn't everyone in this town do everything in public? Apparently they both came in looking a bit prickly. Just before the eggs Benedict arrived, she hauled off and slugged him and then quit the room, as they say. Oh, I *am* good at this, aren't I?'

'Superb,' said Liberty. 'And...?'

'Two weeks later, after she'd gone over to Warner's as their head of production, he called in the decorators to redo his bedroom – their very love nest...'

'And?'

'Well. Again, I wasn't under the bed, but the decorators... found...' He faltered. 'Certain *things*.'

'What things?'

'Oh, God!' He shot Liberty a look that begged for mercy.

'What things did they find in the house?' Liberty repeated.

'I can't!' he cried. 'I may be drunk, but I'm not mean. I couldn't do that to my Kitty Cat.'

Liberty decided to be merciful and signalled for the bill. 'You're very sweet, Jay Scott. Thank you for everything.' She signed the bill and gathered her stuff. 'Wish me luck?'

He sang a muffled chorus of 'Who's afraid of the Bic bad wolf...' as Liberty made her way over to Crawford's table.

'This is Tammy,' Bic Crawford said to Liberty. 'Say hi to the lady, Tammy, and then get lost.'

Tammy looked pretty lost already. She was a Beach Boy's beauty: a chlorine blonde with a perfect tan who looked spectacular in harem trousers and matching bra. Liberty stared at her. She wore an orchid to mask her pubic hairs – barely. Only in El Lay.

'My orchid's wilting anyway,' Tammy said.

'Anything that gets near that pussy wilts.' Bic winked at Liberty as Tammy left.

Pretending not to have heard, Liberty stretched her hand out across the table. 'It's a pleasure to meet you, Mr Crawford.'

'Oooh,' he said, squeezing her hand. 'You're a sexy little fox, just like they said you were.'

Liberty blushed, annoyed with herself for not being more turned off.

'Wouldn't it be easier to talk at my house? What do you say?' Bic signalled for the waiter and hustled her out into the parking lot. His silver Maserati was parked up front.

'Nice car, huh?' Crawford jerked her hand from the car door as she was about to open it. 'God, Liberty, don't touch that. You want the whole police force here?' Liberty waited while he fiddled with the door lock, his fingers moving swiftly. He looked like a glamorous safecracker, a jumbo-sized Bob Wagner.

'Can't be too careful,' he said, helping her into the car.

'You know how I keep my car safe in New York?' Liberty asked him, leaning back, watching Beverly Hills fall away as they followed Cold Water Canyon Drive up towards Mulholland.

'How?'

'I get twelve illegal aliens to stand guard around it.'

'What kind of car do you have?'

'A sixty-seven MG.'

He laughed loudly. Liberty liked guys who laughed at her jokes. It usually meant that the competition would be kept to a minimum.

He drove through an imposing wrought-iron gate monogrammed with a florid BC and up a narrow road lined with cypress trees. Pink gravel churned up beneath the wheels, and there it was: the quintessential stinking pink palazzo.

In minutes a gay houseboy was serving them dinner on the terrace overlooking the reflecting pool and a military assembly of shrubs and colour-coded gravel. The food was what she would expect: cold Maine lobster and dry French champagne. Liberty put up a weak struggle with her lobster and then gave up in favour of basking in Bicness. He was an almost overpowering presence, sitting across from her at the round table, his big face shiny in the candlelight. He'd taken off the blazer and the flaming red ascot before dinner and replaced it with a maroon smoking jacket. Over the cold pasta, Liberty finally steered him towards business.

'How does it feel to run a studio with stockholders breathing down your neck? Instead of the old days with just one rich man to please?'

'It's rough. I loved running my own show at Centurion. I was there before it was swallowed up. Those were the days. More champagne?'

Liberty shook her head, a little surprised by his solicitude. He was a good host in a casual, self-effacing way.

'What was so different at Centurion?'

'In those days I set up my own shots. You know, turn-around jumpers, lay-ups, or anything else I wanted.' Bic pretended to dribble a ball beside his chair. 'Any mistakes just weren't made public. If the team was in a slump and we released a few clunker films, nobody really knew how much we had lost.'

'What's the advantage there?' Liberty asked.

'Oh, Liberty . . .' He said her name as if it had twice the number of syllables. 'In this town, the most important thing is to seem to have an unlimited line of credit.' He helped her away from the table. 'Let me show you the house. It makes great copy.'

They wandered together through one gargantuan room after another. Bic's house was a strange mixture of exquisite taste and horrible nouveau-riche extravagance.

She tried to steer him back to the subject, while Bic kept bending over and putting his big fingers through the strap on her camisole. They settled in the library.

'This is the library,' he said.

'No kidding.'

It was Library, Hollywood style: an investment in books by the yard, with expensive leather bindings.

'Come here. I want to show you something.' Bic held out the preserved penis of a sperm whale, erotic Eskimo scrimshaw, two prehistoric wasps in amber caught forever in the act of copulating. 'They're one of a kind. I like collecting one-of-a-kind things.' He rubbed his hands.

Liberty knew her cue when she heard it. 'Kit Ransome's one of a kind, don't you think?'

He looked thoughtful. 'I liked fucking Kit Ransome, I won't lie.'

'She's an extraordinary and beautiful woman,' said Liberty, unfazed by his quick candour. 'I'll bet you did. That much is obvious from where I'm sitting.'

'Where *are* you sitting, sweetheart?' He leaned over and moved her strap aside. He nuzzled her neck. 'You're not close enough.'

He opened a round box and ran it beneath her nose. 'Go ahead, sweetheart. I dare you to sneeze.'

There must have been an ounce of coke in the box, ground powder-fine. Liberty turned down drinks. She turned down marijuana from time to time. She turned down acid and speed and Valium and even antihistamines. But coke she had trouble saying no to, no matter how unstable the company.

He filled a small spoon shaped like a Hollywood poster girl, arms behind her head, with one leg bent and the other leg out.

'Where's the dwarf?' she asked, looking around.

'Come on and blow your mind, little fox. I want to see that snippity mouth of yours get all soft.'

It was like being in the middle of a *Playboy* fantasy and liking it. Liberty snorted a little into each nostril.

'Holy shit!' Liberty leaned back on the stool. He caught her with his leg and pressed his penis into the back of her head.

'I like dirty talk, Libby. You can talk dirty to me all night long.'

She got up quickly and started pacing. 'Got a track? I think I could run the six hundred.'

'It's either the four-forty, the eight hundred, or the fifteen hundred,' Bic corrected her. 'But I think we can find better ways of testing your endurance.'

'Oh, Bic' – she punched him in the arm and hurt her finger on the muscle – 'the way you talk.'

'You love the way I talk.'

He took her arm and pulled her out of the library into the den, where a fire burned.

'How cosy,' said Liberty. She plopped herself down on some pillows and immediately fished out her tape recorder – her garland of garlic. She ran it through and tested it. 'Shit,' she said when the fast-forward jammed.

'Know any other dirty words?'

'Yeah,' said Liberty, setting the recorder between them. 'Kit Ransome.'

He looked at the recorder on the pillow between them and then at Liberty and said. 'I love women who like to fuck on tape. That's an even bigger turn-on to me than talking dirty.' He pulled her towards him. She moved the machine to her other side. His tongue was flicking her ear. It felt a little too good.

'Listen,' she said, pulling away from him. 'I came all this way to hear you talk about Kit Ransome, and God damn you, you're going to talk.'

He sat up with a sullen look on his face. 'You are a one-track bitch. They said that about you, and it's true.'

He dished her up some more coke and she bent over to snort it, then decided instead to empty the coke into her palm and rub it on her gums. She liked the way her gums and tongue tingled, like they did on the way back from the dentist.

'Why do you want to talk about Kit, anyway? She's dead.'

'I hope not. I have a hard-won interview with her tomorrow.'

'She's still a good actress. She can pass for living.'

'But not for head of Horizon Studios?' she asked.

'She has to go running to Sugar Daddy Ransome for every little thing.'

'Cousin,' Liberty corrected.

'Whatever. She's always been jelly around that dude, and she still is. If she stood up to him the way she used to stand up to me, she'd stand half a chance of keeping herself alive.'

'If Ransome lets them finish *Last Chance*, she's got herself a strong release there.'

'I've got a stronger release.'

Liberty ignored the note of insinuation in his voice. 'What makes you such an expert on *Last Chance*? Studio espionage?'

'Cunt espionage. I used to fuck Monette Novak before Rush Alexander got into her pants.'

Liberty's mouth opened and shut and opened again. 'Rush Alexander and Monette Novak?'

'Strictly behind the scenes, mind you. He was the one who got her hooked on the Big H again. I don't like fucking junkies myself – I'm not that kind of guy. I let Rush have her all to himself.' His smile broadened. 'You like all this talk, don't you, little fox? Come sit on my lap.' He patted his enormous thighs.

She eyed him grudgingly. 'Only if you keep talking.'

He went on, in her ear. 'Everybody in this town loves to talk about how creative Kit Ransome is. Kit Ransome's creative, all right, but she doesn't know how to play team ball. Kit's not a businesswoman. Being creative isn't enough. The sharks will eat her. Rush is just waiting for her to slip. You don't understand, little girl.' He held her by the shoulders. 'You don't understand. Kit's fucked. It's got nothing to do with *Last Chance*. It's got everything to do with who she is.'

Liberty helped herself to some more coke.

He went on. 'I could fuck up twelve times as bad as I did two and a half years ago with that turkey western. Twenty times! And my arse would still be on the court because I can play, that's why. I can play! Kit can shoot pretty but there's no way anybody is going to keep helping her set up those pretty shots.'

'I don't know,' said Liberty, 'it looks to me like she's attracted some pretty substantial talent in the last few months.'

'Sure,' he said contemptuously, 'creative people have always been attracted to Kit – especially oddballs and Europeans – she's Lady Bountiful. But it's an act. It's all an act.'

Liberty eased herself off his lap. 'If it's an act, it's a good act.'

'Take it from me, Kit's weird.' He captured her hand and began tonguing her finger. His teeth pinched the tender skin between her fingers, and she jumped.

'Small and jumpy. I like that. Did you know that my Kitty Cat likes to be tied up?'

'So what? So did Marcel Proust. Does that make her any weirder than the next Bel-Air *hausfrau*?'

'Maybe. Maybe not. But I never saw a woman *love* it like Kit loved it.'

'Yeah, well. I'm not surprised.' But she was. Strangely scandalised, too, as if she had come upon Kit making love in the privacy of her own home. She wanted to close the bedroom door and get out of there fast.

'I played this game with Kit. I would fool her. Get her all tied up and blindfolded and hot, and then I used to tell her I was going to put my cock in her. But you know what I put in her instead?'

'Enough.' Liberty sat forward and sent him tongue-first into the cushions. 'I don't want to hear any more of this.'

'Yes, you do. It's a turn-on. I can see your shoulders rising and falling like a little birdie. A little hot birdie. She had this paperweight thing on the desk in her office. It was something her old lady had sent her as a present when I promoted her to VP. I don't know what kind of trip that old lady is on, but it looked like a cock to me. It looked like *my* cock, as a matter of fact. I used to wonder: how did the old lady know what it looked like? Anyway, I

161

used to sneak it off her desk and fuck her with it.'

'You're disgusting.'

'And you're fucking gorgeous.'

'No, I'm not.' Liberty closed her eyes. Her mind was buzzing. She felt like she was deaf except to the sound of Bic's voice and her own heartbeat.

He moved over her, blocking out the light from the fireplace, blocking out the whole set. She yielded to him, to Bic Crawford, the all-American boy.

The bedside Seiko read one-thirty when Liberty finally put her plan into action. She hoped it would work. Otherwise, she might die right there underneath 210 pounds of roasted sleeping Bic. It felt as if he were asleep when she freed her trapped arm sufficiently to reach the remains of the last cigar-sized joint they'd shared, and the Fabergé lighter next to it. She lit up and waited until she got the ember good and hot; then, taking a few last tokes for the road, she flicked the joint and watched it sail like a tiny meteor over the massif of the sleeping Bic. Now it was just a matter of time. She only prayed the bed would catch fire before he reared up and began another round of pumping.

For the life of her, Liberty couldn't understand what he'd want with her now anyway. The last three times they'd done it, he might as well have been doing it to mud, for all the notice he took of her. His boyish enthusiasm had long since played itself out and now he was a grim professional, stuck on medium speed, pumping away. *Pumping Mud* – a good title for a book about the nature of male sexuality. Bic was a chapter unto himself. What was she saying? Bic was a whole book.

Mud was tired. The fascination was long gone, along with the panic. When panic had initially welled up in her, she told herself to take it easy. She wasn't going to die, for goodness sake. How often did he do this? Coke couldn't keep him going this long. Could it have been the cold water? When he first did it – pulled out of her the second before his climax to plunge both arms into the ice-cold water of the champagne bucket – she had burst into laughter. He had looked at her with a hurt, bewildered expression, reared up on his knees, paws dripping like a betrayed St Bernard.

If she hadn't laughed, Liberty thought, she might have got off with just a couple of dirty-talking rolls in the hay. But laughing had made him mad. It was Hollywood mad, Liberty realised, the kind of rage people there think is therapeutic for you to get out of your system. No est-ian undelivered communications for him.

Around midnight he lifted her up by the heels and poured champagne inside her. The champagne was so cold, Liberty screamed out in pain. He slurped it out of her, letting the stuff run down her body.

And the gadgets, the gadgets she used to wonder about when passing the window displays in sex boutiques. Well, now she'd never have to wonder again.

She could smell it now, an odour of reefer and singed satin. He didn't stir. Oh, well, thought Liberty, this palazzo is poured concrete; I'll probably get away with a third-degree burn or two. She couldn't see – Bic's body blocked her view – but she was sure the fire had caught on the other side of the bed.

She saw the smoke.

'Liberty . . . quick! Get up. A fire!' He emptied the champagne cooler onto the bed in one hulking move, looking like a Boy Scout at a campfire.

Liberty ran into the bathroom, grabbing her slacks and camisole. Even if she got trapped in the burning bedroom with Bic when the firemen and the reporters all arrived in a gaggle, she was going to wash his spit off her face now. Her eyes in the mirror were afraid to meet their owner. She splashed hot water on her face, squeezed a bar of soap through her hands, and soaped off her fingers, her face, and between her legs. The gesture was ridiculous, considering all the other places Bic had been.

When she went back into the bedroom, he was sitting on the edge of the barely burned bed. 'I don't do it in *fire*. I'm not that kind of a guy.'

Liberty grabbed her bag and made her way through one enormous room after another until she emerged onto the driveway. At least I have the tapes, she thought, running towards the front gate.

There were two messages for her back at the hotel – one from Ransome and one from Peg. She didn't want to talk to a man – any man – right now.

'Lib, I'm glad you called. You've got to get back here on the double.'

'So book me on the eight-fifteen United.' Liberty yawned until her eyes watered.

'No, you have to get back here sooner than that.'

'Gee, Peg, I don't think we have charter bucks in the budget, do you?' Liberty stretched out on the bed and stared up at the ceiling.

'I got Freddie at Federal Express to let you take the three-thirty a.m. freight run out of LAX.'

Liberty stared at her watch. It was two-fifteen. 'Does this mean I have to ride with the chickens?'

Peg chuckled. 'I told him you were doing a story on Midnight Flyboys. You can ride in the cockpit with the pilot. Gratis.'

'Peg, you're a gem. But why all the fuss?'

'You've got a two o'clock today with Mrs Novak.'

Liberty gasped and sat up. 'Peg! You're psychic. How did you know I wanted to speak to her.'

'Your friend and mine at the *Post* knows about your Kit quest. He thought you'd be interested to know that Monette Novak's mother tried to ace Kit.'

Liberty stared at the shadows of the palm fronds on the hotel carpet. Suddenly, they looked like daggers. 'When? Where?'

'Late yesterday morning in the lobby of the Sherry.'

'Didn't it make the evening papers?'

'Not the front page apparently. None of the parties was identified.'

'That's strange. Why the blackout, I wonder.'

'Our friend wouldn't say. But apparently, Mrs Novak is willing to offer you an exclusive.'

'Lucky me. From her jail cell?'

'No, she's out on bail. Kit refused to press charges.'

'Curiouser and curiouser.'

'Maybe you two gals can chat about it over tea.'

'Somehow, I doubt it. Thanks Peg. I'd better hang up. If I don't take a shower, syphilis may set in.'

'Before you go, Lib, I thought you'd want to know about that reporter.'

'What reporter?'

'Winchell's reporter. The one who covered Mrs Ransome and got canned. He went out to work for the Toledo *Star*, but this is the real interesting thing. He was writing this three-part construction-site story for the *Star* and he never made it to Part Three.'

'Oh?'

164

'He was crushed to death by a falling girder. They said it was a faulty crane.'

'God.'

'That's not the real kicker. The real kicker is that the building was owned by Ransome Enterprises.'

Liberty felt suddenly sick. 'Thanks, Peg,' she whispered. 'And now I really do need to take that shower.'

10

Rush was up to something. Kit dreaded facing him today at the budget meeting. Would he make his move in public, in the Ransome Enterprises boardroom? The twelve heads of Ransome Enterprises' subsidiaries sat around the horseshoe table, the green felt tabletop glowing under track lighting like Astroturf at a nighttime baseball game. Rush spurned one-on-one meetings. 'The arena,' he would say, 'is good for competition. It keeps people alert.'

Rush sat alone at the centre of the horseshoe at a small table which abutted but did not touch the larger table. A microphone, a pitcher of iced black coffee, and a stack of multicoloured folders sat on the table before him. At the top of the horseshoe was another microphone and an empty chair.

Archer's chair was also empty. Archer always chose to sit aloof in a white leather armchair by the wall, rather than joining the semicircle. It irritated Kit. Today, apparently, he wasn't coming.

Kit had drawn fourth in the lottery, a good number. Being fourth to present and defend her budget would give her time to compose herself beforehand and time to reflect afterwards. It was always better to get it over with in the first half; towards the end of these sessions, Rush's patience tended to wear thin. He would ask more questions, but listen less.

Kit looked around the table. To the right of the microphone sat Shirley Welles, the only other woman in the room. She was head of Ruba, the recently acquired cosmetics company. The other faces were all familiar from the other budget meetings Kit had attended.

'Ladies first.' Rush smiled crookedly into the microphone. There was polite laughter around the table.

Kit didn't laugh. As Shirley Welles rose to come to the microphone, Rush grinned and pulled a pale yellow folder from the stack in front of him. Kit's eyes went to the hot-pink one in the pile: her Horizon folder.

Kit was glad to see another woman at these meetings; she was used to being the only one, but she wouldn't let it daunt her.

166

Hadn't Bic taught her there was power in being different, whether by colour, sex, or outrageous behaviour?

Shirley grabbed the microphone like a Las Vegas comedienne.

'Testing – one, two.' She hit her front teeth with her thumbnail. Shirley was cocky. Hadn't she just hired Rush's daughter, a model, to be 'The Face' in their turn-around campaign?

'Shirley, I notice on page six,' Rush began immediately, before Shirley had got her yellow folder secured under her long fingernails, 'that you've included a contingency fee in the creative-services column. I know you're new, but any of your colleagues here today would be happy to tell you we don't use contingency fees in our budgets.' Rush paused to let the nervous laughter die.

'Fine,' said Shirley without hesitation while clicking open her lighter. 'Let's just boost the outside-design and new-logos column by the same amount.' She let her Newport dangle from her lips.

'I'll accept that.' He made a note. 'And now I have a question on page ten.'

'Fire away, El Jefe.'

Kit had to admire Shirley's style. It reminded her of Bic's, only not as good. At meetings, there was no one better than Bic. She'd learned a lot from him.

When her turn came, Kit walked calmly to the microphone and took her place at the head of the horseshoe. She bent the microphone's long wire neck closer to her mouth. She thought of how thin her fingers looked as she moved it. She had this trick of keeping her composure by forcing herself to concentrate on details: on Rush's maroon-and-green-striped tie, on the small shaving nick below his right sideburn, on the hot-pink folder holding her budget. Rush sent her to the wrong page, becoming snide and condescending. She was patient and polite.

'I'd like to know who you got this figure on page seven under development costs from.'

'I got it from Randy Sheridan, of course.'

'Well, I just happen to have a copy of Sheridan's original prelim budget for production here.' Rush fingered a piece of paper. 'And the figure reads more like eight hundred grand than a million-five.'

Kit flushed. 'I'm fairly sure my figure is correct. Randy revised his preliminary estimate several times. I *know* he revised up.'

'Revised up?' he mimicked her. 'I hope this isn't another example of your creative financing, Kit. I must have back-up for this.'

Kit groped around in her mind, but she couldn't remember now where she got the figure. Was it from Randy's secretary? Was it from Randy when he called her at home the night before she left for New York? She couldn't have made up the figure, As Rush was trying to make everyone in the room believe.

'Kit, this bears an uncomfortable resemblance to that game of hide-and-seek you played last quarter. Do you have anything to say about this?' He ran a palm over his high forehead and across the top of his head.

The room was quiet. All faces turned towards Kit. She had absolutely nothing to say. If he was going to rip her apart, Kit was going to have to let him. She waited, paralysed, like a cornered rabbit.

'Why don't you check with Sheridan and get back to me before we finalise. Everything else here seems okay. It looks like Horizon is surviving your reign.' He flipped the folder closed and smiled sweetly.

Kit thanked him weakly and slid back into her chair. For the life of her she didn't understand why he hadn't ripped her to shreds and left her bleeding on the green felt. Bic would have. Bic would have said something like, 'You're taking mid-court shots, Kitty Cat.' But he would have left her bleeding.

Kit walked slowly back to her seat and gave Meyer a wan smile as he rose to take his place at the microphone.

For several minutes the room seemed strangely silent, as if everyone were stunned that Rush had spared her arse.

'I own your arse.'

Bic had never, not even for an instant, let her forget it. She had begged him to let her make *The House on Haight Street*. The story of a young establishment lawyer whose life is turned around when he smokes his first marijuana cigarette, *Haight Street* was a relatively inexpensive movie to make: unknown actors, easy locations. Bic wasn't interested. She told him she could make it for 2.9 million in about twelve weeks and have it ready to release for summer – before any other studio had a chance to come out with its 'hippie-dope' picture. Against his better judgement, Bic finally let her make it, but in ten weeks' time and for only two million.

It was a box-office smash. Bic happily took the credit.

When *Haight Street* swept the Academy Awards – Best Picture,

Best Direction, Best Screenplay, Best Original Music – everyone who got up to accept that night thanked Kit first, middle, and last. The reporters backstage after the ceremonies were eager to know how it felt to have backed a long shot and won, but it seemed to Kit that Bic physically prevented her from speaking to them. Then, later, at the Awards Ball at the Hilton, she heard Bic admitting to John Spiers of *Variety* that it had been he – Uncle Bicky – who had encouraged Kit to make *Haight Street*. Kit herself had been doubtful. *Fearful*, even. Kit left without a word, astonishing the table of Bic's vice-presidents, their assorted spouses and molls, and the *Haight Street* company.

'You expect me to just sit there and listen to you lie?' She hissed at him in the parking lot where he finally caught up with her.

'You should have spoken up if you didn't agree with my version of things, Kitty Cat.' He grinned smugly.

That moment, she hated him. 'You know I never disagree with you in public.'

'Of course you don't. It'd be beneath your dignity, right? You haughty bitch. You deserve to have it all taken away from you. You can't handle it.'

Tears came to her eyes. 'Why, Bic? Why did you have to lie?'

'I wasn't lying, Kitty Cat,' he said innocently. 'I just wasn't drawing undue attention to your star play. You ought to know my philosophy by now. The team takes credit, not the player. A lot less ups and downs that way. A stronger team. More winning seasons.'

She turned her back on him while he was still talking and climbed into her limo.

The next morning, Warner Brothers called and offered twice what Bic was paying her to be their head of production. Kit accepted on the spot.

Her letter of resignation was on Bic's desk before lunch. By one o'clock, Rita had the Port-O-files in. They were in the middle of packing when Bic sauntered in, her letter in his hand, burning at one corner.

Kit blew it out and went on packing. Rita slipped out of the office.

'All right. You've made your point.' He came up behind her and held her tenderly. 'I know you're hurt. I lost my head. You know you're my most valuable player. We make a winning offence. It's balls against the wall from now on, Kitty Cat. You can't trade yourself to another team.'

She worked out of his embrace. 'You should have thought about that last night. It's too late, Bic. I've made up my mind. I'm going to Warner's.'

He yanked her around to face him. 'What do you mean? Your place is with me. You can't make it alone. You're a *cunt*, Kit, do you understand? You operate by cunt instinct. Without me, you'd dissolve in a heap, walk into walls, lose millions. You need me.'

'Maybe so,' she said, avoiding his eyes, 'but it's time I tried to make it without you.'

'But we're Goldwyn and Thalberg!' His plea was almost boyish. 'We owe it to the industry to stay together.'

She leaned against the desk and began to laugh.

'What's so funny?' He shook her by the shoulders. The harder he shook, the wilder her laughter became. Finally he slapped her across the face.

When Rita came back, she found Kit alone, tilted back in her chair with a Kleenex to her bloody nose.

'That pig!' Rita went to get a wet cloth for her boss's nose. 'I'm glad we're getting out.' Rita's hands were trembling, so Kit had to apply the compress herself.

The next morning, Rita came into Kit's office holding a blue interoffice envelope in one hand and a piece of paper in the other. The tears were streaming down her face, the mascara staining her cheeks blue. 'Oh, God, Kit. I'm sorry. I'm so sorry,' she sobbed.

Kit prised the piece of paper from her hand and carried it over to the window to examine it. Bic had made a Xerox copy on interoffice stationery, obviously taking great care, for it was perfectly centred on the page below a neatly typed 'To: KR From: BC Re: See Below'. And below the Xerox copy of the photograph were typed the words 'I own your arse.' The sight of the picture made Kit sag against the window blind and stare out through the slats at the lot below. She would never be able to go to Warner's now. Centurion would be her prison.

Bic probably hadn't taken the photograph; that was her next thought. Whenever he tied her up like that, she always insisted that he never break his physical contact with her; otherwise she'd panic, cry pitifully, and spoil the fun. No, he must have had someone else come to the house to take it from a place somewhere up in the eaves, for it was a bird's-eye view of herself splayed naked on the bed, bound and blindfolded. She found herself straining to remember when this picture might have been taken, on exactly what night.

Then she thought: so this is what I look like. So this is how I appear to him. Then she thought: I look beautiful. Then she panicked again; she didn't know what to do. Rita was hysterical, so she picked up the telephone herself and sent a telegram to Kitsia. 'Bic blackmailing me to stay at Centurion.' Then she dialled Bic's secretary and made a date for breakfast at the Polo Lounge. She would try to white-flag it until help arrived.

'You're mine!' Bic banged the breakfast table the next morning. 'How dare you give yourself away.'

'How many times do I have to tell you?' she explained as sweetly as she could, terrified he'd cause a public scene. 'I'm going to *work* there, not sell my body.'

He didn't seem to hear her. 'Warner's is a shambles. You'll be so busy putting out fires you'll never get any of your own work out.'

'I'm willing to try,' she said quietly.

'You're better off staying where you are. I'll set things up any way you want. You've earned it. *Haight Street* is all the proof anybody'd need. You're ready to run your own show.'

That he was willing to give her credit for *Haight Street* was small comfort at this point. 'Yes, but working with Mace, Phil, John – even with you, Bic – it's . . . well, it's old habit. Habit is the great deadener.'

'My dick is dead.'

'Bic, *really*.'

'Why don't you just be honest and admit that it's because you don't love me any more? Why don't you just say it? You're leaving because you've had it with me. Go ahead! I can take it. I'll tell you what, though. You don't even have to fuck me anymore. How would that be, Kit? You don't have to fuck me, and you can make whatever movies you want to make. Only stay, Kitty Cat. Please stay.'

Kit realised that not only was he serious, he was scared. So, his business need of her was greater than his sexual need! She felt oddly disappointed then, as if all those multiorgasmic flings with him were nothing more than a sort of athletic competition, an extension of what had gone on in the office, none of it having anything to do with love. Maybe the real truth of the matter was that Bic didn't love *her* any more. Maybe he'd never loved her.

'I'm going.' She couldn't stand to look at him. She'd never before seen him this defeated.

'I wish you'd make this easier for me.'

'I suppose you want me to hand you to Marty on a silver platter?'
Marty Rosen was the head of Warner's. 'Why should Marty get
you?'

He stopped. Kit could just *hear* him thinking.

'Tell me, Kitty Cat, will you be taking your manacles and your
blindfold with you now, or shall I have them delivered to your new
office at Warners?'

She slapped him as hard as she could and ran out.

Help finally arrived that afternoon in the form of Kazimir 'Rush'
Alexander, whom she'd never met before. She had hoped Archer
would come, but when Rush presented himself, she was relieved.
Archer would have judged her. Here was a stranger, someone who
might hear her story and feel sorry for her.

They dined that night at Chasen's. Rush charmed Kit. He was a
wonderful conversationalist. He talked of his art collection, of his
Russian icons, of a novel he'd just finished reading that day on the
plane, of his young daughter. He ordered their dinner, selected the
wine. He refused to take any phone calls. Kit was relaxed by his
voice. His movements were slow, deliberate, calming.

While they waited for coffee to be served, he said, 'I need to
know everything if I am going to be able to help you. Think of me
as your lawyer. I need to hear everything, even if it seems trivial or
unimportant.'

Kit described her unsuccessful attempt at reconciliation with
Bic. Rush nodded and encouraged her to go on. She told him about
the photos, the Xerox, the office games, the sex games.

Because he was so serious, so staid and formal in his white dinner
jacket, so totally unlike Bic, she told him every single intimate
detail.

He listened to her in absolute silence. She sensed he was
listening attentively, but she couldn't tell whether he was
sympathetic or contemptuous. When she'd finished, he just sat
there and didn't say anything.

'You know,' she said, 'you're very difficult to read. I keep
thinking you must think me the world's biggest fool.'

'No.' He smiled strangely. His eyes were so deeply set, it was as if
nature had given him a place to hide.

'Well, then, say something. Speak to me! React! Don't just sit
there smiling secretly to yourself.'

'I was just thinking how much alike you and Archer are.'

'What do you mean?' She was caught off guard by the comment.

'You both come on so strong, but when you need help...'

'I'm not so sure I like the sound of that,' she said.

'Don't get me wrong,' he went on. 'I respect Archer more than any other man alive. After all, he saved me.'

'Saved you?' Kit asked.

'From fifteen years of hard work.' He grinned boyishly. 'Anyhow, I'm grateful enough to help him keep his business in the Fortune 500 and his name out of the press.'

'And *my* name as well?' Kit arched a brow.

'I've told you, I owe him everything. If it hadn't been for Archer...' His voice trailed off. He ordered another straight shot of vodka, looking at Kit doubtfully. He seemed to want to gather her into his confidence, but he wasn't sure whether she'd come.

'You see, Kit, I've led a life that's been far from conventional,' he began.

Having just revealed to him her most carefully guarded secrets, she welcomed a chance to share any intimacy of his. The air was ripe for confession.

'Few people of any real character have lived conventional lives.' She smiled encouragement.

'My father was something of a maverick. He was the son of a landowner in eastern Russia who deserted the czar's army and ran off with a girl from belowstairs. A maid. They made it to Istanbul, where they boarded a ship for America.'

He stopped to order another vodka. To make him feel comfortable, she joined him, though it wasn't her drink. She ordered espresso, too, to counteract it. His recessed eyes seemed turned inward, totally intent on his story. Kit was determined to miss nothing.

'I was born in steerage, just before the ship put into New York.'

'Born in steerage!' Kit's eyes widened. 'How romantic.'

He grinned grimly. 'Rats and putrid water and people so closely packed they breathed the same fetid air, Kit. I don't know what you call romantic...'

Kit blushed, ashamed. 'I sound dreadfully naive, don't I? Go on, please.'

'We settled in a tiny two-room apartment in Providence, Rhode Island. The floors were so tilted, I didn't learn to walk until I was three.'

Kit imagined a frail, dark-eyed boy lurching across the floor.

'My mother died of tuberculosis when I was three. I still have the shawl she used to wear in her last days.'

She bent to her vodka and threw it back, wanting Rush to think the tears were all vodka. But Rush hadn't noticed.

'After my mother died, it was just me and the old man. But something happened to him after she died.' The grin again. 'He took to hating America, hating everything, hating even me. He'd come home from working all night as a bouncer in a speakeasy to find me hunched over the wood-burning stove, studying with my hands wrapped in rags, balancing my books and papers on my knee on a length of broken board. He'd go berserk. He'd swear at me in Russian. He refused to learn English. Then he'd tear the place apart.' The grin broadened into a smile. 'Whenever he broke a chair or a bureau or a table, I used it for firewood. Those were the coldest winters I'll ever know. And my hands, you see, developed frostbite. By the time I was ten, they were terribly scarred. I was so ashamed that even in summer I wore gloves to cover them up.'

Kit picked up his hands lying on the white tablecloth between them. 'But your hands are beautiful, Rush. Perfect, in fact.'

He held them up and turned them around. 'Yes, they are, aren't they. Another thing for which I am grateful to Archer. He paid for plastic surgery before I could afford it myself.'

'So what happened to your father?'

The grin took over. Kit was getting the idea that it preceded some harrowing, macabre detail of his early life. 'My father worked as a bouncer at a speakeasy, as I said, but he started one fight too many and they finally kicked him outside to serve as a night lookout. My old man would sit up in a tree night after night, with a handful of small rocks in his pocket. If he saw the police coming, his job was to throw the rocks onto the tin roof of the speakeasy to warn the owners inside. One night, one of these bitterly cold winter nights I've told you about, he drank a gallon of bathtub gin. They found him shortly after midnight, passed out. He was frozen solid in the crook of the tree with the gallon jug hooked on his thumb. The two men who brought him home to me the next morning told me how they had to remove him from the tree with a pick and shovel. They had to cut off his thumb to get the jug loose.'

'My God! How horrible for you!'

'Yes.' He grinned. 'Yes, it was. I was furious with the two men who brought him home. I jumped up and began punching them, kicking them. I wanted them dead instead of my father.'

'Of course you did!' Kit said.

'They ran off and left me to get rid of the body by myself. I was small for eight, and my father was over six feet – a regular Peter the Great.' His voice was bitter. 'It took me four hours to get his body down the stairs and over to the police station.'

He tossed back his vodka.

'Not to mention three years of working after school as a clerk in a pharmacy to buy a marker for his grave. I had it engraved just as they would have in Russia. I never knew where he buried my mother, so I put her name on the headstone too. I went to live in the back of the pharmacy. I studied hard and earned a Latin scholarship to Harvard.'

'Where your life changed?'

'Yes. Having Archer Ransome for a room-mate was a poor boy's dream come true.'

'Did you become friends right off?'

'I suppose you could say that Archer took instant pity on me. I imagine I was a pitiful sight compared to the average golden Harvard boy. Compared to Archer.' He smiled thoughtfully. 'To begin with, there were my hands. I was even skinnier than I am now. Archer took one look at my suit and made me throw it in the bin. He gave me his castoffs.'

'Weren't the trousers a bit short?' Kit's eyes roamed over the lanky body in an impeccably tailored tuxedo and smiled.

'Quite.' He smiled back. 'But he had his tailor alter them for me.'

'That was considerate.'

'Archer is nothing if not considerate.'

Was he being sarcastic? She couldn't tell.

'Archer thought of me as a sort of soulmate. He might have been a Choate boy, but he was still a foreigner.' He looked critically at her. 'Like you.'

Kit blushed.

'Archer taught me all the things that had been neglected in my education. He taught me how to tie a Windsor knot, how to comb my hair, which forks to use, how to come on to women.'

Kit smiled dryly. 'Archer has always known how to do that.'

'Yes, but I was too busy with my prelaw and my night work at a restaurant to do anything with that particular lesson. Nevertheless, I was staggeringly happy. You see, I realised that for me, the worst was over. Life could do nothing but improve. And I was right.'

He shifted in his chair and held up a finger to the waiter. While the waiter brought them each another shot, Kit could swear that

Rush was avoiding her eyes. Then, fortified by a sip, he went on.

'I met her the spring of freshman year. She was the most enchanting creature I had ever seen. She was nearly as tall as I, copper-haired and leggy with the most delightful laugh. It seemed to bubble up from deep within her, out of a throat as long and white and perfect as a swan's. I used to spot her crossing campus between classes. She was always surrounded by girls far less pretty than she was, like a princess with her handmaidens. She held her books up to her chest as if they were a shield. And she always seemed to be laughing. Night after night I came back to my room tempted to tell Archer about this girl, but something kept me from doing so. Perhaps I was afraid that sharing the infatuation would cheapen it. Perhaps I was afraid Archer would laugh in that mocking way he has and say, "You're just hard up for it, old man. Let me fix you up with a date just this once and you'll see how easy it is."

'And it *was* easy. For Archer. Archer dated lots of pretty Cliffies. But I had only my copper-haired beauty from afar.

'One night in the Widener Library, I was sitting at my usual table studying when I looked up from my reading and there she was, sitting two chairs away from me. I held my breath. I was barely able to make my fingers turn the page. She was reading *Tess of the d'Urbervilles*. When she got up to leave at eleven o'clock, she put a daisy in her book to mark her place. I called her Tess.'

'That *is* romantic!' Kit murmured.

He ignored her. 'I became even more obsessed with her now. I rescheduled my hours at the restaurant so I could go to the library every evening on the chance she'd show up. I wasn't disappointed.

'She was there again the next night. This time, when she got up to go, she put a daisy in her book, and when she passed behind my chair, she dropped another daisy on the page of my book.

'I was too astounded to turn around. I could only sit there staring at that daisy.'

Kit swallowed her vodka without blinking, absorbed in the tale.

'The night after that, she was there again, only this time she was sitting in the chair opposite mine. I'd never been so close to her before. The colour of her skin took my breath away. It was suffused with rose, like a Titian Madonna. The words swam on the page before me. I got up and followed her. We went out in the yard and sat on a bench holding hands. We never spoke much. Sometimes she read me poetry. She had a beautiful rich voice.

'We met like that, night after night, in the Widener Library.

176

Every night, I'd beg her to tell me her name, but she never did. Then, one night, she didn't show up at the library. I was frantic! Desolate! I couldn't look her up at the registrar's because I didn't know her name.'

'And you never saw her again?'

'Now you see that you're not the only one in the world with secrets.' He rubbed his hands together and grinned at her. 'Should you ever feel the need to tell your cousin Archer about my little secret romance, I assure you, Kit...'

Kit was indignant. 'Why, Rush, I'd never dream of betraying a confidence.'

He looked thoughtful as he lit up his pipe. 'Actually, now that I think of it, I'm not at all sure why I did tell you. Maybe I wanted you to know that you're not the only one who's been betrayed.'

'You just wanted to make me feel comfortable in my own... plight.' But Kit wasn't sure that she believed this.

'I've never told another living person,' he said, as if realising this for the first time. 'Well, Kit, I guess you're one of the lucky few who've been privy to a weakness in Rush Alexander.'

'I won't call a press conference about it, I promise.' She got into her car. 'Seriously, Bic's threatening to call his own press conference. I don't think you realise how determined he is. He's extremely powerful in this town.'

Rush made a gesture of dismissal. 'Don't worry, he won't do it. Even if he does, he won't do anything to embarrass you in front of your colleagues. Trust me and call your own conference.'

As she dropped Rush off in front of the Beverly Wilshire Hotel, Kit realised she had no choice but to trust him. She scheduled it for Thursday – three days off.

Bic called her up every hour to ask if she'd changed her mind yet. It got more and more difficult to say no.

Rita kept busy spying to see when Bic had scheduled a meeting with Rush, but dug up nothing. Could it be a secret meeting? Kit pictured Rush cornering a baffled Bic in some LA warehouse. Finally, the night before the press conference, Rita called Kit at home. Rush would be having breakfast with Bic tomorrow morning. 'I guess he likes to cut things close, eh?' said Rita.

The next morning Kit was in her office finishing her packing when a duplicate of the original memo arrived in the interoffice mail: 'I still own your arse.'

She set a match to it. Could even Rush save her arse now?

She got her answer a half-hour before the press conference. Rush sent a messenger over, carrying the three golden statuettes *Haight Street* had won, and a message: 'Crawford's photo library reduced to ashes under my personal supervision. On with the show'.

Kit was speechless. When Rush showed up, along with the first members of the press, she hugged him tearfully. Rush gallantly took over the press conference, reading a written statement by Crawford.

'I'm happy to tell you, gentlemen, and ladies' – he turned to grin crookedly at Kit – 'that Kit Ransome has just concluded an amicable release from her contract. Mr Crawford has given me this statement to read to you today: "Let no one ever say that I tied Kit Ransome down".'

Kit had blushed furiously at these words, but they seemed to satisfy the press and Warner's. All that afternoon, her body had been on fire with shame. That evening, she had gone to see Rush to retrieve the ashes of her negatives. She was even willing to *buy* them. And she did. Kit let Rush Alexander make love to her standing up against the cool sink in his bathroom. When she left the hotel room late that night, she had forgotten to ask him for the ashes and the next morning she was too embarrassed to call him.

Rush adjourned the budget meeting, saying, 'Kit, I'd like to see you for a moment.'

Kit was hardly surprised, but she was curious. Why save the kill for an empty arena? She waited patiently in her seat as the others filed out.

Rush lay down lazily on the table in front of her and leaned on one arm. He smiled crookedly. 'Fooled you, didn't I?'

'In a way.' Kit pushed her chair away from the table and looked at him warily. She smiled uncertainly. 'Why'd you go easy on me today? Getting soft?'

'I wouldn't want Arch to miss out on any fireworks.'

'How considerate of you, Rush. By the way' – she gestured to Ransome's empty chair – 'where was he today?'

'Oh, much too busy for our little show. He's got his hands full with Senator Pierce.'

'Are we in real trouble, Rush?'

Rush rolled over onto his back and stretched, cracking his wrists.

'Trouble, Kitty? Not sure. I told Archer to let me talk to Pierce. I sometimes have a way with politicians. But he wanted to handle it himself. And you know your cousin.'

Kit eyed him suspiciously. 'I'm sure he can handle it.'

'Sure he can.' Rush got up lazily and ambled over to the door. 'Oh... I almost forgot. I have a favour to ask you.'

Kit waited as he strolled back and sat down in the chair next to her and dangled one long leg over the chair's arm.

He was silent for a long time, grinning at her.

When she couldn't stand it a second longer, she asked him. 'All right, Rush. What's the verdict? Will you let me finish *Last Chance* or are you opting for the insurance? Don't you two gentlemen think you've left me dangling for long enough?'

He ignored her question and asked one of his own. 'You know my daughter Verena?'

Kit nodded. 'She's a good-looking girl. Going to turn Ruba around. But look, Rush, I don't see what this has to do –'

'Yes, she's a beautiful girl,' he mused. 'She's been taking some acting classes with Max Rugoff. Old Max says she's very... special.'

What was Rush getting at? 'Rugoff's good,' she said cautiously. 'He ought to know.'

'Kit, you know this part you're having trouble casting?'

Kit narrowed her eyes at him.

'I'm going to help you fill it,' he finished with a smile. His dangling foot made small circles. He bent to fill his pipe.

Kit closed her eyes and heard Sam Rothman's voice: *You gotta step up to this, Kit-honey.*

'I want you to give Verena the Lacy part in *Last Chance*.'

'I can't do that. You don't understand, Rush. It's totally out of the question.'

'*You* don't understand, Kit.' He puffed at his pipe. 'Remember the favour I did for you?' He puffed. 'Well, this is the favour I want in return.'

Kit put her hand on his knee. 'I'll be glad to give Verena a part, Rush. I'll do that for you. But please don't ask me to put her in *Last Chance*.'

Rush smiled and groped under the table for the shoe he had slipped off.

'I've had enough trouble on this set, Rush. Don't give me any more. Be reasonable.'

'Do you see my shoe under there?' He ducked his head under the table and went on. His voice sounded muffled, as if he were underwater. 'My daughter is talented. She'll help *Last Chance*.'

'For God's sake, Rush. Listen to me. The child's never been in a movie. I'll be happy to do you a favour –'

'I know you will be,' he said.

'Why *Last Chance*?' she said. 'Why this movie? You weren't even interested in seeing the footage.'

'I'm no movie critic, Kitty Cat. You told me it's going to be a great movie, and I believe you.'

'Rush, please, please. Think about it!' she pleaded.

He eased himself out of the chair and walked to the door. He fiddled with the light switches and the boardroom went black.

'Nothing to think about, Kit. Have your business-affairs guy draw up the contract.'

Kit summoned her will and shouted, 'I will not! I'd rather see you collect the insurance.'

'Hey, Kit. I've got some negatives. Know a good twenty-four-hour developer I might take them to?' The embers in his pipe flared, and she saw him grin. She stared at him, hands glued to the arms of her chair.

'Just in case you ever had any doubt, Kit. Now *I* own your arse.'

11

Liberty stood at the bottom of the seven-floor staircase. The buzzer next to 'Novak' read '7B'.

'Just my luck.'

The white limo had picked her up at the Federal Express terminal and desposited her here in the East Eighties at the address of Mrs Dorothy Novak. There hadn't even been time to go home and shower. The thought of dragging her duffel bag with her to the day's appointments made her feel even wearier, but she dismissed the limo. She didn't want Archer to know what she was up to all day.

On the third-floor landing she paused to rest. The stairs pitched inward, the greasy walls seeming to cave in upon her. After a few deep breaths she trudged upward. At the fifth-floor landing she heard a wispy voice call down: 'Keep coming, Miss Adams. Don't give up!'

Liberty panted, 'I won't.'

At the top of the stairs she came face to face with a smallish, meek-looking strawberry blonde with a large bruise on her chin. She didn't jibe at all with the raving harridan on the cover of the *Post*: 'MOM SHOOTS KITTY AT SHERRY'.

She put out her hand. 'How do you do, Mrs Novak? I'm glad you could take the time to see me.'

'Oh, I had to!' the woman assured her. She wore a lime-green cocktail dress and carpet slippers, her hair freshly teased and sprayed. She peered at Liberty shyly. 'Are you sure you're her? You're such a little bitty thing. I was expecting someone ...'

'Hulking, with fangs?' Liberty smiled and stepped into the gloomy space beyond the doorway.

'You know, "Stocks & Trades" was *it* as far as Monette was concerned. She turned right to it every week – even before she read the *Enquirer*.'

Liberty didn't see the point in telling her that someone else had taken over 'S&T' nine months ago. 'I'm glad to hear that, Mrs

Novak.' Recoiling from the odour, a mixture of Raid and Shalimar, Liberty followed her hostess through four rooms of a railway apartment. Time had turned everything – walls, furniture, ceiling – a tired tea brown. They came to the end room. Liberty took it in at a glance: low brown couch, shot with gold, gilt-edged marble-top coffee table stacked with bulging scrap-books, large colour television set. She couldn't help staring at the bad abstracts on the walls.

'My late husband did them. Can I get you something cool to drink? It's warm for October, isn't it?' She fanned herself with a copy of *TV Guide*. 'Seems like ever since we put a man on the moon, the weather –'

'I'll take a glass of water, please.'

'All right.' She tiptoed back to her kitchen.

Liberty sat down on the couch, opened her bag, and switched on her tape machine. A photograph in a gilt frame sat on the end table. She tilted it towards her. A pale-eyed Mary Francis girl smiled shyly into the camera, wearing a white dress and veil and clutching a small bouquet tied with ribbons. Liberty recalled her own First Communion at St Mary's: the too-big second-hand white dress with no petticoat, getting tipsy on the blood of Christ – all in all, a grotesque ceremony.

'Beautiful, wasn't she?' Mrs Novak handed her a tall green plastic glass. The water was tepid, tasting the way the apartment smelled. After one sip, she set it down on the end table and looked around again. 'Was Monette raised here?'

'My late husband, Richard, and I moved here a year after we married. When Richard passed away – that was ten years ago – it was just the two of us. Now...' She trailed off sadly and then came back to Liberty. 'You must think I'm the most terrible person.'

'Of course not!'

'Yes, yes, you do. I can see it in your eyes. That was a terrible thing I did to Miss Ransome.'

Liberty touched her arm lightly. 'We sometimes do terrible things when we're grief-stricken.'

She bobbed her head absently. 'Yes ... I suppose we do. It's just that ...'

'Mrs Novak, is there something in particular you'd like to talk to me about?'

She seized Liberty's hand with surprising strength. 'That man loved my Momo. He told me so himself, sitting right where you're sitting right now.'

Liberty pointed to the brown carpet at her feet. 'Who sat here?'

'After the funeral, he sent me a huge bouquet. You should have seen the mountain of flowers all the stars sent my Monette.'

Liberty cut off the litany of men who had used and discarded Monette Novak in her too-short stardom. 'She was an actress, Mrs. Novak, but tell me, please, who is this man who told you he was in love with Monette?'

'I don't think I should say.'

'Sure you should.'

'I don't want this misrepresented to her public.'

'I'd never do that, Mrs Novak.'

'He worshipped her, you know. In fact, he was going to leave that society wife of his for her.' As if relishing Liberty's impatience, she persisted. 'He was going to leave his wife – yes, he was. You don't believe me, I can tell. You have very expressive eyes, did you know that? I didn't believe it myself at first. I never imagined they'd got that close until . . .' She plucked at her chiffon lap excitedly. Her hair had come unstuck from its helmet of spray and flew out from her head as if electrically charged. Liberty was beginning to feel the interview slipping out of her control.

As firmly as she could, Liberty said, 'Who was the man in love with your daughter?'

'Why, Rush Alexander, of course.'

Liberty just stared at her.

'Stop looking at me like that. It's true!' she cried. 'Do you think he would have given it to me in the first place if he didn't love –'

'Given you what, Mrs Novak? The flowers?'

'Of course not the flowers! The gun!'

'The gun!' Liberty exploded, then quickly got hold of herself. 'What gun, Mrs Novak?' It came out in a whisper. 'The gun you tried to –'

'The gun the police have right now,' Mrs Novak whispered back, mimicking her. 'The gun he gave me to avenge my Monette's death.'

Liberty rubbed her face and took a deep breath. 'Rush Alexander gave you the gun, Mrs Novak?'

'Mr Alexander, Rush Alexander, gave me the gun. He told me to do it in a public place and then to act like a crazy woman when the cops came to get me.'

'Rush Alexander?'

'He told me he'd get me off on an insanity plea and have me confined to a mental institution in New England somewhere. Some of those places are in old mansions rich people used to live in ... I asked him if he could put me in a place like that. I always wanted to live in a mansion. What is there for me here?' It was easy to see how Monette came by her flair for the dramatic; her mother's eyes, when they came to rest on Liberty, were brimming with tears.

'Don't you see, that's why I tried to kill her.'

Liberty cleared her throat. 'No, Mrs Novak. Frankly, I don't.'

'Miss Ransome was the one who got my Monette hooked on drugs again. No!' She slammed her fist into her knee. 'Monette didn't need anyone to hook her. She was perfectly capable of ... of ... Mr Alexander told me it was Kit who put needles and packets of drugs in her trailer. But I don't believe it. Not now.'

'Do you know who did, then, Mrs Novak?'

There was a sudden look of triumph in her eyes. 'I'm not telling. That's enough for you, little Miss Stocks & Trades.'

Liberty made a pleading gesture. 'Mrs Novak! This isn't enough for me to go on.'

She looked disappointed, then sulky. 'Oh, all right. I'll tell you. Somebody had it in for my Monette.'

Liberty spoke through gritted teeth. 'We know that, but who?'

'You see, I was there when the delivery came.'

'What delivery?'

'It was addressed to her, but I opened it. I never showed it to her, of course. I put it out the back in the rubbish and never said a word about it.'

'What was it?'

'Can you imagine? Sending a nasty, hideous thing like that to a lovely young thing like my Monette? It was female, too. I checked.'

'What was, Mrs Novak?'

'Why, the dead cat in the Kotex box, of course.'

Liberty felt her lunch lurch towards her oesophagus. 'Who would have done a thing like that, Mrs Novak?'

'I thought it was Miss Ransome. He said she'd done it. He said she was jealous of Monette because she was a fresh young starlet like she was once. But all I had to do was look in her eyes outside her hotel the other day ... That lady's too classy to have done anything like that ... no offence to Mr Alexander, you understand.' She touched the bruise on her chin.

184

'I understand. So did you tell the police about Mr Alexander and the gun and the' – she swallowed – 'dead cat in the Kotex box?'

She wheeled her arms, angrily now. 'Of course not! What do you think you're doing here? This is an exclusive! It's yours to tell the world. From my lips to –'

Liberty had to think fast. 'Mrs Novak, I can't print this story. It's a police matter.'

'But you promised!' She grabbed Liberty by the shoulders and began to shake her.

'I know I did, Mrs Novak, but that was before –'

'You little bitch! I saved it for you. Monette died without getting into "Stocks & Trades" ... and now you sit here and enjoy my hospitality and tell me all high and mighty that you can't get Momo into "S&T" because it's a police matter?'

'I'll do what I can, Mrs Novak. I'll do what I can. All right?'

The woman stopped shaking Liberty and sniffed. 'All right.'

'Do you think you could release me, Mrs Novak?'

As her hands fell away, Liberty rubbed her shoulders.

'Now, where were we?' said Mrs Novak, smoothing her skirt.

Liberty looked at her watch. 'I'm afraid I'm going to have to leave now, Mrs Novak. I've got another –'

'Oh, no you don't. We're just getting started. What about these?' She slid the topmost scrapbook off the pile and opened it, but Liberty was already on her feet, backing up into the next room.

'Look, Mrs Novak, I'll have my secretary call and schedule a follow-up.' She kept backing up towards the kitchen, towards the door. 'I can't thank you enough, really.'

Mrs Novak, carrying the scrapbook, followed a room and a half behind her. Liberty turned and swivelled the locks on the door, relieved to find no resistance. She stepped out into the hall. 'Have a nice day, Mrs Novak, and thanks again.'

Mrs Novak stood at the top of the stairs, resting the open scrapbook on the railing, chatting with Liberty as if she were at her elbow and not fleeing down the stairs. Her voice echoed in the stairwell. 'Here, look! Isn't she cunning? Here she is at her tap dancing classes. And here she is winning the Beautiful Baby Contest. And here she is ...'

Liberty swung open the door to the street and closed it behind her, exhaling at last. She stared down at her tape machine and swtiched it off. What was she supposed to do with that mess? It would be impossible to separate fact from wild fantasy. She might as well erase the whole thing for all the good it would do her. She hailed a cab going west. As she was giving him the address of the Berkshire Place, she glanced in the rearview mirror and saw the slight dark man in the blue suit, her shadow, climbing into a Checker. She tapped on the plastic partition.

'Do me a favour, mister, and lose that Checker back there?'

'You gotta be kidding me, lady! Do you think you're in the movies?'

'Yeah, *The Andrew Jackson Story*,' she said, slipping him a twenty dollar bill. He accelerated, flinging her back into her seat, and swerved into the park.

'I'd like to sit over *there*, instead.' Liberty pointed to a corner table.

'That table is for four. You said you were a party of two.'

It was after four o'clock, the tea trade at the Berkshire Place was already brisk, and the maître d' was on edge.

'I'm interviewing someone and we need *privacy*,' said Liberty, emphasising the last word. 'My duffel bag and my pocketbook will be the other two.' She slipped a ten-dollar bill into his clipboard.

'Very good, miss.'

Liberty settled in and ordered tea and scones. She needed energy; Mrs Novak had successfully sapped what little had remained after the flight. She was still trying to figure out whether the woman was completely crazy or just halfway there. What was it someone had once said on the subject? Neurotics only dreamed of castles in the air. Psychotics lived in them – and their mothers came to clean? Mrs Novak's mother definitely came to clean. She couldn't believe Rush Alexander was the type to leave his wife for a chippie on the side. And even if it were true, surely he wouldn't rely on such an unstable pawn as Mrs Novak. She'd have to find a way either to prove or to discount everything Mrs Novak had told her, and that would be no easy task.

Slathering strawberry jam and then whipped cream over her scone, she propped her feet up on the lower rung of the chair next to hers and waited for Kit Ransome to arrive. The room's oversized flower arrangement made her feel suddenly like an elf perched at a little pink toadstool about to take tea from acorn tops. Then, like a large black crow, a vision of Bic Crawford swooped down upon her and she shivered uncontrollably. What a night! The timing was terrible. A revolting evening with Bic was managing to overshadow a very special afternoon with Kit, an interview that meant more to her than she cared to admit. It wasn't just the culmination of three hundred telephone calls to Kit Ransome's office. It wasn't just the means by which she would now be able to wind up her Kitsia profile with a flourish. It was the completion of the mission that had begun a month ago on Zwar in Kitsia's studio. She reached into her bag and felt around for the small cold body of the turtle for reassurance. When her hand hit upon the tapes, she brought them out with a shudder: the record of her hours with Bic Crawford.

When she saw the cassettes, she nearly screamed. He had replaced her tapes with a two-volume set of Wayne Newton's Greatest Hits. That prick! She called for the phone and dialled his office in a rage, able only to leave the number of the restaurant. Still fuming, Liberty tucked the phone under her chair and signalled to the waiter that she'd be keeping it.

The woman who appeared at the door gave her an unexpected jolt. She was the same elegant lithe brunette who had appeared at the mouth of Stewart Granger's tent in *The Storm Heiress* twenty years ago. She caught Kit's eye and lifted a finger in salute.

Kit had a cat's stealth, a cat's erect, velvet-pawed way of passing through a room. Liberty noticed heads swivelling to take her in. If they weren't recognising the actress, they were acknowledging the beauty.

Kit stood over her, dressed in a sleek black suit, blouse of pearl-grey silk hanging in a soft V between her breasts, skin tanned flawlessly, a smoky brown. She extended her hand. Long tapering fingers, ringless, bare of polish. No nonsense about this woman.

'I'm sorry I'm late. I hope you haven't waited too long. Good. I see you've had some tea.'

Tiny cross-shaped pupils were swallowed up by jungle green: eyes that Technicolor was *invented* for. And there, piercing her right earlobe, the object Kitsia had prepared her for: the single black-pearl stud. Liberty's head reeled.

Kit settled herself fitfully, signalling the waiter with such authority that he bounded across the floor to her.

'This chair is sprung. I'd like a new one, please.'

The waiter switched her chair with the empty one right next to hers. If that had been my chair, Liberty thought, I'd have switched it myself.

'People must tell you this all the time, but you really do look as beautiful as you did in your movies.'

'Thank you.'

The fact was, she looked better, more substantial. On film she always looked so fragile, all ivory and cellophane.

'You work out, I hear?'

Kit tilted her head regally. 'Pardon me, Miss Adams?'

'You swim.'

'Yes.' She nodded slowly. 'I swim.'

'I swim too, but not seven miles every day,' Liberty cracked. 'It's more like seven miles every seven years.'

Kit smiled without involving her eyes. Her coal-black hair was so shiny it looked wet.

Liberty remembered a Xeroxed page from an old *Life*: Kit, dripping wet, pulling herself up on a mossy bank on the set of her most successful movie. The caption read, 'Who Says Kats Kan't Swim?'

'I'm glad we've finally got together,' Liberty said to the beautiful heart-shaped face that was a softer version of Kitsia's.

'You do understand, Miss Adams, that this is only an exploratory interview.'

'Miss Ransome, you know as well as I do that there is no such thing as an exploratory interview.' She had finally hooked Kit, thanks to Archer. Did Kit actually believe she'd settle for one interview? No, Liberty would reel her in slowly over a series of sessions, whether Kit liked it or not.

Kit smiled tightly. 'Then why don't you tell me what kind of piece you're writing?'

'A double profile of you and your mother. You make a most unusual team.'

'We hardly work as a team,' Kit cut in softly.

'I meant that loosely, of course,' Liberty hastened to add. 'Until now I've talked to a lot of secondary sources, got a lot of different angles – what I call the *Rashomon* approach. Now that you've consented to be interviewed –'

'*Rashomon*, Miss Adams? I do hope you don't intend to rape us?'

Liberty laughed. 'That would hardly be treatment befitting a birthday girl. The article's coming out in December. On your mother's seventy-third birthday.'

'How perfectly charming.' Kit was deadpan.

The waiter hovered over them.

'Would you like some tea or something?' Liberty asked.

'A pot of Earl Grey, please,' Kit told the waiter.

'I thought I might concentrate on *Last Chance*,' Liberty went on. 'After all, it's been part of your pattern to back losers and win.' Start from *Last Chance* and build out, she had told herself. Skirt the personal stuff – that would make her too skittish.

'Losers, Miss Adams?' Kit looked at her watch, an oval face with Roman numerals. 'I'm afraid I don't know what you mean.'

'All right, Miss Ransome ... I mean *Haight Street*. I mean *The Dakotans*. I mean *Last Chance*.'

'If you mean I am averse to the bandwagon philosophy of movie-making, then you are correct. And call me Kit, please.'

'All right, Kit. I guess that's what I meant.'

Liberty brushed some crumbs off her pad and rummaged in her bag for a pencil. Her fingers hit upon the turtle. *Not yet*, she told herself.

She looked up and blushed. Kit's gaze was steady, unblinking. 'Are you concerned about *Last Chance*'s hiatus?'

'Yes,' she said slowly, 'But not overly so. We've had some problems and we have chosen to close down until they are solved.'

'Isn't it costing Horizon nearly $150,000 each day shooting is delayed?'

'It's not my policy to confirm budget figures. A movie ought to be judged on its own merit, not by its budget.'

'Are you saying, then, that *Last Chance* isn't heading over budget? Aren't you going to have to go into golden time to finish it?'

'*Last Chance* isn't a particularly expensive film to make. The book rights were expensive, but the above-the-line costs are average. There have been some problems due to the tragedy on the set.'

'Why do you think Monette Novak committed suicide *on* the set, as opposed to somewhere else? Doesn't that make you curious?'

'"Curious" is such an inadequate word for my feelings about Miss Novak's death.'

'Have you recast the role yet?'

'Why, yes, we have. Just yesterday.'

'Oh, really? Who did it go to?'

'It isn't for publication, but we've cast an unknown actress, Verena Alexander.'

Liberty paused with her scone halfway to her mouth. 'Verena *Alexander*? Rush Alexander's daughter?'

'Yes.'

'Small world.' She bit down on her scone and chewed it quickly.

'Very,' Kit said. It was as if a door shut behind her.

Liberty nudged at it. 'I thought his daughter was a model. Isn't she committed to the Ruba campaign?'

'*Last Chance* will be her film debut.'

'I see.' Liberty wiped the crumbs off her mouth and pulled out a Camel. She pressed on. 'Have you any idea why Miss Novak might have gone back on drugs?'

Kit recoiled visibly. 'I don't meddle in people's private lives, Miss Adams.'

'Mr Scott thought perhaps she might have been having romantic difficulties.'

'I wouldn't know.'

'She was seeing Bic Crawford. He claims he broke up with her because of drugs.'

'Did he really? How interesting.'

'He said Rush Alexander also took up with her, after he dropped her.'

Kit twisted her earring. Liberty guessed it was a nervous habit – probably her only one.

'I said that Rush Alexander –'

'I heard what you said, but I don't believe you. There are no secrets on a movie set. I would have heard –'

'I'll admit, it doesn't make much sense, a happily married man like that. What I don't understand is why he would go to such lengths to get his daughter a part when the plan is to close down the picture and collect the insurance.' Liberty's mind raced ahead. If Lacy had gone to Rush's daughter, did that mean Rush had something to do with Monette's death? Could mad Mrs Novak have been on the level? But then why kill off the starlet to give his daughter the part if they were going to close down the movie for insurance? It just didn't make sense.

'I said, who told you that?' Kit leaned forward.

Liberty came back from her thoughts and shrugged.

'I don't believe Archer has reached his decision yet,' Kit went on.

'Perhaps not.'

Kit looked at her directly for the first time.

Liberty bent to sip her tea; it was bitter and lukewarm. 'They say Brendan Marsh is threatening to pull out.'

190

Kit's eyes widened. The pupils shone like tiny black daggers. 'Brendan is threatening to quit?'

'Yes, or so I heard in LA last night.'

'From whom?' she demanded.

'I can't say.'

'Why not?'

'Because it was told to me in confidence.'

'Is that so?' Kit stirred her tea slowly and never took her eyes off Liberty. 'How can you keep something this serious confidential? After all, it's not something you are even remotely involved in.'

'When you put it that way...' Liberty tried a weak smile.

'What other way is there to put it, Miss Adams?'

'Please call me Liberty.'

Kit was silent. She held herself very still, like a panther ready to spring.

Liberty decided it was more than time to change the subject. 'When I was in Zwar, your mother –'

'Liberty, *Last Chance* is extremely important to me, to Horizon, to everyone concerned, and when you bring up something as serious as this, I can hardly let it pass.'

'And *I* can hardly betray a trust. I clearly should not have brought it up. Can we go on?'

If Kit had a tail, she would be switching it.

Liberty dragged deeply on her cigarette and took her silence as permission. 'I've just returned from Zwar. I found it dramatic, but so barren. How did you amuse yourself?'

'Zwar was often quite lively.' She warmed quickly to the memory. 'Mother imported friends from Europe and the States and kept them at our house for months at a time. She used to throw enormous parties in our courtyard. There were artists, actresses, adventurers, vagabonds... some real characters. I remember one woman who dressed herself up as a man and hopped freights across America.'

'Sounds fascinating,' Liberty cut in, 'but not exactly appropriate company for a little girl. Were there any kids your own age? Any other little girls?'

Kit shook her head. 'The Arab girls weren't allowed out. I played with boys. Sons and nephews of the emir. I was so tanned, some people thought I was one of them.'

'Are you?'

191

'No,' Kit answered softly. 'Do I look that dark to you?'

'No.' Liberty wanted to say more. Since Kit didn't know who her father was, she might be half Arab for all she knew. But Liberty didn't dare.

'I found your mother fascinating.'

'Most people do.'

'Do you think she was a good mother?'

'I don't know what that means. Do you think your mother was a good mother, Liberty?'

'Is it true that you and your mother aren't speaking?'

'To each other? That's really none of your business.'

'But it does make my job more difficult if it's true.'

'I didn't ask you to take it on.'

'No, but your mother did.'

Kit recoiled visibly. 'So that's it! I should have known this was her idea. Only Kitsia could get *Metropolitan* to cooperate with her machinations.'

The phone under Liberty's chair rang.

'Excuse me, Kit.' Liberty picked up the phone. 'Hello?'

'Oh, Miss Adams. Mr Ransome calling.'

'I can't talk right now. I'll have to call him back later.'

Ransome came on the line. 'Hello. I've been thinking about you. How was Los Angeles?' His voice was so real, so sexy, that for a brief moment Liberty wanted more than anything to talk to him.

'I can't really –' Liberty started.

'I wanted to invite you to a party tomorrow evening. My god-daughter Verena is celebrating –'

'Yes, I know all about it. I'd love to. Look...'

Watching her from across the table, Kit seemed to enjoy seeing Liberty wrestle with an awkward situation.

'Liberty, I have to ask you something that can't wait.'

'Sure, fine, what is it?'

'Do you know Eben Pierce?'

Liberty hesitated. 'Listen, can we discuss this later? I'm in the middle of an interview now and –'

'Do you know Eben Pierce?'

'Yes, but –'

'I'm disappointed in you, Liberty.'

Liberty blushed. 'I ... I ...'

'I wish you'd told me yourself, Liberty. But no matter. We can take this up again later.'

192

Liberty hung up, feeling chastened, and smiled sheepishly at Kit. 'Sorry. Where were we?'

Kit merely raised her shoulders.

As a last resort, or perhaps to wipe the smile of satisfaction off Kit's face, Liberty lunged into her bag and brought out the turtle at last. She set it down on the table between them and watched the colour recede from Kit's cheeks. She didn't know what she'd expected to see registered on Kit's face at this moment. Delight that the long-awaited moment had come? The shock of recognition? But what she saw was utter and complete mortification. Slowly Kit began to work her chair away from the table, away from the turtle.

Liberty stammered. 'I... I'm sorry to be so abrupt... I was hoping to broach the subject a little more subtly. Maybe if I just –'

'*Get that thing out of my sight!*'

'But your mother –'

'I don't want to hear it, do you understand? I don't want to hear anything that woman has to say to me.'

Liberty spoke as quickly as she could. 'Look, Kit, I wish I didn't have anything to do with your and your mother's private lives, but... How can I put this? Kit...' She leaned forward, pressing her palms against the marble. 'I think your life –'

'Is in danger? Oh, please. Not you too!' She snatched her purse off the table.

Liberty blundered onward. 'There are men who want you dead. Your mother gave me this turtle as some kind of a sign to prove to you that I'm telling you the truth.' Liberty cast around for the right cinematic metaphor. 'Sort of like the ring in *Elizabeth and Essex*?'

'And I'm asking you to take it back to her and tell her that I am not in the least interested in hearing her Byzantine plots, nor in anything else she may have to say to me.'

'But, Kit –'

'Stay out of it, Liberty!' She gave herself a final heave away from the table, sending china and silver spinning and clattering onto the carpet, and walked briskly out of the tearoom.

Only vaguely aware of the rising level of chatter in the room, Liberty sat there and stared at the teacup, overturned and dripping into her lap. She was trembling so violently that she couldn't even pick up a napkin and blot up the tea soaking into her culottes. The waiter was on the floor at her feet, picking up the service.

'Is this yours, madam?'

'What?' Liberty shook herself and looked down. He was holding out the turtle to her. For a split second she debated whether or not to take it. After all, it wasn't really hers. Yet she had failed in her effort to pass it on to its rightful owner. Failed. *Mission Not Accomplished*. She took it, mumbling thanks, just as the phone underneath her chair buzzed. She leaned down and picked it up, still staring at the turtle.

'Yes.'

A man's voice asked, 'Who is this?'

'Bic!' Liberty felt the blood return to her face. 'This is Liberty. Liberty Adams. Remember? I had dinner at your lovely home last night?'

Silence.

'I was wondering if I might have left a little something behind when I left so abruptly after dessert. A couple of tapes, perhaps?'

Silence.

'The tapes, Bic. They're mine and I want them.'

Silence.

'Come on, guy, give me a break. It's the words I want. Not the heavy-breathing passages. I promise. I'll return them when I've finished with them. For your archives.'

Silence.

'Bic, they're my property.'

More silence.

'Come on, Bic, for crying out loud,' she pleaded.

'Get fucked, babycakes.'

Click.

Liberty walked into the amphitheatre of the Ransome Building, then wanted to turn right around and walk out. Brendan Marsh was in the middle of bellowing at some poor gofer and the sound brought her headache back. So much for the three Tylenols she'd popped in the ladies' lounge of the Berkshire Place where she'd gone to change out of her tea-stained clothes and recuperate from the fiasco with Kit. Lord knows, she didn't want to go through with this. She'd even called up Jay Scott on the lounge phone to see if she could postpone this interview until tomorrow, but Scott told her that if Brendan had agreed to see her for his sake, she'd better show up as scheduled.

She squared her shoulders, got out her thermos, and went over to offer him a cup of cappuccino. At least she'd had the presence of mind after taking her Tylenols at the tearoom, to have the kitchen fill up her thermos. Marsh took one look at the Tiffany cup she held out to him and burst into laughter, twirling the tips of his handlebar moustache.

'You must be the young woman Jay sent. It's about time *Last Chance* got a fair shake in the press.'

Liberty nodded, smiling, suddenly glad she hadn't postponed after all.

'I like your style, young lady.'

She followed him up to the back of the room and sat down on a metal folding chair. He stood with his foot on his, resting the delicate cup on his knee, like a bear at a tea party.

'I've been here since eight-thirty this morning. I have talked to twelve groups, with no less than fourteen to a group. I have interviewed at least twelve in earnest, chatted avuncularly with over fifty, and read eight. I am just about to take on a baker's dozen, and I can tell you, little lady, I am *not* amused.' A grin broke through his scowl.

The first question on Liberty's mind was: If Verena Alexander already has the part, what are you all doing here? But there were some answers you went for right away and others you waited for.

She gestured to the women being herded out of the room. 'What kind of young woman are you looking for?'

He inflated his cheeks and blew out slowly, rubbed the back of his neck, and then stroked his moustache.

'I don't exactly know, honey. I'm looking for a human being as opposed to a –'

Looking at the new line-up of women filing in, Liberty said, 'A Marilyn Monroe clone? I call them Norma Jean Baker Dolls, myself.'

'Say,' he grinned. 'I like that. That's very good.'

'I'm afraid it isn't exactly mint-fresh.'

He stared at her blankly.

'Oh, that's right,' she said. 'I forgot that you pretend you don't read.'

He grinned. 'Just reviews.'

She'd heard how some years ago he'd thrown a reviewer for *Variety* through the window at Sardi's. Or was it into the mirror over the bar? In any case, Liberty, for one, would never dream of red-flagging this bull.

'Do you think there's a shortage of good actresses today, particularly ingénues?'

'You might say that. But then again, I don't think this is a business that attracts actresses. It attracts narcissists and divas, megalomaniacs and nymphomaniacs, but actors . . .' He blew his nose on a faded blue bandanna and stuffed it back into the pocket of his khaki trousers. His trousers, Liberty noticed, looked pre-World War II, but well cared for. You wouldn't find Brendan Marsh shopping in those European boutiques on Rodeo Drive or Madison Avenue. He probably wouldn't wear another man's label on his arse unless it was L. L. Bean. What had Liz Smith called him once? 'The last *real* man in Hollywood, maybe even America.'

He put on a pair of steel-rimmed glasses and studied the women. She liked his profile, the angular bends in the bridge of his nose, the gnarled scar tissue built up there. As a young man he had hired himself out as a sparring partner to professional boxers, and he looked it.

'Tell me, how has a man like you survived in Hollywood?'

'Because I'm a worker, that's how!' he said aggressively, daring her to challenge him. 'Because I've always worked. People can say what they will about me – that I have run with the right pack, or worked with the right people, or got myself involved in the right projects. But I was never out of work for very long. I raised five kids from three on up without much help from anybody, and I made sure they had nothing but the best.'

Liberty recalled that one wife had left him, another had committed suicide, and a third had run off with a TV-exercise jock, leaving him to raise the five children, the youngest a toddler. It couldn't have been easy.

'Do you think it hurt your career, having had to take care of children all those years? Or did you enjoy family life?'

'Hell, no, there were times when I really hated it. I worried. Jesus God, how I worried! I worried about them growing up in that den of sin. Getting in with the wrong crowds. Taking drugs. But most of all I worried about money. I used to work myself up into the most Godawful sweats in the dead of night. Would I be able to keep them all in college? So I drank. I drank like a son of a bitch. It was the one way I could control the tension.'

'What did your children think about your drinking?'

He laughed heartily. 'They hated it. Jesus Christ, my daughter especially. They used to take turns coming down to my study. My "stewdio" was what Lily, my daughter, called it. You'd like Lily, she's about your age. And a lot like you, too, now I come to think of it: a righteous little bitch.'

'Fuck you, Mr Marsh,' Liberty said mildly.

He put his paw on her hand. 'Don't get me wrong, darlin', I love her dearly. But she's proud and prissy, just like you. She used to stand toe to toe with me and bawl me out. She must have poured thousands of dollars of good bourbon down the sink over the years. Like that Cheever story, what the hell was it?'

'"The Sorrows of Gin",' Liberty replied.

'Anyway' – he patted her hand earnestly – 'that's all over with now. I've almost given up the bottle. They're good kids, though. Three of them are up in Frisco, one's down in Baja – that's Lily, my daughter – and the youngest is still in school. He's at MIT, and damn, but I'm proud of him. Goddamn, I'm proud of all my get!'

'Are any of your "get" going into show business?'

'The three in Frisco are. My three oldest boys. One's a playwright. Or rather, he was a playwright until Kit convinced him to write for the screen instead.'

He stopped and stared sadly down, as if the very mention of Kit had opened up a gaping hole before him. Liberty was sorry that her line of questioning had led him here. Carefully she led him away.

'Do you think staying busy is the secret of staying sane in LA?'

'Absolutely.' He slipped past the hole and went on. 'The problem is keeping your mind busy while you're working. When you're working, you spend an hour, maybe two at the most, actually in front of the camera, acting. The other fifteen, sixteen hours a day you're fighting off everything else. You're fighting boredom. You're fighting sin. Good God, it's a regular Shanghai! But I have my family and I trust a few colleagues – very few – I've known for years and trust as buddies. And I tell all the rest to go fuck themselves. And if they don't, I go and get myself a two-by-four with rusty nails in it and persuade them to go and do so. That's what you have to do to survive.'

He said this cheerfully, almost elegantly, as if he were describing some ritual out of Emily Post.

'Well,' he said, putting down the cup and turning, 'time to get the show on the road. This is the next-to-last batch of the day. Excuse me, madam, while I go and be a dirty old man.'

It was a half-hearted lechery that Liberty saw in Brendan Marsh as she watched him at work from the third row, where she now sat. He went among the girls, taking their hands and asking them their names, what they'd done, patting their heads and calling them 'honey' and 'dear girl' and 'darlin'' as if they were all his children. When he'd finished learning their names and telling them all how lovely they were, he turned on them like a drill sergeant, so that the whole group visibly jumped to attention.

'You!' He pointed to the girl in front, a girl with dyed black hair and a scrawny neck, wearing black stretch trousers and a pink and black polka-dot tunic. 'Are you a waif or is the fly-blown look still in this year?'

Having undoubtedly made it to this point in the day believing that she was the very epitome of fashion, she blushed and pointed to herself, cork earrings bobbing.

'Yes, you. What's your favourite stage role to date?' he asked her.

'Cassie?' she asked.

'Are you asking me or telling me?' he said gruffly.

The girl stood there trembling.

'Can somebody please tell me who the hell this Cassie is?'

'*Chorus Line!*' several of the girls chimed in.

'Oh, really?' He nodded politely. Liberty could tell this didn't impress him.

'You!' He pointed to a girl in a pink shirtwaist who was obviously doing her best to look like what she thought the part called for. 'I want you to come here and kiss me. See if you can arouse me without actually touching me with any part of your body except your lips.'

She blushed and came up to him without hesitation, fastening her lips over his. Liberty detected a mingling of tongues. They broke apart at length. There was an audible sigh among the girls. The girl who'd done the kissing looked flushed and excited.

'Say!' he said, standing back and twisting his moustache, 'That's some acting! I like that. Let's do that again!'

They all laughed at him as if he were a girlfriend's father, being silly.

This went on for over forty-five minutes, during which time he badgered them, rebuked them for their shoddy training, railed at them for their weaknesses, physical and otherwise, and generally carried on like a gruff old man. None of them seemed to mind it, though. It was the price of their admission.

'Enough!' he told them at last. 'Thank you, lovely young ladies, for indulging the whimsy of a tired old man.'

They giggled as they filed out of the room, but they were clearly awed. Fifteen seconds later another twelve filed in. A young man ran up the stairs to Brendan and handed him a list of their names, which Brendan promptly crumpled up and threw on the floor.

'Look at these girls.' He backed up to Liberty.

'Women,' Liberty corrected him automatically. 'None of them can be under nineteen.'

'These aren't women,' he said contemptuously. 'They're just kids. They haven't even lived!'

'Doesn't the role call for a sixteen-year-old?'

'I've never yet met the sixteen-year-old who could play a sixteen-year-old,' said Brendan. 'Desdemona, Juliet, Richard's Queen – they've all been played by full-blown women. It takes a woman to play a woman-child.'

Liberty tried to look at this new batch more carefully. They certainly looked womanly. But maybe Brendan was right. Maybe they were arrested, in a way. Certainly any semblance of natural bearing had been cut short.

'It's not their fault.' Brendan twisted a corner of his moustache thoughtfully. 'They're just looking the way they think we want them to look.'

'What way do we want them to look?' Liberty wanted to know.

'Like little girls dressed up as whores. It wouldn't be so depraved it if were just the appearance we wanted. But we demand the behaviour of them as well, and it's no wonder they don't mature.'

Liberty wanted to ask him why, then, his name was almost always linked to women – girls – young enough to be his daughters. If he believed half of what he was saying, how could he have let Kit get away? Instead, Liberty asked, 'Was Monette Novak a "real woman"?'

He narrowed his eyes at her suspiciously. 'Novak was a mess. And no, little missy, she was not a "real woman". Had she lived on, she most likely wouldn't have amounted to sweet doodily.'

'As an actress, perhaps not. But she could have run a travel agency or played aging ingénues in summer stock, or dealt dope, or *something*. At least she'd be alive!'

Brendan didn't seem to be listening. He leaned back on the hind legs of the folding chair, his fingers hooked into his trousers.

'Lacy was the perfect part for her. Mo didn't have to reach to play her, but she was damned good. Even a stopped clock is right twice a day.'

As Liberty listened to him, she felt his husky voice brush against her. She couldn't resist interrupting him to say, 'You know, it's nice to hear a real actor's voice, a room-shaker, instead of those itsy-bitsy voices' – she pinched her nose – 'so many TV actors have.'

He stared at her strangely then. 'What are you, Liberty Adams? You're no girl. But you're no woman, either.'

'I'm a writer,' she said, and thrust onward. 'Is Kit Ransome a "real woman", Brendan?'

She wasn't sure then whether he'd punch her or throw his arms around her for bringing up that precious name.

'Kit Ransome is one of the most extraordinary women I know. She is absolutely upright and pure. Why, do you know that she actually feeds seagulls on her windowsills? The house is overgrown with wild roses. She jokes that they hold the house on the cliff. But at the back, she has this beautiful little garden. That's the thing about Kit: she knows when to let things grow wild and when to cut them back.'

He paused, ordering his thoughts. 'She's a real blessing to the business, I'll tell you that. And it's because she's a comber of uncultivated places that she brings so much to it. She nurtures the best out of us, and combs up the treasures. This business is full of so many cold-blooded killers, people, men mostly, who are enemies of real art. It's a real pleasure to see another kind of human being attracted to it. Sort of vindicates the whole profession, if you know what I mean. She's got so goddamn much more integrity than all the rest of them, all the rest of those sharks she swims around with...'

'She's got integrity, all right. But maybe her integrity makes her too vulnerable.'

He closed his mouth abruptly, saddened.

'It's a goddamn shame what happened. All of it's a goddamn shame. We ought to be granted a retake. And I must say that I find all this talk about insurance pretty goddamned discouraging.'

There wouldn't be a better opportunity to bring it up. Liberty took it. 'I am correct, am I not, in assuming that you disagree with

200

the Verena Maxwell Alexander casting?' She held her breath, waiting for his answer.

His eyebrows knit. 'I don't follow you.'

'Well,' she said hesitantly, 'what is all *this* about' – she gestured to the girls – 'if you don't disagree?'

He continued to scowl at her.

'All *what*'s about?'

'The cattle call. I was under the impression that the casting was done yesterday. That you'd found your Lacy. Verena Maxwell Alexander.'

He squinted at her as if she were something that had just crawled out from under a rock. 'Where the hell did you hear this?'

She shrugged. 'From a fairly reliable source.'

'Well, I'll be . . .' He stared off into space, and then turned back to Liberty. 'In that case, madam, I'll say good day to you,' he said gruffly.

'But, Brendan . . .'

'I don't think you heard me, little lady. I said good day, and I meant good day. Would you like me to see you out?'

The otherwise chivalrous offer was so threatening that Liberty picked up her pad, her thermos, and her two Tiffany cups and found her own way out before the bull charged.

As she staggered gratefully towards a just-emptied taxi, she wondered whether there might not be something in the air today that had made all three of her interviews go haywire. She needed time at home to review her mess of tapes and notes. What was she going to do about Kit – and about the little green turtle still riding in her bag?

She was so busy wrestling her geometry textbook into her knapsack that she almost didn't see the midnight-blue '57 Packard limousine waiting for her at the corner of Park and Eighty-fifth.

'Shit.'

She walked away. The car followed her. She stopped.

'What's happening?' She spoke to the uniformed driver.

He jerked his head towards the backseat.

The window descended and she looked in.

'Oh,' she said. 'You.'

'That's right.'

He opened the door for her. She stood motionless. 'I was planning to walk. I'm missing gym today. I could use the exercise.'

She made herself look only at his hand on the door.

'Get in.'

'All right. But just for a couple of blocks.'

As she slid in she heard the door locks make an ominous clicking sound.

'You look sensational in that dress. Come and sit a little closer to me.' He pulled down the collar of her trench coat and nibbled at the nape of her neck. She shivered and gave him a hard elbow to the ribs.

'Am I asking for so much?'

'You better not touch me again! Jesus! Some people just can't take a hint.' She rummaged through the silver canisters on the car bar until she came to the one with 'Lemons' engraved on it. She selected a piece of Bazooka bubble gum and unwrapped the comic, reading the fortune aloud.

'"An empty sock can't stand on its own".' She stuffed it into his hand. 'Here! This must be yours.'

They sat there in silence until she said, 'Gee! I just love sitting in traffic. It's such great exercise.'

'I wish the traffic were worse. Then I'd have more time alone with you.'

'Oh, please!'

'I never get to see you anymore. This new schedule of yours –'

'That's the way I planned it!'

'I've waited up for you on more than one night.'

'Yeah? Well, too bad. I told you. You're wasting your time.'

'I want you to be naughty for me again.'

'Forget it! That's over.'

'I don't believe that.'

'Leave me alone!'

'You used to be so perfectly naughty. I wish –'

'Wish all you want. It isn't going to happen.'

'I want you to be naughty for me. I've made up my mind.'

'Well, I don't want to be naughty for you. I've had it. Can't you understand? Don't you see how sick –?'

'Darling girl, why are you going on like this? You know you're the only thing on this earth that keeps me going.'

'Can't you keep yourself going?' She wiped her eyes on her upper sleeve.

'What a naive question! . . . Oh, please don't cry. You know it's no good for me when you cry.'

'Good!' she screamed at him. 'Who do you think I am? Some ten-year-old geek, ashamed of her height and her big tits! I used to be the ugliest, grossest thing on stilts and you were the only one who would look at me. Now people think I'm beautiful. I'm not about to blow it by going back to you!'

'Whatever in the world are you talking about? You know how I value you: not just your body, but your intelligence and your character as well.'

'Value! Listen to you!' She balled up her fists. 'You talk like I'm a piece of art or something. I'm a jade statuette – right?' She shook her head pityingly. 'You don't realise how sick you are. I may not have opened my mouth much since I came back a year ago, but I do know one thing.' She spoke slowly and with meaning. 'You are getting away with murder. People think that because you're so sexy and smart,' she sneered, 'and so cool, that you're the boss. I always thought you were the boss! When you told me to spread my legs –'

It was out before she knew it. She clapped her hand over her mouth and moved away from him.

'I can always depend upon your imaginary audience to bring you around, can't I?'

'Very slick.' She warded him off with her meanest look. 'I've learned something else since I ran away. When I was in stock down in Key West, I learned about real audiences.' She tapped her temple. 'As opposed to imaginary audiences.'

'Ah, but your imaginary audience was always so appreciative of you.'

'Oh, God!' The tears spilled. 'You think I won't remember that for the rest of my life?'

He grasped a lock of hair and began to wind it around his fist, reeling her in. 'Why don't you come out for that audience today, baby?'

'You know why.' She tried to pull away from him.

'You're afraid. Don't be afraid.'

'I'm not afraid of anyone,' came back through clenched teeth.

'That's my brave little runaway.' He gathered her hair into his arms and pulled her towards him.

'Please, oh, please, don't.'

'I can't help it. You're too beautiful!'

'You're wrong.'

'No, you're *wrong*. You're *flawless!*'

'God,' she sobbed.

'You are without sin, my darling girl. Always remember that.'

She nodded her head, cheeks wet and burning.

Then she heard a familiar whrrrrrrr as the the black curtains crossed the windows and the lights dimmed. Soon it was jet black. The limo swerved out of traffic and raced down a side street as she arched upward towards the warmth of his hand.

'Let me feel you,' he begged.

And she did.

12

'*Verena*. Just one word. Don't you think it will look great on a marquee?'

Verena Maxwell Alexander sat in the living room of her parents' East Eighties town house, entertaining Senator Eben Pierce while her mother, Amanda, supervised the cook in the kitchen. Verena was seventeen and built on a large scale, with big cow-brown eyes, a wide mouth, and thick golden hair that fell to the small of her back.

'Sounds great. What acting have you done?' Eben Pierce took a long swallow of his beer.

'Hardly any. I'm studying – you know – taking acting classes.'

'Full-time?'

'I wish. No. I'm a model and a high-school senior full-time.'

'High school, eh? You look much older.'

'I know. Simply everyone says that.' She put on a Southern accent and batted her eyelashes at him.

'You're simply beautiful is what you are.'

'You really think so?' She jumped up and looked into the mirror above his head. 'Really?'

'I said it, didn't I?'

'Might have been reflex.' Verena sat down and brought her hair in front of her face and started to plait one section. 'You know . . . senator talk . . . politics . . . stuff.'

Pierce laughed. 'I've seen your face in lots of ads. I'm a real fan.' He looked at his watch.

'You bored with me? Mandy will be here soon, don't worry.' Verena started another braid on the other side of her face.

'You're very direct. I like that.'

'My mother says I'm rude.'

'You probably are . . .'

Verena's head bounced up. She let go of the half-plaited braid.

'. . . sometimes. We're all rude sometimes,' Pierce finished with a grin.

'Not Mandy. She's perfect that way. Poppup's perfect little princess.'

'Who?'

Verena collapsed over her knees and her hair fell forward into her face.

'You mean to tell me you don't know who my mother is?'

'I hate to sound like a chauvinist, but . . . Mrs Rush Alexander?'

'Mrs Rush!' She chuckled. 'Wait'll I tell her that. No, what I mean is you might be hot American shit, but Mandy's hot English shit, and believe me . . .' She went back to examining her ends.

Pierce swallowed some beer and appeared to be figuring. 'Let's see, now . . . that must make you one-quarter hot shit, and I've got to tell you I find that hard to believe.'

'What do you mean?' She rose to her feet, looming over him.

'I mean, you seem more like ninety-five percent to me,' he finished smoothly.

She shrank back to the hassock. 'Her father was only the thirty-ninth Duke of Scarborough, the screwball Viceroy of Ceylon.'

'It's Sri Lanka now.'

'It Sri is.'

'Did you know your grandfather?'

'No, he croaked before I was born. Did your grandparents croak before you were born?'

'No, as a matter of fact, three of them lived to be quite old.'

'Your grandmother Pierce lived till she was ninety-six.'

Amanda Alexander breezed into the living room, smelling of gardenias, twinkling with sapphires, and carrying a tray. She wore a kimono of midnight blue and her eye shadow was emerald green. She was built on the same scale as her daughter, only she wore her blonde hair in short, soft curls, and her eyes were hazel. She had the squint around the eyes of a woman too vain to wear glasses.

Verena nudged the senator. 'She knows everything. Watch her.'

He jumped up and helped her with the tray. 'You're looking lovely, Mrs Alexander.' Together they set it down on the butler's table.

'There are spring rolls. Call me Amanda, please. So lovely to meet you, Senator. Verena darling, would you go and get the duck sauce? There's a jar in the refrigerator. You can put some in one of those pink dishes.'

'What pink dishes?' Verena stayed where she was dangling her leg.

'The medium-sized ones with the plum design.'

'Which medium-sized ones with the plum design?' She yawned widely.

'The ones in the small sideboard.'

'Ma, can't Anna get them?' Verena jumped up. 'Here, I'll ring for you.'

'Verena!' Amanda warned. 'I'll see about them myself Senator . . . I'm sure my daughter can keep you company.'

'Yes, she can.' He winked at Verena and she batted her eyes at him.

'What are servants for if not to serve?' Verena muttered under her breath.

Amanda gave her a mild look of reproval and left the room.

'I know where I saw your name recently!' He snapped his fingers. 'In *The Wall Street Journal*. You've just been signed to be the new "Face" of Ruba.'

'That's me.' She framed her face with her hands. 'What do you think?'

'What do I think? Did your father get you the job?' Pierce grinned at her.

Her face fell. 'Very funny.'

'It happens.' He shrugged. 'Look at me.'

'You look pretty cute to me. Like you do on the tube, only thinner. Molto cute, I'd say.'

'Thanks, but what I mean is, my father-in-law got me my job.'

'You were a gasoline attendant before?' Verena tucked her legs up under her and smirked at him.

'No. A congressman.'

'So? Big deal.' She tossed her hair over her shoulder. 'Who cares?'

'Don't you like to think all senators have been duly voted in?'

'Duly voted in?' She shook her head. 'You're talking to the *wrong* person. Talk to Mandy about that. She's got definite ideas. I got no ideas. I'm too young to vote, too busy to read, and too old for heroes.' She held her hair ends up to the light.

'You mean that?' He leaned forward on the narrow white love seat.

'I don't know.' She shrugged. 'I just said it. Look, Eben – okay to call you Eben?'

He nodded.

'Okay, Eben. What kind of name is Eben?'

'A family name.'

She said it several times. 'I like it. Anyway, I wouldn't know from politics. I wouldn't even know what state you're from.'

'Virginia.'

'Or what you do all day.'

'I sit on several committees.'

'Or why you're here for dinner.'

'To talk to your father.'

'And to tell you the truth, I'd rather be a –'

'– million miles away.' They spoke in unison.

'You married?' Verena asked.

Amanda came back with two small pink bowls and set them on the tray. 'I'm sorry!' she said.

'What about?' Verena leaned forward and picked up a spring roll.

'Verena!'

Verena stopped with the spring roll halfway to her mouth.

'Aren't you going to offer the senator some first?'

'Oh!' She picked up the tray and swung it towards him. 'Take a spring roll, Eben. They're my mom's speciality. Watch the mustard, though.'

'Thanks.'

'So, *are* you married?' Verena dunked a spring roll into the duck sauce and the hot mustard.

'No,' Pierce answered.

'How come?' Verena popped it into her mouth. Her eyes watered from the hot mustard. She looked around for something to drink, grabbed his beer off the table, and gulped it.

'My wife died three years ago.'

Verena squinted at Eben. 'Really? A widow? You're not that old.'

'Verena!' Amanda's tone was sharp.

'Widow*er*.' He reached for his beer.

'For *heaven's* sake, Verena.' Amanda's sapphires flashed as her hand flew to the soft gap in her collarbone.

'I'm sorry, Eben. Really.'

'It's okay.'

Amanda asked, 'Senator, would you care for another beer?'

Verena spoke over her. 'Do you have a girlfriend?'

'Yes,' said Pierce, 'to both of your questions.'

Amanda got up and the sleeve of her kimono brushed against the carved jade figure on the table. Pierce caught it before it hit the floor.

'Oh ... thank you. This is one of Rush's most cherished pieces.' She replaced it gingerly.

'Yep. Great reflexes. I'll be right back. Don't worry. I'll give you plenty of time to talk.' Verena swept past Anna, the housekeeper, who was carefully positioning each piece of silverware on the already perfectly set table. She tweaked Anna's bottom.

'Just get the senator's beer, Miss Verena.' Anna spoke without looking up.

Verena walked into the pantry, grabbed an apple, and ducked into the refrigerator for a beer. When she brought it and an opener back into the living room, the senator was saying, 'You must be very busy.'

Verena groaned as she opened his beer and refilled his glass. She went to sit next to her mother on the sofa and continued to crunch on her apple.

Her mother took the apple away and cut it up for her with a paring knife.

'Mother's work is never done,' Verena said to no one in particular.

Amanda went on, 'Yes, I like to keep busy. I like to work with Verena, keeping her career on track ... keeping *her* on track.' She hugged Verena. 'She's very talented. A photographer's ideal.'

Verena pulled away. 'Come on, Ma. Eben doesn't want to hear you carry on. Enough already with my career. Can't we talk about something else?'

'By all means, darling, redirect us.' She fingered a small silk pillow.

'What's your girlfriend look like?'

'Verena, a good conversationalist does not ask personal questions.'

'A good conversationalist is Boring City, Ma.'

'But, Verena, you've only just met the senator.'

Pierce smiled.

'Eben and I know each other plenty.' Verena eyed the last rice cake. 'Can't you stop being a mother ever ... just for one teeny tiny minute?'

She blushed. 'Senator, one day when my daughter has a child of her own, she'll see how hard it is to stop acting like a mother.'

'Amanda, I'm sure Verena knows how really lucky she is to have you for a mother.' Pierce stared at Verena's sullen face.

Amanda stiffened slightly and stood up. 'My husband is home.'

'I didn't hear anything.' Pierce looked around.

'It's her sixth sense,' Verena put in.

'I'll just be a minute, Senator. Verena, will you come with me?'

'No, thanks. I'll wait for him here.'

'Will you at least fix him a drink?' she said as she left the room.

'No chance.' Verena lunged over to the bar and opened the silver canister marked 'Lemons'. She took out a piece of Bazooka bubble gum and began to unwrap it.

'You're mother's quite young, isn't she?' Pierce asked. Verena didn't look up. She just shrugged.

'She seems younger than you, in a way,' Pierce finished.

Verena wandered over to Eben and handed him her fortune.

'"Good fortune is in the offing",' he read aloud.

'"Offing" is a weird word, isn't it?'

'Yes, it –'

'Well, well, well! It's a real surprise to have both of my girls home tonight.' Rush Alexander came in with his wife on his arm.

Verena made a face before she turned around and smiled sweetly at her father, snapping her gum.

'Evening, Daddy dearest.'

'Verena's made you a drink, haven't you, dear?' Amanda swept past her.

Verena looked at her father and shook her head with a smile.

'Eben. How are you? Good to see you.' Rush shook Pierce's hand and patted him on the shoulder.

'It's good to see you, sir.' Pierce rose.

Verena sat back down on the hassock and imitated them under her breath. Amanda scowled at her and went over to the bar to make her husband a vodka martini.

'Nothing but champagne will do tonight, my dear.' Rush rubbed his hands together.

'Champagne?' Rush winked at Eben. 'Tonight we have something special to celebrate.'

'What is it, Rush? What are we celebrating?' Amanda watched him.

'Not till we get the champagne.'

Verena's hand hovered over the tasselled cord that summoned the butler.

210

'No, Verena, I'll see to it myself.' Amanda left the room.

Rush stood over Verena with his hands on her shoulders. 'Senator, I hope you don't mind sharing with us some very good news about my lovely daughter.'

'On the contrary.' Pierce beamed at Verena as she screwed up her face. 'I'm honoured.'

'What news?' Verena tried to work loose from his hands.

'Champagne first,' he said, squeezing her again.

Amanda came back in, followed by the butler carrying a tray of tulip glasses and a bottle of Dom Pérignon champagne in a silver ice bucket.

'Thank you, William.'

Verena counted the glasses to make sure there was one for her, and looked at the label. 'Ooh, yummy. Dom.'

Amanda looked at her wrily. 'A seventeen-year-old shouldn't be on such intimate terms with expensive champagne.'

The cork popped gently as Rush eased it off. He barely finished filling the glasses before Verena grabbed one.

'All right,' Verena said. 'Now, will you tell us what the big deal is?'

Rush raised his glass. 'Very well, then: to my daughter's first acting job in Hollywood!'

Pierce clinked glasses with each of them and drank.

'Cheers!' he said. 'Congratulations!'

'What job?' Verena took the gum out of her mouth and looked for somewhere to park it. She settled on the base of her glass.

'What's all this about, Kazimir?' Amanda said sharply. She set her glass down on the tray, untouched.

'I've just had a little talk with Kit Ransome. It seems she's been talking with Max Rugoff. He's Verena's acting teacher, Eben. Kit says she's going to give Verena the lead part in one of her movies.'

Verena jumped up and down, spilling her champagne all over the rug. 'I can't believe it! Is it true? What part?'

'Please, Verena. Calm down.' Amanda put her hand on Verena's shoulder.

'The movie is already under way.' He spoke past her to his wife.

'Oh, Daddy.' Verena kissed him quickly on the cheek.

'Not so fast, Verena. We need to discuss this. We have to consider your school.'

Verena swung around to face her mother. 'Ma, *please*. There's nothing to discuss –'

'Verena,' Amanda interrupted her. 'Our guest does not want to hear you whine.'

'It's all yours, baby.' He grabbed her round the waist. 'Run and look in my case. There's a script in it.'

'A script! A real script!' Verena tore into the hall and swivelled the dials on the combination lock of his briefcase. The script was lying on top. She read the cover sheet.

'*Last Chance*?' she said, walking back into the living room. 'Now, where have I heard of that before?'

Pierce was over in the corner, looking particularly hard at some French plates displayed on the wall. 'I thought you'd be happy for her.' Rush grinned at his wife.

'Rush, I'm *not* happy about this.' Her voice was calm, but she looked as if she was about to cry. She nodded nervously towards the senator.

'Verena, darling,' Rush said, 'why don't you show the senator the games room while your mother and I ... discuss your wonderful news?'

Verena took Pierce's arm. 'Shoot much pool, Senator?'

She dragged him through the dining room, down the narrow stairs to the games room. An art-deco bar, salvaged from an ocean liner, ran along one wall. Besides the pool table, there were a couple of video games and a row of old wooden slot machines. In the back, behind the stairs, were the Betamax and the movie screen.

She pulled a cue off the wall. 'Are you by any chance a hustler, son?'

Pierce took down a stick and rolled it back and forth on the table. 'It's a good table.'

'My mother always buys the best of everything.' Verena said, bored. 'She studies all these magazines, and asks people's advice, and then she takes her money and buys the best. I'll break.'

The senator stood across the table and said, 'Mind if I take off my jacket?'

'Of course not. Mandy keeps it too hot down here. She thinks the heat will get rid of the damp smell.' Verena inhaled deeply. 'Musk city.'

'Eight ball, all right?'

He nodded.

'I'm solids, then,' Verena said as the seven ball went into the side pocket. 'I'll get you another beer, on one condition.'

'What's that?' He grinned.

'That you give me sips.'

'You're on.'

She went behind the bar and opened the refrigerator.

Returning with the open bottle, she took a gulp.

'Sorry.' She wiped her mouth. 'I love the first sip. You can have the rest. You could be arrested for corrupting a minor, you know.'

'Some minor.' He bent to shoot. 'Your parents always have these little conferences?'

'Oh,' said Verena, waving her hand, 'isn't that what marriage is all about? Little summit meetings? Subcommittees? Isn't that what your marriage was all about?'

The senator shook his head.

'Well, take my advice and don't remarry. I think marriage is a drag. I mean, look at them.' She pointed to the ceiling. 'He works fifty billion hours a day. I mean, they almost never *do* it.'

The senator cleared his throat.

'And look at my mother! All she does is redecorate our house every six months. And wait for him to come home.'

'She's busy managing you, isn't she?' Eben's ball careened off the three ball and missed the corner pocket.

'Good shot, EP. Sure, but not for much longer, if I can help it. I don't need her any more. I can take care of myself.' Verena sat on the edge of the table with her arm behind her, trying to make a tough shot. She missed.

'Tough luck, kid. Good try.' Pierce waved his cue at her to get her off the table.

Verena moved behind Eben, studying his shot. 'If my mother doesn't let me take this part, I'll kill her.' The eight ball fell into the side pocket.

'Don't do that,' said the senator. 'It would wipe you out as an actress.'

'Very funny.'

'Your mother doesn't want you to be an actress?'

'No. She thinks all actors are crazy nuts. But she's just got to let me do this. She's probably angry it was Rush's idea and not hers.' He shot while her head was turned. 'You just cheat.'

'What else would you expect from a man who believes in marriage?'

'Why?'

'Probably because I'm in love, Verena.'

'Good for you,' she said absently. 'I wish they'd get it together up there. They're upstairs talking about my life like I don't exist.'

'Is that what it feels like to be the daughter of such a powerful man?'

She snapped her gum. 'Why do you care?'

He shrugged and broke. 'My father was a powerful man, too. I know it isn't always easy.' He spun a ball into the corner pocket.

'Actually, it sucks.' She began to blow an enormous bubble.

He stood up and held his finger to the bubble. 'Sucks?' he echoed. 'He just got you a part in a movie, didn't he?'

She popped it and gathered it in. 'Yeah, he's great. A perfect dad. Guess I should be glad I'm not still in Key West.'

'What were you doing there?'

Verena stared at him, her big eyes blinking. 'I ran away.'

Pierce cleared his throat. 'Your shot.'

She bent to shoot and missed. 'What else do you want to know about him?'

'Oh, I wonder why your father wanted to see me here instead of at the office.'

She popped another bubble. 'That's a cinch. He wants to screw you.'

She took another sip of his beer while he pocketed three balls and missed one.

He winked at her and gave her the table.

'So, tell me about her.' She leaned over the table.

'Her?'

'This girlfriend of yours that's so special.'

'Oh, her!' he finished off his beer. 'She's smart, she's funny . . .'

'Pretty?'

'Very.'

'Tall?'

'Tiny.'

'Blonde?'

'Red hair. Violet eyes.'

'Violent eyes?'

'Vi-o-*let*.'

'Oh! Nice. Work?'

'A reporter.'

'What kind?'

'First-rate.'

'What kind?'

'She writes about famous people. About how they make a place for themselves and how the rest of us fit around that place.'

'You mean how people like *me* fit. You're already famous.'
Verena made her last shot. She had put seven balls away in a row.
'I'm hungry. To hell with them. Let's go upstairs.'

At dinner, Amanda smiled brightly at everyone but said very little.
After making sure they had enough meat, she excused herself
before the final course.

Verena raised an eyebrow to Rush. 'She all right?'

'Why shouldn't she be?'

'I think I'll check on her anyway.'

'Do as you wish, but feel free to join us later in the library.'

'Can I have some of that fifty-billion-year-old brandy?' she
asked.

Without waiting for his 'yes', she went into the kitchen to fix a
nightcap.

Her mother was sitting at her vanity unit when Verena knocked
softly and went in carrying a glass of warm vanilla milk and a
Valium. 'I thought you could use this.' She put the glass and the
pill down on her vanity unit and stood back.

Amanda was tissuing the cold cream into her face in tiny little
circles, the way she did it to Verena. She stopped long enough to
swallow the valium with a little milk, using a tissue to keep her
greasy fingerprints off the glass.

'Is this one of my Valiums or one of yours?'

Verena smiled at her little joke.

She spoke to her own reflection. 'You're going to take your
father up on his offer, aren't you, Verena?'

Verena said in a small voice, 'I'd be nuts not to, Ma.'

'Without an audition? I didn't hear him mention anything about
an audition.'

She stopped and turned around to face Verena.

Verena blushed.

'Do you know what movie this is?'

'Yeah,' she said slowly, '*Last Chance.*'

'Do you know anything about it except its name?'

She shook her head and stared at her mother. Now that her
make-up was off, her face looked shiny like a worn pearl. *She looks
old*, Verena thought. *And it's my fault.*

'*Last Chance,*' her mother said carefully, 'is the set on which
Monette Novak took her own life.'

215

Verena sank to the carpeted floor and crossed her legs. 'I knew I'd heard of it.'

Amanda began to slap at her hair with her brush. 'Lots and lots of people are talking about it, my dear. I wouldn't mind it if I thought you were coming by the part honestly. Do you actually think Max Rugoff had anything to do with this?'

'Gimme a break, Ma, I'll work hard.'

'Verena you're young. You don't see what I do.'

'I don't? Like what?'

'The acting world is filled with misfits, with crazy sad people. A break like this could start you off on the wrong foot. People might get the wrong idea.'

'Stop it. That isn't fair. You should be happy for me.'

'Happy to have your name linked to Monette Novak's and Brendan Marsh's?'

'Brendan Marsh!' Verena jumped up. 'You mean Brendan Marsh is in the same movie I'm going to be in?'

Amanda went to the closet and took off her kimono, draped it neatly on a padded hanger, and took down her chenille robe, the pink one that matched the flowered border on her bedspread.

'I didn't realise you were such a fan of his.'

'You kidding me?'

'I forget that you stay up all night watching movies instead of studying.'

'Watching movies *is* studying, Ma, and anyway, I hardly do that any more. Brendan Marsh – wow!'

Amanda went to the bathroom and ran the water. She came out with a cold cloth. She put it on her eyes and lay down on the bed.

'Ma, please! I want this part. You know how much I want to be an actress. How can you do this to me? I hate modelling.' Verena was near tears. 'Please, Ma.'

'I suppose if your father wants you to have it on these terms ...'

'Yippee!' When she went over to kiss her mother, she saw the tears seeping out from underneath the cloth over her eyes.

'Don't worry, Ma.' She touched her hand. 'I'll be all right. Really. I won't do anything to embarrass you. Promise.'

'Will you, my baby?' Verena felt her mother's body begin to tremble. 'Will you?'

Verena tucked her mother in and went down to the library to say good night to the senator. She didn't feel so much like celebrating now.

'I won't hear of you deserting us again.'

'But, Dad . . .'

'Daughters' – he smirked to the senator – 'they give you a run for your money. I don't care what anybody says about sons. Stay and have some brandy.'

Verena made the worst face she could and walked over to pour herself an enormous snifter full.

She plopped down in the old chair next to her father's and chugalugged a quarter of the snifter. Her eyes smarted and her vision began to swim.

'Rush,' the senator said, 'are you sure we shouldn't postpone our talk?'

'My daughter and I have nothing to hide from each other. Isn't that true, my dear?'

She answered him with an upraised glass and a hiccup, then dropped her head on her arm, her hair falling over her face. She was drowsy, but she managed, within the space of five minutes, to feign sleep without giving into it. Max Rugoff would have been proud of her.

After a while, she heard Rush say, 'She's asleep now – my girl's had a busy day.'

'All right, Rush. I know you've asked me over here to try to fix the Ransome Enterprises case. I know you're the best lawyer in New York and I hate to be rude to you after you've shown me such lovely hospitality, but I'd just as soon you saved your manipulation techniques for someone else.'

'Is that why you think I've asked you here?' Rush lit up his pipe. Verena was roused by the smell of Balkan Sobrani.

'Well, it doesn't take a whole lot of deep thinking to figure out why Ransome's best friend and business partner would ask the senator leading the investigation over to his house for one of his notorious "library chats".'

'Greenhause is going to testify before your committee next week – right?'

'Is he?'

'Come on, Senator. *I'm* not being investigated. It's no secret that your committee has offered Greenhause a very sweet deal to start naming names.'

'If you say so, Rush.'

'I think I have some information that may help you and your committee.'

Verena opened her eyes and peered at them through her hair. She saw Pierce reaching for his glass of Drambuie, grinning at her father.

'Information that's going to help me? Or information that's going to help your client?'

'Archer Ransome is not my client.' Rush picked up a bulky folder.

Pierce folded his hands over his stomach. 'But he is your best friend.'

'In this folder you'll find papers that document consistent corporate fraud by Archer Ransome. Bribery, illegal manipulation of markets, violation of anti-trust laws, conspiracy, violation of currency regulations. Among other things.'

The senator sat up straight.

'See for yourself.' Rush threw the folder onto his lap. Pierce caught the folder and opened it slowly. He began to read the top sheet. He looked up. Rush was slouched in his chair, shoes off, pipe dangling.

'Why give all this to me?' Pierce leafed gingerly through the papers.

'A junior senator looking for re-election. Excuse me, looking to be *elected* in his own right.'

Pierce looked at Rush and closed the file. He stood up. 'Well, I have to hand it to you, Rush. I'm surprised.' He picked up a gold-framed photograph from the mantelpiece. 'Is that Ransome's wife?'

'Yes, that was Cassandra Wentworth Ransome.'

'She's beautiful ... She died years ago, didn't she?' He still held the picture.

'Yes ... a tragedy.'

'You realise you'll have to testify yourself. These alone aren't going to be enough.'

'I'm prepared to.'

'You're prepared to testify against Ransome ... your business partner, your best friend? To do a John Dean? You're prepared for that?'

'Look at those papers, Pierce, and you'll see the systematic fraud that A. J. Ransome has committed. Several of those papers deal with his tax shelter in the Bahamas where he launders money. This cash is used to chase the stock up or down, depending on what he wants. That piece there, that dark grey paper marked "eyes only" –

that's the memo outlining the planned coup in Macao.'

'I suppose you want immunity?'

'Yes. Even though it's not really necessary.' Rush grinned.

Pierce replaced the photograph.

'Look, do we have a deal, Pierce, or not?'

Without turning around, Eben answered. 'I'll have to see the originals. No copies. If they check out... then I guess we do.'

13

Liberty stood with her keys in her hand and listened to the music playing on the other side of the door to her loft.

It was the Beatles singing about Old Flat Top.

Making as little noise as possible, she fit her three keys into her three locks and nudged the door open with her shoulder.

She wasn't sure what she was expecting to see, but it certainly wasn't Eben Pierce lying on her sofa in the dark, balancing a bottle of Beck's on his bare chest, with a six-pack lying on the rug by his dangling arm. She walked across and stood over him. He was listening to the Beatles with his eyes closed. He opened one eye and said, 'You're late. I was beginning to worry.'

'I'm touched. I didn't realise we had a date.'

'I brought a peace offering. A bottle of champagne. It's on ice. And mashed peaches, Lib. For your favourite drink.'

'Points for memory, Pierce. *Ex*-favourite drink.' The driest of dry champagnes poured over pulverised peach: a Bellini. They'd discovered it together in Italy, years ago. She stuck her hand wearily on her hip. 'Now, just how did you get in?'

He held up a finger and chugged his beer. 'That would be telling!'

'Look.' She blew her hair out of her line of vision. 'Do you mind if I turn that off?'

She strode over to the stereo and yanked the needle off the record. When she stood up, he was there behind her, locking her arms softly behind her. His lips feather-brushed the bones behind her ears. She mashed her ear into her shoulder to kill the sensation and pulled away.

'Cut it out, Pierce. Technique doesn't count any more.'

He followed her back to the couch, where she sat down and began to take off her boots. He took over for her, and kissing her shinbone, pulled off one boot. She shivered. He pulled off the other boot and kissed her leg again.

'Mmmmmmm,' he said, 'I've sure missed that flavour.'

She shook him off. 'Oh, please, Pierce!'

'Please what? Your wish is my command.'

She screwed up her face. 'Make me a cup of coffee. There's instant on the shelf above the sink.'

He leaned back and consulted an imaginary wristwatch. 'Caffeine this late, Lib? If you're not ready for your Bellini yet, how about a spritzer instead? One of your bachelorette specials? With a hit of Triple Sec?'

'I give up, Pierce. Go make it.'

He stood up with her and took her chin into his hand as he ground a kiss into her lips. She felt his cock hard against her stomach. She pulled away with an effort.

'Spritzer!' she gasped, propelling him towards the kitchen. She went to her vanity unit and removed the photograph of the 1940's fairy-tale princess and put it in the bottom drawer. Her hands were shaking. She had never tried to explain that snapshot and she wasn't about to try tonight. She tore off her blazer, her slacks, and her blouse, stripping naked. 'So what?' she spoke to her reflection. 'This is my house.'

He came back with a tall iced glass. 'My Little Red Flag,' he said tenderly, holding out the glass.

She took the drink and slipped past him on her way to the bathroom. Taking a long slug of the spritzer, she looked in the mirror and said, 'You never told me how you got in, Pierce.' She switched on the shower and adjusted it to cold.

'Can't we keep it a mystery?' he called from the bedroom.

'Fuck you, Pierce!' she hollered over the noise of the shower as she stepped into it. 'A single woman living alone on the outskirts of civilisation needs to know why her security system is inadequate.'

'Got the keys from an old lover boy.'

Liberty gasped.

'Aren't you going to ask me which one?'

Liberty shook her head, speechless.

'One of my aides paid a visit to a certain penthouse –'

'Not to Broadway Bob!' Liberty found her voice.

'Broadway Bob. Now, isn't that chummy. My aide told him it was a matter of national security.'

Liberty tore aside the shower curtain and marched out to him, dripping wet. He was sitting at her vanity unit, opening bottles of perfume and sniffing them. He turned to look at her.

'He what?'

'Do you actually expect me to answer you when you're standing there like that?'

Liberty's face grew hot and she stormed back to the shower.

Eben went on. 'He's a good man, this aide. I told him to do whatever he had to do to secure the key.'

'"Secure the key"? Christ, Pierce, you sound like Haldeman and Ehrlichman.' She didn't hear a reply, so she went on, hoping to get a rise out of him. 'Marvellous use of the taxpayers' money.'

'Frankly,' he spoke up at last, 'I'm surprised you actually gave a duplicate to anyone.'

'Kiss my arse,' Liberty growled, but she couldn't help grinning. 'Poor Bob,' she mused, 'he must have coughed up the key and made a beeline for his heart pills.'

She heard Eben laugh and then yell back. 'What do you keep in some of these little tiny bottles? LSD?'

'You're really an arsehole, Pierce, when you try to be funny, you know that?'

'I guess you're funny enough for both of us.'

'Fuck yourself.'

'You know, Lib, this really is a nice vanity unit I got you. I'm glad you kept it.'

Liberty turned off the shower and grabbed a towel before heading back to Eben, who was blithely going through the drawers of the unit. Barely missing his fingers, she closed the bottom drawer.

'I don't believe you!' She shoved him off the vanity stool and planted herself in his place, glaring at him in the mirror. He was grinning.

'Out with it, you smug scumbag.'

'And to think she was raised by the highest order of nuns!'

She ignored him. 'What other gentlemen did your happy helper try to hit on for the key?'

He ducked into the bathroom. 'Beautiful, Lib. Super tub. Super shower head. Hey, how come you didn't soak in your tub? Come on, Lib. Full day of being mean? A little hydrotherapy'd do you a world of good. I'd-a kept you company. It's the perfect size, this tub. Did you have it custom-made?'

'Yeah,' said Liberty, following him in, 'and I'm gonna get in it and slash my wrists if you don't tell me what else you've done.'

'Let's see.' He sat, musing, on the edge of the tub. 'What other boyfriends of yours did we visit tonight? A psychiatrist. The one with the *haute clientèle*.'

'You went to Gavin! He must have thought you were psychotic.' She went back to cream her face and legs.

'Not *me*, my dear. But he threw my aide out of his office. A pretty well-developed guy for a shrink.'

'Yes, he is,' she said dryly.

'A *sixty-year-old* shrink, Lib. Don't you sleep with anybody who isn't a senior citizen?'

'Drop it, Pierce!'

'Then there was the writer.' He came out carrying her loofah sponge, sniffing at it. 'You know, the skinny, nervous one. He was real cooperative.'

'Really?'

'He put us on to good old Bob. "Check with Ross," he told us. "If anyone has it, Ross has it." Dressing so soon, Lib? I was just getting used to your lovely nakedness.' He leaned against the door jamb and his eyes travelled slowly up from her toes.

Liberty wrapped her silk patchwork robe around her and shook her hair out of a towel.

'You're hair's so gorgeous!'

She edged past him and caught his smell: lime and beer. 'Look. Are you hungry? I'm hungry. All I've had today was some horrible aeroplane food, two pots of tea, and a cup of luke-warm espresso.'

She felt him close behind her as she went to the kitchen.

'This is an amazing place, this loft of yours.'

Liberty yanked open a cupboard and pulled out a jar of peanut butter and an open package of saltines.

'Well, it's hardly a Georgetown town house, but it suits me. Just give me a dozen closets and a hundred cubbyholes and I'm a happy chippie.'

Eben put a hand on her arm. She stopped spreading peanut butter on her cracker and stared at his hand, gritting her teeth.

'Look,' he said gently, turning her to face him, tipping her chin up to look into her eyes, 'why don't you just ease up a little bit, Lib? I know this is difficult for you. You want an apology? I'll give you an apology. I'm sorry I broke in, Lib. But I knew it was the only way I was going to get to see you again. I know how stubborn you are, girl.'

Liberty blushed. 'Eben. I –'

'I know, Lib, I know.'

'It's just that I can't seem to *deal* with your being here. Look at me.' She held out a trembling hand. 'I'm shaking all over. And, Eben, I don't shake.'

'For Bob, and Gavin, and What's-his-name the writer you may not.' He laughed gently and brought her towards him. 'But for me...'

They kissed. This time she couldn't pull away. She leaned weakly against the kitchen counter.

'Woman can't live by sex alone,' he said hoarsely. Lifting her onto the high stool, he set about plundering the refrigerator, the cupboards, the drawers. When he was finished, the counter between the two stools was laid out with caviar, lemon peel, thin wafer crackers, cream cheese, two crystal goblets, a pitcher of pulverised peach, and a bottle of Pol Roger '42 in a bowl of ice.

He turned down the lights, lit a candle, and put on the soundtrack to *A Hard Day's Night*. Liberty wolfed down crackers and cream cheese with just a film of caviar on top and washed it down with the Bellini, which was so dry it melted like peach-flavoured snow on the tip of her tongue.

She was light-headed after one glass. Perched there in her own cosy kitchen, feeling bathed and full and vaguely but not uncomfortably sleepy, Liberty stared at Eben. He stared back, chewing, grey eyes friendly and mild. He grinned at her and she wanted to kiss him.

Instead, she hoisted her glass and said, 'So. Congratulations on your graduation from the Hobo Jungle. Up with the August Hundred, eh? I'm impressed.' She was referring to his recent appointment to the Senate.

'The governor appointed me, Lib.'

'Ah, yes, the governor appointed you.'

'Yep.' He swirled the champagne around in his glass.

Just like he appointed you to marry his daughter.

'How is it up there in the Senate? You were looking pretty comfy down there in the House.'

'True,' he said.

'The other senators resent the new boy on the block? The nonelected pariah. Goodness, Pierce, this must be a totally new sensation for you: rejection.'

'I'm doing okay.'

'Sure you are,' she laughed.

'I've missed you, Lib.'

'I've missed you,' she told him. 'I won't lie. You were the best friend I ever had.'

He was the *only* friend she'd ever had. They were quiet for a while, listening to the Beatles. Liberty realised she lacked friends, just as she lacked family. At St Mary's on the River she'd made no lasting ties. Most of the girls had gone on to be waitresses or correction officers. The few eggheads who'd befriended her because they admired her ability to score high on tests without ever studying had also gone the way of all flesh: one had run off with a roadie when the Who came to Nyack to play junior year, and the other two had gone on to take vows. When Liberty got to college, it seemed she was too busy catching up on all the reading she was supposed to have been doing in high school. Then, the job at *Mademoiselle* and the affair with Eben had taken her out of the college's social circles.

Liberty pushed herself back from the counter. 'Look, Eben, I really don't know what you're doing here.'

'I told you. I think we should start over. I didn't want you to mistake our get-together at the Oak Room for a shakedown, but I guess you did. So now I'm here.'

'For another shakedown?' She wandered away from him over to the kitchen window. 'Don't look now,' she said, 'but one of your bodyguards is playing with himself.'

'What?'

Pierce came up behind her and, resting his hands on her shoulders, looked out the window onto the street below. Beneath the blinking red light of a garage three doors down, a small dark man stood idly fanning playing cards. 'He's not my bodyguard. No cards, no dames, no booze.'

'Well, he's not mine!'

He whirled her around to face him. 'What do you mean, "not yours"? Why would you be needing a bodyguard?'

'It's just a joke, Pierce!' She pushed past him and started to clean up. 'I don't have a bodyguard. I may have a tail, but that's not my tail. Who knows? Maybe I have a new tail.'

He blocked her way and took the sponge out of her hand.

'Are you serious? What do you mean, "tail"?'

She examined his socks. 'I don't think I like that look on your face, Pierce.'

'What look?'

She forced herself to look at him. 'Like somebody's dad on prom night. Proprietary. Yes, I am serious. Ever since I took on the Kitsia story, there's been this little guy . . . He follows me wherever I go. But he never bothers me. I said, stop looking at me like that, Pierce. I can take care of myself. I've done all right so far, *n'est-ce pas?*'

'I don't like strange little men following you everywhere you go. I'm giving you one of my guys first thing tomorrow.'

'More squandering of the taxpayers' money? No, thanks, I don't want one of your guys. I just want to finish my story in peace. Jesus' – she threw up her arms – 'I'm beginning to feel like a pterodactyl going down in the tarpits.'

'A what?'

'The harder I struggle, the deeper I get sucked in.'

A lewd gleam came into his eye. 'Did somebody say "suck"?' He picked up her hand and pulled the tips of her fingers into his mouth.

She pulled them back and went to the bathroom to brush her teeth.

'Go to my vanity unit, will you?' she called to him over the sound of running water.

'What's that you say?'

'I said, go to my vanity unit and open the drawer.'

'Which drawer?'

'Top one, far right.'

She heard him rummaging around.

'Wait a minute, Lib, this is a controlled substance you've got in here. You know I can't handle that.'

'Force yourself. For me.'

'What do I do with it?'

She yelled over the sound of the tap. 'Twist me up a joint, of course!'

'What with?'

'Your little fingers and the rolling papers in the second drawer down in the centre.'

'Well, I'll try.'

'Attaboy!' she said through the toothpaste.

When she came out of the bathroom, he was sitting on the bed with his lap all covered with reefer, grinning sheepishly. She relieved him of the folded newspaper full of reefer and a pathetically lumpy joint.

'That's the best I could do, Lib. Afraid I'm out of practice.'

'Well, Senator.' She patted him on the shoulder. 'It's the effort that counts.' She poured the rest of the marijuana back into the plastic bag and put it away in the drawer. Then she struck a stick match and lit up, toking so hard that she began to choke. He took the joint away from her. She found herself staring at the muscular ridges on his belly and wondering what had been so attractive about Archer Ransome. *This* was her type; this had always been her type. He held out the joint for her again. She exhaled and said, 'We had a totally contrived relationship, you realise that. The Liberty you think you know is not the Liberty that was, or is.'

'What kind of talk is that?'

'Listen to you. Listen to what you just said. "What kind of talk is that?" Why don't you listen to what I said and respond?'

'What did you just say?'

Liberty looked at the joint burning in his hand. 'Have you had some of this yet?'

'Can't you tell?'

She looked at the joint again. She looked at his eyes. 'Guess you have at that. What do you want to know, again?'

'I wanted to know what you just said.'

'Tenacious, aren't you?' Liberty gathered her grey matter together and squeezed hard.

He laughed at her dramatic effort.

'This is serious,' she said.

'Yeah?' He reached out to grab her, but she swung away.

'Don't distract me. I'm trying to think of what I just said. I hear it. It's coming. It's almost here. It was ... let me see if I got this right: the Liberty you think you know – the Liberty of your memories, and the Liberty I represented myself to you as – isn't the Liberty you see right now.' She pulled the joint out of his hand and inhaled, blowing the smoke into his face. 'I was the world's biggest faker. I lied to you. The statute of limitations is up now, so it won't hurt to confess. So if you want to leave right now, you're welcome to.'

'I don't want to leave,' he said quietly. 'I want to hear about the "real" Liberty.'

She took a deep breath. 'The real Liberty wasn't raised by patrician nuns up at Maryknoll. The real Liberty was raised at St Mary's on the River.'

'Sounds like a decent enough place to me.'

'It was a down-at-the-heels Catholic-charities orphanage. Up in Westchester County, they call it River Mary's. River Mary's is the *other* institution Ossining is known for.'

'It's got to be nicer than Sing Sing.'

'Oh, it was okay. But it was no Maryknoll. The nuns didn't have PhDs like I told you they had. And I wasn't the diligent little student I said I was. You want to know what I was in high school?'

'What?'

'I was a greaser.'

His eyes widened, but he smiled.

'I used to sneak out after dark wearing shoplifted make-up from the drugstore in town. I used to wear thick dark blue eye liner and white lipstick and black net stockings. Once this other girl and I stayed out late drinking stingers at a townie bar after we'd watched *East of Eden* at the local movie house. The night-duty sister caught us sneaking in at three o'clock in the morning and told us we were sinning and would go to hell if we didn't confess the next Friday. I stuck my hand on my hip, hitched up my black net stockings, and said, "That's a lot of bullshit, Sister, and you know it." Sister was so blown away that she never said anything about it. No matter how many nights I stayed out late, she never threatened me with hellfire again.'

'I can imagine,' he grinned.

'And there's another thing I lied about. Remember I told you I had this secret benefactor? Remember I told you that you didn't have to worry about what would happen to me after college because I had this benefactor looking after me?'

'I remember.' He wasn't grinning now.

Tears stung Liberty's eyes. 'There wasn't any secret benefactor. Or if there was, he never showed himself. Oh, there were presents. On five of my birthdays I got presents, but they were never *from* anybody. They just came. I was a *rotten* kid,' she said, looking at him. 'I was not the goody-goody I pretended to be. I was a greaser... and a terror to the sisters who didn't... understand me... which was most of them. There was this one sister, Sister Mary Beth. Now, *she* understood me. She should have been a beautician or an air-conditioner repairman's wife, but never a bride of Christ. She was a real tube-head. All she wanted to do was watch television. We used to sit down in the rec room together and monopolise the tube watching old movies. I learned most of what I knew from watching old movies. There was another sister there,

Sister Bertrand, a cut above the others, who helped me with my reading and encouraged me to apply to college. When I got into Sadie Lou, she was so proud of me! She took all the credit. She deserved it. She'd practically filled out my application for me, see. Anyway, she told me that if I didn't start studying now, I'd be in for a shock when I got down to Sarah Lawrence.'

'Were you?'

'I sure was. It wasn't because I hadn't done my reading, though. I was shocked because there I was with my dark blue eye liner and my white lipstick and my black net stockings and there they all were, *oozing* upper-middle-class rebellion. I looked down at myself and didn't see the point in being rebellious where it was so trendy.'

'I see your point.'

'The first day there, I went to the bathroom and washed off the make-up and ripped up the stockings and threw them away. But once a greaser, always a greaser.'

'You just have a guilty conscience because you never honestly told anyone about that part of your life. But to anyone really watching you, you reveal that side of you all the time. Deep down, you're a tough little greaser. I mean, I'll bet you were really something to run into in the girls' room in those days. A real tough cookie.'

She sat back on the bed and stared at the ceiling for a while before speaking. 'You mean it's not such a big deal that I lied to you?'

'In the first place, you weren't lying. You were merely not telling the entire truth. You told me you were raised somewhere *like* Maryknoll. If you'd told me River Mary's, I would have accepted that just as easily. But the fact was, I learned all about you the second year we were together.'

She pressed her face to his. 'You what?'

'I learned all about you. I ran a check on you.'

'What?'

'I found out all about you.'

'Well.' She leaned back on her elbow thoughtfully. 'You shithead.'

'I wanted to see if I could track down any living relatives, if you want to know the truth.'

'Really?'

'Really.'

'That was really nice of you.'

'I thought so. I wanted to give you that as a birthday present.'

'And?' She nudged him with her knee.

'And, it was hard to find out anything about you.'

'What do you mean?'

'I mean you showed up at St Mary's on the River as a doorstep case.'

'Doorstep Daughter, that's me,' she said wryly.

'I love you, Liberty Adams. I don't care if you have no living relatives. Or if you were raised in some dump up the Hudson. Or if you were the world's biggest greaser. I love everything you've ever gone through, because it's what made you you.'

'What a romantic thing to say.'

'I thought you'd like it.'

'Been working on it for a while?'

'Oh' – he shrugged – 'my writers pitched in.'

'Want to try some more of it on me?'

'I'd like to do more than that.'

She pulled away from him. 'I may have been a greaser, you know, but I never had sex. The day Kennedy got shot, I was down in some townie's basement with a boy who was trying to wedge his middle finger up me. I took Kennedy's getting shot while this was happening to me to be a very definite sign that I should keep the old cherry on ice for a few more years. Know what I mean?'

'I know what you mean.' He was nuzzling her neck.

'Are you enjoying this?' she asked him.

'I'm having a fine time,' he said into her hair.

'And there's no doubt in your mind that I came to you pure?'

He shook his head, helpless. 'You know, I have a hard time trying to figure out why such a New Age Woman as yourself would worry about that.'

'I guess it is a little strange,' Liberty admitted. 'I guess it's because . . .'

'Because what?'

She shook her head. 'I'm not going to say it.'

He played at twisting her arm. 'Say it.'

'Fuck you. I won't say it.'

'Then I'll say it for you. You're concerned – retroactively, if I read you right – about having been pure when you came to me that weekend in DC, right?'

She nodded her head, and it suddenly occurred to her: she'd

230

never loved anyone before then. And she'd never loved anyone since.

'It's just that I compare every man to you. He's older than Eben. He's flabbier than Eben. He doesn't have a sense of humour like Eben's. His teeth aren't white like Eben's. His tongue isn't as...' She trailed off.

He was snaking his tongue between his teeth.

'His tongue isn't as...'

'Come here,' he said. He held out his arms and she rolled over into them as his tongue came into her mouth. God, he had the best mouth in the world. It was like drinking in a mountain stream.

'What's wrong?' he said, pulling away from her and looking at her closely.

She covered her face. 'I'm still in love with you.'

Gently he pulled her hands away and looked at her tenderly. 'Why do you think I'm here?'

'It makes me nervous, having you here.'

'*Still* nervous? I think I can take care of that.'

She shook her head violently.

'What's the matter now?'

'I guess I just don't want to have a fabulous time in bed with you tonight.'

'I guess not.'

She rolled back to him and sighed as she felt his arms come around her. It was like riding down a river, years after you'd been there, and coming to that familiar bend. They lay there just hugging. He seemed content to wait for her nerves to settle.

'So, have you been having a really miserable time?' Liberty said at last.

'No, it's just been busy. So busy I haven't had time to stop and think.'

'Not *any* time?'

'Just these quick rest stops. Corny's funeral. When my father died –'

'Oh, that's right. Your father died.'

He shrugged. 'No big deal. He was a mean old bastard. He came from the old school that said you weren't a good father to a son if you weren't a motherfucker. He was a motherfucker, all right. And he died thinking he did a great job. After all, I'm in politics. He always wanted us to get back into elective politics, I'm the first

Pierce in the Congress since Cousin Freddy corked on the House floor in aught-eight.' He grinned.

She nudged him. 'You and your fucking family tree.'

'Speaking of fucking, Adams...' He pulled her on top of him. 'Let's.'

She felt him hard beneath her. She knew, when they finally would get around to making love again, that it would be fantastic: better than ever. But she wasn't ready.

'No,' she said, 'you have to hold me some more first.'

'I'll hold you for as long as you like.'

'Sounds like a lifetime commitment to me.'

He didn't respond. Instead he nuzzled her with his chin. The stubble made her shiver.

'I remember exactly where I was the day I read Corny's obit in the *International Trib*,' she said. 'I was in Wiesbaden, Germany, covering the hostages' return for *Flash*.'

'I remember the piece,' said Eben. 'I thought what you said about solitude and purgatory was wonderful.'

Liberty shrugged off the compliment. 'I was sitting in the cafeteria at the Air Force base, staring at this picture of Corny. You know what I was thinking about as I looked at that picture?' She looked at Eben and her eyes filled with tears. 'I thought she might have suffered in her life, but I had absolutely no sympathy for her.

'You know how many dinners I threw in the river because you were too busy to come up to the cottage? There were times when I thought of throwing myself in, too.'

Eben winced.

'It wasn't for you that I didn't. I just couldn't stand the thought of the headlines: 'GIRL DROWNS DINNER, THEN SELF''.'

She was lying naked on the bed and Eben was down below, flicking her with his tongue. She found herself softening faster than she had in years, until her thoughts began to drift. She was a young female warrior, Joan of Arc, lying on the battlefield, wounded. A young soldier bent before her in his armour, licking her wound clean. The pain eased and she began to feel better and better and better, until the pain burst into flame, delicious and hot and she was burning and melting and writhing gloriously on the grass and calling out. He entered her then, whole and hard.

Liberty opened her eyes. She turned and looked at Eben lying next to her. A lock of blond hair had fallen into his eyes and he was smiling innocently, eyes closed. She nudged him with her big toe.

'I think I have just about enough energy left over for a grin,' he said.

'Have enough energy to answer a question?'

'Depends.' He sighed.

'What's this business with A. J. Ransome?'

'You read the New York *Times*.'

'I'm serious.'

He opened one eye and looked at her. 'You don't believe in taking off much time, do you?'

'Come on, Eben. This isn't work. It's strictly personal. I like the guy. I get the feeling he's being set up. I'd hate to think that you were helping.'

'Christ, Lib. You talk like the guy's a blue-eyed babe with the dew still damp on his MBA. He's a seasoned, ruthless financier. He'll know how to defend himself when and if the time comes.'

'Ruthless,' Liberty murmured. 'Does that mean he doesn't have Ruth?'

'He sure doesn't have the support of somebody inside his own company.'

'And that somebody is Rush Alexander. Right?'

'Between us, yes.'

'What can you tell me about him?'

'He's a brilliant, complicated, vital man.'

'That I know. Tell me something else.'

'He'd sell out *anyone* to get what he wants. Why do you want to know?'

'Because I'm interviewing him the day after tomorrow.'

'Whose idea? Yours or his?'

'His, actually.'

'In that case, I really *am* going to give you one of my guys.'

'What else can you tell me? What do you know about that daughter of his?'

'Verena? An armful of girl. Sure wouldn't have to shake the sheets to find her.'

She kicked him. 'What *else* do you think?'

'I'll tell you what I think: I think Rush Alexander's got a thing for her.'

'Very interesting. Just how do you come by that little theory?'

He shrugged. 'The way he behaved towards her this evening at dinner. And these photographs of her he has on his office wall. They're practically soft porn. And I'll tell you something else...'

'Yes...?'

'He's got an even bigger thing for Archer Ransome's dead wife.'

14

Kit Ransome pressed the doorbell in the centre of the big black gate. It was late. Circe might be asleep. She waited, turning around several times to see if anyone had followed her there. She rang the bell again.

'Kit Ransome? Is that you, Kit? I hardly recognised you, you look so tired. Come in and let me help you.' Circe pulled Kit into the marble entranceway. 'Are you all right?'

Circe Nikos-Sekotra was the ninth daughter of Stavros Nikos, once the richest, most ingenious whoremaster in the world. On an island in the fertile crescent where the Tigris and the Euphrates emptied into the Persian Gulf, within a bustling complex of several city blocks known as the 'Beehive', Nikos boasted a beautiful woman from every nation on earth. For a brief time his own daughter had represented the legendary charms of Greece, while her friend Kitsia Ransome, then a runaway of nineteen, had embodied La Belle France.

Now, at age eighty-seven, Circe owned Kalypso, Manhattan's poshest health spa, hidden away on top of a midtown skyscraper. Here in the midst of the world's most impersonal city, Circe provided a most personal service. With its twelve private rooms – each with its own private, exquisitely designed meditation garden – its saunas, steambaths, whirlpools, sensory-deprivation tanks, and a small army of impeccably trained service personnel, Kalypso accommodated an exclusive clientele of professional women only.

'I'm sorry I've come so late. It's just that I needed...'

'Come with me.' Circe towed her gently along behind her. 'Are you all right? You look as if you've seen a ghost.'

Without speaking, Kit followed the tiny, delicate woman, pacing her own steps to match Circe's. Kit knew Circe was Greek, and yet she had always seemed Oriental to Kit. She dressed in kimonos, wore her iron-grey hair piled high on her head, and spoke in a soft voice. An aging geisha, she smelled of eucalyptus and aloe.

'Come into my office and I'll give you something to wear.' She handed Kit a moss-coloured kimono. 'Put this on and give me all your clothes.'

Kit looked around for a room in which to change, her fatigue making her unduly modest.

Circe turned her back and studied the calendar on her desk. 'I'm glad you've come.'

Kit took everything off save the single black pearl. She fingered the ear nervously, then handed all her possessions to Circe.

Shining out of a gnarled and wrinkled face, Circe's eyes reminded Kit of pools of water evaporating on the desert. She looked away. 'Are those tears, Little Kit?'

Kit nodded and stood with her hands limp at her sides, letting Circe pull the ivory sticks out of her hair. Circe shook her head sadly. From a desk so small it might have been a school-child's, she counted out four wooden beads into a small leather sack.

'Stay here for twenty-four hours. You've got to promise me, though, that you won't run off to some emergency meeting or to meet your boyfriend.'

Kit nodded humbly and accepted the leather sack. The four beads, she knew, would allow her four telephone calls during her stay. Circe was strict, but not unreasonable. She would not be completely denied access to the outside world.

Together the two women walked up the sweeping stairway to the upper level of the duplex penthouse that sheltered Kalypso. As they climbed higher, Kit began to hear the birds. There were over a dozen species – coloured toucans and tiny parrots, canaries and lovebirds – living up here on a steaming tropical plateau where flora and fauna flourished year-round beneath an enormous plastic bubble. Overhanging the swimming pool was a balcony, where the bedrooms were. The rushing of a fountain in the pool at night provided a white-noise inducement to sleep. Water, sleep, massage – Circe's classic prescription for the overwrought working woman.

Kit's pace quickened as she glimpsed the pool through the trees. She'd always harboured suspicions of vicious blue swimming pools radiating chlorine. But this pool she trusted. Faced in Carrara marble, it was as pure and cool as a mountain lake. 'Who but a whore could care so much about cleanliness?' Circe liked to say.

'Have a swim first, Kit. It will lengthen your muscles. You are so very taut.' She pressed her fingers into Kit's deltoids to prove her point.

Kit shed her kimono and stepped quickly down the pool's dark green stairs, starting in on an easy sidestroke. Circe stood at the pool's edge and followed Kit from end to end with her eyes.

Stretch, contract. Stretch, contract. 'So much has been happening ... I need to sort things out,' Kit explained tentatively, reaching the edge.

All her life, she had waited for Kitsia's sign. Yet today, when she had actually laid eyes on the turtle, she'd felt nothing but terror. Twenty years ago – even ten – she would have welcomed the sight. But now it was too late. She was a grown woman – too old to become some man's daughter just like that.

'How is your work, Kit? How are you faring with *Last Chance*?' Circe called out to her.

Kit smiled to herself but didn't answer. Circe and her staff were avid followers of the gossip columns. She switched to a slow, measured crawl. *Stroke, stroke, breathe.* With each breath, Kit spotted the pool's tiled border – pink flowers against white. Shouldn't she welcome a new parent? Especially since she'd cut herself off from the one she had.

Kit heard Circe's birdlike voice echo off the dome above them. 'I read about that young woman dying. Very sad,' she said, more to herself than to Kit.

Kit tried to remember what the reporter had said, but all she saw were the bright eyes of the turtle.

'I feel the pressure, Circe.'

'Turn over and float on your back,' Circe instructed her. She walked over and touched a button and all the lights went out except for two tiny blue spotlights deep inside the pool. 'Look, Kit.' She pointed to the dome above their heads.

Kit stared up at the night sky, a tender pink colour. She longed to dissolve into this currentless water, to stop time. Her body was a spindly starfish. She tried to find her centre, but it was too much: Rush's threat. Archer's withholding comment on the footage, Brendan's face just after she slapped him. She thought about Liberty Adams, her quick mouth and her wide, slow violet eyes.

'It's Kitsia, Circe,' Kit finally said. *Kitsia.* She wanted to tell Circe how impossible it was to be her daughter, but she didn't. 'What's it like being her friend?'

Circe sat down on a white wrought-iron bench flanked by lemon trees. She pulled some birdseed out of her pocket and sprinkled it on her arm. Two canaries and a lovebird alighted to eat, and she made soft kissing sounds at them.

'When I worked for my father, I had a regular customer. A handsome Australian boy, a dockhand. He would come every Saturday and ask for me. He would send me flowers every Sunday morning. He never had sex with me – I would undress for him and he would just kiss me. I did what no whore should ever do: I fell in love with him. One Saturday he didn't come, but the next morning the flowers arrived. They made me happy. I missed him. He didn't come again, but every Sunday the flowers came. Three months later, the flowers stopped coming, but I didn't care. I had stopped missing him by then. Years later I found out that the Australian had gone away without a thought for me. All those Sundays, Kitsia had sent the flowers.'

She floated, feeling disoriented. Circe's Kitsia was a person she had never met. She swam to the edge of the pool and trod water.

'You've known her a long time, haven't you?'

Circe nodded and shelled a sunflower seed.

'She plays games.'

Circe nodded again and popped the meat into her mouth.

'Why can't she behave like everyone else?'

'Because, Little Kit, she is not like everyone else. She is special. She is apart from most of us.'

'Did you know that we're not speaking? Did she tell you?' Kit got out of the water.

Circe stood up and shook her head sadly. 'I'm sorry to hear that. She is old.'

Accepting a towel from Circe, Kit looked at her sharply. 'She's not *that* old.' *Anyone who can seduce Brendan Marsh isn't old at all.*

'You ought to have more regard for your mother.'

'Why should I? She has none for me! Besides, she doesn't want respect, Circe, she wants control.' Kit slipped back into the kimono and headed upstairs to her room.

Circe overtook her, frowning. 'Respect. Control. Words, Little Kit, just words.' She opened the door to Kit's room. 'What matters is that you feel good about yourself. Do you feel good about yourself?'

It was a rhetorical question, yet Kit bridled. Circe shook her head and went on. 'You were just beginning to relax, and there I went and challenged you. You'd think I'd know better.'

She lowered the lights, and as she did, the lights behind the rice-paper walls came up, revealing a tranquil country landscape. Kit longed to be somewhere peaceful and far away. 'Oh, Circe! I want to run away.'

Circe began to massage Kit's arms.

'No, I don't want to run away. I just want to be able to cope with it all. Will you give me a brighter light bulb so I can read tonight? I've let the scripts pile up since –'

'Does your office know you're here?' Circe interrupted.

'I telephoned Sasha from the booth downstairs. I didn't want to waste a bead on it.'

Circe was unsmiling. 'Then give it up for twenty-four hours.'

'But Circe!'

'Your shoulder muscles are like iron! Do you want to lose your health? Now, do as I say!'

'Yes, Circe.'

That meant no scripts, no correspondence, no newspapers tomorrow morning. No trades with breakfast. The thought was unbearable and yet Kit knew she had to obey. She sat up and took several sips of an herbal tea, concocted to soothe her nerves and bring on sleep.

'Circe?'

'What, lamb?'

'I miss Brendan.'

'I know you do.' Her voice was tenderer now. She turned Kit over and started to massage her back.

The effect was immediate. 'I miss Brendan!' She repeated the words, as if Circe's hands were literally pulling them out of her. 'You know, he's come to New York. I realise now he came to make up with me. But I treated him so badly.'

Kit closed her eyes. She'd been so wrong; she realised that now, expecting Brendan to behave in ways she herself could not.

'Here I am a grown woman, and my mother still frightens me, angers me . . . possesses me!'

'Easy, easy.' Circe kneaded her lower back. 'Don't work against me!'

'If I can't withstand Kitsia's powers, why should Brendan? You know what Kitsia's problem is? She's never known what it means to be in love.'

'I think she has.'

'No, she hasn't – and I feel sorry for her, because she doesn't know what it's like to love someone so much, so much . . .' Kit's voice cracked.

'Kitsia was in love once.'

'When?'

'A long time ago. But her love was not returned. Now, go to sleep.' Circe gently pressed her back onto the futon. 'It's late. Tomorrow we will heal you. But for now, rest.'

Kit felt the tea taking its effect: her face seemed to be melting back, leaving the bones in her cheeks brittle and too large. Again she saw the small green turtle with sapphire eyes, and her heart fluttered. 'Who, Circe? Who did Kitsia love?'

But Circe had disappeared into the shadows and Kit was too drugged to pursue her. Instead, she lay there, her thoughts drifting, carrying her back to her girlhood, to Zwar.

They used to ride on horseback over from the palace on the far side of the harbour: the four sons of the old emir's youngest wife. No one ever heard about his daughters, who were said to number a dozen. Kit sometimes felt like the only girl in the world.

Each with his own purebred Arabian stallion, they dismounted and tethered their horses together, leaving the reins with Cassim, the old stablehand. They ran to the screen door of the kitchen, where they knew Little Kit would still be eating breakfast. It was safe to fetch her now, since Big Kit would be busy working in her studio. They were known as Big Kit and Little Kit among the Zwarians. But Big Kit was sly and sometimes surprised them by lingering a little longer over her coffee, visiting with her daughter. Whenever the boys saw her, they'd drop their youthful posturing and walk shyly up to the screen, pressing their noses and palms to the mesh.

Little Kit let out a high, shrill call: their special signal. Never so much as covering her ears, Big Kit turned slowly and regarded them through the screen with black, merciless eyes.

'My friends are here,' the girl said eagerly. 'I have to go now, Big Kit.'

Her mother glared at her. 'How many times have I asked you not to call me by that name?'

Little Kit stared back, green eyes unblinking. Her small sharp shoulders came up. 'That is who you are, Mother. Everyone knows that.'

'Little Kit, indeed!' Kitsia rose to her full height. 'Why. you're taller than I am – at twelve!'

The girl giggled into her palm. 'Soon I'll be Big Kit and you'll be Little Kit, eh?'

Her mother smiled bitterly. 'Never! Now, go.' She smacked her bottom. 'I know you prefer their company to mine, little heathen.'

'Thank you, Mama.' Kit hugged her mother and, behind her back, to the boys waiting beyond the screen, made a circle of the fingers – the American 'okay' she'd learned from the oil drillers who'd recently come to Zwar.

'Tell them I said to keep their hands off you,' Kitsia whispered.

'We're just playing games. Touching is a part of our water games. Everyone knows that.' Kit skipped to the screen, and when her mother followed her, the boys pulled back as one. They were naked save for striped loincloths.

'Good morning, little braves,' Kitsia said snidely.

'Good morning, lady.'

They burst into chatter then, practising their British-schoolboy manners all at once, topping one another – 'Hullo!' 'Splendid weather, eh, what?' – until Kitsia, silencing them with a hand raised to the screen, spoke. 'Take good care of her, boys.'

The boys smiled back innocently. Although they'd had some schooling in Great Britain, even the two eldest – Akmed, thirteen, and Dhali, eleven – seemed young for their age, impossibly unsophisticated. 'I suppose I ought to be grateful that you don't have sports cars. Yet,' she added gloomily. Opening the screen door, she set her daughter free and watched them gather her into their midst, like bright ravens.

Swarming over to their horses, Akmed, the leader, sprang agilely onto his mount's back, and Kit leapt up behind him. Clinging with bare knees, she clasped him around the waist and spurred his horse with her bare heels. Swinging their arms over their heads and whooping wildly, they rode off to the widest swath of beach, where the sun ricocheted off the wet sand like lightning off a mirror. Here, fifty yards from shore, the rocks rose up out of the deep like underwater monsters, shaggy with seaweed.

Dismounting, they skipped out into the shallow breakers and, diving like dolphins, swam out to the far side of the largest rock.

Whenever the tide was right, they played 'Genie of the Lamp'. Kit was the genie, the boys shipwrecked sailors. In order to save themselves from certain doom, the boys had to find the lamp and claim the genie – and the three wishes she could grant them. Akmed and Dhali were highly competitive with each other.

No matter where she hid, Dhali was always the first to claim her, and Akmed always the next and the last. Yet in spite of its predictability, the game held an almost hysterical suspense for its players. Dhali, who was capable of holding his breath even longer than Kit, would swim along the hull of the sunken Portuguese steamer where Kit often swam to hide amid the semi-submerged hatches and would gently pluck her loose, bringing her safely to the rocks. Always a tender captor, swimming with one arm encircling her waist, Dhali would then bring her down to the Magic Grotto.

To reach it, they had to dive twenty feet down under the lip of the rock and swim another twenty feet up into a small phosphorus-lit sea cave. Only at low tide was this possible. At high tide, even Dhali could not hold enough air in his lungs to make it. Once he was alone with Kit in the cave, Dhali hunched on the grotto bank and stared at his knees, too frightened or too shy to ask for his three wishes. Then Akmed's shiny black head broke the surface of the pool and he heaved himself upon his younger brother, punching him and twisting his arm until he surrendered the genie of the lamp.

Under the rules, Kit was not permitted to touch land until she had given Akmed his three wishes. In the meantime, she could touch only the body of her master. She clasped him around the waist. Once she touched him between his legs by mistake. She'd seen male models, nude in her mother's studio so she knew what men and boys looked like down there. But still, she was startled. Another day, he had held her hand there, not letting her move it until she stroked him beneath the linen. It felt like a bony fish trapped in a net.

It was about this time that her mother had a houseguest named Caroline Ainslee.

'Caro-*line*.' Her mother used to drawl the name, and half-close her eyes.

Caroline, who had come for a month and stayed for six, longer than all the rest, was a tall straight young woman with yellow-red hair and yellow-red eyebrows shooting up towards her temples over blazing brown eyes. Kit secretly called her Shiva after one of the pictures in an Indian artbook: the destroyer.

Shiva wore white open-neck shirts, jodhpurs, and black boots and had her pick of the emir's stables. Her mother had first taken her on four years earlier when her best friend, Cynthia, died in Ceylon. It wasn't that Kit disliked Shiva. She simply didn't like the way her mother behaved in Shiva's presence. She became less direct; if not shy, then sly and slinky, calling Kit 'darling' instead of 'daughter' or just plain 'you'.

Kitsia was far less likely to go off to the studio on mornings her friend was about. They always seemed to be laughing together over some private joke. They lay in the cool terracotta parlour on their separate carpet beds, feet almost touching, smoking hash-laced black cigarettes. Their breath when they leaned over to let her in on their private joke smelled like that of the greybeards in the *souk*. She shrank from them, and when her friends came to collect her, gladly left them to their jokes.

But they laughed about her friends too, until Kit, outraged one morning, stepped over to Shiva's couch and demanded to know what was so funny.

'About the Little Princes?' she said, as she abruptly stopped laughing. 'Nothing at all, really. I was just saying to Kitsia that it was a pity they are so nice and good to you now, considering they'll grow up to want to cut your clit off.'

'What are you talking about? What is a clit?' Kit wanted to know.

'Rosebud, darling; bijou; sugar lump ... that tender little tip of flesh ... right *there*.' She touched Kit so that she jumped back, doubly horrified. Then she began to have the nightmares about Akmed and his father, the old emir, coming in the night with a knife.

The week after Caroline left, Kit had been having the nightmare when she woke up in the morning with blood on her sheets. She tore the sheet off the bed and ran with it out to the studio, where her mother was already at work. When Kitsia saw the bloodied sheet, she pushed up her goggles, put down her blowtorch, and climbed down off the scaffold.

'So! It's happened, has it? I thought it would. Did you know that some women actually slap their daughters' faces at such a time? Don't worry. I wouldn't do that. This is slap enough.'

They went to the courtyard, where she showed her daughter how to wash the blood out with a paste of cold water and sand.

'*I* feel dirty too,' Kit had said.

'Then you'll shower.'

'But haven't I already had my weekly shower?'

'Now that you're a woman, you're entitled to shower every day that you bleed.'

243

'That's all right. I won't need to. I can always swim.'

'Yes, with those horrid boys. That's another matter we must discuss.'

Kit stood under the trickle from the shower and watched her blood mingle with the water and run down the drain. Afterwards, when she dried and oiled herself, Kitsia gave her a pad of gauze that hooked onto a peculiar little belt. She felt as if she were a baby again, freshly nappied and comfortable enough to confide in her mother about the recurrent dream. Kitsia listened without comment until she had finished.

'Well, now, isn't it obvious why you dreamed that dream?' She held up her stained nightgown. 'Perhaps now that you've actually begun to bleed, you will stop having the nightmare. But listen to me, daughter: to become a woman is to enter a sort of nightmare. Which brings me around to that other matter.'

Kit, who had been drying her hair, peeked out at her mother from beneath the towel.

'If you ever let Akmed or any of his brothers put their penises inside of you where the blood flows, you will have created for yourself – for both of us – an even greater nightmare.'

Then Kitsia pulled something out of her trouser pocket. It glinted in the morning sun and Kit had to shade her eyes to see it. It was a beautiful bejewelled turtle, a special magical object that drove away all thoughts of nightmares.

'It's magnificent. Where did you get it? Where did it come from?'

'From far, far away. Now, take it. It's yours. A consolation prize of sorts.'

Kit reached out and took it into her hand, holding it up and admiring it from all angles.

'It is not only beautiful, but functional as well.' Kitsia turned it over and pressed its belly. The creature's multicoloured shell popped open and a single black pearl stud fell into Kit's hand.

'Another prize?'

Before she could thank her mother, the houseboy came out carrying a tray that he set down on the bench between them and went back into the house.

'Which ear do you want pierced?'

'Must I choose, Mother? Isn't there a second earring?'

'Greedy girl. Take just the one and thank me for it.'

'I don't understand.'

'The day you receive the second pearl earring is the day you'll learn who your father is. I hope for your sake that day never arrives.'

The hole in Kit's ear healed easily around the black pearl stud and she continued to swim with Akmed and his brothers almost every day. They admired her new – her first – bit of adult adornment and enjoyed making insinuating jokes about it.

One day she was hiding behind one of the smaller rocks, the one shaped like a hunching giant, playing a game they called 'Sardines', when Akmed slipped up behind her and began to kiss her neck. She was not surprised. Even the youngest of the boys was forever kissing her. But then she felt his fingers thrust past the elastic of her swimsuit and work its way up inside of her. She trod higher in the water, but his finger only followed her, battering its way farther inside of her, hurting her, but also striking fire deep inside of her.

'I'm getting you ready,' he had whispered in her ear. It was as if he were issuing her an instruction from one of their games, and she obeyed, letting him pursue this mysterious preparation.

In the days that followed, they played 'Sardines' regularly and she returned to the same rock, knowing he would come to her.

One day at the rock, she felt something bigger and harder than his finger work its way inside of her. She cried out, but he clamped his hand over her mouth, not wanting the others to hear and come after them. The young ones had become distracted by an impromptu game of water polo in the shallows. She listened to the crash of their horses' hooves in the surf, the wild whoops and screams as gradually she felt herself widen for him. The salt water around them seemed to grow slicker, warmer. She clung to the back of the rock while he moved in and out of her.

'I'm beginning to think those games of yours are getting a little too serious,' Kitsia said one day.

'Oh, Mama,' Kit sighed. 'You just wouldn't understand.' She ran her fingers through her salty hair and went to her room to oil her skin and dress for dinner. Kitsia followed her and watched her as she took off her suit and began to spread oil over her body.

'You've developed into an astonishing beautiful young woman.'

'Thank you, Mama.' Kit blushed at her mother in the mirror and

245

bent to smooth oil into her legs. Soft down had begun to sprout between her legs. When she straightened up, she caught her mother looking there, too.

'I think I'll wire Posy and have her find you a suitable *all-girls'* school in America,' she emphasised darkly. 'Your tutors here have all been fools. What is more, I don't want you getting pregnant by the local rabble.'

Kit pulled herself up haughtily. 'That rabble, as you call them, Mother, are princes. Why, one day, when his father dies, Akmed will become the emir. And he happens to be my best friend.'

Kitsia spoke through her teeth. 'He is not your friend. He will never be your friend.'

Kit turned upon her mother. 'You just hate him because . . . because . . .' She could not finish.

'Say it,' her mother prodded her. 'You might as well come out with it.'

'Because you hate all men,' Kit finished with narrowed eyes.

Her mother looked mildly affronted. 'I do not hate all men. That's the most absurd suggestion I have ever heard.' She threw up her arms.

'Well, then,' Kit added sulkily, '*most* men.' She turned to the mirror to brush her hair.

'Most men, it's true, are idiots,' Kitsia said reasonably. 'Then again, so are most women.'

'Yes, but you'd rather hug and kiss an idiot woman than an idiot man. It's true, isn't it? You're nothing but a . . . a *lesbian*.'

Kitsia grabbed her and spun her around. 'Where did you hear that word?'

Kit pulled away and shrugged, marching over to the closet and yanking it open.

Her mother came after her and slammed it shut. 'Tell me where you heard that!'

Kit turned away, remembering the night she'd gone to say good night to her mother. She'd burst in the door and, in the light from the hall lamp, seen her mother, wild-haired, crouching at the foot of the bed, her mouth glistening. Caroline had drawn her nightgown down over her raised knees and cried: 'Oh, shit, Kitsia! I knew it! I knew it!' What had shocked her – more than the wetness of her mother's chin, more than the strange, moaning noises she'd heard before opening the door – was seeing her mother's hair in disarray. Kitsia had always kept her hair tightly wound in a bun. What was wrong with her? Disturbed, Kit had described the scene the next day to Dhali, who had blushed, claiming to know nothing of these matters. But Akmed was only too happy to explain to her exactly what it was that her mother and her houseguest had been doing and what they were called. 'Lesbians. Lots of English ladies are lesbians,' he told her matter-of-factly. 'When he was at Oxford, my cousin Ali used to pay to watch two of them doing it.'

Remembering Akmed's words, she had no answer for her mother. And when she went off to school in America the next month, she wasn't sorry to leave. Forbidden by her mother to see Akmed and the boys, she found nothing to make her want to stay on the island – certainly not her mother.

15

Kit is dreaming again. She is back in her car, driving down the shore road from the studio to Clara. Moments ago, a dazzling sunset ended, magenta streaks fading towards the horizon, leaving the world drained of colour – chill. She has been excited about coming home early to him, but now, for some reason, she feels as dull and empty as the sky. Her chest aches because she has missed sharing the sunset with him.

The lights of Clara aren't on. She is afraid, as she always is, that he may have grown tired of waiting for her and gone to some bar down the coast where the people are loud and warm and full of life, unlike her. But the front door is open and she runs down the hall, eager for the feel of his warmth and burliness. She halts, bracing herself in the doorway of the living room.

Their bodies are naked, locked, dark against the white wicker. She will never forget the details – the sound of the wicker groaning beneath their knees, the look of his back, arched in ecstasy one minute and then, when he senses her standing there, deflating like a sniper's victim. He falls back and stumbles away. His companion, Kitsia, turns around slowly on the wicker with her brazen look ready, as if to say: 'Well, Little Kit, what did you expect?'

Kit woke up with the memory of the dream still clinging to her like a fallen canopy. Her anger and her fear had mysteriously evaporated while she slept. In her dream, Kitsia had seemed so old, so frail. Kit could still feel her mother's bony shoulders in her hands. Brendan could not be blamed. And Circe was right: Kitsia would always be beyond blame.

This morning, Kit felt capable of taking control. Even though Rush was blackmailing her into giving his daughter the part in *Last Chance*, she could make it work. But she had to find a way to prevent Rush from using the negatives again and again – a way to free herself from him.

248

Liberty Adams. Kit had to see her: to retrieve the turtle, to find out at last who her father was. And – who knows? – perhaps she and he could even become friends, if never properly a daughter and father.

Kit sat up and rang for her breakfast. She was lonely for Brendan. She had to talk to him about all this.

'You want me to do *what*?' Rita's voice on the phone was incredulous.

'I said I want you to get to Liberty Adams' secretary as soon as you can and set up a series of interviews with me out in LA next week. Tell her she can stay with me at Clara.'

'Kit, are you sure?' Rita asked her.

'Just tell her I'd prefer several relaxed interviews at home rather than one long... *intense* one in New York.'

'Okay. I'll schedule her a flight on the company jet then. It's good to hear you sounding like your old self again.'

'It's good to *be* my old self again.'

A half-hour into a massage, Kit used the second bead to call Jay Scott at the studio.

'Where have you been?' She could tell it was an effort for him to keep his voice this even. 'I left messages all over town for you last night. Why didn't you call me back?'

Needing to hear a friendly voice, Kit was thrown off. She proceeded lightly. 'I had an interview with Liberty Adams yesterday. I'm at Kalypso recovering.'

'Great. The studio's falling down around your ears and you check out for a mud pack.'

'Actually, it's a massage.' Kit closed her eyes. *Don't let him bring you down,* she told herself.

'Don't be cute, Kit, it doesn't suit you. You know what I'm looking at here on my desk? Apart from my heart, that is?'

'What's that supposed to mean? Ouch!' Kit winced as the masseuse crunched into her calves.

'It means, Kit, that I'm sitting here in my office at seven o'clock in the morning –'

'Eight o'clock.'

'*Eight o'clock*, staring at a piece of yellow paper.'

'Scottie, please, no more build-up. What piece of paper are you talking about?' Kit felt the iced cold-cream run down her legs. The small room began to smell of pine.

'It's a contract requisition form, Kit. A Horizon Pictures

contract requisition for one Verena Maxwell Alexander for the part of one Lacy Jones. Now, just what the fuck is going on?'

She had wanted to break it to him personally. She could just see him sitting in his tiny all-blue office wrapping the royal-blue telephone cord around his wrists, preparing to strangle her. Kit steeled herself. This woman was trying to relax her, and all she did was tense her muscles more. The masseuse loomed over her, about to apply a circularly vibrating machine to her thighs. 'Oh, that,' she said simply.

'"*That*"? Kit, are you crazy? Have you lost your mind? What are you doing? I'd give *anything* to know what's come over you. Why am I the last to know? Why am I getting this information inter-fucking-office? Does Brendan know yet?'

'Scottie, calm down. You know I've been trying to reach you. This *just* happened.'

'I'd give *anything* to know who this girl is!' he cried.

'You *will* know her. I'm flying her out in just a few days. And then you'll see how groundless all your objections are.' How convincing did she sound? 'I tried to reach you, but I had to move fast to wrap her up.'

'I suppose her agent held a gun to your head? We all know when agents say boo, Kit Ransome jumps. Come on,' he bore down on her sarcastically.

Kit moved the masseuse away and sat up on the table, pulling her towel around her. She signalled one of the maids for a cup of tea. 'Scottie, Verena Alexander is going to be wonderful. She and Brendan will look fantastic together.' Kit couldn't even remember what the kid looked like, but she hoped this was true.

'Fantastic? I'll just bet,' Scottie muttered. 'What's she done that you're so all-fired sure she's going to be fantastic in my movie? In the pivotal role in *my* movie?' His tone was still exasperated, but Kit sensed him softening.

'She's new, Scottie. She's a model. She works with Max Rugoff and he swears by her.' Kit's tea tasted of violets and oranges.

'A model? Great! Rugoff's schtupping her in his office after class, right? And you're schtupping me right now. I'd give *anything* to know what you're up to. Revenge, Kitty? This is revenge, isn't it?'

'What are you talking about?' Kit felt panic well up.

'You never forgave me for hiring Monette. You hated her in that part. You were always hounding her, badgering her. She could never relax. She was petrified you were going to fire her. You drove her –'

'For God's sake!' she broke in. 'Stop it! Do you hear me? Stop it this instant.' The masseuse stared at Kit guiltily, as if it were she who were being reprimanded.

'I will not stop it, Kit,' he persisted in a spoiled voice. 'You're ruining *Last Chance*. You're ruining me, and I don't know why. And you're ruining our friendship.' He lowered his voice. 'I thought we were friends.'

'Friendship has nothing to do with it,' Kit said evenly. Her hand was over her heart, which was thudding so that it hurt to breathe. She exhaled shakily. 'I chose the best person for the part, and as soon as you see her, you'll agree. She's fresh. She's innocent.'

A woman was on her knees before Kit trying to fit slippers saturated with cream onto Kit's feet. A stainless-steel bowl filled with hot water steamed at the woman's elbow. Kit stared down into it, then drew her legs up underneath her and sat on them. She pressed on, 'She'll be great with Brendan. The chemistry is there, I know it.'

She heard him heave a sigh. 'I hope for your sake Brendan knows it too, Kitty. Wait a minute...' He paused. 'Verena Maxwell Alexander. She isn't by any chance Rush Alexander's daughter?'

'Yes.'

'What a coincidence! You really are one of the Blue Suits, aren't you?'

'Brendan will back my decision, Scottie. I know it.'

'You mean you haven't told him?'

'I was hoping that you'd –'

'Oh, wonderful. Fine. I'm so glad you've asked me. Kit. After all, what are friends for?' he said sarcastically.

Kit unfolded her legs and laid herself back down on the table. She stared gratefully up at the cedar-planked ceiling.

'Please, Scottie.' She scarcely breathed.

'Please, nothing, Kitty Cat. First you shove this no-talent, no-credits, no-brain bimbo down my throat, and now you want me to break the happy news to our high-strung, oft-intoxicated, lovesick leading man. He's threatened to quit, our leading man. Did you hear that, Kit? I said he's threatening to walk out on me. Tell me you didn't know that. Tell me you heard that gossip and still went

251

right ahead and did this terrible thing. Oh, that's right. I forgot. You don't believe the things you read in the press. You don't believe in gossip.'

'Scott!' she pleaded one last time.

'No. I guess you wouldn't have believed it,' he said meekly.

Kit began to breathe normally again. He had thrown in the towel.

'You're an angel, Jay Scott,' she said, and she meant it.

'And you, Kit, are a ferocious feline devil. Listen to me, Kit. I'll accept this fuzzy end of the lollipop you're sticking me with, but only on one condition.'

Always conditions, Kit thought. She closed her eyes. 'I'll do anything, Scottie. Anything you want,' she whispered.

'I've just got the exact figures from your *faithful*' – the emphasis was sarcastic – 'comptroller, and it looks as if we'll be going into fucking *golden* time to finish this flick. The figures are on their way to you by pouch. You'd better get together with your sugar cousin and do some serious hustling. You hear that sound, Kitty Cat? It should be me scratching out my eyes, but it's me signing your precious contract req.' He hung up.

She had actually got Scott to believe her! Relaxed at last, she treated herself to a whirlpool. As she sat in the tub, awash in green bubbles, Brendan flashed in and out of her mind. He was a perfect partner to fantasy, only his presence made her body slow down and her mind become crowded with thoughts of her love for him. Let those thoughts come, she thought. I'll be with him again before long.

She emerged from the whirlpool so relaxed that the two women who came to fetch her nearly carried her back to her room. She felt like a mummy as she lay on the chaise while two of them wrapped her body in the sopping, greenish swaths of cheesecloth. When they had completely encased all but her nose, mouth, eyes, and the bottoms of her bare feet, they left her alone to listen to the dripping of the fountain in her meditation garden.

Money, always money. It seemed she could not escape it. Everything in business could always be reduced to money. This one wanted more money. That one wanted her to spend less. How could she now ask Archer for more money? How could Rush have implied she was cheating the company, playing with figures? Kit wanted to be involved in something that was indivisible by money. It was a naive wish.

'Miss Ransome?'

Kit peered through the cheesecloth at the young woman interrupting her meditations. She was a great golden-haired oaf of a girl, impossible to take in at a single glance.

Kit's eyes travelled up from big feet in red cowboy boots, over long legs in bright blue corduroys, to a thick waist and big braless breasts slung in a yellow polo shirt, and finally to that gold hair and soft brown eyes. Now she knew who this young woman was. She'd seen the pictures. The big brown eyes staring out from the covers of magazines: *Vogue, Bazaar*. A face that might have been on a totem pole, a powerful face that was born for the big screen. *All right*, Kit thought, *all right so far*.

'What do you want?' Kit asked grouchily.

'Hi.' The girl smiled bashfully. Her voice was throaty, a natural stage voice. *Good*.

Kit remained on the chaise but she no longer felt comfortable. 'You haven't answered my question,' she said coldly. 'This is my private room and my private garden. You realise I could have you arrested.'

The girl shrugged. 'My mother comes here. They know me. They sneak me extra carrot cake from the kitchen.' Then, as if she were irritated to actually have to introduce herself, she thrust out a big hand and said, 'I'm Verena Maxwell Alexander. I'm real pleased to meet you, Miss Ransome.'

Kit sat up stiffly and began to unwrap the bandages.

The girl stammered. 'Sasha told me where to find you and I just wanted to come over and introduce myself and say thank you for giving me the part. I'm *so* excited.' The girl bent her knees in a childlike way to show her enthusiasm.

Kit continued to struggle with the mummy casing, and got off as much as possible before pulling on her robe and standing up to face the girl. She must be at least six feet. *She'd make Brendan look ridiculous!* She sat down again. The robe clung to the remaining herbal strips unpleasantly.

'Well,' Kit said, 'don't thank *me*, young lady. Thank your father. If I had my way, you wouldn't be allowed to *read* for the part, let alone land it.'

The girl backed away and sank into a chair against the wall, shaking her head. 'I don't get it.'

'Your father forced me to cast you.' Kit chipped the words off, sheer ice.

'Wow,' was all the girl could say.

'Wow, indeed,' Kit added dryly. 'I think it's important that neither of us pretends. It won't do you any good and it certainly won't help me. So I'll tell you at the outset that I didn't want you for the part. In spite of the fact that I would seem to have no choice in the matter, the very idea of casting you horrifies me.'

The girl kept shaking her head, as if struggling to awake from a bad dream.

Kit let her words hang in the air. She knew how cruel they sounded, but she couldn't stop herself. Seeing Verena face to face was unravelling her composure. She had been ready to make the best of things, but why had the girl come here to push her face in it?

'Wait a second.' The girl seemed to be reviving herself slowly. 'Wait a second.' She stood up. 'I'm not wrong for the part. I'm *right* for the part. I could be really good!' She sank to her seat once again.

'Really?' Kit asked sharply, looking at the young, beautiful girl. 'I'd like to know how –'

'I've studied,' the girl said defiantly.

'Oh, I see,' Kit said sarcastically. 'Your two nights a week with Rugoff have made you the Monroe of the eighties. Is that what I'm expected to believe?'

'I'm not sure the part would be really right for Monroe.' She considered this seriously. 'I've had some acting experience.'

'Hah!'

'You don't understand. I'm good. I *know* I can do this part. I know I can play Lacy.'

'Actually, I don't think you could play one of the daughters on *The Brady Bunch*. You come in here like Katherine Hepburn in *Stage Door* – only you're not Hepburn.' Kit's voice rose on every word.

'Why don't you just try me!' The girl jumped to her feet and stared down on Kit, clutching and unclutching her fists, every inch the thwarted infant. It was hard to feel sorry for the girl. Her father must have given her everything she'd ever wanted, and now he was giving her the most luminous gift of all: stardom. Well, she might have to hire this girl, but nowhere did it say she'd have to make it easy for her.

'Try me!' the girl pleaded again.

Kit smiled cruelly. 'Try you? I'll try you. I'll let you fall flat on your face and embarrass Horizon, embarrass me, yourself, and your father – if your father is capable of embarrassment, which I sincerely doubt...' This wasn't true, of course. She wouldn't let her fall. She'd call in Rugoff for support. She'd work miracles to get the very best out of this enormous child.

The child's eyes widened and she began to back away from Kit. Kit followed her.

'Oh, absolutely, Rush will get his way. Hasn't he always got his way? But this time it'll be at the expense of Horizon. At the expense of Brendan Marsh's career. At the expense of his own overgrown daughter.'

Tears fell on the girl's cheeks. She lifted a shoulder to wipe them off on the sleeve of her polo shirt.

Not even tears daunted Kit. 'This is a grown-up world you're in now, my dear. There's no place for your adolescent tears. Save them for Lacy.'

The girl stared at Kit as if she were a madwoman and backed out the door. 'Maybe this wasn't such a hot idea after all, coming here...' She backed farther away, muttering, and then turned around and ran down the hall.

Seconds later, Circe came through the door with a sprout salad for Kit and found her hunched on the chaise out in the garden, seething.

'What is all this?' She put down Kit's food and took her in her arms. But Kit, furious, would not permit herself to be held. She turned on Circe. 'How could you, Circe! I trusted you.'

'Whatever are you talking about, my child?'

'I'm not your child. And I'm talking about *that* child.' Kit gestured towards the door. 'How could you let that child in my room?'

'She's a beautiful, harmless creature,' Circe said. 'Her mother is a dear –'

'I don't care how old and dear her mother is. How *dare* you let her invade my privacy!'

Circe sat down beside Kit.

'You're even worse than last night. What am I going to do with you? Oh, I almost forgot.' She took an envelope out of her pocket. She sighed and handed the envelope to Kit. 'There's a messenger outside and he will not leave without an answer.'

Kit tore open the envelope.

'"Rush and Amanda Alexander request the pleasure of your company at a special celebration this evening for their daughter,

255

16

Liberty slid into the white limo. Seeing her tuxedo, Archer whistled softly. Liberty smiled. 'Barney's of Boys' town. One of the advantages of being small. You don't look so bad yourself. I haven't figured out yet whether I want you to marry me or just adopt me.' He looked taken aback. She grinned and chucked him on the arm. 'Just joking, Arch. Relax.'

He recovered himself. 'I'm glad you could come. This is a very special evening for all of us.'

'Does "us" include Kit Ransome?'

'I imagine so.'

'Good, I need to talk to her. I haven't been able to reach her all day.' Without Kit, she would have bowed out altogether. Now that she had seen Eben again, a date with Archer Ransome was more temptation than treat.

'Liberty,' he began. 'I wouldn't want anything to interfere with our evening together.' He gathered her hand into his and brought it into his lap. 'Suppose you tell me about Eben Pierce.' He looked at her. 'And what you're up to.'

Liberty felt herself colour and her hand go clammy in his. She took it back and folded her arms across her chest, speaking to the seat in front of her.

'I used to be in love with him,' she said flatly.

'When was this?'

'Oh. God,' She blew the hair out of her face. 'A billion years ago. When I was a kid . . . in college.'

'And . . . ?'

'And for a little while after he married Cornelia Hays. But not for long,' she assured him. It was suddenly very important that he not take her for a home-wrecker.

'And that, as they say, was it?'

'Yes, Hercule Poirot, that was it.'

His eyebrow remained upraised. 'All?'

'All right. I'm still in love with him.'

'And . . . ?'

'I had lunch with him the day before yesterday.'

'Anything about that lunch I ought to know?'

'You're good at this, aren't you? I've got the perfect career change for you. Anyway, he wanted to pump me about you. But have no fear.' She covered her heart with her hand, then, growing serious, touched him lightly on the shoulder. 'I didn't tell him anything.' She looked at him, then quickly away. 'My lips are sealed.'

He took her hand with renewed feeling. 'I knew I had nothing to worry about. I *knew* it.'

Liberty sagged into the leather seat, vastly relieved that she had passed the test. And, in fact, he probably didn't have anything to worry about. Telling Eben of Tony Alvarro's whereabouts was no big deal. Only yesterday the *Times* had carried the story.

Archer went on talking as he looked out the window, about nothing in particular. Unexpectedly, she heard him say, 'Seeing you this week has been . . .' He broke off.

She squeezed his hand. He went on, still looking the other way. 'My whole adult life,' he said, 'I've worked for one thing, and one thing only: business. And business has been good for me. But I have a vast blind side, a deep, hollow space. Alone, at the end of the day, I can hear it echo.'

Liberty had a sudden wild impulse to open her evening bag, take out the turtle, and say, 'Here! Look! This is evidence that you're not alone'. But she knew she didn't dare. She had to give Kit another chance to hear it first.

The Alexanders had rented the Crystal Room at Tavern on the Green, the big white one overlooking the garden. Although it wasn't even eight-thirty, there was already a sizeable glitzy-looking crowd clustering beneath the chandeliers. As Liberty entered the room on Archer's arm, the jazz combo – bass, drums, guitar, piano – struck up the vamp to 'New York, New York'. There was scattered applause, which Archer ignored.

'Tell me . . .' She went on tiptoes to reach his ear. 'Does everybody here know the guest of honour is Verena – or do they think it's you?'

He spoke over the music. 'Mandy's thrown lots of parties for Verena since she emerged from her Ugly Duckling phase. After she modelled the Paris collections. She was fourteen then. And last year, when she landed the Ruba account –'

'Landed?' Liberty cut in. 'Didn't Rush set that up for her, like he's set up this movie?'

He eyed her quizzically.

'Surely nobody's pretending nepotism isn't alive and well in your little group?'

He shrugged. 'Verena got her first modelling jobs because of connections, I'll admit, but she landed Ruba on her own. Believe me, nobody tells Shirley Welles who to hire. As for Lacy, I have to confess that was my idea.' He lifted two glasses of champagne off a tray and gave one to her. 'From the look on your face, Liberty, I'd say that surprises you.' He raised his glass. 'To taking you off guard. I rather like the sensation.'

Liberty shook her head. 'I was so sure it was Rush's doing.'

He seemed to be enjoying her momentary confusion.

'Who do you think persuaded Rush in the first place? He was afraid Mandy would disapprove. I told him I'd take care of Mandy if he set up the audition.'

'And here I was working so hard on my Big Conspiracy Theory.'

'How's that?'

'Never mind. You'd lose all respect for me.'

'Try me,' he grinned.

'Someone I interviewed persuaded me that Rush might have had something to do with the Monette Novak suicide. You know . . . that he engineered it to clear the boards for his daughter.'

Archer laughed. 'To begin with, Rush is a very economical guy. He never performs tasks unnecessarily. To get Monette Novak fired would have been the simplest thing in the world. Even Kit wasn't all that sold on her.'

Liberty's gaze ran over to the bar, where Rush Alexander, lithe and athletic-looking in a white dinner jacket, stood talking with his hands bulging in his pockets. Every so often he stooped to listen to the iron-haired dowager who had his ear, giving her a grin or laugh.

'He looks like he's having a high old time tonight,' Liberty commented.

'Rush? Why shouldn't he? He's very proud of Verena. That also happens to be one of our chief stockholder's he's with. If I'm not mistaken, she's the one he taught to smile.'

'No mean task. So much for the conspiracy theory, although you must admit that Rush does lend himself to speculation.'

'Yes...' His voice trailed off as a tall blonde woman in a bright red chiffon dress came towards them, working her way through the crowd like a swiftly spreading flame. He held out his arms to her. 'You look absolutely –'

She clasped his hands and cut short his compliment. 'I'm worried, Archer. Verena was supposed to be here at seven-thirty.'

Liberty detected the delicate trace of an English accent, and deduced this was her hostess, Amanda Alexander.

'I'm sure there's nothing to worry about.'

'You don't understand.' She drew nearer and lowered her voice. 'Rush handled the whole thing terribly. He told Verena she actually *had* the part – no audition, no interview. Apparently he *forced* Kit to take her, sight unseen.'

'What?!'

It was the first time Liberty had ever heard the man exclaim.

'When Verena went to thank her, Kit just sliced her to shreds. I have a good mind to tell that woman...'

Archer rubbed his jaw. 'What the hell's got into Rush? I knew I should have handled it myself.'

'He's denying the whole thing. He claims Kit misunderstood him.'

Archer frowned. 'She's under a lot of pressure, but I seriously doubt...'

Archer broke off as a small, dyspeptic-looking man whom Liberty recognised as the publisher of Herman Miller's *Last Chance* elbowed his way into their company.

Amanda Alexander put on a warm smile for him.

'Where's Kit? She's the only reason I came to this bar mitzvah.'

He looked, Liberty observed, like a man whose blockbuster was imperilled. His distress somehow offended Mrs Alexander, who turned suddenly chilly.

'I'm sure she'll be along by and by,' Amanda replied. 'In the meantime, Harry, have you sampled the buffet? I think you'll find some of your favourites.' Her tone was enough to send him away.

Liberty found herself suddenly a target of the other woman's stare and made a rather lame show of listening to the band.

Archer spoke up. 'I'm sorry, darling,' he said to her. 'I didn't think you'd mind my bringing the young woman you'll be meeting tomorrow.'

'Why, Miss Adams!' The charm switch was thrown and Liberty was instantly dazzled. 'How do you do? Archer's told me so much

260

about you.' She went on graciously and at length, as if the previous conversation had never taken place.

Amanda Alexander had the softly glowing look of a woman who, when it comes to pampering herself, spared no expense. She looked like a kept woman, but one who kept herself *for* herself. Liberty decided this woman and her husband would have separate bedrooms, and, like Archer at this moment, her husband should be content just to look. Liberty felt suddenly like an interloper, but Mrs Alexander was too polite to let her feel that way for long.

'I'm so happy you could join us tonight, Miss Adams. I'm looking forward to our little chat tomorrow. You know, *Metropolitan* is my favourite magazine, and Kitsia's the most marvellous woman I know. Will you two excuse me? I'm going to telephone some of Verena's friends. Perhaps she's turned up there.'

'She seems worried.' Liberty turned to Archer.

Archer watched Amanda make her way across the room. 'So am I. The poor kid . . . And we meant so well. But she's tough. She'll work it out.' He turned to her and summoned a smile. 'After all, didn't somebody once say that children succeed in spite of their parents? Verena's a prime example.'

'You sound proud of her.'

'I am. And I wouldn't have suggested her for the part if I didn't think she was damned right for it. And *ready*, in spite of what her mother thinks.'

'Let's dance, Archer.'

He relieved her of her champagne glass and laced his fingers with hers. 'That's what I like about you.' He smiled into her eyes. 'You're so direct.'

'You got to watch me, though. I try to lead.'

'I'll be my most domineering.'

Liberty growled in her throat. 'I love it when you're domineering.' She tried to steer them away from the band so that she could still carry on a conversation with him. 'Mrs Alexander is certainly a beautiful woman.'

'You're leading,' he teased.

'I warned you. Amanda seems so young.'

'She is young. She had Verena before she was twenty. You think Mandy is beautiful, you should have seen her mother when she was alive.'

'Whose mother?'

'Mandy's. I met her only once, but she was *smashing*. Then again, I was a rather susceptible adolescent at the time. I begged Kitsia to carry a love note to her. They were best friends, Kitsia and Cynthia. Kitsia brought her to Zwar the New Year's she came to stay. For moral support.'

'Did Kitsia deliver the note?'

'No.' His thoughts seemed to drift. 'Kitsia never did get around to it. She had other plans.'

'I can imagine.'

Liberty wondered whether he could feel her body temperature rise through her hand, betraying that she not only imagined, but *knew* just what had happened that night. Still, she wanted to hear him tell it.

'About that New Year's, Archer . . .' she began. Before she could finish, an enormous golden girl lunged between them.

Liberty hadn't seen a dress that short since 1966. A gold sheath, it was suspended by two straps no thicker than necklace chains, forming a filigreed web above her left breast. Her legs were long and muscular, encased in glittery hose and flat gold slippers. Her hair hung over one shoulder in a thick gold braid; her cheeks were rosy without benefit of blush. Good health exuded from every pore. If her mother was a hothouse special, she was farm-grown.

She pulled Archer across the floor, out onto the terrace, and, throwing herself into his arms, burst into tears.

'Why did he do it to me, Uncle Archer? He's made her hate me. No matter how good I am, she'll still hate my guts . . .' She stopped when she saw Liberty had followed them, and pulled away from Archer, slipping the handkerchief from his pocket and wiping her face.

'Great party, isn't it?'

'Verena, honey, this is Liberty Adams. A reporter,' he added quickly, as if cautioning her.

'Yeah?' She stuffed Archer's linen back in his pocket.

'She's the one who's doing the story on Aunt Kitsia.'

Her face fell. 'Too bad you're not the investigative type. I'd have a real scoop for you.'

As Rush shoved through the doors, Verena clapped both hands clumsily over her mouth.

'Did somebody just mention my favourite word?' Rush grinned at Liberty.

'Yeah,' said Verena. '"Poop".'

Archer dropped his cigarette and crushed it under his heel, taking Rush by the arm. 'Have a minute, Rush?'

'Oh-oh,' Verena said loudly. 'That's my cue. Yours, too.' She grabbed Liberty by the elbow. 'Uncle Archer wants a "moment" with my father. That's code for *alone*.'

'No need to rush off, Verena.' Rush grinned. 'How nice to see you again, Miss Adams. I'm looking forward to tomorrow.'

Me too, Liberty thought, and to hearing all about whether you were behind Mrs Novak's scene at the Sherry.

Verena was tugging at Liberty's arm. 'Come on, Miss Adams.' She pulled her through the French doors and slammed them shut behind her. Spying the waiter with a tray of champagne glasses, she chased him halfway across the floor and came back with two glasses, sloshing one towards Liberty and downing her own in one gulp.

'Mmmmmmmmmm,' she said, wiping her mouth on the back of her hand. 'Isn't this dress wonderful? It's perfect to drink champagne in. Too bad the company isn't nicer.'

'I don't know.' Liberty looked around. 'If I were seventeen and all these people came to *my* party, I'd feel pretty special. Several producers, a few Broadway angels, some soapy aristocrats, a few all-purpose society types.'

'Pu-lease ... those society types are Mandy's, not mine.'

'Isn't that Max Rugoff over there talking to Joe Papp?'

Verena shrugged and wound her gold braid around her wrist. 'Probably talking about money. Want some gum?'

Liberty shook her head, watching Verena reach into her tiny gold bag, and take out a piece of Bazooka. She unwrapped it carefully, withdrawing the fortune.

She read aloud, '"You will soon be sitting on top of the world". Hah! That's a joke.'

'Is there something the matter?' Liberty asked carefully.

'Something the matter? With me? No, nothing's the matter with me. I'm just fantastic. My father is an arsehole, but I'm fantastic. He always does this, my father: turns a perfectly good present into a piece of shit. Don't get me wrong, Miss Adams, I want the part, it's just that I wish he hadn't done it the way he did it. I could have *earned* that part, given half a chance.'

'By auditioning, you mean?' Liberty asked.

She flipped her braid over her shoulder. 'Never mind. I'll tell you tomorrow.'

'Tomorrow?' Liberty asked.

'You're coming to see Mandy, aren't you?' She hauled the braid back over her shoulder and examined the ends.

'Yes.'

'Well, I'll be waiting for you afterwards.'

'Oh!'

She towered over Liberty. The long yellow rope of braid made Liberty think of mountain climbing. Yet there was something overpoweringly vulnerable about this giant child.

'You can give me a sneak preview, can't you?'

'I can't tell you here!' She looked at Liberty as if she were impossibly thick. 'He's *out* there! And it happens to involve high-level people in the government.'

'*What?*'

She whispered, 'Senator Eben Pierce, if you want to know. I forget which state he's from . . .' She screwed up her face trying to remember. 'But he was over the other night, and, *boy*, did I get an earful. No kidding. I'll tell you all of it tomorrow.' She backed up into the crowd. Just as Liberty went after her, a circle of flashbulbs exploded around Verena. She smiled into the glare as if born to it.

Archer returned shortly, his jaw muscles working.

'Everything okay?' she asked.

'Just fine.'

'I don't suppose I can expect to see Kit this evening?'

The jaw muscles tensed again. 'No I don't suppose you can.'

The band began to play an old, slow song. Without even asking her to dance, he took her in his arms. His face had softened noticeably and he was singing in her ear.

'You have a nice voice,' she told him.

'Are you kidding? The first time I heard Sinatra sing this was over thirty years ago.'

She looked up into his eyes, which were sad and a little distant. There would be no better time to ask it.

'What was your wife like?'

'Lovely,' he breathed.

'I know she was lovely,' she said gently. 'That much I can guess. But what was it about her, Archer?' They had stopped moving. People were dancing around them awkwardly.

He looked at her strangely. 'I don't know what you mean.'

She squeezed his hand. 'Yes, you do, Archer. You know exactly what I mean. You know, after breakfast with you on Tuesday, I tried to look up Mrs Archer Ransome. According to the newspapers, she never existed. What do you want to bet when I go to look her up in the City Hall records, she'll be equally missing. Now, I figure something pretty heavy must have happened to make a person get erased like that. Either that,' she added softly, 'or you made the woman up.'

He let go of her in the middle of the floor.

'Let's go outside.'

Liberty snatched two glasses of champagne and followed him through the French doors out into the terrace, eager to hear what he had to say. Would he restore his dead wife to the record?

The garden was furnished with white wicker furniture upholstered with pink cushions. The trees were strung with delicate clusters of lights. It wasn't a very fitting setting for a man, yet it made Archer seem attractive in a new way, somehow more virile. They found a bench and sat down side by side.

After a long silence, he spoke. 'I met Cassie at a party at Ham Barclay's summer house in East Hampton. The fountain shot purple water and there were lanterns strung down to the beach. That was all Ethel's doing. Ethel was Ham's wife. She and Ham had taken Cassie in. I never knew the whole story of how Cassie came to live with Ham. I knew she was from Boston and that she and her mother, her foster mother, didn't get along.'

'Her *foster* mother? What happened to her real mother?'

'I've forgotten.'

Liberty leaned in to him, a silent questioning.

'You don't believe me. If I ever knew, I have forgotten. Cassie loved secrets, loved to keep her own and loved to hear other people's. Anyway, I was telling you how we met. At Ham's.' He closed his eyes and inhaled. 'Every man at that party wanted her, but after Ham introduced us, she wouldn't dance with anyone but me. She said she trusted me not to step on her feet. She was barefoot, you see. There were burs in the hem of her dress. She told me, fifteen minutes after we met, that we'd get married.'

'She didn't waste any time, did she?'

'No, she was startlingly direct. We saw each other every day for the next two months. We couldn't stand being apart. We were married after an extremely brief engagement.

'And the society columns ate it up. MYSTERIOUS BOSTON BEAUTY WEDS YOUNG TURK.'

'They never let us alone. Then again, we weren't exactly

inconspicuous. Cassie loved to dance and loved public places. Everywhere we went, people adored her. The waiters at Twenty-one used to line up to wait on her.'

'Sounds like a musical comedy to me. Too good to be true.'

'Perhaps it was,' he said wistfully.

'I mean, no one could be *that* perfect.'

'But that's just it, Liberty.' He turned to her, eager as a young boy. 'Are you familiar with the practice of Arabian rug weavers?'

Liberty blinked, 'Which is . . . ?'

He smiled and explained. 'In order not to offend Allah with the spectacle of absolute perfection, each weaver is careful to work into his pattern a tiny flaw.' He brought his hands together as if in prayer and murmured, 'So as not to outrage Allah.'

Liberty nodded. 'And Cassandra came complete with a flaw.'

'It was nothing permanent, you understand. But she always had a smudge on her face, or a spot on her dress, or a crooked hem. And her hair: it was wild, like yours, only women weren't wearing it wild in those days. She looked as if she'd never seen the inside of a beauty parlour. And when we used to walk down the street . . . Most women are always watching the windows to catch their reflections, but Cassie never did that. This carelessness of hers, coupled with her natural beauty, had the effect of making every other woman I'd ever met seem vain and pretentious. Even Kitsia – who's rather jaded about physical perfection – was intrigued by her.'

He fell suddenly silent, brooding.

Liberty prodded him. 'When was this – that Kitsia knew your wife?'

'When Cassie was pregnant.' He hesitated. Liberty looked at him but refrained from prompting him this time. The reporter in her was beginning to feel embarrassed.

Then he began to talk more easily. 'Strange. Sometimes I'll picture Cassie in my mind, pregnant with our child . . . all belly . . . and it's as if I were still waiting for that child to be born.'

'What happened to the child?' Liberty asked, almost shyly.

'She lost it. She lost the baby.'

'I'm sorry.'

'What am I saying?' He stood up and fumbled with his cigarette case. 'She didn't lose it.' He lit the cigarette. Smoke caught in his eye and he turned his back to her to wipe it away. She could barely hear him. 'It's a long story, Liberty. I wish I knew you better.'

266

Liberty felt her throat tighten. 'You do know me, Archer.'

'You seem' – he turned to face her – 'so ...' He dragged on his cigarette and handed it to her for a puff.

'After Cassie and I had been married a few months, this woman, her foster mother, wrote to me demanding money. In her letter, she said I owed her money – a sort of reverse dowry – for taking Cassie away from her. I refused to give her anything, naturally. That is, my lawyers refused for me. She began to come around our house. We had a town house in Gramercy Park then. I never saw her. She came when I was at work. Kitsia couldn't always stand guard. She had her work to do. She was often at her studio on Fourteenth Street.'

'What do you mean, "stand guard"?'

'When Cassie became pregnant, she became even more ...' He groped for the right word. '... highly strung. I had invited Kitsia over to take care of her, of *us*.'

'I didn't know you and Kitsia were so close at that time.'

He turned, distracted by a car's headlight, raking the chainlink fence behind them as it passed through the park. Then he looked at her. 'Someday perhaps you'll understand, Liberty. Right now, you can't. You're a young woman who is, if my guess is correct, unattached.'

Liberty stared at him as he ran his finger along her chin. At this moment she felt more drawn to him than ever before. He seemed to be considering whether or not to kiss her, thought better of it, and dropped her hand, turning away. Liberty wanted to go after him, to pull him back. But she also wanted him to go on. She led him back to his story. 'Just as *you're* a completely unattached man? Not like you were then.'

'Yes.' He nodded thoughtfully. 'I was in love. And when you're in love, you feel' – he filled his chest with air – 'expansive. I loved everyone. Even Kitsia, whom I'd vowed never to speak to or deal with ever again.' He let the air out of his lungs and collapsed back onto the bench. With his elbows resting on his knees, he stared forlornly into his flat champagne. 'Sometimes I wonder where my mind was at the time. Inviting that woman into my house.'

'Expectant Father Forgives All.'

'Invites Meddlesome Auntie Back,' he finished bitterly. 'I suppose I felt I had no right to deprive Cassie of Kitsia's acquaintance. Cassie had, after all, studied art and was working at the Met when I first met her. Kitsia was already a legend in the art world. Besides, Cassie wouldn't leave the house after she began to show. She didn't want to be seen by reporters in her condition. She didn't want them to know.'

'So when Cassie requested an audience, who were you to deny her?' Liberty finished for him.

'She was dying to meet her. She'd heard all the stories. You know, I've never met the man – or the woman, for that matter – who wasn't fatally drawn to Kitsia.'

'You maker her sound like a black-widow spider. She's not so bad.'

He greeted this with a hard little laugh.

Liberty went on. 'She's just used to living alone. Having her way. But getting back to the foster mother: what do you think she wanted of Cassie?'

Archer heaved his shoulders. 'Money, I imagine. At least that's what she demanded in her letters. As I said . . .'

'The lawyers told you not to pay.'

'Yes. She was obviously insane.'

'Did you yourself confront her when she came around to your house?'

He laughed again. 'How could I? Until after Cassie died, I never even knew about the visits. Cassie kept them from me. As she kept many things from me.'

'When people die young, they die with their secrets. We save our secrets to tell when we are old.'

He peered at her strangely. 'That sounds like Kitsia.'

'I think it is. Did Kitsia know about the visits?'

'Of course she did. Cassie took her completely into her confidence towards the end. They grew quite close in the short time they knew one another. Female bonding, I suppose you'd call it today. I felt rather closed out, myself. Sometimes they'd look at me in the strangest way. As if I were an impossible blunderer, a fool to have got my wife into this condition.'

'I take it then that Cassie didn't want to be pregnant.'

'That's just the thing. That's all she ever talked about . . . before. We made love constantly. Then again, that never stopped. Even at the end . . .'

Liberty blushed, but he didn't notice, lost in his thoughts. 'Later, the doctors said it was a common syndrome. Resenting the pregnancy after it's too late to do anything about it.' He turned to her, like a blind man, not seeing. 'She died in childbirth.' He stopped, then went on. 'That night, I was lost. I went from one bar to the next.' He paused. 'I never even went to look at the baby. How could I look at the baby when my Cassie was dead? I never did see it.'

The silence drew on for so long, Liberty finally had to speak. 'And the baby . . . ?'

'Was stolen by Cassandra's foster mother. She got her dowry after all.' He stood up restlessly. 'The police report said that she jumped in the river with the baby in her arms. There were witnesses. They never found the bodies. I often wonder what would have happened if I had just given her the bloody money when she first wrote asking me for it. Would my Cassie be alive today?'

Would the baby? Liberty finished for him silently, and took his hand. He looked down, startled to find her there, like a sleepwalker wakened mid-stride. He finished the story mechanically.

'Rush did what he could to keep it out of the papers. Like have the *Mirror's* society snoop fired. Later, he went back and removed every mention of Cassie from all the records. He did it for me. To save me from the pain. She existed only in the memory of the people who knew her. I've always been grateful to Rush for that little bit of surgery. It made it much easier for me to forget her.'

'But don't you see?' she said softly. 'You haven't forgotten her. You haven't forgotten anything.'

17

The party at Tavern on the Green had dwindled down to a die-hard few when Devin Lowe hoisted Verena off the piano and dragged her out onto the patio. Her hair had fallen loose from her braid and she looked like a rag doll dressed in gold lamé. Rush and Archer, black ties loosened, were lounging on a big grey rock near the bushes. Rush had a bottle of champagne between his legs. If it weren't for their evening clothes, they would have looked like men who had wandered off from the women and kids at a family picnic.

'This little girl needs her daddy.' Devin pushed her up on the rock, hoping one of the men would unburden him.

'Who are you?' Rush heaved himself up and Devin flinched as if he were going to get hit.

'Devin Lowe.'

'That still doesn't answer my question, nor offer me the slightest clue as to why you are holding my daughter so familiarly.'

Archer got up and relieved him of Verena's weight. 'He's from Horizon. Thanks, Devin, we'll take her from here. Where's her mother?'

'Out front saying good night to the guests. Verena was fine until a couple of minutes ago. We were all around the piano singing musical-comedy medleys. She's got a terrific voice. But I guess the champagne finally got to her.' He backed off under Rush's menacing glare and returned to what was left of the party.

'Down, Rush. Give me a hand, will you? She's not a little girl any more, is she?'

From beneath the hair, a rash of drunken giggling erupted, ending in, 'That's for sure!' Verena held up a declarative finger and collapsed onto the rock, Rush and Archer breaking her fall at the last minute. Rush returned to his side of the rock and took a sip of champagne. She thought she saw it slosh in the glass. They'd had a lot to drink too.

'Everybody's smashed,' she mumbled.

Archer chided her softly, 'I don't know about everybody, Verena –'

'Nah!' She hiccuped. 'I've had just about enough. Now I'm ready to talk to my daddy.'

'Why not wait?' Archer patted her hair.

'Okay,' she said, resting her head on his shoulder, as docile as a child. 'Maybe later is better.'

'That's a girl. Close your eyes and rest now. We'll take you home. You'll feel better if you close your eyes and sleep now.'

She pulled her hair back and stared at him blearily. 'But when I close my eyes, Uncle AJ, the ground comes up like this!' She held her hand in front of her face and then flopped back on Archer's shoulder, 'Oh-oh.'

Archer began to smooth her hair slowly and rhythmically. How many times had she fallen asleep like this, as a little girl, in her father's library or up at AJ's house in Millbrook? It might be just the three of them, or there might be a whole room of businessmen. And she'd lie there, eyes closed, mouth slack, taking a sleeper's big breaths, listening to the endless droning of men talking business . . . or pleasure. Once Gary Gareth talked about a gambling club in Venezuela where a woman would give the players random blow-jobs under the card table while they played. No matter what the size of your winnings, you lost it all if you let on to your fellow players that you were getting blown.

At the time, Verena couldn't figure out what a blow-job was. She thought it might have something to do with a personal service, like getting your nails buffed or your shoes polished. Gradually she came to understand their conversations, as she did tonight, nestled on her Uncle AJ's shoulder, pretending to be asleep.

'Rush, I might as well say it. You know I'm thinking it. Why didn't you tell me you and Novak were involved? Why did I have to find out from a third party?'

'You're too busy for third parties lately, Arch.'

'Just trying to stay on top, Rush. You know I never doze during crises.'

'We're sure as hell in the middle of one of those, aren't we, buddy? Don't you think we're both a little too busy putting out fires to concern ourselves with who I've been banging lately?'

'Normally, yes, but with Monette, there's a difference. Monette is dead. You know as well as I do that we don't need this now.'

'Don't even think about it, Arch.' Rush's words were followed by a silence during which they both listened to Verena breathing deeply.

'How did we ever let things get this far, Rush?'

Rush puffed on his pipe and didn't answer.

'And didn't I ask you where do we stand with the senator? You never did answer.'

'Sure I did. I said the senator is ours.'

'You did?'

'I did, old buddy. I did it all for you.'

'That's right. You did say something about that.'

They both fell silent. Verena was just beginning to drift off when Archer stopped smoothing her hair and said, 'Rush, there's another thing.'

Rush waited to hear.

'I know I've asked you this before, but isn't there some way you could start toning this SEC stuff down?'

Rush puffed some more. 'How can I do that?'

'I need time. *We* need time. Rush, it can be handled. I'm sure it can be.'

'I'm not sure. I've tried to keep the papers fair ... but can you expect them to ignore all this?'

'Do you mind if I prefer not to be convinced before the trial starts?'

'I don't mind a lot, Arch, but Greenhause goes before the Senate committee on Monday. We don't have to worry about the senator, but' – Rush lowered his voice and spoke quickly – 'that son of a bitch Greenhause is going to tell them without even being asked that Ransome Enterprises paid him three hundred thousand in cash to look the other way on our recent stock ... uh ... stock trading. Cash.' Rush spoke the word slowly, almost as if he didn't understand the word. 'Three hundred thousand dollars in cash.'

'What good are gambling casinos if we can't use the cash?'

'You are drunk, aren't you? I couldn't agree more.' He spoke around the stem of his pipe. He always smoked a pipe when he was drunk: it made him look sober.

'We've been in tight places before, Rush. If we can just engineer one more infusion of money to prop up the stock. It's fallen nine points. Do you realise I've lost ten million dollars on paper?'

'I suppose this means you're destitute now.' Rush let the burned tobacco fall out of his pipe.

After a while, Archer spoke up. 'If we could arrange to transfer the money from –'

'Forget it, Arch.'

'No, hear me out. Just one more time. You call the bank...'

Rush was irritated. 'Good God, transferring laundered money from the Bahamas to a paper company to prop up the stock is exactly what the SEC is investigating.'

'Exactly. And they'll figure we wouldn't possibly do it again.'

'And I thought I had balls. Forget it, Archer, there is no money.'

There was a new, a sober edge to Archer's voice. 'If the stock falls again...'

'There isn't enough money in the account to do what you want.'

Verena felt the heat of his lighter as he lit a cigarette.

'Well, maybe we have to sacrifice *Last Chance*, after all.'

Verena dug her fingernails into her palms.

'Don't bother with *Last Chance*. The insurance isn't enough money and the movie might win you some supporters down the line.'

'This is a nickel-and-dime process, Rush, and you know it. And with the Trips cash, have you any idea how much that'll give us?'

'A better idea than you, Arch, and I tell you, it isn't enough.'

'Why isn't it enough?'

'I'll spell it out for you tomorrow.'

'I want to know why, and I want to know now.'

'Would you like to go back to the office now? We can go over the books so you can –'

'Jesus, Rush, I'm sorry. I didn't mean to... It's just... you know, we've got to find some way out of this mess without losing the company. Maybe this is Allah's way of punishing us for the way we got control of the company in the first place.'

'I can't see the humour in that, Arch.'

Rush began to rock back and forth on his heels.

'I suppose you're right, it's not very funny. But you know, Rush, we really made something. When I was young, all I wanted was to make enough money so I wouldn't have to go back to Zwar. But after we went out on our own, I realised I could really make something.'

'And we did, Arch.'

'If we could get the money together, and get a little time, we could make Ransome Enterprises stronger than ever. I know I can turn this around.'

'Let's call a meeting first thing tomorrow morning with Adler and Hahn. Let them in on the problem and get them to advise us legally.' Rush hooked the tip of his hands in his cummerbund and

273

clutched his pipe in his teeth. He looked as if he were smiling, but Verena couldn't tell for certain as she peered at him secretly through the veil of her hair.

'I don't want any of your counsellors, Rush. I want *your* opinion.'

'All right, buddy boy, you'll get it. There is a way to boost the stock, to save Ransome Enterprises, but it means sacrificing us. And it means your giving me your decision on it tonight.'

Archer leaned forward again. Rush seemed to lean backward, away from him.

'Sacrifice *us*, Rush?'

'We'd both have to sell most of our stock. You, mostly, since you have so much more than I do ... Sell your stock to the consortium in Canada ... they'll give you half, maybe three-quarters of a point higher than the board price.'

Archer leaned back.

'I must tell the consortium tonight, so that as soon as the market opens, they can start to buy ...'

Archer still didn't say anything. Verena felt his arm tighten about her.

'I can handle it quietly, so it doesn't get out. But you should tell me tonight.' Rush continued to rock.

'I heard you the first time, Rush. You don't need to tell me again.'

'Prickly, aren't we?'

'How do you think it feels for a man to have to save his company by selling his entire stake in it? Do you thinks that's an easy decision to make?'

'I wouldn't know, Arch, but I do know one thing. It's *the* decision. If you blow it now, Allah won't give you another shot ... Now, why don't you let me hold that girl of mine for a while? She looks awfully heavy and you've got burdens enough, don't you, old man?'

'Cassie,' he sighed aloud. He hadn't forgotten a thing.

She had asked for nothing but to be loved. She craved reassurance constantly and he'd given it to her gladly, loving her more each time she asked.

And the plans they had made: to have children – hordes of them – to ward off the loneliness each had suffered as a child; to buy an old house out in the country that would swell and grow as the children came – a games room here, a bedroom/bath for the twins there, a hideaway in the attic for the girl who would want privacy from her brothers.

From the moment he met her he had wanted to take her to Paris. She would wear a long white dress and they would ride through the Bois in the back of an open car, eating pomegranates. Who knew – perhaps he'd even take her to Zwar. He had had this idea that all she'd have to do was set foot on the island and his anger would vanish. But they never got to Paris, and they never got to Zwar.

He spun around, realising suddenly that the tiny twinkling lights in the trees around him had gone out. The big party room was dark and deserted now. Rush and Mandy, the last to leave, had tactfully left him. 'To his glum old Mumms.' Verena had come to, mumbling as Mandy led her off to a cab. He went over to the champagne bucket and pulled out the Mumms, taking a swig from the bottle. He turned the label towards the light: 1957. Tonight, the only meaning that date had for him was that Cassie was gone seven years by then.

He took the bottle with him back to the bench he'd shared earlier with Liberty, as if it were the only safe spot on which to receive the memories.

First they'd bought out Ham Barclay. Then they'd bought a chain of plastics factories. He and Rush had made a pact not to have anything serious to do with women until the operation was established. How was he to know that at the party Ham threw to celebrate the acquisition, he would also introduce him to his smashing-looking young boarder? As ecstatic as he himself had been to meet Cassie, Rush had been hurt, even resentful of her. But Rush had softened, much to his relief, and by their wedding day he had been his sly, charming old self. Even Cassie noticed the change and began to warm to him. At the end of the evening, Rush had come up and locked him in a fierce handshake. 'You're one lucky bastard,' he had said.

Cassie had been so funny about men making advances towards her. She'd turn gruff and tomboyish, rebuking them in a way that never damaged their ego but which nevertheless made her feelings well known: she loved only Archer. He had been a jealous man before he met Cassie, but with her he knew jealousy was a coarse, inappropriate reaction, in spite of the way men looked at her. Passing her in the street, men would look away and then turn and stare, hungering after her. And those same men eyed him with envy. Whenever he met her in a public place, she'd run towards him, flinging herself into his arms, the heat from her body travelling into his, inflaming him. He had felt all-

powerful with her. Yet her beauty awed him.

They'd had to fight for their time alone together. It seemed everyone wanted to be with them. Rush had said it once: it was as if they gave off this golden glow. Had Rush felt cheated of the glow? Was that why he'd said those things to him that night in the hospital waiting room? Talking to Liberty tonight, it had all come back to him: the pain, the lies... Was there some hidden malice there, even then? He turned away from the thought and back to the memory of their best times together: evenings when he had had her to himself out in public. Hands locked, bodies pressed together on the dance floor, they had swayed to the old songs.

She'd sung along to the music, the merest whisper, in his ear. After a while, he had been unable to help himself. He'd hustled her off the floor and out of the club so quickly people remarked on it. In the taxi on the way home he never touched her. They had sat apart, like children trying to be good. But the cab-driver knew, everyone knew that they couldn't wait to be alone together in bed. Bed! Sometimes it was a chair, sometimes a sofa, a table, a new carpet. They'd inaugurate every new piece of furniture by making love on it.

He closed his eyes, swallowing the cold, still-bubbly liquid, and then opened them, remembering the line of her throat, the way her skin went all rosy as she eased herself onto him and leaned into her long ride.

'It's a pity you never get to see yourself... how lovely you look at these moments,' he had said to her once. And she'd widened her eyes at him as if he were slightly mad.

But she had been so fine, with her head thrown back and her eyes closed. Every now and then she had stopped and opened her eyes to reassure herself that he was with her, and then she was off again, bringing on that moment he now lived for: when she broke into moans, writhing above him, when she began to suck on his fingers as if they were teats and she some wild, starving cub. And then she'd fall on him, netting his head and chest in her wild, wild hair, calling out his name so sweetly. And always it was as if he were hearing his name spoken for the very first time.

He had never confided in her his greatest fear: that he would come home one night and find her gone, the dream vanished. Every time he made love to her, he held on to that dream. Every time he walked in the front door and heard her cry greetings from some quarter of the house and saw her come running to him in one of those too grown-up dresses Ethel Barclay bought for her because she was never able to shop for herself, the dream was alive again.

She might not have been able to shop for herself, but for him she was tireless. She had even shopped for their house in Gramercy Park, with its green copper mansard roof, its four French windows on each floor. How she had loved the tiny wrought-iron balconies on each window, the wind trap in the bedroom eaves! She claimed the sound of the wind at night made her feel cosy. And yet, nights when the wind blew hardest, she never slept. He'd wake up to feel her arms tightening quickly around him, as if she were afraid she was about to slip and fall.

'I'm sorry I dropped you, Cassie,' he said aloud.

She'd had such fun decorating that house, slowly, in the form of presents for him. Each night, he'd come home and find some new surprise awaiting him. The small bronze Degas ballerina bending to tie her toelace; an original lithograph poster of the Folies Bergère by Toulouse-Lautrec. She'd found that poster in a junk shop whose owner didn't realise its worth. Taking pity on him, she'd paid him three times what he was asking. Her stories pleased him as much as her gifts.

She'd been so brave those last months, so strong and confident – glowing with maternal feeling. She had wanted them to share their happiness with others. Although ignorant as to its cause, she had begged him to bury this irrational hatred for Kitsia. He had thought it was for his sake that he'd sent for Kitsia in his wife's fifth month. How could they have known it was for hers, too?

He knew now that whatever her past life or lives, he'd been a fool ever to doubt her love for him. How could he have believed those lies? Lies from his friend! He had felt he was losing her. He couldn't bear to listen, and yet he was too frightened to cover his ears.

'But all this time, Cassie, I never blamed you. You, my dearest darling angel, will always be blameless.'

18

Verena let herself into the kitchen as quietly as a cat burglar.
Locking the door behind her, she put the key back into her jogging
bag. She stood in the middle of the floor with both feet inside one of
the large tile squares. She tested herself and walked the deep red
line that separated the rows of white tiles. At least she wasn't drunk
any more. Rush had stayed to tip the help at the Tavern, and
Mandy had brought her home, undressed her, and put her into her
granny gown because it had turned cold. As soon as Mandy was
gone, she'd got up, pulled off her nightgown, put on sweats, and
gone outside again. She had this idea that to lie senseless and
drunken in her bed was dangerous. She had to be sober, alert, on
guard. She'd gone running, sweating out the alcohol, running until
her sides ached and she'd had to lean against a tree and throw up
and then run still more. Coming back now, she had to be careful
not to make any noise that might wake either of them.

She started up the first of three flights of stairs, feeling queasy.
How could she have let herself get so drunk? She knew how. She'd
done it to get up the courage to tell Rush off for the way he'd
handled getting her the part, but the drunker she got, the less sure
she was of what to say. She never did get around to it.

Verena came to the first landing. The back stairs, narrow and
covered only with a thin rubber runner, could easily have been in
another house. The main stairs were wide and covered with a thick
beige carpet with a border of tiny blue flowers, and on each step a
brass rod held the carpet in place.

Verena stopped short. What was that? Her heart beat faster. She
held her breath to listen. It was the clock bonging three-thirty a.m.
Verena sat down on a step to recover.

She stretched her long legs down the steps and felt like Alice in
Wonderland after she'd finished the 'Drink Me' bottle and grown
too big for the house. She imagined her head pushing through the
roof. Verena stretched her arms from one wall to the other. She *was*
too big for this house.

She looked down the steps and began to count them. One, two, three, four ... Why had she ever come back? Once she'd been free of them, free of Mandy and Rush. Why hadn't she just stayed free?

'I don't see why you want to go back.' The boy, her fellow runaway, sat cleaning grass on a Police album cover.

Verena was trying to fit tiny violets into her pierced ears. She was perspiring. She kept wiping off her upper lip and between her breasts, and then when she touched the violets, they got all damp and flat. She walked over to the far side of the deck to pick more.

'I'm not sure ... exactly,' she finally answered.

'Give me a hand, willya, Verena?'

Verena held the wooden match over his pipe. She took a toke herself. Just a small hit. The sun was making her spacey enough.

'Something horrible might happen. They're my parents. I have to try to make it up to them. Something terrible ... you know.'

'Verena, something bad's going to happen to you if you do go back. Take it from me. That father of yours is a sickie.'

Verena's eyes filled with tears. 'I don't know why, but I'm going back to New York.'

He reached out for her, but she moved back and kept talking.

'Don't you see, they're still my parents. Can't you understand that? I can't just keep running away.'

'Whatever you say, Verena. You got to do what you got to do.'

'Fuck you!' Verena shouted, and he put his earphones on.

Verena lined up the six stacks of coins on the silver ledge in the phone booth. She cupped her fingers around the nickels to make them as neat as the two dime stacks and the three quarter stacks. She lifted the receiver, and the wire cord knocked into the dimes and they fell all over the ledge and onto the dirty floor of the booth.

Verena bent down to pick up the dimes. It was hot in the booth, but she kept the door closed. It was safer with the door shut.

Some days, she thought, I can go almost the whole day without thinking about it. Then, out of nowhere, I see him or I hear him talking to me. God! She felt so guilty. She stacked the fallen dimes into smaller columns, four in all.

Verena had been gone nine months. Nine months. She used to wonder if Rush had pulled the detectives off the search or whether they were still looking for her. She'd run away with a boy from school who'd run away six times already. He was an expert. She told him everything and he never touched her. Key West had been his idea. For the first six weeks in Key West, Verena made him steal the New York papers at the fruit stand every morning to see if there was any mention of her disappearance. But there never was. Rush could control writers better than he could control daughters.

Someone knocked on the phone booth. Verena jumped and turned around.

'Are you finished?' a young man asked her.

'No, I'm not.'

'Will you be much longer?' The man stuck his tennis shoe into the door to hold it open.

'Yeah. I got a few calls to make. Parents, you know.' Verena saw her friend over the guy's shoulder. He was pointing to himself and to her, asking if she wanted him to come over. She shook her head.

'There's a phone booth one block down there.' Verena tossed her head.

The man stood looking at her. Then he smiled. 'Thanks.'

Verena turned back to her bank. She took one dime and scrutinised it, looking for the date. It was a 1973. And this whole nine months she had felt like a spy, an undercover agent who had been given a temporary identity. But now it was time to come in out of the cold. Sometimes the 'company' didn't like to let undercover spies back in – it was dangerous. But she had to try.

She dropped the dime into its slot and dialled ten digits.

'Please deposit two dollars and twenty cents for the first three minutes.'

The phone was ringing.

'May I speak to Mr Archer Ransome, please?'

'Mr Ransome is on another line. May I ask who's calling?'

'This is . . .' Verena hesitated. 'A friend of his.'

'Well . . . is there a message, or can I give him a number where he can reach you later?' The woman's voice was nice, but this was just another call to her. She had no way of knowing how important this call was.

'Can I hold on? I don't have a number.'

'I really don't know how long Mr Ransome is going to be. He has a meeting to attend as soon as he finishes this call.'

'Please . . . this is very important. Long distance.'

'Please deposit one dollar and five cents for the next two minutes.'

'Yeah . . . okay, operator, just a sec. Can I hold on?'

The phone line popped and Verena was cut off from Ransome's secretary.

'You will have to deposit one dollar and five cents or I will have to disconnect your party.'

'Wait . . . wait!' Verena fumbled with the change.

'You've deposited one dollar and twenty-five cents instead of one dollar and five cents. I'll credit you the extra time.'

'Thanks a heap.'

'You're welcome. Your party's on the line.'

'Please let me speak to Mr Ransome. It won't take a second to tell him something!' Verena pleaded with the secretary.

'What is your name, young lady?'

'I can't tell you. But please, I really do know him.' Verena weighed her options. She wasn't getting anywhere with this woman, but she was so afraid of tipping her identity and being transferred to Rush's office. 'He's *kind of* my uncle.'

'Just a moment, let me see if he's free.'

'Verena?' Archer came on the line.

'Oh, Uncle AJ!' Verena bit her lip. Spies don't cry. 'I want to come home.'

'I want you to come home, too. We've missed you.' Ransome spoke slowly, as if she were his only care in the world.

'Don't tell Daddy yet. Or Mandy. Okay?'

'All right.'

'Promise?'

'Yes, I promise. Your coming back will be our secret.'

'I love you.'

'I love you, Verena. Now, how shall we start?'

Verena had guessed right. Because he didn't have any kids, he was calmer. He didn't feel compelled to tell her how bad she had been.

'Please deposit an additional ninety-five cents for two minutes.'

'Uncle AJ, can you hear me?' Verena raised her voice nervously.

'Please deposit the amount or I'll have to disconnect you.'

'Fuck you, lady!' Verena jammed the rest of her quarters down the telephone's throat. *Bong. Bong. Bong. Bong.*

Archer was laughing. 'Have you a plan, honey?'

'No, I thought you might –'

'Here. How are you getting back to New York?'

'Flying.'

'You have enough money for the ticket?'

'Yeah.'

'Before you leave wherever you are, you call my office and tell Susie what time the car should be at the airport to pick you up. Will you be alone?'

'I'll be alone.'

'Okay. How about if my driver takes you up to my house in Millbrook and I'll come up and we'll figure out together what to do next.'

'How are they, Uncle AJ?'

'Oh, Rush is a little rocky. Your mother is desolate. But don't worry, everything will be fine as soon as you come home.'

'Uncle AJ, I'm so sorry.'

'Don't, Verena. You have nothing to apologise to me for. Everything will be fine.'

Verena hung up the phone and wiped her nickels off the ledge into her palm. How could everything be fine?

'We can't fit the armoire up those stairs, Mrs Alexander.' The moving man stood in the kitchen wiping his face with a red checked handkerchief.

'Well . . .' Mandy looked from the armoire to the moving man and back. 'Bring it around and go up the main stairs. They're wider. Please watch the pictures on the walls.'

Verena sat at the kitchen counter on a bar stool eating a bagel with cream cheese, sliced onion, and tomato. It was her first day home.

'Are you thinner? You look thin.'

'When's Rush coming home? Late, as usual? I sure wouldn't want my homecoming to fuck up his work rituals.'

'Verena,' Mandy said, then checked herself. 'I'll go see how the moving men are getting along.'

After Mandy left, Verena poured herself a little white wine in a jelly glass and sipped at it. Forty-eight hours ago she was saying good-bye to her friend. Thirty-six hours ago she was in Millbrook waiting for Archer. Twenty hours ago she was asking Archer if she could have some of his old furniture in the attic for her new bedroom in Mandy's attic she had decided to take. Three hours ago she was hugging Mandy and telling her not to cry and at the same time telling her the new ground rules.

'I want to live up in the attic. I'm furnishing it myself with Uncle

AJ's help. I'm going to take acting classes with part of my modelling money. And you and Rush are going to leave me alone. You are not allowed to ask me why I ran away or where I've been the last nine months, or I'll run away again.'

Mandy had agreed to everything. Verena felt like a terrorist, with Mandy the frightened hostage.

Verena pulled her knees up and rested her head on them. She remembered how sweet Rush had been when he came home that night. She had come back on Labour Day, a holiday, but Rush was at the office. He took only Christmas and her birthday off. He was so nice, so polite, so glad to have her home. She took him aside and explained to him that if he ever touched her again, she'd kill herself.

It didn't take Verena long to see how things had changed between her parents. They'd always behaved like strangers, but at least before they'd had the cues down. Now they seemed to have forgotten even the cues. Rush seemed not to know that Mandy only used pepper at the table; he persisted in passing her both shakers. Mandy served coffee with cream and sugar on a tray every night, even though Rush always drank his coffee black. Verena felt responsible. She didn't feel sorry for them; they were probably better off this way. But she did feel responsible that the house was so cold, and boring, and creepy. Maybe with time things would get better. And they had got better . . . until the other day, in the back of the car.

Verena stood up. Thinking back had made her smaller. Maybe she could still fit in this house for as long as it would take her to graduate and get the money she had coming to her when she turned eighteen. She stopped and leaned against the railing. *How could he have done that to me in the car?* How could I have let it happen? Verena thought how she had been on her guard, testing him, always ready. But he'd never once tried anything since she was back. They had watched movies together in the dark without Mandy. They had sat on the couch talking. They had sat together in his library. And all the while, he had behaved himself. So after over a year of watching him, Verena decided he'd learned his lesson. But it was a trap. It had been his plan all along to lure her into thinking he would never lay his filthy hands on her again.

'How fucking stupid can I get?' She stood up and shivered.

There was a draught coming out from under her bedroom door. Her floor, the topmost of the house, was in general about ten degrees hotter or colder than the rest of the house. She opened the door and stood in the doorway looking at her room. It was almost like a nun's cell – white and brown, bare. A double bed was in the far corner. It had white sheets and a brown and white striped satin comforter. A wicker rocking chair without arms stood near the bed. A low pine dresser with a small bookshelf over it was against one wall, and a high, honey-coloured armoire stood beside it. The last wall was filled with a ballet barre with full-length mirrors at each end. Only one thing from her old bedroom was up here – one of Rush's presents, a Matisse litho, a red and pink picture of a window opening onto a harbour. She loved it. She'd take it with her wherever she went.

Verena closed the door and switched on the overhead light, a simple pewter chandelier. Rush stepped forward and she pulled back, seizing her throat.

'You scared me. For Christ's sake. What are you doing here? I'm tired.'

'I'm tired too, Verena.' Rush's voice was low, almost unrecognisable. 'I've been waiting here for a long time.'

'Yeah? . . . Well . . . Good night.' Verena walked back over to the open door and stood by it.

He ambled over, his balding head bent to the floor. Just as he got to the door, he slammed it shut. 'I want to talk to you!'

Verena turned and walked into her tiny bathroom. She pulled the string and the fluorescent light came on. She turned on both taps full blast. She knew he was angry. His fists were balled in his pockets.

She looked in the mirror and saw him standing right behind her. 'Rush, there's not enough room for me in here, let alone you. Go wait in there.' Verena spoke to the mirror.

He said nothing. His black eyes fixed her with a long stare.

Verena opened three jars of cream and dipped her fingers into each, scooping up a little white blob from each and putting it on her face.

'Let me help you.' Rush turned her around by the shoulders and sat her down on the toilet. She waited tensely while he took several cotton balls from a basket on the shelf. Gently he wiped the cream off her face.

'Thanks, Daddy. I can do the rest.' Verena got up and bent over the sink to rinse her face.

'You hardly ever call me Daddy. Why not?'

'Be serious. You know why.' She pushed past him. 'Drop it. It's late.'

Avoiding his eyes, she grabbed her flannel nightgown off the hook on the bathroom door and threw it over her head and undressed beneath it. She knew he was staring at her. She could feel his eyes going right through the flannel. She prayed she'd be able to get into it without showing him anything.

Following her back into the bedroom, Rush accidentally caught her nightgown under his shoe. It ripped. Verena looked down. The back of her thigh was visible through the tear. Neither of them spoke.

She went and sat in the rocker. She had to be careful now. She knew Rush hadn't meant to tear her gown, but she was afraid it might get him started. Rush had more patience for a fight than anyone she knew – except maybe herself. She was a lot like him that way. She rocked and watched him.

He stood over by her dresser. He was holding the green ginger jar he'd given her after she had come home from Key West. He put it back on the shelf and slowly and carefully began to fold the clothes that lay in a heap on the floor. He made a neat pile of them on her dresser: the slips in four folds, the blouses all buttoned in halves, the tights neatly folded in half, toes aligned just so. She had always been a slob, never hanging up her clothes. Verena thought of Rush's own dressing room downstairs – so organised it was creepy. The socks all sat in a drawer in little square piles, the shoes were all shined and waiting in flannel bags. The shirts hung in one closet (never folded), while the trousers and jackets hung in another, like well-pressed soldiers at roll call. As Verena watched him fold her things, she found herself fascinated, as always, by the quick movement of the perfect white hands.

She knew all about his hands. If she really wanted to think about it, she knew just about everything about him. He'd told her about his life while they were hacking around, in the car, down in the rec room. Before he'd got around to making her be naughty for him. She used to think something was wrong with her that she couldn't feel sorry for Rush, the little Russian boy he'd told her about.

Some part of her knew it was sad, his stories, the ones he had told over and over. She stared at him, certain he was telling the story over again, to himself, silently. Right about now, she thought, he's remembering how scarred his hands used to be. Before the plastic surgery. He was so poor, he had no coal for the stove and his hands would get so chapped from the cold that they never healed. He'd wrap his hands in pieces of old sheets and study in front of the fire. Uncle AJ had seen those hands. In fact, Uncle AJ was probably the only other person who knew so much about Rush. To everyone else – even to Mandy – he was a mystery. How could Rush betray him like this?

She rocked, pushing off with her bare feet. She was thinking of the story he'd told her of his first day at college, of his coming into Harvard Yard and feeling like a dark misfit in a sea of golden boys. He had one suit then, but his room-mate, Uncle AJ, had made him throw it away. Verena picked up a nail clipper and concentrated on a hangnail. AJ had given Rush his own slightly altered hand-me-downs. AJ was an inch shorter than Rush. Rush was much thinner. Verena's cuticle began to bleed where she had cut off the torn skin.

Then she remembered the high point of his days at Harvard, his affair with the beautiful redhead. Tess, he'd called her.

Rush carried a straight-back chair into the centre of the room. He turned it around, and straddling it, stared at her. Verena started rocking again. She didn't take her eyes off him for an instant as she filed away. She wondered if he were thinking of Tess right now. He thought about her all the time.

'Rush, I have to get up and go to school in three hours.'

'And you want me to leave, I suppose?'

The sound of his voice startled her. It sounded so calm, so reasonable. Verena's mouth was dry, her heart fluttered. *Don't be fooled.*

'Daddy, I just want you to postpone this little talk till tomorrow. No big deal.'

He said, 'I'd like to know why' – he took a deep breath – 'why you called me Daddy just then. Is that your way of flattering me?'

'I don't want to flatter you. What do you want me to call you? I don't know what to call you.'

'Verena, I love you.'

'Yeah. Okay. Can we talk tomorrow, then?'

'I want to talk about us.'

' "Us"?' Verena laughed nervously. 'What us? I'm going to bed, Rush. Good night.'

'Surely you can spare a few minutes to talk to the man who got you the part in *Last Chance*?'

Verena's eyes roamed the ceiling. 'No comment.'

'Where did you go tonight after the party?'

'Home.'

'Home? I've been here waiting for you.'

'I went running.'

'At two in the morning?'

'Yeah. Why not?'

'Don't you like your gift?'

'At first I did, but not now.'

'Why not?'

'Because.'

'Because why, my darling girl?'

She stopped rocking and glared at him. 'Don't call me "darling". Because it's just a dirty bribe.'

'Bribe for what?'

'For keeping my mouth shut about what you're doing to Uncle AJ.'

He nodded thoughtfully. 'I suppose you're right. When I let you come into the library the other night when Senator Pierce was here, I knew I was deliberately involving you. And I have. You're in this with me, whether you like it or not.'

She started rocking again. 'Fat chance ... or *Last Chance*?'

'Wise off all you like, but it's true.'

'If you think I'm going to stand by and watch you double-cross Uncle AJ you've got another think coming!' She got up from the rocker and went to stand over him. 'That reporter, Liberty Adams? I told her everything. At the party tonight. So you can just forget about it. How can I be *in* with you when I've already *ratted* on you?'

His face hardened but she tossed her head, pulled the satin quilt down to the bottom of the bed, and got under the sheet. 'I swear I don't understand why you'd want to do this to the man who fixed your hands and ... and helped you –'

'What did you tell her?' He rose and came after her, his hands closing around her throat before she could pull away.

'Everything!' she gagged. 'I told her everything!'

Just as abruptly, his hands fell away from her neck. She rubbed it. He began to pace around the room restlessly. 'I'm sure she wouldn't believe you, no matter what you told her.'

'You wish.'

He stopped pacing. He saw something on the floor. He stooped to pick it up. It was her gold lamé dress. He held it in his fists and stared at it curiously.

'Mandy said every woman at the party...' Her voice died as she watched him tear the dress in half. It made a sound like a paper towel being ripped off the roll.

Verena began to cry.

He let the pieces of the dress drift to the floor, staring at them sadly. When he lifted his head again, she saw that his cheeks were wet with tears.

'You bitch! You little bitch!'

He came over to the bed and collapsed on it, burying his head in his hands. His shoulders heaved.

'Daddy, please... please don't cry.'

She patted him helplessly. The back of his head where the hair grew finer than on the rest of his head made him look helpless. She wanted to pick him up in her hands and set him down somewhere where no one would step on him. 'Daddy, I'm sorry I made you cry.'

He lifted his head and rubbed his face with the back of his hand. 'I can't ever forgive you,' he said dully. The tears had vanished. 'I had plans, Verena. I thought that you'd be happy to be a part of them. But now I see that you're not.'

'What are you talking about?' She pulled back against the headboard and drew her knees up to her chest.

'In another couple of weeks I will have all the money any man would need. We'll have the rest of our lives. We'll go away... we'll live together as a man and woman have every right –'

'*Holy shit!*' she exploded. 'You're really flipped out, you know that?'

'We have something special. We belong to each other.' He lowered his voice. 'You're mine!'

'Rush,' she warned, 'you better quit it.'

'You'll never belong to anyone else. I thought you'd already come to that conclusion when you came home after having tried to make a go of it with that punk. No one else will have you.'

'Shut up!' Verena clenched her teeth. She put her hands over her ears, shut her eyes, and began to hum loudly.

'Tell me, Verena' – his voice penetrated the hum – 'do you think it's wise to turn me down?'

She hummed louder, but his voice rose. 'Tell me, did you tell little Liberty about you and me? Did you tell her about your dear daddy and the special relationship we share?'

'We don't have a special relationship!' She took her hands off her ears and glared at him. 'We *had* a perverted, sick relationship, and it's over!'

'It didn't seem to be over the other day in the car.' He smiled crookedly.

She slugged him then, with all her might, right in the middle of that crooked smile. His tooth cut her hand. His smile was bloody now. 'Why, you ungrateful little bitch!'

She threw herself at him then, pummelling him with her fists, pinching handfuls of flesh, digging deep to draw blood. She sank her teeth into his shoulder and tore the silk of his dressing gown.

He grabbed her arm and pinned it behind her. As he pushed it to the breaking point, she opened her mouth and began to scream, the scream growing louder the farther he pushed.

Finally she managed to knee him in the groin. He released her arm and sent her flying off the bed, spinning painfully across the floor.

'Oh,' she said, grabbing the chair and holding it out like a lion tamer. 'Oh, how I love to hate your disgusting, filthy guts. I love it! You make me sick! Did you actually think I'd ruin my life and go away with you? Don't you know you make me want to puke? You know what I did the other day after I got out of the car? I puked. I puked my guts out. You know where you belong? You belong on the funny farm, that's where!'

He came at her and rammed the chair up against her, pinning her to the wall with it. His eyes were dark, furious. She lowered her voice to a coarse whisper and said, 'You're a pig. A pig with a curved spine and ugly hands and a crooked smile! And I hate you, I hate you, I hate you, *I hate you, I hate you*!'

The back of his hand hit the side of her face like a brick. Her head cracked against the wall and the mirror next to her slid to the floor with a crash of shattering glass. Verena slid right after it. For a minute, all she saw were red stars.

'All right, you two, what's going on up there!' Mandy called from the bottom of the stairs. 'Rena, honey, what's the matter?'

Rush flung the chair away and yanked Verena to her feet. Her head and arm throbbed. She felt as if she were held together by threads. 'Whoa!' She put her hand to the back of her neck, but

Rush grabbed her arm and pinned it again.

'Truce!' she screeched. 'Truce!'

His hand came over her mouth and nose and she tasted fresh blood. He whispered furiously into her ear, 'Tell her you're fine. It was just an accident.' He twisted her arm still tighter. 'Tell her!'

'Verena? What's going on? Do you hear me? I'm coming up,' Mandy called out loudly. 'Are you hurt? Is Rush up there with you?' Verena could hear her start to climb.

'I'm fine, Mama. Really. We were just talking. Really. Go back to sleep.'

'What was that noise?'

'I dropped a glass. It's just an accident, Ma,' Verena called out weakly. The pain in her arm was unbearable. She thought she might pass out. 'Everything's just fine, Ma.'

Rush called out lazily, 'Your daughter and I are having a small discussion. Did you know she'd taken to midnight jogging?'

Mandy was silent, seeming to consider this. 'I wish you two would talk tomorrow,' she said finally. 'Rush, let her alone. She needs her sleep.' They heard her shut the door.

Rush released her. 'There. That wasn't so bad. Thank you, my dear. You're most cooperative and quite family-spirited not to worry your poor mama. She's been worried enough already, what with you taking that movie part against her wishes. Shall we do a good deed and tell her the news together at breakfast?'

'What news?' Verena was testing the bruise on her cheek with her good hand.

'Why, the good news that you've decided not to take the part, of course.'

'Oh no you don't! That part's mine. I want it, Rush. And besides' – she smiled slyly – 'if you don't let me keep it, I'll tell Uncle AJ about your plan. I'll tell everybody. I'll write a regular publicity release.'

'No you won't,' he said easily.

'I won't? What makes you so sure?'

'Because you wouldn't want me to go to your mother and tell her everything. All about the games room and the car. Everything. I'll tell her everything. And she'll tell Archer. She always does. And you won't be their little darling any more.'

Verena started to say something, then stopped. What could she say?

'So, my dear,' he said cheerfully, 'can I expect you to help me break the news at breakfast?'

Verena felt the tears fall, stinging the cut on her hand.

She is back in the treehouse. It is a beautiful sunny summer afternoon. She can smell dinner cooking and Rush has gone off to play squash with Uncle AJ. She is all alone and lying in an old rubber tyre AJ has hoisted up there to 'furnish' her treehouse in proper style. The tyre fits Verena's body as if it were made for her. She lies there looking up into the sun-dappled oak leaves, wearing last year's shorts, skintight this summer. Her legs fall naturally apart as she lies in the tyre, and her fingers, just as naturally, slip up inside the shorts. She feels safe beneath the canopy of leaves. Then she happens to look out a crack between the boards. Her heart stops. Rush, who is supposed to be playing squash, has laid a piece of timber from his study roof across to the treehouse. He crosses the wobbling bridge in three bounds and is suddenly standing over her in his white tennis shorts, panting.

'I've come to watch you be naughty.' He grins and tells her to take off her shorts. The tyre is perfect, he says: perfect. This is not the back seat of the car or the couch downstairs in the rec room. This is a platform of two-by-fours enclosed on only three sides, thirty-five feet off the ground. Up here with Uncle AJ, she has never felt it, but now, alone with Rush, she is suddenly terrified of falling. Fearfully, she obeys.

'Perfect,' he keeps saying as she squeezes out of the shorts. 'This is so fine. You have no idea,' he says. 'Go ahead,' he says, 'let's see you stir up a little of that sweet cream.'

She begins to make her circles with her fingers, clumsy circles since her hands are stiff from fear. She cuts herself on a hangnail. He hears her sharp intake of breath and misunderstands. 'Let me, please,' he says. He pulls her hands away and she draws them up, like paws. Now his fingers are in there, slipping in and out, rubbing her. But she feels nothing. She tells herself that it does not hurt. If it hurt, she might writhe and roll around, and then she'd fall and die for sure. When his fingers come too far up inside of her, she cried out, 'Too far!' But he isn't listening. He doesn't understand. 'Please, stop!' she says, and her voice wobbles.

'I can't stop, Cassie!' he tells her. Her eyes open when he calls her by that name, and she sees the thing she has never wanted to see. All the

times he has made her be naughty, she's never actually seen it. It is sticking out of the bottom of his tennis shorts. It is purple and swollen, polished as a club. Something glistens at the end of it. 'I'm sorry, Cassie,' he says, 'but I have to.' He braces himself above her on stiffened arms. The muscles are long and hard, like metal bands on either side of her. She will never be able to get away. If she could only fly, she could escape. He lowers himself upon her and buries his head in her neck. Still, she cannot smell him even though she feels the sweaty dampness of his skin. She feels strangely sorry for him, but she knows she cannot, must not, ever touch him in return.

She gasps as the hard purple club works its way up inside of her where his fingers were. He winces and closes his eyes. 'Oh, now,' he says. 'Oh, now, that's it, Cassie. That's all I ever wanted. I'm dying.' He is jabbing her now, over and over again, faster and faster. All she can do is pray for it to be over before she rolls over the edge to her death. But how can a prayer work when she can't close her eyes? Her eyes are stuck open.

'I'm gonna fall,' she calls out. Her voice sounds lost and small.

'You won't fall, Cassie,' he grunts. If only he would open his eyes and see who she is. But he's concentrating on the movements of the hard, stiff club. Or is it a snake now, loose between them? Whatever it is, it has broken her open. Is the snake bleeding, or is she? When Rush finally gives up, he pulls away from her, and hides his face in the leaves above her, which are now almost black. Mandy calls for them out the kitchen window. It's dinner time.

Verena gets up on an elbow and looks at the blood smeared between her legs. 'She's going to kill us.'

He squats before her and holds her so that it hurts. His features are sharp. 'She can't ever know,' he tells her. 'You understand? She can't ever know.'

19

Kit opened the door and grabbed the jamb to steady herself. She inched forward to switch on the overhead light. What had at first appeared to be a body turned out to be her clothes from the valet service hanging on the closet door. She touched them lightly to reassure herself, then stooped to pick up the telephone messages that had been slipped under her door.

In spite of all of Circe's tender ministrations, she was rigid, trembling all over. She'd left Kalypso and gone to the Ransome Building to pick up the package Sasha had left for her – the day's mail and call sheet, Sheridan's analysis of the past weekend's box-office figures, and three scripts. While the driver ran in to pick up the package, Kit waited in the car. Moving to the edge of the seat, she'd strained for a look at her reflection in the rearview mirror, when something unexpected had caught her eye.

A small man wearing a dark blue suit stood behind the limo. She'd nearly turned around to signal him, but something told her not to. When the driver returned with the package, she'd felt a sense of relief to leave the man in the blue suit behind. She'd gone on to a shabby, half-lit commercial building just below Columbus Circle to work with the director of one of her pictures in the cutting room. But all the while she'd stood hunched over the Kem machine helping the director to isolate frames, all the while she'd pored over the script suggesting dub changes, she'd been nagged by the memory of the man in the blue suit. Hadn't she seen him before? Why was he following her?

Still clutching the phone messages, she went into the living room.

Liberty Adams, dressed in a tuxedo, was curled up asleep on the love seat. Kit slumped against the door and thought to herself: Don't tell me we're scheduled to re-enact *All About Eve*. Because if we are . . .

The petite redhead jumped up and shook her head. 'I can't believe I fell asleep!'

Kit said, 'I gather my assistant contacted you. Maybe *your* assistant got it wrong. I believe we specified *next* week in LA, not this week in . . .' Her voice trailed off.

Liberty was opening her bag. She took out the cloisonné turtle and a sheaf of papers. 'Before you say anything, Kit, maybe you should read this.'

Kit stared at the turtle and started to reach for it, but changed her mind. She eyed Liberty sharply, reached over and took the papers. She sat down at a table by the window, and putting on her glasses, glanced at the typewritten pages.

' "Kitsia/Liberty"? What is this? A transcript of your interview with my mother?'

'Yes. Part of it.'

'Why are you showing this to me? Now.'

'Please, Kit, just read it.'

Kit started to read:

Liberty: Why do you think you were so attracted to your nephew?

Kit stopped and looked up uncertainly. 'What is this? I don't understand.'

'You'll see.' Liberty nodded, encouraging her to continue.

Kitsia: He was a beautiful young man, it's true. But more than beauty, I saw in him the infant who used to sunbathe naked with me in my rose garden in Paris. The first time I saw my nephew, he was six months old. Angus had brought him to stay with me because Helen was in the hospital.

Liberty: Helen was Archer's mother?

Kitsia: The only reason she left Zwar in the first place was that she was ill. The few times she did come to Paris, she never stayed in my house. She was ever the proper society lady.

Liberty: I don't understand. Why wouldn't she stay with you?

Kitsia: I was a whore. She was the same thing, but hers was a legal arrangement: marriage.

Liberty: Why did you choose to become a . . . a prostitute?

Kitsia: You mean why didn't I become a stenographer? A factory worker? A wife? I had no trade, no profession. I had to earn a living. I had worked in Circe's father's house when I was very young . . . Besides, I liked it.

Liberty: Why?

Kitsia: It paid well. I was rich . . . comparatively. I worked when I felt like it. I enjoyed the company of wealthy gentlemen.

Liberty: Did you have other friends?

Kitsia: Other whores.

Liberty: Seriously.

Kitsia: For Christ's sake! Is this what I must endure? Endless stupid questions?

Liberty: I told you I would have to ask you a thousand questions. It's the only way –

Kitsia: Stop! You must learn to ignore criticism. Don't waste time defending or explaining anything . . . even to me. If the profile is good, it will have been worth it.

Liberty: I suppose you feel your art – your sculpture – has been worth any sacrifice you may have endured.

Kitsia: Absolutely! But it took me a long time to realise it. When I left Paris, it was to devote myself to my work. But I wasn't sure of myself. Not completely sure. I had to come to the desert to avoid temptation.

Liberty: But hadn't you been drawing and painting for several years before you left Paris?

Kitsia: In secret, yes. My habit was to work all summer, autumn, and winter.

Liberty: And in the spring?

Kitsia: The spring I saved for Archer. I was like Persephone.

Liberty: Every spring?

Kitsia: For seven years. The first spring Angus left him with me, his nurse had run off, but I convinced Angus I could take care of him. Archer, poor thing, missed his mother dreadfully and used to suck at my breasts. I let him. What harm could it do? And it did comfort him. After two weeks of this hopeful priming, wonder of wonders, I began to lactate!

Liberty: Really? I've heard of that. They say it can even happen to men.

Kitsia: I doubt that.

Liberty: How long did he stay with you?

Kitsia: About two months. It was heaven. I never missed my work when he was around.

Liberty: What happened that he stopped coming to visit you?

Kitsia: Helen wouldn't permit it. And Angus refused to stand up to her.

Liberty: Were you upset?

Kitsia: Yes. I was very upset.

Liberty: Why?

Kitsia: 'Why?' Are you so dense? I loved him. He was like my first child.

Liberty: When you saw Archer again – what, after eight years? – you remembered nursing him. You had a mother's love, I take it, with none of the mother's fear of incest?

Kitsia: Yes. I suppose you could put it that way.

Liberty: But you were telling me last night that Archer, the teenager, wasn't interested in you at first. He had eyes for your friend Cynthia.

Kitsia: Yes, at first. I introduced them at Angus' New Year's Eve party. We'd arrived in Zwar only the night before. Cynthia had come along to protect me.

Liberty: I can't imagine your needing protection. What from?

Kitsia: My brother. I knew he would disapprove of my coming to live with him on Zwar. It had taken him years to get used to my being a well-paid whore. Now I wanted him to see me as a serious artist who was giving up the fleshly pleasures.

Liberty: I didn't realise your brother's opinion meant so much to you.

Kitsia: Well, Angus was always more like a father, and perhaps I wanted a father's approval. Away in Paris, it didn't matter. But living under his roof, let's just say I wanted things to be harmonious.

Liberty: And Cynthia was to pave the way?

Kitsia: Yes. Cynthia had a powerful respectable streak in her. Angus was a little in love with her, so I knew he would welcome us. Two days later, Cynthia was to go on to Ceylon to marry the viceroy. [Unintelligible.] A viceroy – when she could have had any man!

Liberty: Was Cynthia a whore in Paris?

Kitsia: No. We had been lovers for a while. But that was over. We were just friends.

Liberty: You were afraid of something besides your brother?

Kitsia: I suppose I was afraid of my own lack of resolve. I was afraid I would turn around and go back to Paris, or at the very least to the South of France. Cynthia said the first time I couldn't get champagne for my breakfast, I would pack up. She laughed at my plan to go to the desert to be an artist, just as I laughed at her plan to go to the jungle to be a wife.

Liberty: Getting back to that New Year's Eve . . .

Kitsia: I was surprised that the son was so much like the father . . . right down to wanting the same woman. Archer took one look at Cynthia and wanted her desperately.

Liberty: And you found this profoundly attractive?

Kitsia: Yes. I hadn't really thought of Archer sexually that night until he asked me to deliver a love note to Cynthia that he had scribbled on one of Helen's linen napkins. I read it aloud and embarrassed him. Perhaps it was his blush that made me suggest my plan.

Liberty: Perhaps you wished he had written such a note to you.

Kitsia: There is something so alluring about a boy on the brink of becoming a man!

Liberty: And you wanted to help him?

Kitsia: Better me than someone else, don't you think? I proposed that he meet me at the guesthouse that night while the party was still going on and that I teach him a little something about women.

Liberty: And he agreed?

Kitsia: He was eager to learn. You see, a boy knows when he is ignorant, whereas a man . . .

Liberty: So he came?

Kitsia: Yes. A beautiful golden boy knocked at my door.

Liberty: Wait a minute, it's beginning to sound like Archer seduced you.

Kit looked up from the page. Liberty was perched on the edge of the love seat, watching her with round eyes.

'I never even dreamed . . . Of all the men I imagined to be my father, I never dreamed . . .'

'Keep reading, please.'

Kit glanced back at the transcript doubtfully. 'I think I'd like a glass of water.'

Liberty jumped up and went to the bathroom. She came back and set a glass down on the table.

Kit raised it to her lips with a trembling hand and emptied it. Bracing herself, she read on:

Kitsia: I taught Archer everything a man needs to know about giving a woman pleasure. I taught him how to draw a woman out; how to carry her upon wave after wave of ecstasy –

Liberty: It's a pity there aren't more women like you around today.

Kitsia: Pity? That's a laugh! The world wouldn't know what to do with another one of me. And I myself certainly wouldn't

297

tolerate another me. Now, where was I? Hand me the hose, will you, and the taper? Thank you.

(Several seconds of silence.)

Liberty: No, thanks, none for me.

Kitsia: I knew that I would become pregnant that night. I was fertile. Sap had been running down my legs all evening.

Liberty: Do you mean you purposely made love with Archer in order to become pregnant?

Kitsia: No, not purposely, but halfway through our lovemaking, when I was still the teacher and he the student, I decided: Why not? When would I ever have the opportunity to become pregnant – and by a not-quite-man whom I would not have to take on as a husband or even as a lover? It seemed ideal. Archer would be returning to school at the end of the holidays, and I would be alone.

Liberty: So you never thought of having an abortion? No second thoughts?

Kitsia: No. I had decided to let this seed grow. But, as I said, I was never going to involve Archer. I wasn't going to involve anyone.

Liberty: How ideal … just you and your art and your baby.

Kitsia: You needn't sound so smug. You think it's easy to create? Would you ever be willing to close yourself off for your art? I was. I still am! I had to dismiss everyone from my life except those few people I could use in connection with my work.

Liberty: Use?

Kitsia: In the sense of: Was I doing what I set out to do? Was the work honest? I permitted only a few friends to visit me – Vernière-Plank, Circe, Berenson of course, a few others. I edited my work beneath their eyes. I was ruthless in extracting the truth from them.

Liberty: How was a baby going to be part of your life? I can't see where you'd find room or time for a baby.

Kitsia: I see that now. But at the time I thought I could have everything … on my own terms. I certainly didn't count on Archer's returning so soon. I was so sure that the war would keep him away long enough for him to outgrow his schoolboy crush on me. But Angus was determined to bring his son home from America one more time. It almost seemed to me that he wanted to see if he could do it, wrangle the necessary papers, the special permissions, the passage on ships so tightly booked. So Archer came home at the end of the school term. I was five months pregnant. It turned out to be a fatal error. Archer ended up killing a man ... or should I say, another boy.

Liberty: Are you telling me that Archer Ransome is a murderer?

Kitsia: Yes. And no. He doesn't know it. Very few people do. Some members of the emir's family. And now you know it.

Liberty: Why *doesn't* Archer know? I feel like I've just joined a very exclusive club, and I have a funny idea I don't want to belong.

Kitsia: But you do belong now. And there is a great responsibility in knowing about the vendetta.

Liberty: What vendetta?

Kitsia: The vendetta against Archer's children.

Liberty: I don't understand.

Kitsia: Of course you don't. Be still and let me tell you. When Archer returned and found me pregnant, he was overjoyed, planning our future together. When I told him he wasn't the father, he was hurt. Deeply. I wouldn't tell him who the father was, but he believed the rumours that it was the emir's son – one of my most frequent models. In a jealous fit, he fought the boy and wounded him. Archer was also wounded badly – in the leg. I remember asking myself as I watched the two of them rolling in the sand: Is this the *other* part of becoming a man? No wonder I want nothing to do with men.

Angus came down from the main house and pulled them apart, but there was too much blood. He knew instantly the trouble Archer had caused. He hustled him aboard a *dhau* away from Zwar. Now, you must understand, the most important priority in my brother's life was maintaining his relationship with the emir. His business, his standing on the island, his very safety, *everything* depended on his relationship with that man. Just that New Year's they had completed a deal to mine phosphorus in Zwar.

He went to the emir as soon as Archer was safely away from Zwar with instructions not to return until he was told to do so. They say my brother Angus flattened himself in the dirt before the emir and begged for his forgiveness. It looked as if his son would survive the fight, so the emir forgave him. Angus burst into tears of gratitude. They turned out to be premature. The boy's small chest wound became infested, and pneumonia took him a week later.

I was certain when I heard that he had died that all the Ransomes would be murdered in their beds. But the emir delayed payment for his son's life. Angus and Helen and I were to be spared.

Liberty: What about Archer?

Kitsia: In spite of his grief, the emir was also looking for a way *not* to spoil his relationship with Angus. After all, they had a delicate symbiotic relationship. Angus had made him a very wealthy man. The emir was not educated in the Western sense, but he was a shrewd businessman. He knew that if he killed Archer he was throwing away everything that he and his family had gained since Angus settled here.

Besides, it wasn't Archer he was angry with. It was me.

Liberty: Why you?

Kitsia: Because I had caused his son's death.

Liberty: Did the emir forgive you?

Kitsia: Yes. And no.

Liberty: I don't understand.

Kitsia: Why should you? Yes, I was able – at the small cost of one breast – to save Archer's life. But, no, I cannot save his child's life. I'm afraid the emir's sons have found out she is Archer's daughter, so now she has to know. You are the one I have chosen to tell her. Take this.

Liberty: Why me? Why should I tell her? Why don't you tell her yourself? What is this, anyway?

Kitsia: What does it look like? It's a cloisonné turtle. Open it and look inside. Listen to me carefully.

Tears rolled down Kit's cheeks. She did not wipe them away. When she finished, she set down the papers and stared before her. 'I always thought she'd lost the breast to cancer. I was afraid to ask her. Afraid it might happen to me.'

Kit looked up. Liberty was standing over her, holding the turtle out. Kit took it and rose slowly, turning it over in her palm, examining it.

At last she had it. It was identical to the box Kitsia had given her on the day she had had her first period, except that this turtle had sapphire eyes. Hers, in her jewellery box at Clara, had emerald eyes. She reached underneath and pushed the middle joint of its golden belly. The shell popped open, and there, lying in a green velvet nest, was the other black pearl earring.

She took it out and held it up to the light, admiring its smoky lustre. She walked around the room slowly, with her head down, as though she were trying to find something. Finally she spoke.

'I haven't thought of this in years, but I was sitting out on a rock in the Persian Gulf when Akmed first told me that we were cousins.'

'How old were you?'

'Oh, I guess about twelve. Maybe younger. But I remember every word he said. He told me that he had a big brother who had died when he, Akmed, was a baby. The family rumour was that he'd got the crazy Western woman pregnant, and a jealous lover had killed him. Akmed was a beautiful boy with yellowish-brown eyes rimmed with black lashes so fine that they made his eyes always seem open. Like the eyes of a dolphin or a bird. I held my arm up next to his, comparing our colour. He was charcoal black; I was the colour of milky coffee. I remember wondering if his blood ran in my veins. I told him I didn't believe him, and he laughed and said I would when he came to claim me as one of his wives.'

'Were you scared? Did you believe him?'

'I didn't want to believe him, but I wasn't sure. A few weeks later, I had a dream that Akmed came to claim me for his wife. I woke up, and, frightened, I ran to Kitsia's studio. Suddenly I felt foolish. I was bigger than my mother. I was this large gawky animal hiding behind a small scrub bush. I told her my dream and what Akmed had told me.'

Liberty interrupted, holding out her tape machine. 'You don't mind, do you, Kit?'

'I'm not sure. She said that I was not Akmed's cousin and that I would never be his wife. "But you must never tell any of them that. Let them believe what they want. They aren't to be trusted." At that point, I wasn't listening to her; I was trying to summon my courage to ask her who my father was. Finally I asked her. She just shoved me away from her and said, "You needn't worry about who your father is. He doesn't even know you are alive." "But I want to know who he is," I told her. I begged her, naming every man I could think of that I had met or heard about. "So many questions about a tiny little seed." That is how she answered me. "But I want to know!" I told her again. "Not now," she said. "When?" I asked. "Later," she said. "When is later?" I was whining by that time, and she always hated whining. "When I'm ready to tell you!"'

'She never told you. She never even made up a story, did she?'

Kit stared at the reporter, who seemed to know more about her than she knew about herself. Liberty was a brilliant handmaiden helping her unravel an ancient mystery. 'Yes. She gave me a turtle with emerald eyes and told me that the day I got this one as a gift

301

would be the day I'd know who my father was. I waited so many times, so many Christmases and birthdays, wondering would *this* be the day? Would *this* be the day? I finally gave up waiting.'

'What did you think when you saw it yesterday at the restaurant? Coming out of my bag?'

Kit stared before her. 'I . . . I . . . don't know. Nothing rational, really. I just saw Mother . . . looming before me, and all I wanted to do was run . . .' Kit drifted over to the windows but didn't see the view. 'Mother has always been an acute embarrassment to me. I remember, when I went away to prep school in America, being so ashamed when she visited . . . of how she dressed, and those tiny cigars of hers, and her language. I used to complain about her to one of her friends who –'

'Which friend?'

'Posy Crowther. They were always feuding, Posy and my mother. Posy used to visit me secretly at school, take me shopping. She had this idea that Kitsia was the world's worst mother. We used to tear her apart together. Anyway, I asked Posy once who she thought my father was.'

'So you hadn't given up yet.'

'I had this fantasy that I would find out without Kitsia's help, and the next time she came to the States to see me, I'd arrange a luncheon for the three of us.'

'What did Posy tell you?'

'Nothing. I could tell that she knew, though. I always wondered why she wouldn't tell me. Perhaps she knew about the vendetta. Perhaps she was protecting me.'

'Perhaps.'

'I began rather scientifically to figure out who my father was. I made lists of the house guests who'd visited over the years. Other than Vernière-Plank – and I simply *refused* to believe it could be he – they were all artists. She couldn't tolerate any other kind. That I was the product of the union of two artists was a satisfying conclusion for me. It was just a question of which of the men who'd held me on their knee it was. Was it Stieglitz? Was it Miller? Was it Stravinsky? The hours I used to spend in my room at prep school imagining.'

She stopped and heard only the whir of the reporter's machine behind her.

'Kit!' Liberty burst out. 'You don't really believe in this vendetta.' She sounded to Kit like a young girl who had been up all night listening to ghost stories, and now that it was time to go to bed, she wanted someone to tell her there was no such thing as ghosts.

Kit laughed shortly. 'Here we are, two thoroughly modern women, standing in the heart of the world's most modern city, trying to cope in our very modern ways with a situation that comes to us right out of the Arabian Nights. But Zwar is an island out of another time, and Zwarians are a strange and intense people. I don't know, Liberty, to answer your question. But I can't help but feel that Mother withheld the identity of my father up until now, not because of the danger of the vendetta, but because, over the years, she has come to think of me as her immaculate conception.

'And what about you, Liberty? Do you believe it? Did she lure you to her island and bewitch you with her mumbo jumbo and her hashish?'

Liberty shrugged uneasily and leaned over to turn off her tape machine. 'Archer is your father. I believe that much. As for the rest . . . It makes a good story.'

'Are you planning to put all of this into your piece?'

'Wouldn't you?'

'But what if it's true? Aren't you putting my life in danger?'

'What better way is there to protect you than to get the story into print?'

Kit wasn't convinced. She shivered and rubbed her arms. The temperature had dropped at least ten degrees in the last hour. 'If it is real, and if Akmed is the one stalking me, I'm not afraid. Akmed won't kill me. He may set out to, but once he sees me . . . he won't be able to do it. I know it.'

Liberty was packing up. She rose to leave, but Kit stopped her.

'There's still something I don't understand. Something left out of the transcript. I'm not even sure you can tell me.'

'What's that?'

Kit came over to her and aimed a finger at her chest. 'Why *you*?'

It is her first birthday off the island, away from home. Her mother's nephew invites her down to New York for lunch at Twenty-One. One of her classmates has an older sister who dated him when she was at Radcliffe. The report is that he is a living doll. She wants to prove to this living doll that she is an all-American girl – not at all like her mother.

She has seen photographs of him and images of him as a child in her mother's work, but nothing prepares her for the sight of him standing outside the wrought-iron gate of Twenty-One, for this magical quality he has. She feels suddenly dark and dowdy by comparison.

'You're the image of Kitsia!' he tells her, compounding her embarrassment.

'There's someone inside I want you to meet.'

She follows her cousin into the club, where everybody – even the hat-check girl – greets him with a smile.

'This is my bride, Kit. This is Cassie.'

Her arm advances mechanically to shake hands. Something in the other woman's eyes tells her not to cry out.

She remembers a tiny blue matchbox filled with miniature shells that was once pressed into the palm of her hand by a young woman with wild auburn hair on a day when the sea was flat as slate.

'Little Kit, you've grown so tall?' the woman whispers, lifting a finger to her lips to show they have a secret.

Her cousin turns back from the waiter and says, 'How are you two ladies hitting it off?'

She remembers the young woman following them back to the island, and how the day Posy came to take her back to America she had cried until she was ill. Now the young woman is grown, wearing a shockingly low-cut gown. And her cousin stares at her in such a way that she says to herself: To have a man look at me that way . . . that is what it means to be loved.

For the second time, the waiter asks her what she will have for lunch.

'She's just like her mother,' he says. 'She'll probably want to go into the kitchen and tell the chef how to prepare it.'

'An artichoke,' Kit says, her eyes watering so that the menu blurs beneath her gaze.

After another silence, the waiter asks, 'That's all, miss?'

The bride and groom giggle. She blushes furiously.

'Yes, please.'

Later, they let her have a glass of champagne. They are celebrating not just her birthday, but the fact that they are expecting a child. She is the first to know of it.

'We're thinking of contacting your mother,' he says. 'It looks as if we'll be back on speaking terms, thanks to this angel of light.'

'To my husband.' She lifts her glass. 'The world's most wonderful father.'

Seven months later, mother and baby will both be dead.

20

Liberty banged open the glass door of Madelon Weeks's office and sat on the edge of her cluttered desk. Madelon's fingers fluttered up from her word processor like birds interrupted in their feeding.

'Let me finish my thought, angel, *such as it is*. There!' Madelon rolled her chair against the wall, shooting Liberty an exhausted look. 'Angel, you *don't* want to *know*! Your replacement – your *third* replacement – tells me she's stuck at the airport in Cairo. You never did that – leave the Old Girl high and dry. She's got a parasite. "Bacterial or *social*?" I asked her. *Well*!' Madelon clasped her hands together and her rings interlocked. 'Now I'm *reduced* to *writing* again.'

Liberty leaned over and rested a hand gently on her woolly sleeve.

Madelon gave her head a quick little shake, capturing Liberty's hand in hers. 'Come home, angel. *All* is forgiven.'

'Do you mean it?' Liberty asked.

Madelon smiled. 'So what brings you here? More "Mystery of the *Dead* Bride"?' She fingered her chin, where her wattles had lived before a Texas plastic surgeon was handsomely paid to tuck them away.

Liberty grinned and brought the manuscript out of her bag.

Madelon's eyes took on a decidedly ravenous gleam. 'Is that *it*?'

'It's not finished yet, but I'd like you to take a look at it.' Liberty held it out of her reach. 'Promise me you'll read it right away and keep it in the vault.'

'In the vault?' Madelon's nostrils flared, cracking her powder. 'Isn't that going a *bit* far, angel?' She wiggled her fingers impatiently.

Liberty deposited the manuscript between them and hopped off the desk. 'I gave Lily my numbers so you'll know where to reach me if you finish today. Madelon?' She paused in the doorway. Madelon was already reading. 'Yoo-hoo, Maddy? I'd like *you* to print this story.'

Without looking up, Madelon said, 'Why, angel? Isn't *Metropolitan* good enough for you any more?'

'I want you to like this piece, Maddy, and I want you to print it in the next issue.'

'Why, Libby darling, you sound positively *melodramatic*.' Madelon flicked the ash of her Gitane jerkily against her Texas-shaped ashtray. 'What's the matter with you? *Flash* doesn't print articles *this* long.' She riffled through the manuscript.

Liberty held the door open with her foot. 'I'll have the rest of it to you by tomorrow at noon.' The door closed behind her.

Liberty had to run the last couple of blocks up Sixth Avenue to make her ten-o'clock appointment at the Café Rue de la Paix in the St Moritz. A cosmopolitan mixture of Arab, Japanese, and German businessmen and tourists spilled out onto the outdoor tables. Inside at the far end of the row of tables on the park side, a lone gentleman, slight and elegant, sat staring out the window. A leather *bourse* sat on the table beside his cup of café au lait, which he sipped delicately, his pinkie crooked.

Bruno Vernière-Plank had already explained to her over the phone in flawless English that he could spare her only a few minutes. He was due at the Metropolitan Museum at ten-thirty for a consultation on their new show, *Americans in Paris*. Liberty went right to his table, introduced herself, and got down to business.

'Next to Henry Moore and Brancusi, Kitsia Ransome has done more to raise the acceptance and price of modern sculpture than any artist of the twentieth century. How do you think Kitsia feels about the connection between art and money?'

He bowed stiffly. 'I *am* that connection. She never thinks about money. She just endorses the cheques.' He smiled impishly, reminding her for a moment of a figurine in a Swiss clockworks: rigid, precise, and precious.

'Is it true that you have a corner of Kitsias because you once had a corner on Kitsia herself?'

He raised an eyebrow and slowly poured more hot milk into his coffee. Liberty was sorry she had been so flip, so American. She wanted to draw him out, not turn him off with her early-morning stabs at humour. Humour was so hard to translate.

'I have a long acquaintance with Kitsia Ransome, yes.'

'I'm curious, if you don't mind my asking, how much you paid for the first Kitsia you acquired?' She smiled at him sweetly.

'Not a centime. In fact, I have never paid for any of them.'

'Can you describe your arrangement?' Liberty took out a Camel and Monsieur Vernière-Plank leaned over and lit it for her with a thin silver lighter no bigger than her little finger.

'I took over the contents of her apartment on the Île St Louis when she left for Zwar. Then, as now, I took her work on consignment. My commission comes off the top.'

'Who knew then what you'd be letting yourself in for?'

'*I* did, mademoiselle.' He bowed slightly.

'Then you control the disposition of all her works?'

'Yes,' he said, and then he seemed to hesitate.

'You sound unsure, Monsieur Vernière-Plank.'

'Some more coffee, mademoiselle?'

Liberty shook her head.

He proceeded cautiously. 'There are certain pieces I cannot sell without her approval.'

'Which pieces?'

'The Cassandra Series, for one. And other single pieces.'

'And where is the series right now?'

'Well, let me think.' He laid his finger lightly beside his right temple. Liberty noticed his cufflinks were made of pink marble. Kitsia originals, perhaps? 'Here, in the Sculpture Garden. On Zwar. At the Kimball Art Museum in Fort Worth. At the Beauborg. The National Gallery in Washington. And in private collections all over the world. I believe her daughter has one.'

'Do you know Kitsia's daughter?'

'Naturally.'

'Can't these pieces be resold at the original buyer's discretion?'

'How astute of you, mademoiselle. No, they cannot. They carry a special stipulation.'

'Which is?' Liberty stubbed out her cigarette.

'If the owner wishes to sell, we have the right of first refusal.'

'Why all the ironclad control?'

'Ironclad,' he repeated. 'How humorous. Because Kitsia has some old associates whom she never tires of punishing.'

Liberty grinned. 'I think I know at least one of those associates.'

If Archer Ransome's office was Winter Wonderland, then Rush Alexander's was the Black Forest. The carpets, the walls, the heavy velvet drapes at the windows were all deep forest green. The furniture was dark brown suede, Internationale, but barely.

Liberty registered with interest the absence of a desk. She found Alexander lounging with one leg draped over the metal-pipe back of a Le Corbusier chair. He rose when he saw her, very like a cobra from a basket, headfirst, slow and easy, to take her hand.

'I can't tell you what a pleasure it is to see you again.' He steered her over to the couch and recoiled back into the chair opposite her with his leg again flung over its arm. It was not a very executive pose, but it worked for him, because he wasn't really relaxed. He was merely conveying to his visitor his readiness to spring.

Liberty looked around and said, 'So where's the Executive Desk? Ransome has a Louis Quinze *escritoire*. I'd expect you to have at least a Le Corbusier to go with the chairs.'

'Your knowledge of design is charming, Liberty. I prefer to use a lap desk. As a boy, I had no desk – among many, many other amenities – and learned to balance books and papers on a sheet of wood. It is a working habit that has never left me. Besides, a desk restricts movement. You certainly are looking lovely today. Is that a miniskirt? It certainly is daring.'

'Not all that much more daring than what your daughter was wearing last night. By the way, how is she? Recovering from her little bash, I hope?'

He gave her a long look. 'She's just fine. Only I'm afraid she won't be able to see you as planned.'

She watched him carefully, saying nothing, and took out her notepad. The questions she had prepared on Monday night seemed all wrong for today's interview. She was no longer writing the sort of descriptive, gossipy, detailed portrait of a mother and daughter that she had been assigned. Everything had been thrown off course. She had a new focus now. Now she was writing about a family's personal history – so intimate, it was deadly. Liberty cleared her throat.

'Some water, Liberty?' Rush was staring at her notes. She could tell he was reading her writing with perfect ease from that angle.

Shaking her head, she thumbed to a blank page and asked: 'So, what have you to tell me?'

'Ah, a refreshingly low-key approach!'

Liberty cut him short. 'About the Weird Sisters. Didn't I hear you call them that earlier this week?'

'Marvellous memory skills.' He grinned and packed his pipe, methodically tamping down the tobacco. It was a Meerschaum, very clean.

Ever since Liberty had returned from Zwar she had felt as if she was on a roller coaster. It was exhilarating – taking the deep dives without flinching, banking the dangerous curves. Seeing Rush and preparing to ask him questions – not impersonal business questions, but personal questions that she had to find a way to mask as impersonal – was like standing up as the coaster took its steepest plunge.

'I got the idea on Monday that you know both the mother and the daughter equally well.'

'I do. Although I haven't seen Kitsia in years. Who has?'

'I have.'

Rush nodded, and leaning over, offered her an open cigarette box stocked with different brands. Liberty took out a Camel. His manners were impressive, as were his hobbies. He collected old Russian icons and a mixed palette of great art, ranging from Rembrandt to Rauschenberg, jogged four miles each day, spoke seven languages. She knew the facts cold, but when she got right down to it, she knew very little.

'I imagine Kit must be relieved that *Last Chance* is going ahead. And you must be pleased for your daughter.'

'I'd prefer not to discuss this right now. There'll be a release –'

'You prefer not to discuss it? But I thought you orchestrated the whole thing.'

'Then you're mistaken. I wouldn't want my daughter to be associated with the project. I blame that on Kit. There's been so much negative publicity about the movie. About her. All in all, it's been very bad for Ransome Enterprises. Hardly a wholesome set.'

'Hardly,' she agreed hollowly. She was completely baffled.

'I'm afraid that in spite of all her experience, Kit's naive about the press. She doesn't have her mother's shrewdness.'

Liberty spoke up. 'Was there really a way to contain the fallout after Monette's OD?' Liberty was trying to ease into the subject. Her heart began to beat faster.

'I think there was.'

'What about your affair with Monette Novak? In fact, didn't your affair with Ms Novak have something to do with her overdose?'

She had been hoping to catch him off guard, but Rush grinned broadly, appearing almost flattered by the question. 'No. I believe I met Miss Novak only once. I can't imagine my effect was so devastating as to drive the poor girl –'

'Why do you think Mrs Novak tried to kill Kit on Tuesday?' Liberty was pleased that her voice kept its normal register. As long as she acted as though she didn't know the answers to her questions, she might just get Rush to stumble over his own smugness.

'Kill Kit? Is that what she tried to do? Well, I suppose I shouldn't be surprised. Mothers are so obsessive about their offspring.' He dismissed it lightly.

'I don't know what *you* call it when someone waves a loaded gun in your face.'

'I'd call it a bluff.'

Not wanting him to see how frustrated he was making her, she got up and said brightly, 'Mind if I prowl? You can tell a lot about a person from what he hangs on his office walls.'

His voice followed her. 'Are you interested in telling a lot about me?'

'You never know...'

Liberty stared at the display of about thirty two-by-three photographs individually matted in a six-by-three-foot frame that ran eye level along the green wall. They were studio shots, probably out-takes from a commercial shoot, recognisably the work of a well-known but daring fashion photographer, and they definitely told her something about Rush Alexander. Eben was right. Rush Alexander had a thing for his daughter he could neither hide nor control. They were not the sort of pictures your average proud dad shows off of his little girl. These were pure Lolita times thirty. For the first time, she found herself feeling sorry for Rush Alexander.

'What do you think of her?'

She laughed uneasily as Eben's words came back to her. *You sure wouldn't have to shake the sheets...* 'She's a photogenic girl,' she managed to say as she moved on quickly to study the photos of Rush Alexander – most with famous men, a couple with Archer – and in all of them he looked the same: well-dressed, reserved, unsmiling. There was one small sepia print of him with a beautiful middle-aged woman. Liberty heard the door open and turned to see a waiter wheeling in a tea trolly, complete with white linen and napkins rolled into copper rings: service for two. Liberty eyed the proceedings grimly.

'Ah, the birthday feast has arrived!'

She turned back to look at the photo: it was Kitsia. She turned away. She could feel him watching her face as the waiter brought out two steaming Wedgwood plates: one holding thickly cut flank steak, whole poached carrots, and several large french-fried potatoes; the other, two crisply meunièred soft-shell crabs, a pile of baby green beans, and a dab of green sauce in a poached apple.

'I had my girl call your girl and ask her what your favourite meal was.'

'Oh, boy!' She managed a small smile for him. This inordinate attentiveness made her feel strangely uneasy. He knew her weakness for Maryland crab. Was he aware of her other weaknesses?

He dismissed the waiter and pushed the chair in behind her.

'I hope you enjoy your birthday lunch, Liberty.'

He sat down opposite her and flapped out his napkin.

She looked at his plate and noticed that everything – steak slices, carrots, potatoes – had been served in fours.

'Something special about the number four?' she asked.

He smiled as he began to slice his steak. 'Very observant, Liberty. As a boy I had four candy bars to last me from rising to bedtime. I don't like to forget that I once lived on four candy bars a day. You see, you're not the only one with an underprivileged childhood.'

'I'm beginning to get that idea,' she said dryly, picking up her fork and poking at one of the crisp crabs.

'I hope you have a birthday appetite. Or are you one of those women who scorn the whole process? Now, my daughter ... my daughter loves food. I often think ...' He waxed thoughtful now. '.. she could eat the world if we let her.'

'I like food fine.' Liberty popped a microscopic string bean into her mouth to prove it. 'I just don't like to make a big deal out of it. Do you think Kit had an underprivileged childhood like ours?'

He looked at her, seeming not to understand her question.

'Not having a father, I mean,' Liberty clarified.

'Oh, I don't know. Kitsia would seem to be parents enough.'

'Do you ever wonder who Kit's father is?'

'Wonder. Why, no. I know who Kit's father is.'

'You do?' Liberty leaned forward, curious to know what he knew. 'Who?'

Rush grinned. 'Liberty, *really*. Arch was right about you in *that* respect as well. You are charmingly direct.' He paused to eat a piece of steak. Clearly he thought he was still in charge of the interview. 'Getting back to *Last Chance*. This business has been very hard on us as a group.'

'Stock-wise or morale-wise?' Liberty asked absently. She wondered if he really knew about Kit. Who could have told him?

'Both, actually. Until recently, Horizon was the member of our group of which Archer felt the most proud.'

'I can see that.' Liberty picked up a crab leg in her fingers and contemplated it. 'No enslaved populations, no young Taiwanese girls going blind from assembling teeny-tiny components. I can see how he would be proud. After all, movies give people happiness. Not cancer or white lung.' She put the claw back on her plate uneaten.

He held his knife and fork still for a moment, looking at her.

'Seems that Kit isn't the only one having trouble containing the press,' she said casually.

He grinned slyly at her. 'No, she isn't. This SEC business is extremely difficult.' He sipped his wine so carefully, she thought for a moment he was going to send it back.

'I'm surprised at just how bad things look in the press for Ransome. You have quite a reputation for handling the press. Have your powers deserted you?'

'My powers? How flattering.'

'I don't mean to be.'

'Surely, Liberty, this isn't germane to your profile on the Misses Ransome?'

'Well, I wouldn't have thought so a few days ago, but now it all seems relevant. After all, this SEC business might very well affect Kit's career.' Liberty knew her answer was a bit weak. She hadn't counted on Rush's being quite so slippery. She wiped her mouth with a napkin and set it beside her plate, as the servant came in and removed the lunch, stepping over Rush's outstretched legs. He tossed his napkin on the pile of dishes and called for his pipe. She wanted to stay as cool as Rush.

'Would you care for some coffee or tea?'

'Some tea, please.' She'd eaten half a crab and four string beans. Her stomach growled as she returned to her corner of the couch.

He went to sit sideways on the other side, packing the bowl of his pipe thoughtfully. His extremely white hands were almost devoid of wrinkles. In their weird way, his hands were perfect and yet she noticed that he usually kept them in his pockets, flung them out of sight, or kept them busy with his pipe.

'By the way, how is my lift mate, Tony Alvarro?'

'Recovering nicely, I'm told.' Rush's eyes were mild.

'I'm almost finished. I know how busy you are.'

Rush was silent.

'I'd still like to hear more about the Weird Sisters. Besides shrewdness, what other qualities of Kitsia's do you think Kit lacks?'

'Kitsia Ransome is a brilliant artist. She is an old, good friend of mine.'

Liberty dragged on her cigarette. She thought Rush might use her question to criticise Kit, but this was better. 'Is that so?' she said casually, feeling a surge of power. 'If you're such old friends, I'd like to know why she refuses to sell you any of her pieces.'

She might have told him his daughter had run off with a Hell's Angel, he was caught that off guard. She persisted mercilessly.

'According to Monsieur Vernière-Plank, you have repeatedly tried to buy several of the Cassandra Series. I believe you offered triple the market price.' She watched him carefully. His face remained smooth; only his voice, when he finally spoke, betrayed that her question had surprised, even saddened him.

'Yes. I have tried. I find that series particularly beautiful.'

'That series? I'm curious as to why you would want a statue of Archer Ransome's wife.'

'How did you find out about her?' His voice penetrated the office and seemed to echo about them.

She was about ready to hit him again when the intercom buzzed, interrupting her.

He gave her a warning look and picked it up.

'I'm sorry, Mr Alexander, but Senator Pierce is on the line and he's very insistent –'

Rush punched a button viciously and managed to work up a jocular grin as he said, 'Eben, my boy! What can I do for you? Oh, really? Sorry, I had no idea.' Rush pointed to the extension at Liberty's elbow. 'It's for you.'

'Hello, Senator,' she said, avoiding Rush's ever-darkening look.

Eben's voice was low. 'I hope you don't mind my putting a little scare into your interviewee.'

'How's that, Senator?'

'If I'm not mistaken, he's bound to throw a paranoid fit as soon as you hang up the phone.'

'Gee, thanks a lot!'

'Listen, I talked to Tony Alvarro. He claims the falling lift was no accident. Stay cool. By the way, you were fantastic the other night.'

'Really?' She blushed as Rush's eyes never left her face. 'That really helps me stay cool to hear that. I'm glad you could make it.'

'Make it?' he said. 'I must have made it five times. I feel like a kid again.'

'Congratulations, Senator,' she said stiffly.

'What about you, Lib? Those wonderful noises you made . . . you weren't just trying to make me feel good.'

'No, I really appreciated all the help you gave me.'

'I'm getting hard just talking to you.'

Her blush deepened and she looked down at her notepad to avoid Rush's eyes.

'I want to see you tonight. And not just about the Ransome thing.'

'Absolutely. We'll work something out, but I really must hang up now.'

'Watch his reaction carefully – he's bound to get jumpy about my calling you – and report back to me.'

'I hear you, Senator.'

'But play innocent, whatever you do.' He kissed the receiver before he hung up.

'I don't know how you arranged that, Liberty, but I find it distastefully transparent.'

She pushed the phone away and felt the colour draining from her face. Pierce was right. 'I don't know what you mean, Rush.'

'You really shouldn't get into things that are none of your business,' he went on.

'I *really* don't know what you're talking about.'

'If you're planning anything with that young senator . . .'

She got un uncanny impression of the skull glowing beneath his olive skin. She laughed a little, amazed at his lack of subtlety, yet frightened. She tried to reassure him. 'Senator Pierce is nothing more than my next profile piece. He's anxious for me to get started. You know what a media Lothario he is. I don't have to tell you.' She put her pad into her bag and stood up. 'Look, I think I've got all I need. Thanks for the lunch. Don't bother. I'll find my way out.'

He got up and followed her to the door, opening it for her.

'Leaving so soon, Liberty?'

She avoided looking at him and smiled tightly at his 'girl', a smouldering brunette with nails that flashed like short pink knives.

'Oh, Liberty!'

She turned and looked at him. He was lounging against the doorjamb with his hands stuffed into his pockets. Such nonchalance as his at a time like this just had to be studied. 'Mrs Alexander won't be able to see you either today, after all. She asked me to apologise for her.'

'Oh, yeah. That's too bad.' She hadn't missed a beat. 'And I was really looking forward to our interview. Some other time, I guess. Well, thanks again.' *It's been better than a dead cat in a Kotex box.*

She turned and walked down the hall past the nurse's station.

She realised as she rode down in the lift that she was perspiring. Surely he wouldn't try the lift trick twice.

Walking through the cool marble lobby, she looked at her watch. It was over an hour before she was expected at the Alexander house. Since she was too twitchy to sit in a cab, she would take her time and walk through the park. She had no intention of missing this interview, in spite of Rush Alexander's paranoid fit.

She was barely into the south side of the park when the sky began rapidly to cloud over, making the autumn leaves turn suddenly, garishly bright. She shivered and stopped to take her red llama wool sweater out of her bag. She poked her head through just in time to see him, her shadow, crossing the street at the entrance to the park. Panicked, she looked around her for help and was relieved to see a team of policemen on horseback within shouting distance. She'd never find a better opportunity. She hurried round a bend and dropped behind a clump of rhododendron, counting the seconds until he would pass her. Sixty-five, sixty-six, sixty-seven. She jumped out in front of him.

'All right, mister. Don't you think it's time you cut the crap and told me why you've been following me?'

In his dreams, Rush sees her again as he first saw her on campus. Nearly as tall as he, she is copper-haired, golden-legged, long-throated. He imagines her sunbathing naked on the roof of her Radcliffe dormitory, laughing with her girlfriends, the way she does when they are escorting her across campus. Far less beautiful, they surround her like dull, fawning handmaidens. He thinks he will never be any closer to her than he is at this moment. It is enough.

Then he is sitting at his customary place in the library, trying to read. He looks up and finds her there, sitting at the head of the table. She is reading Tess of the d'Urbervilles. When she gets up to leave at the eleven-o'clock bell, she drops a daisy in her book to hold the place. The vision now has a name: Tess.

Tess is there again, and this time when she gets up, she walks behind him and drops the daisy on the open book in front of him. He is too astonished to turn around.

Then she is sitting directly across from him. He forces himself to look at her. The skin on her cheeks is suffused with rose, like a Titian Madonna. He feels a slight pressure under the table between his legs. That part of his body has taken on a life of its own. Then he realises what it is. He closes his eyes and opens them again. Both her hands are holding the book, but her eyes are closed and her lips parted. She is bringing him off, ever so slowly, with her bare feet.

Then Tess is spiriting him away from the table. He follows her as she weaves in and out of the stacks, leading him farther and farther up into the highest, most dusty reaches of the library. He wanders among the stacks, afraid he may have lost her. As he passes a broom closet, she shoots out an arm and pulls him in. She is sitting on the sink with her skirt gathered up and her legs spread. A moist pinkness glistens in the dusky light. He is helpless to do anything but stare. She makes soft reproving noises as she draws him towards her and pulls him out of his trousers. He nibbles at her throat as he feels her, slippery and hot, surrounding him. As he drives himself into her, her head is thrown back, her arms are flung behind her, grasping the handle of a broom, stroking it. He thinks he will go mad with pleasure. Each time he opens his mouth, she covers it with her hand. He cannot even ask her what her name is. His eye falls on the cover of her notebook and he sees it, written in a fine, earnest hand, the letters neatly bent at the same angle, like wheat shocks in a wind; her name. At the moment of his climax, he calls it out.

'Cassandra!'

She freezes and pulls back, levelling a look at him he will never forget. She pushes him away and jumps down from the sink, taking her books to her breast as if they are a shield. Then she is gone.

For months, years afterwrds, he searches for her. On more than one occasion he runs after the copper-haired one of a group of girls, calling out, 'Cassandra! Wait!' – only to discover some other, duller face beneath that glorious hair.

One day it happens. Out at the end of Long Island at a huge affair at

Ham Barclay's. The fountain shoots purple water and the lanterns are strung along the path to the beach. He looks up and there she is on a man's arm. Archer. When introduced to him, she cocks her head and says, 'We've met before, haven't we?' He searches her face and finds it innocent: bearing no hint of the knowledge of what they'd shared years ago in the library closet, up against that cool white sink.

'No,' he tells her sadly, 'I don't believe we have met.'

He dreams they are at the Rainbow Room, celebrating Archer and Cassandra's thirty-third wedding anniversary. Archer whirls her around in the centre of the floor. Mandy watches them, swaying absently to the music. Mandy leans in to whisper something to Liberty Adams. Liberty giggles uncontrollably. Tony Alvarro, in a hospital nightshirt, is there too, waltzing by himself, holding an IV bottle in one hand.

He goes over to the band and pays them to switch songs. When Archer and Cassie drop arms and stop dancing, he seizes the opportunity: he must see what she looks like now after all these years. He takes her away from Archer, into his arms, burying his face in her red-gold hair. But she is laughing at him. He pulls away and sees that it isn't Cassandra after all. It is Verena, and she is saying, 'Ugh! Not you, Rush! Oh, please, not you!'

Amanda Alexander sat at her desk in a pool of golden light reading a book. She held her reading glasses by one corner, as if she expected to have to take them off at any time. Verena cleared her throat. Her mother looked up. Off came the glasses.

'Verena! Come in here. I want to speak to you.'

'Later. I can't talk now.'

'Verena!' She raised her voice. Verena turned around, surprised by her mother's tone. She walked into Amanda's study and sat down heavily on a blue wing chair.

'Where have you been? I've been worried about you.'

'I tried to get in to see Kit Ransome, but they wouldn't let me. Then I tried to see Uncle AJ, but Susie said he was out of town for the day. Then I came home. I didn't know what else to do.' She stared at the tips of her cowboy boots and pulled her ponytail around to examine her ends.

Mandy got up and swung the reading lamp towards Verena to get a good look at her face. A small sigh escaped her. She shook her head. 'Is this what happened last night?'

Verena was silent.

'Is it, Rena? Answer me!'

'Yeah, yeah, yeah. Why didn't you come upstairs last night? Why didn't you save me from him? I swear, sometimes you're the world's yellowest –' Verena clamped her hand over her mouth, but it was too late.

Her mother began to cry.

'Don't, Ma. It's too late for that.'

'No. Don't say that, Verena.' Mandy pulled a handkerchief out of her sweater sleeve and dabbed at her tears, sniffing. When she switched off the light, her little study with the wall of miniature paintings looked eerily dark, as if it might storm at any moment. 'Come into the kitchen,' she said. 'I want to make sure that cut is clean.'

Verena got up and backed away. 'Oh, no. No, thanks. Really, Ma, you don't have to bother.'

'March!' Mandy pushed her out of the study into the hall and down five steps into the kitchen. Mandy sat her at the table and came back in a few seconds with alcohol and cotton.

'No way, José!' Verena shoved the swab away. 'That stuff stings.'

Mandy ignored her. Verena winced as the alcohol hit the cut.

'He'll never hit you again, I'll tell you that much. If he tries it, I'll call the police.'

Verena laughed. 'On Rush? He practically owns the precinct. Come on, Ma.'

'I'm serious, Verena.'

'You can't control him. You've never stood up to him in your life!' Verena shouted.

Mandy went on cleaning her cut as if she hadn't heard.

Verena tried again. 'Rush wants to take me out of the movie, you know,' She pointed to her face. 'What do you think *this* is all about?'

'Last night I had the photographer pick out the best photo of you taken at the party. Then I told him to drop it off at the *Entertainment Tonight* office. They're already in LA. Verena Maxwell Alexander celebrating her entry into the cast of *Last Chance*. "Lovely new Lacy brings luck and new life to *Last Chance*".'

'Ma, you did that for me?'

'I decided to accept your new career with grace. Tonight everyone will know you're in the movie. It will be too late for Rush to reverse himself. He'll have to go along with it.'

Verena sighed. 'It's no use. Kit hates me.'

'Archer will take care of her.'

'Don't be too sure. I overheard them talking last night. Uncle AJ expecially.' Verena rolled her eyes.

Mandy lifted Verena's ponytail to free it from her collar. 'Yes, Verena. What did they say?'

'Well, Uncle AJ said something about collecting the insurance money, but Rush said that wouldn't be enough.'

'Enough for what?'

'I don't know.' Verena didn't want to tell her mother any more about what she'd heard. Her face ached and she was tired.

'Your hair is so tangled. Go and get me your brush and I'll fix it for you.'

Verena went into the hall and came back with her brush. She

handed it to Mandy and sat down cross-legged at her feet. No one brushed her hair the way Mandy did. Everybody else just touched the top layers. Only Mandy got under and pulled out the deep tangles. 'Weeding', she called it.

Verena slumped back against Mandy's knees, relieved. It was just like Mandy to see her face all swollen and pretend ten minutes later that it never happened.

'I wish I had never got you started in modelling.'

'Oh, that's okay, Ma,' Verena said quickly.

'No, really, if I had it to do over again, you'd be going to a nice normal high school and having the time of your life. Hamming it up in school plays, making friends your own age, instead of mingling with fashion photographers, single-minded advertising people, and beauticians with crooked haircuts.'

Verena pushed her mother's hand away. 'Don't say that, Ma. Everything's fine. I like the modelling.'

'I wish everything *were* fine, Rena. I don't know why I ever started the modelling business in the first place. It's just that you'd grown into such a special young woman. And it gave us something to do together. I always thought as long as I was there to ward off bad influences, it couldn't hurt you. Maybe if my mother had been younger or not as sick, I would have known how to be a better mother to you.'

'You're fine, Ma. Come off it.'

'Then why did you run away? Your father said I drove you away. I didn't drive you away, did I?'

Verena turned around and faced her mother. 'He told you that?' She felt something well up inside of her, dark and swarming and too big to keep down much longer.

She bit her lip and nodded rapidly. 'I've pushed you too hard since you came back. I suppose I was punishing you for running away, when I should have been rewarding you for having the guts to come home.'

Verena felt a rushing in her ears. She could barely hear herself speak above it. 'It didn't take guts. I knew I had to, that's all. Ma, listen to me: I have something to tell you.'

'No, Rena, you don't have to tell me anything. We can just forget what's happened and go on –'

'Mother, for Pete's sake, listen to me!' Beads of perspiration popped out all over Verena's forehead.

Mandy got up, walked over to the sink, and let the water run for several moments. Then, without turning around, she went on talking as if Verena weren't there. Her voice was calm. 'I had just decided to tell you that you could quit the Ruba account and stop all this, when your father offered you that role. I was so angry with him. I just didn't want to see you get any deeper into that crazy world. Now I see how much it means to you and I'll do anything to make sure you keep this part. I love you so, Verena. Maybe you could love me a little and forgive me my foolish mistakes.'

Verena went over to the sink and put her arms around her mother. 'I do love you, Ma. But I'm such a horrible daughter I don't deserve your love.'

'Rena. Don't say that.' She patted her daughter's arm. 'You're so beautiful –'

Verena interrupted her sternly. 'Come here, Ma.' Taking the glass of water out of her mother's hand, she steered her over to the table and sat her down. She placed the water next to her. 'I want to tell you something so you'll really know who I am.' She squeezed her eyes shut and spoke through clenched teeth. 'I'm a hideous, disgusting, gross daughter. And I wouldn't blame you if you never wanted to look at me again.'

'Verena!' she cried. 'Don't say such things!'

'I'm a disgusting *cunt*!' she screamed, and opened her eyes. But now she was blinded by tears. She fell down and began to beat her head against the tile. With each bounce of her head, she said, 'I'm hideous. I'm horrible. I'm sick. I'm mean. I'm a cunt. I'm a cunt. I'm a *cunt*!'

'Verena!' Mandy grabbed her wrists, but Verena fought her off and scuttled away from her backwards, like a crab.

'Oh, God, Ma, don't come any closer. Don't look at me. I can't stand it. Rush and I did naughty things. We did. We did a lot of times. He *made* me.'

Mandy knocked the glass of water off the table. The pink drained from her face. She sat staring ahead of her with water dripping into her lap, seeing her husband and her daughter together, talking or watching TV, out riding, just fooling around. She dropped her head into her hands.

Utter shame paralysed Verena. A small voice begged, 'Don't hate me, Mama. Please don't hate me. I wouldn't want to live if you hated me, Mama. I'd die. I'd die. Please don't kill me. I didn't mean to do it. It wasn't my fault. He made me do it. He made me do it and he watched. He found me playing in my playhouse once. He

321

used to sneak up to the window and look at me, then one day I sneaked up to the window and caught him. He said what I was doing was naughty and that if I didn't let him watch, he'd tell you. He said you'd hate me if you heard. He said you'd send me away to some place where they send little girls who are naughty. I didn't want to be sent away, so I . . . I let him watch me. It wasn't those little boys who burned down my playhouse. It was me. I burned it down, Mama! But then he took me out in the car. He'd make me be naughty there. I was naughty on the rec room couch, too.'

'Verena, Verena, Verena.' Her mother's whispering was just loud enough to silence her. 'Please, not all at once. Don't tell me all at once. Verena, please answer me one question and I'll never ask you another question about this, I swear. Did he ever . . . ?' She held her hand over her mouth and looked as if she were about to be sick.

Verena reached up and touched her mother's face ever so gently, knowing that she had to lie. 'No, Ma, never.'

'Never?'

'We never did *that*.'

'Oh, thank God.' Tears soaked Mandy's face and yet she made no crying sound. She was like a silent screen actress.

Verena peered at her timidly. 'Do you still love me, Ma? A little?'

'Verena, why did you tell me? Why today?' She held her index fingers to the corners of her eyes to stop the tears.

'He threatened to tell you, and I couldn't stand thinking what he might make up. I didn't know I was going to tell you today. It . . . it just came out.'

Mandy gulped. 'I love you, Verena, very much. I'll always love you.'

Verena embraced her mother and cried into her neck, her whole body shaking. Her long hair fell over her mother's shoulders like a shawl.

Mandy patted her hair. 'Don't cry, honey. Now I have to tell *you* something.'

The phone rang and Mandy crossed the kitchen to answer it, leaving Verena still crying at the table. 'Hello. Yes, Rush.'

Verena's head shot up. She threw back her hair.

'Yes, fine. Whatever you say. Good-bye.' She hung up and looked at her daughter. 'Strange. He's cancelled my interview with that young reporter, Liberty Adams. I wonder why.'

322

'He's afraid of her. Of what she might find out.'

'About what?'

'I thought you were going to stand up to him from now on.'

'About what? Cancelling this interview? I don't really want to see her anyway. She wants me to sit around and reminisce about Kitsia. I couldn't keep my mind on it. Not after what you've just told me.' Mandy put a kettle of water on to boil and started to get out the tea service.

Verena watched her standing in front of the cabinet contemplating which of several sets she should choose. She selected the white dishes with the dark red poppies. Verena watched her mother closely. She wanted to be like her: to be graceful instead of clumsy, and calm instead of crazy and loud. How could someone like Mandy stand having Rush make love to her?

'Rena, now *I* have something to tell you. Only I don't quite know how to tell you.'

'What is it, Ma? You can tell me,' Verena encouraged her.

'When my father died, I went to live with Aunt Kitsia.'

Verena nodded.

Pulling two white linen napkins from a cabinet, Mandy went on. 'I closed up the house on Ceylon where I had lived all my life and took a boat to Zwar, to Kitsia's. She was the only person I really knew besides my parents. She was my mother's best friend. I was sixteen years old when I showed up at her house. She wasn't very happy to see me. In fact, for the first month I was there she hardly spoke to me. But fairly soon she remembered how much she had loved Cynthia and, I guess by extension, me.'

Verena began to pace about the kitchen, hopping up onto cabinets and then slipping off. She had no idea what her mother was trying to tell her, but she wished she'd make it snappy. Mandy never told her very much about her childhood, though. Rush told her all the time about his.

'I'd been there awhile when Kitsia turned to me one day and looked at me with those eyes of hers and said, "So, what are you going to do now? Read books for the rest of your life?" Reading books for the rest of my life sounded like a perfectly splendid plan to me. After all, I didn't have to work. I was rich. Poppup saw to that . . .'

Mandy broke off as she began to pour tea leaves out of a canister into the strainer of her silver teapot. Verena had seen her do this before: get herself through a difficult emotional situation by concentrating on some menial task. 'When Kitsia went to the States in 1964 to oversee a gallery show, I tagged along. Don't ask me why we travelled together. We squabbled constantly. She couldn't stand that I always had my nose in a book or that I looked at life and made "bookish observations", as she called them. I couldn't stand that she was totally subjective and emotional about everything she looked at: from the design of the jet we rode in over to America, to the cut of my hair. For her, aesthetics were a matter of life and death. I wanted to be free of her and yet I lacked the courage to leave. Lacking courage is really what my life is all about.' She paused to look at Verena. They both knew how hard that admission had been.

'As long as I remained with Kitsia, I didn't have to speak to anyone. I could carry on as I had back in Sri Lanka, eating my meals alone whenever I liked, rising at two in the afternoon, and staying up all night to finish a book. I was merely another member of her motley entourage. Then I met Archer.'

'Was he the handsomest man you'd ever seen? I'll bet he was.' Verena was sitting on a counter, swinging her legs. She had the peanut-butter jar out and was licking crunchy bits off her finger.

'He was certainly worth taking my nose out of a book for.' Mandy smiled. 'We ran into him by accident at Chumley's in the Village. "This is my nephew, Archer, with whom I am barely on speaking terms. This is Cynthia's only daughter and an impossibly bookish toad. I doubt very much you'll have anything in common." Hardly Cupid's arrow.'

'When did you meet Rush?'

'Not long after I'd met Archer, but it was Archer that I liked. There was something about him... He was a widower, used to being alone, and so distracted by his own thoughts that he left me alone with mine. We kept each other company in our mutual solitude. I had a room at the Barclay Hotel while Kitsia was staying up on Madison at a small place near the gallery where they were showing her sculpture. She couldn't bear to be far from the work while the show was in progress. While she busied herself at the gallery, Archer and I quietly fell in love.

'We spent every weekend at his house in Millbrook. We'd take long walks across the pastures and return at sundown to have martinis out on the porch overlooking the meadows. I loved this new country. It wasn't steaming and damp like the rain forests of Ceylon. It wasn't a crumbling pile of sand in the Persian Gulf, like

Zwar.' She laughed and shook her head. 'I felt at home there. More so than in this house.' She looked around the kitchen. 'This room is mine, I think.'

Verena jumped off the counter and went over to her. 'For crying out loud, Ma. Who gives a flying fuck about the kitchen! Tell me. Tell me what you want me to know, or so help me...'

Verena's voice died away as she looked into her mother's eyes.

'All right,' her mother said in a voice Verena no longer recognised. 'All right. I'll stop beating around the bush and tell you. I'll tell you everything. And I hope to God that you're strong enough to handle it.'

She remembers Ceylon: a steaming garden inhabited by snakes so big they feed on human babies. She and her family live, barricaded, in the house with the dark green louvred windows. There is her mother, always ailing, eventually bedridden. Standing at the door outside her room, she hears her mother calmly discuss with the doctor the worms that are eating her alive. Afterwards the doctor, a squat red-faced man with an emerald ring, walks down the hall to her father's end of the house to drink gin and wait with him for the worms to finish their work.

Her father is white-haired, as tall as a tree. She calls him Poppup because it is a name a smaller, less frightening man might have. Poppup leaves her with Nurse after her mother dies. He doesn't know what to do with a girl. She hears him bark at Nurse: 'A boy would be different!'

'How would a boy be different?' she asks Nurse.

'Boys have snakes between their legs.'

Are they poisonous? Do they eat babies? she wonders secretly.

When her father dies, her first thought is: Now I will have to go outside. She closes up the house with the green louvred shutters and goes to the only person who can help her: her mother's best friend, the artist who lives on the island. But the artist is contemptuous of her ignorance, impatient with her fears.

Then, almost by accident, in a pub one night, she meets the artist's nephew. The artist and her nephew are not on speaking terms. Yet he likes Amanda. He is touched by her fears, charmed by her ignorance. He takes her up to his house in Millbrook, and he teaches her not to be afraid. The meadows of Millbrook are spongy underfoot and fragrant with wildflowers. When they troop in together from their walks, both are muddy to their knees. Never has she known such happiness.

It is his birthday. She wants to surprise him. His aunt suggests the perfect setting: the Sculpture Garden.

On the afternoon before the party, she is there checking to make sure that everything is just right. The garden, a setting for the aunt's art, has been decorated for the occasion with baskets of fresh white lilies and gardenias. She returns to her hotel room to prepare, changing into a long white dress and weaving lilies of the valley into her hair.

'Did you know lilies of the valley are poisonous?' his aunt asks. Poisonous? She begins to think she has made a terrible mistake, but it is too late. His car is already on its way to pick her up.

His driver has been told the address in advance to keep the surprise a secret. They sit in the back of his limousine, sipping champagne. He lays his hand in her lap, pushing the soft material between her legs. She feels herself grow damp. He nuzzles the lilies of the valley in her hair. Poisonous. The car stops in front of the wall. They get out and it is as if she has slapped him in the face. He stands looking at her, hurt, not believing she could plot such a scene.

'What did you think you were doing? Why did you bring me here?'

She shrinks from him, her fears confirmed. 'Darling, it's a surprise for your birthday. All your friends are waiting for you inside. Please don't be angry.'

'I'm not angry with you. It's her, isn't it? This is her idea. It's always been her idea. You're even her idea.'

She doesn't understand. All she can say is, 'I'm sorry, I'm sorry.' She pulls at his hands, pleading.

He looks at her and says, 'No. Good night. Good-bye.' He ducks into his car and rides off.

She tells everyone at the party that business has kept him away from his own birthday celebration. It is a relief that everyone seems to believe her. The party goes on anyway. Only one man there does not believe her! The dark one with the beautiful hands, his best friend. Every time he catches her eye, she flushes, hot and ashamed. All night long, he hovers near her, as if he were taking his friend's place. His eyes are dark and there are shadows across his face. She sags against him and lets him kiss her neck.

Waiting for her lover to call, she sits in her room. His aunt tells her that he will not call. They are finished, she explains to her, looking almost pleased as she packs her suitcase to return to her island.

'Drive with me to the airport. The air will do you good.'

'No. He might call. I have to be here.'

'Then you will be here for the rest of your life. Aren't you sorry you didn't make other friends? Now you'll be alone. Just you and your books.'

326

She stays in the hotel room, drinking tea, reading. The dark one comes to her one afternoon, the friend, dressed in a dark blue suit, a white shirt, and a grey tie. He speaks hardly at all. He puts his hand down her blouse and squeezes her nipple. She lets out a small scream. He pulls her up out of the chair, and, pushing her against the wall, makes love to her, still wearing the dark blue suit, white shirt, grey tie.

He visits every day, but they don't always make love. He teaches her what American life is about: how to pay cab fares, order meals, deal with tradesmen. How to dress. He takes over the management of her money.

'Will you marry me?' he asks her one day.

'I don't love you,' she answers.

'Will you marry me?' He asks her every day and her answer never changes.

Finally she says, 'Yes.'

As if by some unspoken agreement, they stop making love. Instead, they make arrangements for the wedding. Or rather, he does. He picks out her dress, reserves the church, orders the flowers, plans the reception, handles the invitations.

On the day the invitations are to be mailed, she goes to his office, and when no one is looking, flips through the sealed, stamped squares until she finds a certain one. This one she will deliver in person.

She musters all her courage and calls his office. She hasn't spoken to him since the night of his birthday. 'Can you come and see me? It's an urgent matter.' She gives him her hotel-suite number.

He knocks and she tells him that the door is open. He appears angry to be called away from the office, but when he sees her, his face softens. She sees in his eyes that he still loves her. She is lying naked on the bed. He lays his body over hers, as if to hide her nakedness. She feels his erection through his clothes.

When the marriage, as planned, takes place a month later, she knows she is a month pregnant. He comes to the wedding, the best man, dressed in a morning suit. She thinks he is the handsomest man there. And he is forever lost to her.

22

Kit turned off the shower and stood still, letting the water drip slowly off her body. She looked down at herself. Her nipples were erect. Her breasts were white against her tanned chest and arms. Gooseflesh ran up and down her body. No pain. Kit touched every part of her body, her stomach, her thighs, her crotch, her buttocks, seriously expecting to turn up some bruise, some sore spot, some place where all the pain must surely have collected. But there was no pain. There was only a sense of relief, and a miraculous sense of wholeness.

She stepped out of the shower and began to pat herself dry with the hotel's terry robe as she went to put the telephone receiver back in its cradle. The telephone rang immediately. It was Sasha, running down the morning's calls. Archer wanted to see her at three-thirty.

She hung up and went to the closet, pulled on a red silk blouse, knotted the tie in a loose bow at her neck. She stepped into a navy-blue skirt that hugged her hips and flared at the knee, slipping on a pair of red high heels. She stood up and looked at herself in the mirror. Whatever else was about to happen to her, with her job or with Brendan, she now had the answer to the question she'd been asking since she was a little girl.

She picked up the telephone and called room service.

'Good day. I have a rather specific and unusual request, and I'll need it filled rather quickly. I'd like a raw potato. Yes, raw. A bucket of ice. A sharp needle. No, I won't need any thread. And a bottle of rubbing alcohol. That's Room 821. Thank you.'

While she waited for the knock at her door, Kit organised her papers and packed everything back in her attaché case, unread. When the knock came, she opened the door cheerfully, took the tray with its peculiar contents, and tipped the bellboy five dollars.

'Thank you, Miss Ransome.' The boy grinned, backing away down the hall, tipping his cap.

Kit smiled. It was as if everyone nowadays took their models from some old Hollywood type. This one was a Mickey Rooney. Was she Bette Davis?

She took the turtle off the nightstand and set it on the bathroom counter, along with the tray. With a ball-point pen she made a dot on her right earlobe, making sure it lined up exactly with the hole in her left ear. The second black pearl earring stood ready in its green velvet nest. She let the needle rest in a pool of alcohol while she held a piece of ice to either side of her ear, waiting until the throbbing gave way to numbness. Then, holding the raw potato to the back of her ear, she took the needle and shoved it through the ball-point dot. She heard the crunch of cartilage as the needle pierced her ear. Quickly she pulled out the needle and threaded the earring through the hole the needle had just made. She brought the potato down and saw a single red dot of blood on it. She screwed in the back of the stud, gently. Then she opened the medicine cabinet, emptied out three double-strength aspirin, and swallowed them with tap water, one after the other. She looked at her flushed face in the mirror. She looked exhilarated. Yes, she was ready.

'Susie says Mr Ransome's not reachable right now, but I'll keep trying for you. You look really great, Kit. Did you sleep well?' Sasha asked.

'I didn't sleep at all, as a matter of fact.' Kit looked over yesterday's figures, the opening day of *Straight Flush*, frowning at the columns of neatly printed figures. 'Has Jerry Braxton called for these?'

'Yep,' Sasha answered, flipping through her book of phone messages. 'You have a very nervous producer there. He called at nine thirty-five ... that's six thirty-five LA time! Can you imagine? He tried to get me to read him the figures, just like you said he would.'

'Get me Sheridan first. I want to find out if any movie did business yesterday or whether we're the only flop in town.'

Sasha dialled from the phone extension. 'By the way, Verena Alexander stopped by.'

Kit felt resentment spread through her as if dye had been injected into her bloodstream. She took a quick breath. 'Oh?'

Sasha pushed down the hold button and said, 'She's very upset, Kit. Poor girl, she thinks you hate her. Mr Sheridan is on two.'

'Hate isn't exactly ...' She picked up the receiver. 'Hello,

Randy . . . Fine, thanks. Could you give me the numbers on the competitive movies yesterday? . . . Yes, per-screen average is fine.' Kit scribbled a column of figures on her pad. 'That bad, eh? . . . Yes, well, I think it's a bit early to say that, Randy . . . Well, Randy' – Kit's voice grew softer, then harder – 'that's your job, isn't it, to make the theatres hold the picture?' Kit hung up before Randy could argue.

'Get me Braxton,' said Kit. 'Let's get this over with.'

'Before I forget, Mr Alexander called twice and even dropped by once in person.'

Kit stiffened. 'What does he want now?'

Sasha spoke into the receiver, 'We'll hold for Mr Braxton . . . Yes, Ms Kit Ransome calling from New York.' And then to Kit, 'I thought you might like to know – Verena seemed to think he wants you to take the part away from her.'

'That certainly doesn't make sense. Rush was the one who twisted . . .' Kit paused. 'Rush was eager enough for her to have the part two days ago. Now he wants to take it away?'

'Look,' said Sasha, wedging the receiver into her shoulder. 'You didn't hear this from me . . .'

Kit nodded.

'. . . but you know that big party Rush threw for Verena last night – the one you didn't go to . . . ?'

Kit nodded again, thinking that Sasha, like any good secretary, treated her boss as if she had no memory.

'Well, Susie went,' Sasha continued. 'She said Verena acted really wild. And it was pretty obvious to everybody there that Mr Alexander wasn't exactly pleased with her.' Sasha spoke into the receiver. 'One moment, Mr Braxton, for Miss Ransome.'

'Jerry, honey,' Kit said kindly. 'How are you?' Kit swivelled in her chair away from Sasha, pulled out the lowest drawer in her desk, and propped her feet up. She concentrated on her conversation with Jerry, trying to be patient and supportive. After nearly five mintues of 'stroking', Kit read him the figures for *Straight Flush*. Figures, the all-important 'numbers', were so definite, so cut-and-dried, so unforgiving.

'No, sweetheart, it didn't open very well. But listen to these.' Kit read Braxton the competitive movie figures. 'It looks like people were staying home and watching football last night instead of going to the movies. It's too early for us to get depressed. It's the second weekend that'll really tell us. I want you to know, Jerry, that I've already been on the phone,' she lied, 'and I'll be seeing some new ad concepts in a couple of days. And if the grosses don't pick up, we'll introduce a new advertisement campaign next weeked . . . No, just print ads. Well, Jerry, we'll see about running more television. Okay, Jerry, relax. Go back to your Nautilus equipment and I'll call you tomorrow.'

Kit hung up. She, too, was disappointed with the performance of *Straight Flush*, but she had other things on her mind. Fingering the new earring, she buzzed Rush's office.

'What's up?' she asked coldly.

'Oh, Kitty Cat,' he came back softly. 'Sweet of you to return my ten-o'clock call at ten minutes before two. Busy playing fifty-two pick-up with your *Straight Flush* deck?'

'What is it, Rush?'

'I was wondering if you'd tear up the contract req on Verena.' Sasha was right: he did want out.

'Tear up the contract, Rush? I don't understand. I thought this was your heart's desire.'

'I've changed my mind,' he said.

'And to think I was just getting used to the idea.' She smiled into the phone, enjoying making *him* squirm now. 'That's not so easily undone, Mr Alexander. I guess you didn't catch the announcement on the *Today* show. It's news now, Rush. And it came across as *good* news. Your little party last night really set us up well. We can't afford any more bad news when it comes to *Last Chance*. As a member of senior management, Rush, I'm sure you can appreciate the value of turning the press and the public around on this. To quote the late great Merman, just call me Birdseye, Rush – the deal is frozen.'

She hung up before he could say anything and turned to Sasha. 'I *will* meet with Verena. Give me an hour with Archer and then have her come in. Now, get me Tom Gillan in Toronto, please.'

Kit waited while Sasha put the call through.

'Go ahead, Kit – he's on.'

'Tom . . . So? The people like *Phoenix Waltz*? . . . The film never got there?' Kit made a fist and banged the desk. 'And the full-page ad ran announcing the sneak preview . . . ? Well, yes, I realise you couldn't stop it, but for God's sake, what did Randy say was the reason the print never got there? . . . The plane sat on the goddamned runway in LA for three hours.' Kit got a hold of herself – these kind of things did happen, people made mistakes. Planes from LA carrying prints to Toronto did break down, money did get thrown out the window.

'Oh, well, Tom, it's not your fault. How did you keep the producer off the ceiling last night?' Kit enjoyed a good laugh. 'Okay, I'll talk to Randy and we'll reset it for next week.' Kit hung up. She liked Tom. He was Sheridan's second in command.

Tom was more interested in doing a good job than he was in politicking for Randy. Kit infinitely preferred talking business with Tom. With Sheridan there was always a subtext to their conversations and Kit could usually tell nowadays that Sheridan had called Rush before he called her, his own boss.

'Sasha, get me Scott, and while I'm talking to him, would you get to Price and tell him that *Flush* opened soft and we need new ads? Tell him I said to play up the Las Vegas murder-mystery line and play down the love story. We want sinister slot machines, evil dealers, stuff like that.'

Sasha nodded and closed the door behind her.

Kit waited for Sasha to put the call through. She was worried about Scott: there was so much pressure on him. Being a director had to be the hardest job in Hollywood. He had to be a general, a mother, an analyst, a visionary, a master tactician and technician who could make all the pieces fit together. It was the director's responsibility to make sure the actors were on time and not on drugs, that they knew their lines and were willing to work with their co-stars and not disappear when it came time for someone else's close-up. It was the director's responsibility to make the cinematographer shoot the movie the way he wanted it shot, even when the cinematographer reminded the director that he had won an Academy Award on his last film and knew perfectly well how to set up a shot, thank you. It was the director's responsibility, too, to make sure the grips who were playing poker and drinking beer and didn't give a shit about his movie were doing their jobs. And, perhaps hardest of all, it was the director's responsibility to keep the studio executives, who were complaining that the movie was over budget, happy and preferably *off* the set. Later, he had to duck out of the cutting room to speak with reporters so his movie would get good press. And once his movie was in the can, he had to persuade the studio's marketing executives that he did know something about how his movie should be advertised – *if* they would only let him look at the campaign. Being a director was an almost impossible job.

Scott came on the line. He was almost incoherent. 'They're going to close down *Last Chance*, Kit. It's all over town.'

'What's all over town, Scottie? Calm down.'

'They need the insurance money for their SEC defence.'

'Don't be ridiculous, Jay.'

'Can you tell me for certain that Ransome isn't going to close us down?'

Kit swivelled nervously in her chair. She looked out the window. Clouds were being blown across a slate sky so fast it looked like a special effect. She heard some commotion in her outer office. Loud voices, the loudest painfully familiar to her. She was having trouble concentrating on what Scott was saying.

'You can't! I knew it. You want to know some of the other things they're saying about you? Like ... you're having an affair with Verena and that's why she's in the movie. I'd give *anything* to know what kind of show you're running, Kit.'

Brendan Marsh barged into Kit's office and stood there glaring down at her. Slowly she hung up on Scott mid-sentence.

'You wanted to see me?' His voice was a low growl.

'Why, yes, didn't you get my messages?'

He didn't answer her. His fists were curled tightly at his sides. He looked as if he were ready to deck her. Only once before had she seen this kind of anger in him, and then he had been acting. He wasn't acting now.

'Well, I left messages,' Kit went on nervously. Her voice sounded silly, shallow. He already knew about Verena, but he'd come to hear it again, from her lips.

'I gather you've already spoken to Scott.'

'Scott, *hell*, I heard it from some fucking reporter, Kit. Some reporter tells me while I'm interviewing actresses for the part, for Chrissakes. Imagine how I felt, Kit. Imagine.' His voice was low, but it vibrated the letter opener on Kit's desk. It made a noise like teeth chattering.

Kit kept her eyes on the opener. 'I'm sorry, Brendan. I wanted to tell you myself.'

'The hell you did. You were too much of a coward to tell me yourself. You put poor little Scottie up to it instead.'

They both knew he was right. Kit was too ashamed to meet his eyes.

'Maybe I am a coward,' she said simply. 'But I didn't know what else to do.'

'You're even too much of a coward to stand up to me and tell me right now, aren't you? Why, I'll bet you can't even look me in the eye and tell me you cast that part behind my back, behind Scottie's back, behind the back of every poor goddamn creative slob who's given their heart and soul to this project, Kit.' He leaned an arm on the desk and chucked a finger roughly beneath her chin. 'If you didn't give a damn about how *I* felt, couldn't you at least care about Scottie? The kid's heart's broken. He trusted you. Hell, we all trusted you.'

He pulled back in disgust and waited for her to defend herself.

'Please,' Kit said feebly, 'please understand...'

'Please understand? Please understand what? That some Blue Suit twisted your pretty arm? No, Kit, no. Not you. You're better than that. You're better than the rest of them. You never let them push you around like that. No, this is something different. This is some perverse female plot of yours to get back at me for Kitsia! You women are a bunch of witches. Witches! I'm sorry I ever let myself –'

'No!' Kit nearly shouted. 'You're wrong. There were other factors, Brendan. Other considerations, and if you'd only trust me –'

He exploded. 'Trust you! Holy Jesus, that would almost be funny if it weren't so pitiful.'

Kit tried to remain calm. 'Brendan, look, I know I overreacted about Mother. I realise it wasn't all your fault. You just can't imagine how hurt I was. My own mother, Brendan!'

'For Chrissakes, woman, don't change the subject. This is about business and honour and how I actually – foolishly – believed that you could combine the two ... But now, after what you've done ...' He put his hands on his hips and threw back his head to laugh at the ceiling. 'I've been such a jackass! And to think, I actually felt sorry for you. By God, I even wanted to work my way back into your good graces, and sooner or later, Lord help me, into your bed. But no thank you, Evita. You can keep your precious boudoir by the sea. I have seen the light!'

'You're wrong.' Kit leaned into the desk.

'Oh, really?' His sarcasm was cruelly dramatic. 'Oh, really? Suppose you give me a reasonable explanation for your thoroughly unprofessional, irrational behaviour of the last two days, or should I say, two months.'

'I will if you'll give me a chance.' Her voice was deadly quiet all of a sudden.

'Fine,' he said, folding his thick arms across his chest. 'I'm waiting. Let's hear this pretty speech of yours. Maybe I need a little more priming before I wire my resignation to Scott.'

Shaking with rage, she gripped the arms of her chair and spoke through gritted teeth. 'I was Bic Crawford's lover for four years.'

'Christ, woman, that's ancient history!'

'Shut up, Brendan!' she shouted. Then, more quietly, she said, 'Just shut up and let me speak. I was his lover for four years. I'd never really had a boyfriend before Bic. I know that sounds ridiculous: a thirty-five-year-old and no boyfriend. But I hadn't. Bic was... well, he had a certain peccadilloes. But I naively thought that was just the way people in Hollywood *were*. He asked me to do things for him. I loved him, so I did them without question. I'd do *anything*,' she emphasised as she stared at Brendan's baffled face, 'for the man I love. It turned out that Bic had me photographed in various poses. No, I didn't realise the photos were being taken. You see,' she said delicately, 'I happened to be blindfolded at the time.' She cleared her throat and went on. 'Don't ask me to explain how, but Rush Alexander got hold of the negatives. All I know is I thought they'd been destroyed years ago... until the budget meeting on Wednesday when Rush came up and asked me for a little favour: Give his daughter the part of Lacy or he'd use the negatives against me. I didn't even ask him how he planned to use them. I simply, automatically, and in total panic, did as he directed. There. You asked for it, and now you have it.' She rose stiffly without looking at him and went to the door. Brendan caught her arm.

'Please don't touch me,' she said coldly, without turning to look at him. 'And I'd appreciate it if you weren't in my office when I come back.'

It required all Kit's control to walk the gauntlet of secretaries' desks around the corner to the ladies' room, where she pushed through the door, went to the very last stall, and closed the door behind her. In the last two harrowing months she had done a lot of crying, but these were the most bitter tears of all.

23

He suggested they go somewhere for a drink, so they walked back through the park to the Plaza, where the strange man asked for champagne, ordering a bottle even after Liberty declined to join him. She squeezed the lime wedge into her Perrier while she watched him stir his champagne with a solid gold swizzle stick.

'You've got to be putting me on!' she said as she noticed its diamond tip.

'It spins out the bubbles, miss.'

She grinned. He pronounced it 'speens'. His eyes were yellowish brown. His blue suit, which had always looked like a uniform from a distance, looked sleek and expensive up close. She wondered if he wore a gun beneath it.

'I have been wanting to talk to you for so long, Miss Adams.'

'Then why the Peter Lorre routine? You've been following me . . . how long is it now?'

He chuckled, showing small white teeth: pearls in shell-pink gums. 'Peter Lorre, miss. That is very good. You are very witty, miss, in addition to being very glamorous.'

He went on, 'Other men have begun to follow you, miss. Are you aware of this?'

Her smile froze briefly. 'Since when?'

He uncovered his gold Rolex. 'Six hours, miss.'

'Tell me, did they look American?'

'*Very*, miss.'

'Must be Pierce's goons.' She drummed her fingers on the table and addressed the ceiling. 'Forgive me, fellow taxpayers, he knows not what he does!'

He flicked his ear. 'Pardon, miss?'

'Nothing.' She came back to him and sighed. 'Just ranting to myself. You mind telling where you were night before last? I missed you. And who was the guy shuffling cards beneath my window? He looked extremely suspicious. Is he a Trips dealer by any chance?'

He shook his head apologetically. 'That is my very smallest brother, miss. He has been frequenting the Trips casino on Zwar since he was a young boy. I am afraid he is happy only with cards in his hands. Drinking, gambling . . . I'm afraid we are all very poor Moslems, miss.'

'And where were you?'

'Even I have to sleep sometimes, miss.' He bowed politely.

'Right. Answer me one question before we go on. Which of you fellows is here to kill Kit Ransome?'

He touched his chest, hurt. 'Miss, I worship her. I would never ever do anything to hurt her.'

'Well, that's a relief.' She fanned herself with one hand and reached under the table with the other, pushing up her sweater and switching on her tape machine. She was glad she had not taken it off her belt after her interview with Rush.

'Which brother are you, anyway? I like to know the names of my shadows?'

'I am Dhali, miss.'

'Dhali.'

'My older brother is Akmed, who became, if you will recall, during your stay on Zwar, the new Emir of Zwar.'

'I remember. Your father had just died.'

'Yes, miss, just before you came to visit us.'

'"Us"?' His extreme politeness was suffocating.

'The Zwarians, miss.'

'Well, as a Zwarian, Dhali, would you mind explaining to me why you guys are honouring that old vendetta now? Doesn't anybody there know we are living in the age of Concorde?' Liberty gestured out of the window at Central Park South.

'Yes, miss, but many of us feel that we have no choice but to carry it out. Vendettas, however ancient, must be honoured.'

She stared at him hard.

'You actually believe that? Your father, the late emir, didn't believe it. He left Archer alone.'

'Yes, miss, but there were no children upon which to carry it out. Ransome's only daughter died at birth. Had she lived, I assure you, my father would have –'

'Right.' Liberty waved her hand. She didn't want to hear the gory details of how vendettas were carried out. 'Who told you about Kit, then? Not Kitsia?'

'No, miss, of course not.' He stirred his champagne. 'Our father did some years ago, when he was ill and thought he might be dying.'

'I see, and now you and your brother are carrying out the old man's wish?'

'No, miss, I am trying to explain. Understand, please, that Akmed and I agreed, secretly between us, to lay the vendetta to rest. The way we both felt about Little Kit, we could not possibly –'

'And have you upheld that agreement?'

'It's a complicated matter, miss. The Russian –'

'Rush Alexander?'

'Yes, miss. He came to our father's funeral three weeks ago. He went to the casino with my brother and myself afterwards. You will think we are not very good sons, gambling so soon after our father's dying – and perhaps we are not – but my father was a long time dying . . . years dying . . .'

'And you'd already mourned him,' Liberty put in.

'Yes, miss, you understand so completely. We all drank very much champagne, and the Russian – he brought out photographs.' He stopped and stared down at his swizzle stick, suddenly shy.

'What kind of photographs, Dhali?'

'Oh, miss,' he sighed, 'it hurts me to tell you. Photographs of a compromising nature. Of . . . of Little Kit, in positions no Arab woman would ever permit herself to pose in.'

Liberty remembered her conversation with Jay Scott. When Bic Crawford put his house up for sale, there had been *certain devices* discovered attached to his bed.

'And what happened then, Dhali?' she went on grimly.

'My brother Akmed – how can I describe it? – he went wild. You would have to know him, miss. He is not like yourself . . . I mean, *myself*.' He bowed slightly and went on. 'He is bored. He has no one to love. He does nothing but spend our money. He usually does not like Westerners because he does not trust them. But the Russian he likes. And when the Russian showed him those pictures – pictures of the woman he was hoping to perhaps marry one day . . .'

Liberty gasped. '*Marry*? Had he ever proposed this to Kit herself?'

'Of course not. He was waiting for the day he became emir. Waiting to – how do you call it? – whisk her off her feet? But after he saw those photographs, he wanted to –'

'Kill Kit.' Liberty finished for him.

338

'You understand so perfectly. But there is more, miss. He told the Russian about the vendetta.'

'And . . . ?'

'The Russian offered to carry it out for him.'

'In exchange for?'

'Help.'

'What kind of help?'

'Help in overthrowing Archer Ransome. Akmed made the deal and my family now work for the Russian.'

'Except for you and your youngest brother. It's beginning to make sense . . . sort of. What I don't get is why Kit Ransome isn't dead right now. A smart man like Rush Alexander can have anyone taken out' – she snapped her fingers – 'for the price of a cheap sports car.'

'Miss, have you ever seen the big cats?'

'You mean like lions and tigers . . . ?'

'And panthers and pumas. Once they catch their prey, they never kill it right away.'

Liberty gulped. 'They like to draw out the kill.'

'When you are dealing with the Russian, you must beware of the big cat. He moves slowly, circling his victim. He started with that young girl.'

'Monette Novak?'

'Yes. First, he wanted to destroy what Little Kit loved best – her work. And then . . . But, Miss Adams, if he thought you knew all that you know, he would kill you quickly, without pausing to savour it.'

Suddenly uneasy, Liberty hoisted her cowhide bag onto the table and used it to block the view in from the pavement.

'Yes, miss, you are correct in that we must not sit together here much longer.'

'Dhali, I am planning on printing my story as fast as I can. It is the only way I know to help protect Kit. But you must help me. You must promise me something.'

'Your servant, miss.'

'Until I can get this story out, you must personally protect Kit.'

He finished his champagne and laid a hundred-dollar bill on the table. 'I will most assuredly attend to my part. I will protect Kit.'

She looked at him closely. 'You really don't want anything to happen to Kit, do you?'

'She was like a sister to me. The day for honouring old vendettas is past – and for honouring those who honour them.'

Liberty stood up and they walked together through the lobby of the Plaza to the street. 'Where do I reach you if I need you?'

'Call the Sculpture Garden. Ask for Maroun. He will know.'

Liberty grinned. 'Naturally the guys at the Garden *would* be the good guys. Kitsia's steadfast little soldiers.'

A small smile momentarily lit up his face. 'Not just *Kitsia*'s soldiers . . .'

'Does Kitsia know about this? About Akmed and Rush's arrangement?'

'Yes, miss. I told her. She said she didn't believe me. Big Kit is stubborn.'

Liberty nodded and started to push through the revolving door.

Dhali reached out and placed his hand firmly on her forearm. 'Be quite careful, miss. He is very dangerous.'

Liberty looked up at him. 'Akmed?'

'No. The Russian. His hate kills.'

Liberty's palms were slippery as she rang the doorbell for the fourth time. Amanda Alexander *had* to be home. Liberty had to talk to her to find out whether she knew what her husband was up to. Perhaps Amanda could provide her with something – a weapon, however small – she could use to stop Rush Alexander from completing his part of the bargain with Akmed.

Amanda Alexander opened the door partway and looked down on her coldly. Liberty was struck by how different she looked today from last night at the party. Her nose and eyes were red. She'd been crying.

'I was under the impression we weren't meeting.'

'Really?' Liberty said innocently. 'I've been checking with my office all afternoon and there was no message about a cancellation.'

The woman went on staring at her, but Liberty stood her ground. Finally Amanda sighed and opened the door the rest of the way, stepping aside to let Liberty in.

Liberty followed the tall, soft blonde down a hallway patterned with tiny Provençal peaches and trimmed in high-gloss mahogany. The dark floors were highly buffed and covered with cream-coloured cashmere rugs. Is this the house of a murderer? Liberty wondered silently as she caught sight of herself in a large

Chinoiserie mirror. She pushed at her hair; it was a dishevelled mop of red.

'Would you care for some tea?' Mrs Alexander stood by a pair of dark oak doors. She fiddled with the strand of pearls she wore over an apricot-coloured cardigan, distracted.

'Yes,' Liberty said, slowing to look at two Rembrandt etchings. 'Mind if I use the phone first?'

'Of course not.'

Up close, Liberty could see even more dramatically the evidence of tears recently shed. This was a woman so controlled, so mannerly, it was hard to believe she'd be capable of tears. Liberty wondered whether it was Rush who had made her cry. Did she know what he was up to, and was she also helpless to stop him?

Amanda Alexander swept open the two tall doors and Liberty peered into a room shades darker than the rest of the house. There was no sunny Provençal in here. As long as a boxcar, it was lined with bookshelves floor to ceiling.

'I don't usually entertain in here, but when you called the other day, you said something about Kitsia's wanting you to see my husband's collection of photographs.'

Liberty walked inside. 'How nice of you to remember.'

Mrs Alexander smiled slightly. 'Now, while you make your call, I'll see about the tea.'

Liberty looked around the room. There seemed to be no natural source of light. The dark made her feel claustrophobic. She looked at the red velvet curtains covering the windows at the end of the room and longed to tear them aside. A heavy black marble fireplace dominated the room like an altar, decked with an ornately carved mantelpiece. Crowding the mantel were the photographs in wooden or jewelled frames Kitsia had told her about. Two Windsor wing chairs stood before the fireplace, another faced the shrouded window, and a fourth hunkered down by a little Spanish writing desk on which stood a wine-red Princess telephone.

Liberty dived for it and punched up Kit's office. 'She's not in?' Liberty tapped her pen on the side of the phone. 'What do you mean she's left in an uproar? Jesus! Sasha, if she comes back, tell her it's urgent that I talk to her. I'm at Amanda Alexander's. *Make sure she calls me.*'

Liberty disconnected the line but did not hang up the phone. She groped inside her bag for her small address book and, finding it, punched in Archer's private line. She let it ring twenty times. If he did answer, what would she tell him? That Rush was out to ruin him? Did she have any concrete evidence?

'Have you finished?' Mrs Alexander came in wheeling a tea trolley.

'Yes, I'm finished.'

'It still looks as if it's going to storm. I think a fire might be nice.' Mrs Alexander spoke more to herself than to Liberty. She bent down and lit the fire.

Liberty sat in one of the wing chairs while her hostess continued to poke at the small flame dancing in the kindling.

'I think we're really through with summer.' Liberty leaned over, lifted the lid off the silver teapot, and breathed deeply. 'This smells delicious. Mind if I pour?'

'Not at all. It ought to be properly steeped by now. I take mine with lemon only, thank you.'

Liberty lifted the heavy pot and poured them each a cup. She put cream and lots of sugar into hers. It was a proper English tea with small salmon, cream-cheese, and watercress sandwiches, without crust, cut into tiny triangles, and beneath a silver bell, scones. But Liberty wasn't hungry.

Amanda Alexander was sitting completely still, watching Liberty.

'You know very well my husband cancelled this interview.'

'I know,' Liberty said mildly. 'I was surprised you even came to the door. Your husband strikes me as the kind of man who gets what he wants.' She stirred her tea, conscious of how hard it was for her to be civil to this elaborately mannered lady.

'My husband usually does get what he wants.'

Carefully Liberty started her tape machine. She didn't think Mrs Alexander noticed, having shifted her attention to her teacup: teal blue poised on a white and blue chequered saucer. Sitting in this bloodred library, Liberty had the eerie feeling of what it must be like to sit with a mafioso's wife. It was the feeling that this woman was deliberately out of touch: deliberately ignorant of what her husband did outside this *Architectural Digest* dream of a house. Liberty wondered why, indeed, Mrs Alexander had agreed to see her.

'Why do you think your husband tried to cancel our interview?' Liberty began.

'I don't know, Miss Adams.'

'He gave you no reason?' Liberty persisted. Just how loyal was she going to be to her husband?

'No.'

'It's because I know about Kit, isn't it?'

'Know what about Kit?'

'It's also because I know about the vendetta.'

'I don't know what you're talking about.'

The two women sat listening to the sounds of the fire catching.

Mrs Alexander spoke. 'Miss Adams . . . may I call you Liberty?'

Liberty nodded.

'Liberty, have you something to ask me? This has been a very trying day for me.' She stopped herself. Her hand strayed to her neck again and she fingered her pearls self-consciously.

'As a matter of fact, I do.' Liberty pulled out a cigarette and, lighting it, began. 'How well do you know Kit Ransome?'

'Not very well.'

'How well is not very well?' Liberty's tone was argumentative. She still didn't believe Amanda didn't know what she was talking about.

'I've met her several times. At Ransome Enterprises functions. She lives in California and I do not travel there with any frequency.'

'You didn't know her when you lived with Kitsia on Zwar?'

'No. Kit had gone to live in the States by then.'

'You must be pleased that Verena will be working for her in *Last Chance*?'

'Why should I be pleased?' Amanda's voice broke.

Liberty perked up. She had thought it must be cork that kept Amanda floating in her private ocean, but maybe the woman wasn't cork-filled, after all.

Amanda inhaled deeply, then exhaled slowly. She seemed to be weighing whether or not to tell Liberty something. She spoke with her eyes on the fire.

'The first time I met Kit was at a cocktail party here in New York. I was out on the terrace staring at an incredible view of all of Manhattan. This striking woman came out and asked if she might join me. I nodded and we stood for a few minutes before I introduced myself. Then I said to her, "When you walked in a few minutes ago, do you know what my husband took the trouble to tell me? He told me he had slept with you. Is that true?" She answered me "yes" without hesitation. I asked her what it was like. She said

343

she felt as if it were happening to some other woman! And do you want to know the most shocking part of this conversation? I know how she felt, Liberty. I knew exactly how she felt – and yet I didn't like her for it. I didn't like her for being so intimate with me.'

Liberty was vaguely scandalised. 'How did you meet Rush?' She tried to sound casual. Now that Amanda had opened the door a little, she had no qualms about barging right in.

Amanda poured herself another cup of tea. She glanced up at Liberty and then away, at the fire. 'Archer introduced us.'

'Tell me more.'

'I met Archer through Kitsia.'

'Were you in love with Archer like everyone else?'

'Yes. But only for a short time. Then I married Rush.'

'Hold it a minute. Did I miss something? You were in love with one man and married the other?'

Amanda smiled shyly. 'Well, as a matter of fact . . .' She trailed off and then drew herself up. 'I can't! I can't go into all that again. And I certainly can't go into it with you!'

Liberty tried to catch her eye, but Amanda looked away. 'Are you, by any chance, still in love with Archer?'

Amanda's delicate hands hovered protectively over her breast.

'Come on, Amanda, it's obvious. The look on your face when I mentioned his name just now. And last night at the party. Someone who didn't know any better might think you were married to each other.'

Amanda blushed. 'Well, we have grown to be good friends, that's true.'

'But no longer lovers!'

'Liberty!'

'Why did you break up with Archer?'

'It's really none of your business.'

Liberty couldn't stop herself. 'Did you let Rush catch you on the rebound to get back at your lover? Is that it?'

Amanda's indignation was deep. 'How dare you speak to me like that!'

Liberty pushed on. 'It was Kitsia who broke you up, wasn't it? Kitsia didn't want Archer getting married again. But you blamed Archer.' Liberty was no longer asking questions, she was thinking out loud. 'You blamed him for not standing up to Kitsia. So you got back at him by marrying his best friend.'

Amanda's eyes swam in tears.

Liberty stammered. 'I'm sorry. Please forgive me.' She reached into her bag and pressed a Kleenex into Amanda's hand.

Amanda dabbed at her eyes. 'You see, Archer was my first love.'

Liberty saw a small shudder run through her body.

'They say you never get over your first love,' she went on. 'Long after you marry someone else or that person dies, your feelings go on. They have a life of their own.'

'And your feelings for Archer...?'

'Were, now that I think of it, in their depth of passion, one-sided. You see, I wasn't *his* first love. From the beginning I knew he'd never love me the way he loved her.'

'I see. You didn't marry Rush to get back at Archer, you married Rush to keep Archer the only way you could. If you couldn't marry him, you'd marry his best friend. If you couldn't sleep with him, you could at least sit across the table from him at dinner parties. But there was no more romance, was there, Amanda?' Liberty hesitated and, taking silence for confirmation, went on. 'After all, you were pregnant with Verena by then. What could be more platonic? You brought him into your house – you even encouraged him to be godfather to Verena. Tell me, when Rush was out of town, did Archer attend the teachers' meetings, the recitals, the –?'

'Yes, yes, yes...' Amanda broke in. 'I admit it. It's all true. But it wasn't as easy as you think it was. I never planned it. It took me a long time to get used to him as a friend, much less surrogate father, holding Verena on his lap. A long time not to run to him when I saw him step into my front hall. I even gave up smoking because he had this way of lighting my cigarette...'

'I know,' Liberty sympathised. 'I know. You still love him. And I pity you for being married to Rush.'

'You don't understand.' Amanda's voice rose. 'Rush was good to me then,' she added pitifully. 'He took care of me. And believe me, I needed taking care of.'

'And so, like so many women, you mistook *care* for love.'

Amanda shook her head. 'Never! I was never mistaken about that.'

Liberty nodded slowly. For a moment she felt sorry for Amanda, but she couldn't stop. 'Let's get back to Kitsia. How close are you two?'

Amanda looked suspicious. 'We're quite close. She's my only family other than Verena.'

'What kind of mother do you think she was?'

Amanda looked taken aback. 'I really couldn't say. Women try in their own way to be good mothers – it's just a matter of what that means. I've tried, but if you asked Verena right now, she would say I've failed her.' Amanda glanced at her watch. 'Kitsia tried to give Kit an inner strength – I think. Tried to teach her that she didn't need anyone other than herself.'

'You mean that she didn't need a man – didn't need a husband – because she had no father?'

'I suppose you could look at it that way. I don't think Kitsia ever intended her to marry. Who knows what Kitsia meant for her? It must have been difficult raising Kit alone on that island, without a father.'

Liberty cut in. 'What kind of father is Rush Alexander? Father to twelve companies and one daughter?'

'Yes.' Amanda looked down and fiddled with the Kleenex, spreading it out on her knee, smoothing it like lace.

Liberty leaned forward. 'Yes, what, Amanda?'

'Yes, he is a busy man.' She seemed distracted.

Liberty was reminded of an uneasy little girl keeping secrets. She leaned still closer, trying to get Amanda to look up. 'Verena was pretty upset with her father last night. Have any idea what that was all about?'

Amanda's eyes rose from her 'lace'. They were deadly calm. 'It's none of your business. Verena has nothing to do with your article. If I find you've printed one word against her, so help me, I'll –'

'Have your husband drop a steel girder on my head?' Liberty was more surprised at her own words than Amanda, who kept staring at her.

'Not one word against my daughter.'

'Don't worry. But I can't guarantee the same for her daddy . . . and speaking of daddies,' Liberty barrelled on fearlessly, 'who is Kit's father? Ever wonder?'

'No,' Amanda replied. 'It's not my place to wonder. It is rude to speculate about others' lives.'

'Then you must see what I do for a living as extremely rude,' Liberty couldn't resist.

'No, I'm sure your piece won't be speculative.'

'Don't be so sure,' Liberty tried a smile.

'Liberty, perhaps I'm not expressing myself well. I know I sometimes speak *around* my point. My parents thought conversation was an extremely important part of a young girl's upbringing, only they were determined that no conversation stray outside the realm of what was proper and decent. Many topics were therefore not discussed. It is difficult to go beyond one's parents' teachings.'

'What is your point?' Liberty addressed her as if she were a schoolgirl. She remembered what Kitsia had said about how she wanted to shake Amanda; how she lived in a fog-bound, book-bound world. Kitsia had told her that Amanda had so carefully structured her life that it was virtually empty except for her daughter, but even so, Amanda had never been able to make Verena understand just how much she loved her.

'Only once have I ever thought about Kit's father, and that was a few weeks ago when Rush asked me the same question. I answered him in much the same way I answered you. He was equally annoyed with me.' Amanda looked over into the fire.

Liberty was almost wistful. 'It's pity you didn't marry Archer. It would have made a lovely circle in some ways. Didn't Kitsia tell me that Archer had a crush on your mother, Cynthia?'

'He did. As a matter of fact, I used to wonder if that wasn't part of his attraction to me. Only, of couse, my mother was an extremely dynamic woman. My daughter is much more like my mother than I am.'

'They say characteristics often skip a generation.'

Amanda was thoughtful for a while. Finally she said, 'I don't think there was any need for Kitsia to break us up. He would never have married me. He's never married again. How could he? He's married to his work. Actually,' she added softly, 'I don't think Archer's overly fond of women. Thanks, I'm afraid, to Kitsia.' She stared moodily into the dwindling fire.

'He loved Cassie,' Liberty reminded her gently.

'Oh, yes. He loved her, all right.'

'Did you know her?'

'Know her?' she said faintly. 'Sometimes I feel as if I grew up with her. Sometimes I feel as if I could tell you everything you would want to know – her favourite colour, the sound of her laughter, the look of sunlight on her hair, how she ate corn on the cob with a fork.' Amanda took a deep breath. 'No, I never met her. And yet, I know her intimately... through my husband's obsession with her.' She gestured towards the mantel. 'My husband keeps that photograph of her as if it were one of his icons.'

'Which photograph?'

347

'Isn't it at the front?' she asked dully. 'He usually keeps it at the front.'

'Does Archer know about this obsession?'

'I doubt it. I think he thinks Rush keeps the picture out of sentiment. Rush loves looking at her flanked by the two of them.'

'Amanda, did you know your husband has tried to buy pieces from the Cassandra Series, and Kitsia won't sell him one?' Liberty asked cautiously. She stood up to browse through the photographs.

'I didn't know that. But as you can see, my husband is an avid collector of fine art.'

Liberty peered at the photographs and then looked around for a proper light.

Amanda went on, 'But I'm not surprised. I wonder why Kitsia won't let him have one of her Cassandras. I guess she wants to keep them all to herself.'

'You speak as if she were in love with Cassie too.'

'Weren't they all? And there's another thing I know, Liberty. Had Cassie lived, she would have left Archer.'

'To be with Rush?'

She looked at her strangely. 'Aren't you listening to me? To be with Kitsia, of course. I think she would have gone back to Kitsia.'

Liberty went over and switched on the desk lamp. A greenish light suffused the room. The photographs on the mantel leapt to life.

'Liberty, earlier you said something about a vendetta. What did you mean?'

Liberty walked towards the mantel. 'Oh, nothing. It's just...' She hesitated, unsure whether to tell her. 'Years ago, Archer Ransome killed the emir's son in a quarrel over Kitsia. The emir vowed to kill, or have his surviving sons kill, Archer's children.' Her eyes roved over the photographs: a tall white-haired man in a cutaway jacket with a Victoria Cross on his lapel; Verena, threeish, in floppy sunhat holding up a daisy for Archer, in tennis whites; Amanda and Rush with Beverly Sills at what must be a fund-raiser...

'But I don't understand,' Amanda was saying. 'Archer has no –'

'Will you please show me the photograph?' Liberty blurted out.

Amanda got up wearily and picked it out, drawing it towards her chest, nearly cradling it. 'Who would have thought such a beautiful creature could experience such tragedy?'

Gently Liberty took the photograph away from her and looked

348

at it herself. It was a wedding photograph, although hardly traditional. At first it looked as if there were two grooms. On closer inspection Liberty was able to distinguish Rush and Archer, more than thirty years younger, the best man and the groom. Both looked touchingly, boyishly formal in morning coats and tails. Archer's hair was blond and wavy and he looked relaxed and tanned, like a movie star or playboy. By comparison Rush looked dark and deprived, no different than he had an hour ago, except that here he was bonier and his hairline was lower. She saved the bride for last. Her gown had a plunging Elizabethan neckline. Slightly younger than Liberty, she had long, rippling hair.

Like the princess in a 1940's book of fairy tales.

Although the photograph was black and white, Liberty could tell that her hair was red – auburn. *Flaming but not raging.*

Liberty heard herself crying out. Her knees buckled.

She heard Amanda's voice in her ear, low and almost vicious. 'She's dead! She was so unbearably beautiful . . . If only they would all let her rest.'

Suddenly the air in the room seemed dead, as in the eve of a storm. Liberty felt a heavy, morbid weight on her chest. The deeper she breathed, the more deeply she sank into the chair. It was a strange sensation. She had to fight for her balance. By the time Amanda crashed across the tea tray to rescue her, it was too late. She had already collapsed.

Liberty came to with a sickening jolt as Eben held a plug of ammonia-soaked cotton beneath her nose. She pushed his hand away and said, 'I thought I was dying!'

'You didn't die, baby. You just fainted. Do you know where you are?'

She was in the sunny Provençal parlour, lying on the sofa with her head on his lap. She stared down at the silk stripe on his black trouser leg. Everything looked a little brighter than usual: storm-washed. Idiotically, she said, 'You're wearing your monkey suit!'

He smoothed her hair. 'That's right, my love. Are you feeling better now? We were just about to call in the medicos.'

She looked around. 'Where did she go?'

'The lady tactfully left as soon as you started to revive. I'm glad she had the brains to tell me what was going on when I called.'

'You called?'

'Yeah. From the cocktail party. To ask you how Rush reacted to my call. She said you were having some kind of a seizure or something. I dropped my rubber chicken and ran.'

'Can we get out of here?'

'My car's right outside.'

'I don't think I can walk.'

'You're kidding,' he said. 'Try.'

Liberty got to her feet and sagged immediately into his arms. He picked her up and carried her into the hall. They met Amanda on her way in with a tray. 'It's lamb's broth. I heated it up, but I see you're already on your way.' She looked dazed and a little forlorn. She set the tray down on a hall table. 'Wait just a minute, Liberty. Senator. Please.'

Disappearing back down her peach-coloured hall, she re-emerged from the library carrying a manila envelope tied with a string. She handed it to Liberty. 'This is yours.' Her eyes looked a little wild. 'I think you found what Kitsia wanted you to find.'

She held the door open and Eben carried her out to his car. When he gave the driver Liberty's address, she was surprised that he knew it without asking. He slid in next to her and put his arm around her. Liberty unwound the string from the envelope. She didn't really want to look at it right now. She just wanted to make sure the photo was in there. She opened the envelope and peeked in. Eben leaned forward and asked, 'Who's that woman?'

'That's no woman,' she said, closing the envelope and winding the string back around the button, 'that's my mother.'

He kept his eyes on the West Side Highway. 'I reopened the cottage, Lib.'

'You *are* trying to tempt me back!'

'I even fixed up the gazebo behind the cottage. There's an electric outlet for your word processor, Lib. And a nice big desk with lots of drawers and good working surface to lay out all your papers on. I've even trimmed a view for you, through the brush over to the river.'

Those were the exact specifications of the writer's study she'd envisioned. She smiled.

He went on. 'I added a few touches of my own, of course. I put a bed in there, for one.'

'A bed?'

'What if it gets too dark or too foggy to find your way back through the woods to the cottage? There has to be a refrigerator there, too, just in case you get hungry or thirsty.'

'When did you do all this?'

'After Corny died. I beat my way in there last spring. I cut away overgrowth for three whole days. The ivy had really taken over, Lib, the way you always said it would. Remember, you said the cottage would slowly but surely turn into a sod hut because of the ivy? Well, your prediction's practically come true. It's waiting for you, Lib.'

She sighed and closed her eyes.

'I've been spending all my free time up there.'

Liberty laughed wryly. 'All your free time? Gee, that must be two or three days a year.'

'Very funny.'

The car pulled up to her building. They stood on the pavement smiling at each other as the wind whipped their clothes. They were marvelling at how this reunion had worked. The old flame still burned, only now she wasn't afraid of losing him.

'At least let me come up and tuck you in.'

'I'm not going to bed. Really, I'm fine.' They kissed. Her tongue slipped so easily, so happily into his mouth, as his did into hers.

'Go back to your rubber chicken,' she whispered hoarsely. 'I need time to work this out.'

She unlocked the door to her loft and saw the old woman perched on a stool at her kitchen counter, making a pyramid out of spice bottles. Liberty noticed with surprise that she was wearing a skirt, long and black, with black stockings, like a Greek widow. She looked older than Liberty remembered her.

'I suppose you slipped through the keyhole.' Liberty didn't recognise her own voice.

Kitsia cleared her throat strenuously, and without taking her eyes off the spice bottles, said, 'I told your downstairs neighbour it was an emergency. He believed me. You know now, don't you?'

Liberty took the photograph out of the envelope, walked over and set it down on the counter before Kitsia. 'I know.'

Kitsia picked up the photograph and, bending back the two sides to obliterate Archer and Rush, stared at it.

'Why didn't you tell me when I was in Zwar? Wouldn't it have been easier?'

'You wouldn't have believed me.' Kitsia peered at her. 'Besides, I needed you to tell Kit.'

'Why didn't you tell her yourself?' Liberty persisted.

'Who better than her own sister? Besides, she wasn't talking to me. I'd tried to tell her. That's why I went to California. But I did something very foolish instead.'

'I know. Jay Scott told me.'

'Let that be a lesson to you, Liberty. We don't necessarily get wiser as we get older. In fact, we sometimes set out to prove rather foolish points.'

'When you got back to Zwar, you found out that Akmed wasn't the only one who knew – Rush also knew about Kit.'

'Dhali came and warned me that Rush had struck a deal with Akmed and that Kit was marked. I tried to contact Kit, but she wouldn't take my call. So I decided to use you.'

'Was this business with *Metropolitan* a charade?'

'Yes. The editor-in-chief and I go back quite a ways. She owed me a favour.'

'And you knew the wedding photograph would be on the Alexander mantelpiece?'

'Amanda has been complaining about it for years. I knew if you were a good reporter you'd see it for yourself. If I'd told you, you would have spit in my face.'

Liberty sighed. 'You're probably right, but we'll never know, will we?'

'But didn't you know? Deep down? Didn't the presents at least make you suspect?'

Liberty took the photograph back. 'I remember every present. I cherished each one as if it were a sign.' She stared out the window at the gathering storm. 'I remember being in bed. A metal bed with bars on the sides that were painted white so many times they were knobby with layers. There were sixteen of these cribs along two walls in my room. The windows were too high for us to look out, but from our beds we could see down the hill to the river. I remember sitting at the foot of the bed, gnawing away at the paint to get at the metal underneath. It must have been my second birthday. Sister Bertrand came in carrying a parcel and put it on my bed. She said she really wasn't supposed to pass out presents to us, but she was making an exception and I was not to tell the other girls. I opened the brown paper package and found an illustrated prayer book. I was too young to read the words, and no one ever had time to read it to me except Sister Bertrand once in a while. But I didn't care. For hours on end I looked at those pictures. They were beautiful, with gold powder mixed in with the ink. It was stolen from me before my fifth birthday.'

Liberty scowled at the old woman. 'Why didn't you send me a present every year? The years you didn't give me anything, I wanted to die.'

Kitsia threw up her hands. 'Everyone wants to be spoiled!'

'I was the only girl at River Mary's who actually had *someone out there*. None of them had a fairy godmother, like I did.

'I knew for sure that I had a fairy godmother when on my sixth birthday I got a present only a gay madcap fairy godmother would send. It was a long blue scarf made of the sheerest chiffon. I started out by wearing it on my head to chapel. For the first time, I wanted to look good for Christ. In those days I thought of Christ as a cute, older boyfriend who understood me as no one – except my fairy godmother – did. I had to keep that scarf with me at all times so no one would steal it. I even bathed with it knotted around my head, even though all the girls laughed at me.

'On my eighth birthday you sent me a white silk shirt with French cuffs.'

Kitsia broke in, 'I remember that shirt! A houseguest brought it to me as a present. It must have been enormous on you!'

'At first, it was. But I grew into it after a while. By the time I was twelve, it fit me like a second skin. I loved that shirt.

'On my tenth birthday, you sent me a musical jewellery box. It had a picture of a swan on the lid, swimming on a mossy lake. Someone stole that from me, too. My freshman year at college. I wanted to kill!

'On my twelfth birthday, I received six issues of a magazine I'd seen on the news-stands in town during my secret forays there. It was called *Screen Story*. The sisters were blown away. They thought my benefactor, whoever she was, had gone to the devil. I was mystified but delighted. I kept them in the storage closet up in the attic and pored over them for hours. And when I'd finished reading every caption and looking at every photograph, I cut them up and made a collage for the wall above my head, next to my own little Virgin Mary. Even now, I can't pass a news-stand without picking up one of those magazines.'

'What have I wrought?' Kitsia wondered aloud.

'Soon I widened my search for clues to my benefactor to the big screen. I started going to every picture at the local movie house. The movies may not have been fresh out of the can, but they were magic to me. Rita Hayworth. Marilyn Monroe. Montgomery Clift... Kit Ransome. I watched each movie nine or ten times, grubbing stubs from off the pavement and fast-talking my way past the doorman. I *had* to get in there. I was expecting another sign from my fairy godmother.'

'Actually those magazines weren't intended as a sign at all. Kit sent me those magazines from Hollywood.' Kitsia explained. 'How she hated them! She wanted me to share her contempt, but they amused me. I thought they'd amuse you, too, locked away from the world the way you were.'

Liberty unfolded the photograph and tried to smooth the creases. 'They meant everything to me.'

Liberty heard a rhythmic tapping. Swivelling around on her chair trying to locate the sound, her eyes came back to find Kitsia hitting a spoon against the side of the pyramid of vials.

'Enough!' Kitsia announced. 'I didn't come here to reminisce with you. I came here to give you your birthday present.'

Kitsia brought out a handmade portfolio fashioned out of heavy rag paper, ancient-looking as papyrus. She untied the four knots that held it together and spread it out on the counter. It smelled pungent, musty, like something recently disinterred. They were sketches executed on newsprint in fierce, oily layerings of dark blue ball-point pen. Their edges were black with fingerprints.

Liberty handled them carefully, her fingers trembling. They were studies of a pregnant woman, voluptuous and sprawling, legs wantonly splayed. She came to a sketch of a well-muscled young man embracing the same woman from behind, and caught her breath. From the arching of her back and the way her cheek brushed up against his, Liberty could tell he was having her from behind. These were the most erotic pictures Liberty had ever seen. Her breathing quickened and she let the drawings fall from her fingers. She looked at the date on one of the papers. August 14, 1949.

'Cassie and Archer?' she whispered. 'Did they know you were drawing them? Did they pose for you? Tell me. Kitsia. Tell me about my mother.'

The girl is big with child by the time Kitsia arrives in New York. Vernière-Plank has arranged for a show at a Madison Avenue gallery.

354

It is important to her that the trip have a double purpose. Not wishing to disrupt her work, she rents a space above a theatre on Fourteenth Street and walks there daily from their house in Gramercy Park.

Each day on her way to the studio she asks herself whether tonight she will bring herself to tell the girl the truth about the child she is carrying: that it will be impossible to protect it from the emir's sons when the time comes for them to carry out their father's wish.

But the girl is so happy! They are totally enchanted with each other. She has never seen her nephew so alive. Perhaps they are good for one another. Perhaps there is a way to avert tragedy.

One day, the young woman is sitting on her bed, rubbing palm oil into her belly while Kitsia sketches her from across the room.

'Now will you tell me how you lost the breast?'

Kitsia pauses, charcoal hovering over the paper.

'Yes,' she finally says. 'I will tell you.' Continuing to draw, she tells her the whole story.

The girl's first reaction is one of panic. Immediately she wants to leave her house, her husband, and to hide so she can bear the child in secret. But her husband comes home from work that night, laden with yellow roses and fresh oysters and she knows she must stay.

'How can I leave him, Kitsia? I love him more than my own life. And he needs me so! To have to choose between the two of them is hateful. We must devise a plan,' she says resolutely.

Together they plot. They persuade Archer to keep the pregnancy a secret from prying reporters. Then they send menacing notes to Archer – jumbles of letters cut from magazines demanding money and 'signed' by the young woman's foster mother.

After poring over these letters, Archer and his lawyers decide they should be treated as the rantings of a crazy but harmless crank. Still, Archer begs Kitsia to remain with his wife during the day, just in case.

Since both women know there is no imminent danger, Kitsia goes off to the studio as usual. Cassie remains at home, knitting garments for the unborn child, running their plan through her mind over and over, searching for flaws. The baby is kicking hard now; with each kick she vows that the horrible Arab men won't ever lay hands on it.

One morning when Kitsia is in her studio, an unexpected guest arrives. The Russian with the perfect hands has come to purchase a piece of art. But not just any piece; he is looking for a particular model. He stares at the likeness of the young woman pinned to the wall.

'I'll be satisfied with any one of these,' he says.

She eyes him suspiciously. 'I never sell my own work. Talk to Vernière-Plank.' And she tells him where in New York he might find her dealer.

She calls Vernière-Plank and tells him not to sell to the Russian under any circumstances, regardless of the price.

He is back in two days.

'Archer tells me you've only just met his lovely wife.'

'That's correct,' she says, trying to get on with her work, but finding it difficult.

'In that case I'd like to know how you explain all of these?' He fans out photographs from the catalogue of her work. Much of it contains the likeness of the young woman. Some are over ten years old.

'What of it?'

'She's your lover. She has been for years.' And then, teasing her, he says, 'You're lying to Archer, Kitsia.'

'At the risk of repeating myself: What of it? You're obviously in love with her yourself.'

And then the self-contained mask disintegrates before her eyes and he is weeping.

'I do love her. I do love her. Help me, please.'

'Now who's lying to Archer?'

'All I want is a sketch. Just a small sketch of my beautiful Tess.'

'No. She doesn't love you, you know. Forget her. The sooner you bury your love, the better.'

'I can't.'

As he leaves the studio, he turns to her. 'You'll be sorry.' Afterwards, she wonders if this is true. Could he be dangerous?

She returns home that afternoon to find Posy in the parlour having tea with the young woman. Posy seems to have mellowed, to have forgiven all. She pulls Kitsia off to the side. 'I blame you for this. How could you let this happen? Have you told her?'

'Yes, I've told her.'

There is no time to argue. Now three of them plot. Posy posts the letters from Boston now, from a box in the South End, as if the real foster were actually sending them. Everything proceeds according to plan.

Weeks earlier than expected, Cassie goes into labour. Kitsia wires Posy to come.

Posy arrives and sits in the waiting room. Outside in the back of her car, a laundry basket waits, lined with a new cashmere blanket. Archer and the Russian sit across from her. The Russian whispers to Archer,

Archer stares into space, dumbfounded.

Later, he is at her bedside, whispering to her. He tells Kitsia to get out. Refusing, she merely stands aside and watches helplessly as they both give in to her pain. He kisses her. Between contractions she looks into his eyes. She wants to tell him everything.

Then, smocked and masked, Kitsia stands by the bed, trying to put herself between the pain and the young woman. 'I will take care of everything.'

'Do you think this baby is killing me like I killed my mother?' The pain is too strong. Something is very wrong.

They wheel her into the delivery room.

'Push harder. Don't stop. You're fighting it.'

She screams. A baby cries out.

'A little girl,' someone says.

'She's dead, isn't she? She's dead. I knew it.'

'Hold her. Here.'

'I can't.'

The doctors work furiously beneath a tent over her knees. She stares up tranquilly at the big white lights, resigned. Signs of pain have disappeared from her face with alarming quickness.

'Get her husband. Hurry!'

He cradles his wife in his arms.

'Don't cry,' she tells him. 'This is for the best. Ask her.'

He is crying, but they push him away. An oxygen mask covers her face. Kitsia leans over and whispers, 'Your baby is alive.'

'Save her, Kitsia. Save her!' he cries.

But they cannot save her. When she is gone, Kitsia runs after him down the street. He spins around and shouts, 'Rush told me everything in the waiting room! You've been her lover for years, before I met her. How could you hurt me so? Why, Kitsia, why have you done this to me again? Take the child. I don't want her.'

'It isn't true about us,' she tries to explain. He walks away.

She returns to the hospital. They have to act quickly.

'Go and take her now. I'll handle the nurse.'

Posy hesitates, then moves swiftly, pulling her blue scarf around her face.

Later, Kitsia tells the police: 'I followed her and saw her throw the baby into the river. She jumped in after it. I tried to stop her. She was the baby's grandmother.' The police offer her a chair. She is shaking. She tells the same story four times. They believe her.

The two women drive the baby along the road that follows the river.

The baby lies in a laundry basket between them, unnaturally silent. She has thin red eyebrows and fine red fuzz all over her head.

'Her eyes are violet. She looks like her mother.'

Kitsia nods.

'How will she survive at the convent? Who will look after her?'

Kitsia's eyes are on the highway. 'It's best for her to be left with the sisters.'

'How can you be so cruel? You're the most selfish woman alive.' Breaking down, she sobs. 'We all loved her so much. And now none of us will ever have her!'

24

Kit walked quickly back to her office suite from the ladies' room, her throat raw from crying. The phone on Sasha's desk was off the hook, and Sasha was nowhere to be seen. A note lying beside the phone read, 'Tell Kit I'll come by for her when AJR's ready to see her. Susie S.'

She hung up the telephone and looked around, perversely hoping Brendan had stayed. But he was gone. And she didn't know how to get him back.

She heard a clickety-clicking in the next room.

'Sasha?' She pushed open the door. The telecopier was transcribing a memo onto a printout roll from the telephone. No Sasha. The office was empty except for the ghostly clicking.

The telephone rang. Kit froze. She couldn't move to pick it up. Finally she turned and lifted the receiver, whispering into it, 'Yes?'

'Hello ... Kit? Is that you?'

'Who is this calling, please?'

'This is Amanda Alexander. Is my daughter there, Kit? I must speak with her. It's very important.'

'Verena *was* here.'

'When? Can you tell me? I'm trying to find her.'

'I don't know exactly. It might have been yesterday. Was it yesterday?' Kit began to laugh into the telephone. She couldn't control her voice. Was she getting hysterical?

'No. *Today*. Have you seen her today?' Amanda was insistent.

'No. I've been very busy today. She might have come in.'

'I've got to find her, Kit.'

'I wish I could help you, Amanda, but I really don't know where she is. Have you checked with Rush? Or with Archer?'

'Archer!' Amanda almost screamed. 'Do you think she's with him? Oh, God, no!'

'Amanda, calm down. What's wrong?'

'Kit, do you think my husband is a dangerous man?'

Kit was cautious. 'I'm not sure what you mean.'

Amanda's voice was low, almost a whisper. 'He's been waiting all these years to find a way to hurt him, and now he has it.'

'What are you talking about?'

But Amanda had already hung up.

Susie appeared just as Kit put down the receiver. 'Good God, girl, it isn't going to be *that* bad.' Susie wrapped an arm around Kit and walked her down the hall to Ransome's suite. Inside, Kit was reeling. What had Amanda meant about Rush's being dangerous? Did she know about his blackmailing her? Was she trying to warn her?

'You've had yourself one hell of a week, haven't you?' Susie patted her on the back. She yielded to Susie's mothering, feeling small and childlike. One thing was certain. She couldn't go on working for him indefinitely, knowing what she knew. But for *Last Chance* she'd stay another year, to see it properly released.

'Big Daddy's going to make it all right. You'll see,' Susie was saying.

Kit stopped and stared at her.

'You mean *"Lost" Chance*, if we listen to *Variety*. *"Fat" Chance* is what *Time* called it. Nothing beats the movie business for public failure and humiliation!' *And I'm lucky enough to get it in love as well as in business. Right in front of over a hundred million people.*

'What do you care what people think? By the way, I heard about that man woofing you back there.'

'Brendan? Brendan's woof is worse than his bite.' Kit smiled at her own weak joke. 'But when he was standing there in front of me, I had trouble remembering that. He's a bit overbearing.'

'You're *too* kind. He jumped all over you. Mr Ransome is right about that one. He's bad news.'

'No, you're wrong. He's just been hurt. He's like a wounded bull.' She sank into a corner of Susie's couch and stared at the seashell litho. 'But it's too late now. Brendan's gone. It doesn't matter any more.'

Susie went into Ransome's office and came back out. 'He's run off again. I'll get you some tea. Grab hold of yourself, Kit. You don't want him to see you this way.'

Susie returned a moment later, handing the cup as if to a child who might spill it. 'You'll need this. He's really on a tear today. I think I've worked harder these past few days than I have in months.'

Archer swept past them, signalling for Susie to open his door.

Kit remained sitting on the couch, trying to collect herself. Her hand was shaking so badly that she had to put her teacup down on the mahogany end table.

'Mr Ransome,' Susie spoke up. 'Liberty Adams just called again. She says it's important.'

'Hello, Kit. Sorry I've kept you waiting again. Second time this week, eh?' He was standing over her, holding out his hand. She took it and, pulling herself up, followed him into his office. Archer turned back to Susie. 'Try Liberty for me now.' The doors slid shut.

'I missed you at the party last night. You should have been there.'

He was starting right in.

'I was busy.' She sat down on the white love seat. She couldn't bring herself to look at him.

He was walking back and forth, collecting papers, folders, cigarettes, lighter, coffee. She suddenly realised that his tie was loosened. Was he really her father? He sat down on the chair next to her and loosened his tie a little more. The afternoon sun broke over his back, blinding her. She couldn't see his face. He was talking about the weekend's box-office activity. She couldn't concentrate on what he was saying.

'The sun's in your eyes, isn't it?' she heard him say. He got up and went to the window and depressed a row of white buttons. A fine meshlike shade travelled across the windows like a slowly spreading storm. He walked back towards her. She noticed his limp. She let her eyes travel slowly up his body, finally looking at him squarely for the first time. To the objective eye, he might just be her father. Their noses were identically shaped; both of their lower lips were a bit too full. She'd got her height from him.

'About *Last Chance*. I'm sorry it's taken me –'

The intercom buzzed. Kit watched him walk over to his desk. She began musing what else she might have got from him.

'Yes, Susie?'

'I can't reach Miss Adams, Mr Ransome. She left the Alexanders' number, but Mrs Alexander said she left about a half-hour ago. There's no answer at her home, and her service isn't on.'

'Keep trying her, Susie. Thanks.' He flipped off the intercom.

'Liberty's such a busy young woman.' Kit spoke with her eyes on the rainbow the sun was making through the shade.

'She's stirred up a lot of old memories, reminded me of things I haven't thought of in years.' He picked up a hot-pink folder and brought it back, adding it to the pile on the table between them.

She studied his eyes. How much more open he seemed than Kitsia. Was it the blue eyes that created that illusion? As he lit up a black cigarette, she noticed that his hand was shaking.

'Lately you've begun to remind me of Kitsia.' He snapped his lighter shut.

'I have? How?' Kit moved to the edge of the couch. She was interested to hear his answer. Maybe she could tell him after all.

'Well, I guess you'll just have to wait and read Liberty's profile.'

'She's here, you know,' Kit went on.

'Kitsia? No, I didn't know. She's so secretive about her plans.'

'And about everything else as well.' Kit blushed and dropped her eyes. *This is the time to tell him.*

'There is a power in being secretive. A formidable power,' he went on.

'You use that power too.'

'Is that an accusation?' Archer fiddled with his lighter, pushing up the top repeatedly with his thumbnail. 'You mean because I haven't told you about what I think about *Last Chance*?'

Kit leaned back against the couch. Her head was flooded with voices.

'I have a lot to talk to you about, Kit. Certain things have come to my attention . . .' He hesitated. Susie had come noiselessly into the office. She handed Ransome an index card with a typed message on it. He read it and nodded. Susie left.

'I was pretty rough on you Monday. About the press, the negative coverage about *Last Chance*, and about you and Mr Marsh. I think Liberty's profile will help you . . . turn all this around.'

Kit looked over Archer's shoulder at the steel gate that closed off the screening-room staircase. 'Actually, I don't think Liberty's piece will have anything to do with *Last Chance*.'

'Oh, really?' He raised an eyebrow.

'I think Liberty will write about things that aren't in our best interests. Private things.'

'She's said she'll let me read the draft before she submits it, and I believe her.'

'I hope she does . . . for all our sakes.'

'There!' He snapped his fingers. 'You sounded just like Kitsia.'

'Sometimes I wish I were more like her, but I'm not. She lives in a world without rules or customs. She's completely unselfconscious. I'm all bound with rules. I care more about what people think of me... Well, look at me right now, waiting for your reaction to *Last Chance*. I care so much about what you think about the film... about me.'

He broke in, not listening to her. 'It's not that she's arrogant. It's just that her belief in her abilities and her perceptions is absolute. She has no room for regrets or doubts.'

'Do you have any regrets?' she asked him.

He shrugged. 'I have no regrets. Maybe I would have done some things a little differently. Perhaps I wish I had more time.'

The doors slid open. Two men in aqua-blue jumpsuits walked in looking like a surgical team.

Archer held up the index card. 'Your mother moves quickly. She has asked for this piece.'

The men began to walk the sculpture off the pedestal, rocking it back and forth. Archer watched them intently. Kit watched, barely breathing, bracing herself for them to drop it. But they wheeled it out without mishap.

When the men were gone, she looked around the office. Maybe she could tell him *now*, now that the statue, now that Kitsia, was out of the room.

Archer slipped off his Gucci loafer and they both watched as he emptied a thick stream of sand out of it. Kit stared down at the light brown granules on the white carpet. She began in her mind: *'Kitsia lied to you about the Arab boy. You were the father of that child.'*

'I was in the Bahamas this morning,' she heard him say. 'Quite early. The beach is beautiful.' He leaned forward and lit another cigarette. 'I'm sure you've heard the rumours about my closing down *Last Chance*?'

Kit pulled herself to attention. 'Yes?'

'Do you know why?'

'Because we're way over budget?'

'Yes, and because Ransome Enterprises needs the cash... because of this SEC thing.'

Kit said nothing. He had never discussed corporate business with her before.

'It's Rush's recommendation,' he began.

'Rush will do anything to hurt me,' she blurted out. 'First he

363

shoved his daughter down my throat, and now he wants to stop the movie altogether.' Kit was shouting, her face hot, her composure gone.

'Don't you read the newspapers, Kit? Haven't you been following the SEC inquiry that has turned into a Senate investigation of Ransome Enterprises? Of me?'

Kit ignored him. 'You know why he's doing this to me? He's been waiting for years. Rush has some photographs –'

He raised his voice over hers. 'Stop it, Kit!' He went on in a low voice. 'I know all about Rush.'

She stared at him.

'Do you understand? I know about Rush,' he repeated.

She nodded humbly.

'Listen to me, Kit, *Last Chance* can be finished.'

'Could have been, you mean. I can't pull it off now with that amazon daughter of his as Lacy.'

'I suggested Verena for the part, Kit.'

Her mouth fell open.

'I told Rush that I thought Verena would be perfect for Lacy. I suggested she audition for you and prove herself. He, I gather, was more insistent about your choosing her. But, Kit, you're wrong about Verena. She's very talented.'

'How is it you know so much? How is it you're so right and I'm so wrong?'

'I just am, Kit,' he said quietly. 'Give her a chance.'

'She's a child.'

'Then why don't *you* close down *Last Chance* if you feel that way?' He crushed his cigerette into the crystal ashtray. 'How did *Straight Flush* open?'

Kit grimaced. 'Not very well.'

'That's putting it mildly, isn't it?' Archer threw a piece of paper onto the table in front of them. 'I've seen the grosses, Kit.'

Kit reached for the sheet of figures, but before she could pick it up, Archer tossed another folder on top of it.

'Your overhead budget, Kit. It's way out of line.'

'But Rush okayed it Wednesday at the meeting.'

'No, he didn't. Here's his memo to me recommending you make a twenty-percent cut across the board. He may have done it for his own reasons, but he's right.' He threw the memo before her, then stood up and began to pace. 'Do you remember the deal we struck that day in your office at the studio?'

'Yes.' She closed her eyes and saw it coming.

'And what was it?'

She opened her eyes. He was standing over her.

'I promised to turn the company around in two and a half years or I would resign.'

'And have you turned the company around?'

Kit didn't answer. Two years ago she had thought she could do it. Now she realised that she hadn't been able to gauge the properties, to make the deals *and* work on the scripts *and* keep the budgets balanced *and* reorganise the overseas operation. There wasn't enough time to do it all. It wasn't until that moment that Kit realised just how good Bic Crawford really was at this business. She hadn't done it all by herself. Suddenly her whole body began to tremble.

Without looking up at him, she answered. 'No, I haven't.'

'That's right. You haven't lived up to your end of the deal.' Archer sat down on the couch next to her; his face was so close to hers it was a blur of brown and silver. 'I'm bringing in Randy Sheridan to take your place.'

She let out a cry.

'You're not a very good executive, Kit. You misjudged just how much of yourself had to go to the business end, the nuts and bolts of running a company. I misjudged just how much like Kitsia you really are. You're an artist, Kit, you have an artist's temperament. I need someone with a business temperament.'

'When will Randy take over?'

'Monday.'

'I see. And what about *Last Chance*? Sheridan doesn't believe in the project.'

'I know. You and I seem to be the only ones who do. I love *Last Chance*.'

Kit felt tears welling up.

'What you showed me on Monday was some of the most moving footage I've ever seen. It will be an important movie, and to ensure that, I'm making you producer of *Last Chance*.'

Kit looked up dully. 'What?'

'Producer. I'm making you producer of *Last Chance*.'

She shook her head, baffled. 'What about Scottie?'

'I spoke to him a little while ago. I explained how I thought it would be best for the project if he concentrated his energies on directing and gave up the producer's role to you.'

'He agreed?'

'Absolutely. You know, I still have a way with people.' He smiled at her briefly before he grew serious again. 'Kit, in the next few days Ransome Enterprises will be coming under attack. There are serious problems I don't want to go into, but all the subsidiaries are in trouble. There's a serious shortage of cash. So, here's what you must do. This evening, sit down and cost out the rest of the shoot and all the post-production costs. Everything: editing, scoring, looping – all of it. Don't leave out one single extra. When you have it all down, call Sy Adler and tell him how much you need ...'

'And ... ?'

'He'll deposit that amount into Barclay's Bank in London. They'll ensure completion.' Archer spoke urgently.

'Sy Adler's your personal lawyer. I don't understand.'

'Just call Sy. That way I can be sure to protect *Last Chance*. And I can be sure to protect you.'

Kit blinked the tears away. She wanted more than anything to put her arms around him and tell him everything. But she'd let the moment pass. He got up and walked to his desk.

Would he believe me if I told him?

He was already telling Susie to try Liberty Adams again. She didn't have much time.

'Archer!' Kit called out suddenly.

He looked up from his desk. 'Yes, Kit?'

It hurt to love Kitsia. It must have been awful to have been so young and so in love.

'Archer, are you in trouble too?'

'Yes, Kit, I am.'

25

By the time she got to the Ransome Building, Verena was drenched through to the skin. She scarcely noticed, having run all the way from her house in the rain.

'You mean you were already pregnant when you married Rush? You had to get married?'

'No, I didn't have to marry Rush! And he didn't make me pregnant. That's what I've been explaining. Archer made me pregnant. You're Archer's daughter, Verena.'

'I don't believe you.'

'It's true. Believe me, I know.'

'You're telling me that Rush isn't my real father?'

Verena exploded, coming at her, digging her fingernails into Mandy's soft upper arms. 'Why didn't you tell me? I thought I was hiding something. I can't hold a candle to you.' She let go of her roughly and spoke to herself then. 'Rush knows. Of course, he knows. That's why he did all that to me. He knows I'm not his.' She narrowed her eyes at her mother. 'He was getting back at you.'

'No, no, that can't be. Rush doesn't know.'

'What do you mean?'

'Do you think we'd still be married? Do you think I'd be alive if I told him?'

'I wish you had told him. I wish you were dead. I hate you!' Verena screamed and ran out of the back door.

She pushed against the revolving door of the Ransome Building, pausing long enough to drop her pumps and slip into them. Her feet were wet, making it a difficult fit. Just then the door hit her from behind and sent her lurching forward. The pump wedged beneath the door and the door jammed. She tried to get it loose, but she couldn't. She straightened up and banged on the window, calling to the doorman.

'My shoe's stuck!' She pointed to it. He nodded and bent to work the shoe loose.

Meanwhile, on the other side of the door some maniac was

banging on the window, shouting, 'Get me the bloody hell out of this madhouse!' The man's face was bright red. It looked as if he were about to explode all over the inside of the door. Verena bent over to help the doorman, but popped right up again as soon as it registered who the exploding maniac was.

She tapped shyly on the window and called out to him, 'Brendan? Hey, Brendan Marsh!'

'You're goddamn right it's Brendan Marsh!' he hollered. Even with the glass between them his voice rattled in her ears.

'It's me!' She jumped up and down and shouted. 'I'm your new Lacy. I'm Verena.'

His fists fell from the window and he peered at her. He took his glasses out of his shirt pocket and examined her.

Just then, the door came unstuck and Verena hopped into the lobby.

'Thanks,' she said to the doorman.

'Don't mention it, Miss Alexander.' He bowed and returned her shoe.

Brendan followed her back in with his glasses still on.

'What a face!' he declared. 'Even with the shiner. My God, what a face!'

He moved his glasses down to the end of his nose, and peering at her over their tops, began walking around her. She closed her eyes, crossed her fingers, and said, 'You don't think I'll make a lousy Lacy? I don't think I could stand it if you hated me too, along with everybody else in the world.'

She opened her eyes, and for a terrible instant she thought he'd gone off and left her there talking to herself.

'Look at me!' he bellowed.

She spun around, wide-eyed.

'What makes you think you can play this part?'

She balled her fists and spoke through gritted teeth. 'Because I'm an actress. And if you can't see that, then you're a blind old turd.' Tears stung her eyes and she swung around, heading for the lifts. But he reached out and pulled her back.

'Wait a minute. Get back here!'

'Look,' she said. 'If you're gonna yell at me, you can just forget about it. I'm tired of getting yelled at, and if you'll excuse me, I have some important business with my father.'

'Goddammit, child. I'm not going to yell at you!' Then he said, 'By Christ, if you aren't just perfect.'

'Perfect?' Verena echoed hopefully.

'Absolutely bloody perfect. Come on, I'm taking you to see Kit.'

'You are?'

He lunged ahead of her, pressing the penthouse button next to the lift door.

Riding up, he kept shaking his head. 'How does she do it? The woman's a witch. I tell you! A witch!'

Verena smiled uncertainly.

'By the way,' he said, barely hiding the grin. 'I meant to ask. Who coldcocked you?'

'Hunh?'

'The shiner. Sure is a beaut!'

'Oh, that.' She hesitated. 'My father. I mean Rush.'

Before he had a chance to react, the lift doors opened and Verena ran out, calling over her shoulder. 'Be with you in a couple of minutes. Important business with my dad.'

It gave her a funny feeling to call him that. Uncle AJ.

She ran down the hall, through the solarium, past the reception area, and down the hall to Susie's office, where Susie held up one hand like a traffic cop. 'No way, sweetheart. Your old man's in with him. And they are *very* busy.'

Verena was quick to act. She began to sway weakly towards Susie in a faint. Susie caught her and sat her on the couch. 'Sit down, baby. You're another one in bad shape. I'll get you some water. When you daddy comes out, you'll be sure to catch him.'

As soon as Susie was out of the room, Verena leaned over her desk and punched the button to open the doors. They slid open, she punched the close-lock button, and ran in just as the two halves came together again.

Rush and Archer were over by the windows. Rain washed off the bank of windows in sheets. It looked like the wall of a giant aquarium.

When they finally noticed her, Archer's voice was stern. 'What the hell are you doing here, Verena? I told Susie –'

'Don't blame Susie, Uncle AJ. I sneaked in. I have to talk –'

'You're out of line, young lady!' Rush barked. 'Does Mandy know you're here?'

'No, Mandy doesn't know I'm here. I have to talk to you. Not you!' she said to Rush. 'To you, Uncle AJ.' She went over to him and put her arm on his, making a horrible face at Rush. He patted her arm, but his eyes never left Rush. 'You can talk to me, baby, in a little while.'

'*Now*, Archer,' she insisted, stamping her foot.

Archer's eyes flickered off Rush. He saw her face. 'My God! What happened to you, Verena?'

'What happened to me?' She pointed to Rush. 'He beat me up. That's what happened to me.'   Archer grimaced. 'Go sit down, baby. I have some business with your father. You can stay until I'm finished.' He turned to Rush. 'Why couldn't you leave her out of this?'

'Because she's my faithful daughter, that's why. Because we have no secrets.'

'Shut up!' Verena screamed. 'Just shut the fuck up!' Her voice rang against the crystal vase on the table nearby. They both turned to stare at her.

'I have to talk to you,' she said to Archer in a small voice, 'before it's too late.'

'It's already too late,' Rush said.

'No, it's not.' Archer turned to him. 'All you have to do is hand over the original documents and you can walk out of here a free man.'

'I'm already a free man. I'm clean.'

'Look, Rush, I don't know what I did to make you turn against me, to make you hate me now.'

'Now? I've hated you for a long time.'

'Well, then, since you won't consider me, consider your wife and daughter. If you lose everything – and I guarantee I'll drag you down with me – they'll suffer. But we don't have to go down. Pierce has come over to my side, Rush. He's shown me the photocopies. Now all I need are the originals. The advantage is mine now.'

'Thanks to that little reporter. I knew Pierce was fucking her, but I didn't realise she was that good.'

'Leave Liberty Adams out of this, Rush. Jesus, man, considering the size staff you've used to set me up, why begrudge me a single earnest helper. Where are the documents? I want them. And I want them now.'

Rush blew into his hands and grinned. 'The boss wakes up, eh? Well, it's too late. You might as well roll over and go back to sleep. It's over. I bought you out. This morning. That Canadian consortium... it's mine. My dummy, old chap.'

Archer picked up an ivory letter opener and slapped his palm. 'I

370

know. But supposing I were to tell you that the shares your Canadian agent bought were forged shares. *Forged*. The money we discussed last night, you provided for me this morning. You bought bogus shares in the company you were trying to steal. It's my company, Rush, not yours. It always has been.' Pausing for effect, Ransome smiled and then continued. 'Because you made the deal off the Exchange, without using a broker – man on man, so to speak – you now have no place to turn. What do you say to that, *old chap*?'

Rush was rubbing his chin thoughtfully. 'I'd say, "well done". *If* it were true.'

Ransome sighted Rush along the letter opener as if it were a duelling pistol. 'You'd better believe it's true. I've been a busy man this week, trying to puzzle out your bizarre behaviour of late. Why, I've even been to the Bahamas.'

'Really?'

'Last night.' Archer began to walk around him. 'Early this morning, actually. I took them by surprise. Your man there – Ali Mamoud is it? . . . I always knew you could turn the emir's family against me if you tried – he's very good. But he wasn't prepared for me. All I needed was to look at the books, Rush. They confirmed what I had already been told.'

Rush's face had gone chalky.

'That's right. Alvarro's already made his report to me. You counted on his being slow. He usually is slow, but not this time. It was a wasted effort.'

'What was?'

'The lift. It was too damn obvious, for one thing. Where was your legendary subtlety on that day? And it was too late, for another.'

'Alvarro really filled you in, eh?'

'He drew diagrams for me, Rush. After I took a good look at them, I had to admit they were impressive. The part I liked best was how you'd managed to take all that Trips cash and hide it in your non-existent firm in Canada. To look at the books, it really did seem as if the casinos had been running red for years.'

Rush looked peculiar, as if he didn't know whether to laugh or cry. He pressed his fingers to both temples.

Archer went on circling him. 'What really amazes me is that you've been doing this for years. It wasn't just a spur-of-the-moment idea. It was more than a hobby. Why, Rush? Why? We were friends. You always knew I was a man who didn't make friends easily. Our friendship meant something. Didn't it mean anything to you? We'd made a goddamn pact.'

'You broke that pact a long time ago.' Rush was flexing his hands.

'Oh . . .' Archer stopped. 'That's right. You never did approve of my marriage to Cassie, did you? Deep down, you were one of the non-believers.'

'I was, but not for the reason you think.'

'I think you were jealous.'

'Sure I was jealous. I was jealous of every moment you spent with her.'

'And not with the business? Is that why you told me all those things the night she died? And to think I believed you and thanked you for forcing me to see the truth.'

'Who's holding a grudge now?' Rush grinned. 'You want to talk about truth, Arch? Remember the girl?'

'What girl?' Archer nearly shouted. He began to pace again.

'Easy, Arch, and I'll tell you. *The* girl, as far as I've always been concerned. You know . . . Tess. Remember that night I came back to the dorm and told you about her?'

Archer eyed him warily. 'The girl in Widener you couldn't shut your mouth about. What of her?'

'I always thought it was kind of spooky. All the S's. Tess, Cass.' Archer froze.

Rush went on. 'She was always Tess to me, even after the two of you got married and I had to watch you together, remembering when she was mine, Arch. Long before you ever had her, when she was my sweet Tess.'

Archer's face went ashen. He pointed the letter opener at Rush. 'You were one of the guys she slept with at Cambridge.' It was a statement, not a question.

'What do you mean, "one of the guys"?'

'Hell, Rush, do you think you were the only one? There were *dozens* of you. When I first met Cassie, she was a nymphomaniac. She was getting better with therapy, but basically she was a very . . . unstable girl.'

'You're lying. She told you about me. She must have. And you forgave her. You forgave me. I loved her –'

'I loved her too. But for Christ's sake, man, that doesn't mean I was blind. What you told me that night was probably true. She was ambiguous about her sexuality, to say the least.'

Rush backed away. 'I don't believe you. It's all lies.'

'You actually thought she'd confessed to me! She didn't confess to me about you, Rush, because she couldn't even *remember* you. Do you understand?'

His words seemed to fall on Rush like blows. He slumped against Archer's desk. 'It can't be...'

Verena looked at Archer, but he was staring at Rush, a weird sort of pity twisting his face. She didn't pity Rush. Pity was not the word.

'That's not all you don't know about, Rush,' she whispered hoarsely. Both men turned to her, startled. She felt giddy, as if she were onstage for the first time. She took a deep breath. She had to get the words right. Afraid they'd all come out in a jumble, she concentrated on the pattern on Archer's necktie.

'It started this afternoon when I told Mandy all about you and me, Rush.'

'You what?'

'I had to, Rush. I wanted to play Lacy. You never should have tempted me with that part. I'd do anything to keep it. Even risk Mandy's hatred.

'But she didn't hate me. Instead, she told me all about an afternoon a long time ago, when she gave Uncle AJ an invitation to her wedding. And he went to her room and they –'

'Oh, my Lord!' Archer pressed his hands to his head as if trying to keep it on his shoulders.

'I'm your daughter, Uncle AJ. I'm not his daughter.' She turned to Rush. 'And so all those things you made me do, Rush – all those bad things – don't seem so disgusting to me any more. They just don't seem to matter.'

'What did you do to her? Why, you son of a bitch!' Archer's voice was unrecognisable as he stormed over and grabbed Rush by the lapels. Spinning him around, he pinned Rush high against the window. Verena could see the glass flex.

'You poor sick son of a bitch.' He spoke between his teeth. His face was mottled, his eyes rimmed with tears. 'We were brothers. What was it Liberty called us the other day? Castor and Pollux? She didn't know how right she was.'

Convinced the window would give way at any minute, Verena cried out and ran over to warn them. They ignored her.

'It isn't enough that you've deluded yourself about Cassie all these years.' He let Rush slide slowly towards the floor. 'But to take out your perverted delusions on this sweet, innocent . . .' He turned to Verena and, still holding Rush with one hand, smoothed her hair back away from her black eye with the other. Turning to Rush, he said, 'I think at this moment I could kill you.'

'You stupid bastard.' Rush cut through Archer's grip and edged away. His shirt was out of his trousers. They began to circle each other like two wild animals sharing a small cage. Suddenly Rush seemed to be enjoying himself.

'You really have no idea, do you?'

'No idea about what?'

'That I'm working with the emir, with Akmed.'

Archer stopped and said, 'What are you talking about? I told you Alvarro told me everything.'

He continued moving.

'Not everything. Tony didn't tell you – because he couldn't possibly know – that you're not only gaining another daughter, you're about to lose her, too.'

Archer stopped again. 'What the hell do you mean? Another daughter?'

'I mean Kit, you stupid bastard. *Cousin Kit*.'

'This is your idea of a sick joke, isn't it?'

'You have to admire Kitsia's brilliant charade all these years, passing Kit off as a half-Arab bastard. No wonder she was so good at playing those native girls in the movies. She thought she was one of them. But Kitsia was no fool; she saved her daughter's life . . . for a while. But Kit got herself in trouble, letting Bic Crawford take her picture –'

'What the hell are you talking about?'

'You keep asking the same question, Arch. Boring, as little Liberty would say. You didn't wound that Arab boy as your dear daddy led you to believe. You killed him! Not in cold blood, perhaps, but in a moment of passion. What your father didn't know, but what Kitsia did, was that the emir planned to take his revenge on your children. She's doomed.' He pointed to Verena. 'Kit's doomed. Akmed knows about Kit. Soon he'll know about . . .' Rush faltered.

'I never imagined –'

'Of course you never imagined! How could you? Unless the old woman told you herself. But she never told anyone. Except maybe Cassie.' He grabbed Archer's shoulders and began to shake him furiously. 'Cassie would be alive today if it weren't for you!'

Archer pushed him away and, pulling back his arm, punched Rush again and again. Rush's face was covered with blood. He wiped his mouth on his sleeve, grinning.

'Reduced to brute force, eh, Arch? Okay.' And he rolled up his sleeves.

'Stop!' Verena screamed. 'Don't do this!'

'You should have thought about that before you opened your sweet mouth.'

It was too horrible: they were massacring each other. Frightened, Verena moved out of their way. Both men were staggering, drenched in sweat, and smeared with blood. They backed against the railing.

'You'd better hope your daddy wins, little girl,' Rush gasped at her, 'or you're dead.'

She raced to the door. 'Help, somebody! They're fighting in here. Open the door!'

Behind her, furniture crashed, crystal shattered. She heard someone slip and a skull thud against the rug. She was afraid to turn around.

'Where's the fucking button?' she screamed. 'Open the fucking door!' She heard more glass breaking. 'They're killing each other!' she screamed, beating her fists against the door.

Suddenly she heard a terrible sound of metal ripping. She turned just as the two of them went crashing through the iron railing.

She ran to the edge of the stairwell and took two turns down the spiral into the blackness. She thought she heard a groan, when the telephone began to ring. She backed up the stairs.

26

'Sasha!' Kit called out as she walked down the hall.

Sasha jumped up and stood by her desk. She was running a twisted paper clip under her fingernails.

Kit stood in the doorway. 'Sasha! You know, don't you?'

Sasha shook her head.

'You *do* know. Does everyone know?'

'Oh, no, Kit. Just ... I wasn't even sure. Susie just thought that he was going to ...'

'Fire me?'

'I'm sorry. It's just that there aren't very many secrets around here.'

'Well ...'

'I mean, you hear so many things. You never know if they're true.'

'This one's true, take it from me.' Kit walked towards her door.

'Don't go in there, Miss Ransome.'

Kit stopped. 'Why?'

'He's in there, Miss Ransome.'

'He?'

'Mr Marsh.'

Kit leaned on the door and pushed it open.

'I tried to keep him out ...'

'It's all right, Sasha.'

Brendan was sitting at her desk, watching the electrical storm. He spoke without turning. 'You witch. You knew all along. You knew that girl would be the perfect Lacy.'

He spun around and nailed her with a look.

'No, I didn't.'

'Yes, you did.' He grinned. 'Come on, admit it.'

'Brendan, everything I told you before was true. All of it. I was blackmailed.'

Brendan regarded her thoughtfully, patting down his moustache. 'You wouldn't let yourself be blackmailed. You're stronger than that.'

Kit walked over to the armoire and took out a bottle of Scotch and a squat glass. She poured herself a small drink, took a sip, and looked about for some soda. There wasn't any. She sat down on the couch and balanced the Scotch on her lap.

'Brendan! I'm not strong. You think that just because I'm not one of your "wenches". I'm this *bulwark*. I can't always be that to you.'

'I know that.'

'Do you really? I wonder.' She stared at him until he swivelled back around to face the window, as if the storm were more important than anything else that was happening. She wanted to scream at him. The best thing, she told herself, was just to be honest. If she couldn't be honest with him, she couldn't stay with him.

'I'm pretty tired, Kit,' Brendan said. 'I feel old today. When you ran out on me a little while ago, I just stood here at your desk. God, but I felt tired. I thought maybe I was going to have a heart attack. I couldn't breathe. I was sure you'd come right back and we'd talk everything out. But you didn't. Do you know how it feels to be old? To be alone?'

'Brendan, please.'

'It's funny how things become clear all at once. It's almost like you didn't know things were out of focus. Then, bam!' He punched his open palm and swivelled around to face her. 'You see it. Bingo! I think maybe it's too late for us. We've hurt each other. And it doesn't matter that we didn't really mean to do it.'

'Maybe it *is* too late.' She heard her voice quaver.

'I really thought we were going to make it. We were living at Clara. We ate dinner together. We used the same bathroom. But it wasn't until now that I realised I was on trial.'

'I understand now –' she began.

'Now! She says *now*. But then? Don't you know how fucking hard it was for me to resist Kitsia? What's the use? You hate talk like this. You hate people who aren't as perfect as you. You know why you're so goddamned perfect? 'Cause you've got no feelings. You drown them in water. You work them to death. And every time you might just be ready to give in, something comes along, some bell in your head goes off.'

'Brendan, don't let's start up again. I'm desperately sorry.'

'The hell you are! If it hadn't been her, it would have been someone or something else. You just could never settle down about us. Never admit that we were a couple!'

'Please, Brendan. Not now. There are things –'

'You still don't get it, do you? Do you really think I care that Bic Crawford made you do things? Sick, twisted things? Do you think it makes me love you any less? For Christ's sake, Kit, did you think I didn't know?'

Kit's eyes widened.

'Not everything. Not the particulars ... the photographs. But there was gossip. Everyone in Hollywood gossips. There was gossip about you and Bic – ugly gossip before I even met you!'

Kit felt cold. She wanted to crawl into a deep snowdrift and go to sleep. She didn't want to hear any more. His voice was so loud. His words were stacked against her ears like sandbags.

'You thought it was a secret. A fucking secret! Why did you keep it from me? Why didn't you tell me about this? Why didn't you trust me? Why?'

Tears rolled down Kit's cheekbones.

'I don't know. All my life I've let this need for ... acceptance rule me. I think that's what it is. Kitsia sacrificed respectability. She didn't care what anyone thought of her. I do care. Too much. But I was afraid to tell you. I was ashamed. I do keep things secret. It's childish.'

Brendan walked over and knelt before her. 'Kit, I love you. Totally and completely. You have to believe me.'

She looked into his dear, bloodshot eyes and began to cry again. 'I want to – more than anything.'

Brendan took the Scotch out of her hands. He reached into his pocket and handed her his blue bandanna.

She wiped the tears from her eyes. 'Archer just fired me.'

'He what?'

'Fired me ... a few minutes ago.'

'What did he say?'

'He said I wasn't a very good executive.'

'No, Kit, I mean, what did he say about *Last Chance*?'

'*Last Chance* will be finished. He's making me producer. He's posting a completion bond. I'll need your help tonight. We need to pull together some numbers for *Last Chance*.'

'Oh, Sweet Jesus! You did it. You did it!' He grabbed her hands and kissed her forehead. 'I can see the headlines now: 'KITTY KAT LANDS ON FEET'! You all right about being fired?'

'Yes.' Kit closed her eyes and nodded her head, knowing for the first time that she really was okay about it. 'You think I'm crazy to be fine? I'm almost glad.'

'You're not crazy. You're just sensible. You know what you really want now. I remember when it happened to me, when I realised what I wanted.'

Kit opened her eyes.

'I know,' he went on, 'you'd like me to say it was when I met you. But I already knew who I was then, what I wanted. I just didn't know who. It was one day after I'd been on a bender, a horrible drunk. My daughter, Lily, came into my bedroom. She was all dressed up. She was wearing high heels and pink lipstick. I almost yelled at her for wearing high heels. I was going to tell her she wasn't old enough. But of course she was. She stood in the doorway and said, "Daddy, I'm leaving now. I can't find any reason to love you any more." It took me a few weeks after that, but she got me started. To think there was no *one* thing about me she could find to love.'

'*I* love you.' He kissed her, but she pulled away. She had to open her eyes to make sure it was Brendan and not a dream. 'How do you know Verena will be any good?'

'I just got off the horn with Rugoff. He's very high on her.'

'He is?'

'She'll need coaching, of course.' Brendan pulled the ivory picks out of Kit's hair. 'Don't worry. Scott and I can handle her. We'll get Rugoff to come out and coach. It'll be fine. You look so much softer with your hair down. Now that you're not one of the Blue Suits, do you think you could do me a favour and wear it down?'

'Can we get out of here?' She stood up and looked around.

'We sure as hell can!'

Kit walked over to her desk and took out two folders from the middle drawer, one marked '*Last Chance*' and the other 'Ideas – if I ever get the time'. 'I'm ready. I just have to stop by Archer's office for a minute. There's something I have to tell him.'

Brendan came up behind her. 'Let me make love to you. Now. Here. I want you.'

'I can't. I'm too nervous.'

Brendan's mouth came over hers. She couldn't breathe. She pushed him away. 'Come with me. I need you. There's so much I need to tell you.'

They walked down the corridor towards Archer's suite. The halls were unnaturally quiet. The reception area was untended.

379

The door to Susie's office stood ajar. They walked in.

'Susie, can I get back in to see Archer? Just for a minute or two?'

Susie stared at Kit.

'Susie?' Kit said.

Just then Sasha burst into the office. 'There isn't another key,' she said, panting for air. 'I looked everywhere. He must have it with him!' she cried.

'What about the sliding panel that leads from Rush's office?'

'Connie's at the dentist. I don't know how to trigger it.'

'Shit!' Susie said. 'You didn't tell anyone, did you?'

Sasha shook her head.

'Susie, what's the matter?'

'Kit, please,' Susie turned to her for the first time. 'You've got to help. I can't open the door.'

Brendan walked over to the door. 'Is it stuck?' He heaved a shoulder against it.

'No, it isn't stuck. It's locked from the inside.' Susie was fighting panic.

Brendan walked back over to Susie. 'Just be calm. Tell me what's going on. Why haven't you phoned Security?'

Susie clamped her hand over her mouth.

'We're afraid,' Sasha whispered.

'Susie, who's in there?' Kit asked, pushing aside the papers on Susie's desk. They fell off the desk and everyone jumped.

'It's Rush. Rush is in there. They must have pressed the intercom by mistake. I heard them fighting. But it snapped off, and now –'

An enormous clap of thunder clobbered the penthouse, drowning out Susie's words.

'Why, Susie? Why are they fighting?'

'Mr Ransome knows!'

'Knows what?' Kit coaxed her patiently.

'Mr Ransome knows that Rush has tried to ruin him. He found out everything in the Bahamas. He's been busy all week planning his move against Rush.'

'Oh, my God, Brendan!' Kit gasped and pulled him by his jacket.

'What about Verena?' Sasha tugged at Susie's arm.

'Verena?' Brendan repeated. 'Is she in there with them?'

'Yes. She sneaked in when I left her here alone. She must have pressed "lock in". And now it can only be opened from the inside.'

'Brendan' – Kit tugged his arm – 'We've got to do something.'

Brendan reached over and picked up the phone. He started dialling. 'I'm calling the police.'

'Oh, Mr Marsh. I don't think we should do that. Mr Ransome wouldn't like it,' Susie said. No one responded.

Kit walked over to the door and pressed her ear against it. 'I don't hear anything. Oh, please, God, don't let anything happen...'

Then they heard it: a constant but muffled pounding on the other side of the door. Someone was screaming.

'It's Verena. Susie!' Kit shouted. 'Quick! Call her on the intercom. Tell her how to open the door. Hurry. I hope it's not too late.'

Susie picked up the phone. They saw the light from the extension into Archer's office blink on and off, on and off.

'It's ringing,' Susie whispered, biting her lip. The little white light blinked four times. Five times. Six times. The light stopped blinking.

'Under his desk, Verena.' Susie spoke calmly. Her fingers wound the cord of the phone tightly around her wrist. 'There's a button under his desk. To the right. Do you feel it? Push it. Come on, honey. That's it!'

The door slid open noiselessly. Kit and Brendan were the first in. They found Verena sitting at Archer's desk, looking small and lost.

Kit went to her and guided her out of the chair and onto a sofa. Verena began to cry hysterically.

Rush and Archer were nowhere to be seen.

'Verena. Don't cry. It's okay. What happened? Can you tell me what's happened?' Kit cradled her in her arms. 'There, there. Everything is okay now.'

'Oh, help me! Stop them! It's all my fault. Oh, God, I'm so sorry. I'm sorry!' Verena wailed.

'Brendan, over there.' Kit pointed to the broken railing around the staircase. 'They must be down there.'

Pulling the jagged railing aside, Brendan disappeared down the stairs to the screening room.

'I tried to stop them.' Verena's eyes were swollen with tears. 'They wouldn't listen to me. They just kept hitting each other. I really tried. But it happened so fast.' She was thrashing about so that Kit had to hold her tight to keep her from getting up.

'Kit... quick! Call an ambulance!' Brendan shouted up from the screening room.

'Let me go. Let me go! I've got to see my father!' Verena's face was red and splotchy. She sucked at her fingertips. There was blood on her lips. *'Mandy!'* Verena's cry pierced the room.

'Don't just stand there!' Kit shouted at the two women standing lamely in the middle of the room. 'Susie, go call an ambulance. Then call the medical department and get someone up here. Go on. *Now!'*

Susie ran to the phone on Archer's desk.

'Don't keep standing there, Sasha, get her a blanket. Can't you see she's in shock,' Kit shouted. 'And then call her mother. *Do* something!'

Brendan came up the stairs slowly. He kept looking behind him. He stopped at the top. 'Kit,' he called out hoarsely, 'Where's that ambulance? There isn't much time.'

Kit looked helplessly at Susie. 'Did you hear him?'

Verena lurched forward, breaking Kit's grasp. 'I want to see. Let me see. He's got to be all right. He's got to be ...' She scrambled over to the staircase. She couldn't keep her balance. She kept falling forward, and she had to crawl the last few steps.

'No!' Kit's scream was shrill.

Verena froze. She stared down the steps. Brendan blocked her view.

The police came in, followed by the medics. The five that wore blue uniforms rushed about the room forming a narrow corridor between the door and the staircase. They kept their hands on their hips. The other three men wore suits, grey, dark blue, muddying up the white office.

Kit walked over to the stairs and pulled Verena gently away, leading her back towards the couch. 'Come with me, honey. You don't want to look down there.' It was she herself who did not want to look.

'Please, ladies. Just sit down,' one of the detectives said. Everyone was sitting now except Brendan.

Two men with a stretcher came into the room. They stopped and conferred with one of the detectives, the one with the hat. Kit wanted to scream at them for going so slowly, but she had no voice. It was like watching a movie, a movie projected in slow motion, but with the sound loud, speeded up.

The uniformed men began to stretch wide yellow tape from sofa to chair to desk to sofa. Kit and Verena were being taped in, trapped on the couch. One of the detectives took out a tiny black brush from a case and dipped it into a jar. He began to powder everything and dust it gingerly.

The paramedics disappeared down the stairs, knocking the ends of the stretcher against the broken railing. It echoed about the room. Kit felt a wave of nausea. She swallowed hard. She gagged. Verena stopped struggling and stared at Susie, who was bending over her wordlessly, holding out a glass of water.

Brendan came up out of the hole. He turned to help guide the stretcher. 'To the left. Left!' A blue uniform came up behind him, took him by the elbow, and steered him away.

'I can't get a pulse. Wait. I'm not getting a reading.' The paramedic's voice was calm. Kit thought he might have been ordering dinner.

'Give me some Adrenalin,' the other one advised, equally cooly.

A few moments later they were pushing the stretcher up the rest of the stairs, trying to balance the upturned bottle that was dripping medicine into the wounded man's arm.

'Who is it?' Kit called out, but they pretended not to hear. Four of the blue uniforms melted towards the stretcher, like ink spilling, and took up the corners and heaved the bed high over the couches, over the tape, over the heads of Kit and Verena.

'Let me see him!' Verena cried. 'Please.' One of the detectives came over to her. He stared at her; he didn't say a word. She fell silent.

A flashbulb went off behind Brendan. He whirled around, but before he could speak, a small man in a dark grey suit said, 'I have to.' Then, as if that gave him permission, he started clicking his camera furiously. Flashbulbs sparked and popped.

Two new men came in. They were dressed in khaki. One carried a large black plastic blanket over one arm. 'Where is it?'

The detective with the hat pointed downstairs. 'Wait, I need a picture.' He motioned for the small grey-suited man to go down first.

Kit tried to get Brendan's attention. He seemed mesmerised by the two men in khaki. Finally he looked over at her.

'What happened?' she whispered. 'Which one . . . ?'

The khaki men came up the stairs. The black blanket was a body bag. One of the khaki men lost his footing and the body bumped against the broken railing. The bag caught on one of the jagged spikes and the detective with the hat had to loosen it.

'Brendan? Brendan?' Kit called out.

'I'm Detective Tooey. I have to ask you folks some questions.'
The man took off his hat and put it on top of the glass table.

Brendan spoke first, telling Tooey how he had found them –
Rush and Archer, at the bottom of the steps. Rush was on top of
Archer.

'When I lifted his arm to check his pulse, I saw the letter opener
sticking out of his ribs.'

'Out of whose ribs?' Kit screamed. She had hold of Verena's
hand. It was clammy. 'Won't somebody please *tell* me!'

'Rush, darling. Rush is dead.'

*Ether fills the big white room. The insides of her nostrils are numb. Her
hands are blue. There is blood on her blouse and she wonders whose it is.*

*Verena is calm now. Her mother has come and given her three tablets
of Valium of ten milligrams each from a small mother-of-pearl pillbox.
Strange, how her eye still misses nothing, how it records even the most
trivial of events, like a movie camera. She will re-run it later; perhaps
even edit it.*

*'At least the right man died.' She repeats it like a mantra as she
rocks back and forth on the love seat, her eye returning to the broken
railing like a tongue to a jagged tooth.*

*They have rushed Archer to the hospital. It's too soon to know
whether he'll live. Mandy Alexander waits for the Valium to take
effect on her daughter so that she can leave and go to the hospital to be
with him.*

*'He'll need to see a friendly face when he comes to,' she keeps saying.
If he comes to hangs unsaid in the air between them.*

*Verena has retreated to the corner of the couch, clutching a pillow.
Her face is swollen almost beyond recognition. There is a nasty gash
below her eye. Kit wonders how she got it. Had she tried to come
between the two men?*

*Brendan is still in Susie's office, where Chief Inspector Tooey and
another officer are questioning him. It will be her turn next. She is
grateful it will be in Susie's office, where she'll be able to focus on the
picture of the seashell. She doesn't know how much longer she'll be able
to hold herself together.*

The doors slide open. She expects Brendan to walk out and come to

384

her, but Brendan is nowhere to be seen. What have they done to him? Could they think he killed Rush?

The young officer reads her mind. *'Don't worry, Miss Ransome, Mr Marsh went down to the lobby to talk to your mother and some reporter.'*

'Some reporter!' Kit finds herself furious. *'They're two of a kind, Brendan and my mother, exhibitionistic to the last.'*

'I'm sorry, ma'am,' the officer says, as if it were his fault. A young policewoman comes in to sit with Verena while Mandy gets up gingerly like a mother leaving the side of a sleeping baby. She has the officer hold Verena's hand just as she's been doing.

'You'll stay with her until after the questioning?' she asks, and Kit nods, amazed at how young and vital the other woman looks. She sits on the brown velour couch and Tooey sits on Susie's desk talking to her in a quiet voice laced with street slang and police argot.

'What is your relationship to the deceased?'

Kit squints. Are the lights brighter in here? Surely Susie never had the lights this bright.

He repeats the question.

'I had none,' she says dully; then, thinking of the photographs, she feels a surge of guilt. *'He was the chief operating officer for the company that owned my company, Horizon Pictures.'*

'That's right,' he says, *'you're the lady prez – for how long now?'*

'Two years.' It seems pointless to tell him her time is up.

'And didn't you use to be in the movies instead of making them?'

Kit nods.

'I saw you the other night. I get insomnia Sunday nights. I usually turn on the late show. You were on all last week. I sure enjoyed those flicks.'

Kit smiles politely.

'Maybe later you could give me your autograph? It's not so much for me, but the wife, she collects them.'

'Certainly.'

'Miss Ransome, do you know any reason why these two gentlemen might have gone after each other in there?'

'I really have no idea.'

I know all about Rush, *Archer had told her when she began to explain about the blackmailing. She has an abrupt conviction that they were fighting over the photographs, over her, when it happened.*

When he asks her for the fourth time, she begins: *'There are these photographs...'* The officers listen without interrupting her. They might be production executives being told the plot of a new movie. She tells the story with her usual skill and thoroughness and ends up with,

'He knew Rush Alexander was blackmailing me. He was trying to help me. I'm Archer Ransome's daughter.'

The one officer looks at the other as if they've just been told an ending too outrageous to buy.

'That's what the other young lady said when Officer Ballard pulled her out of the stairwell. She said Ransome was her old man.'

'That's not true!' she cries out, and then wonders why she's protesting so vehemently.

'That's funny, her own mother says it's true. You'd think the lady would know.'

They dismiss her after telling her not to leave town. She gets up mechanically and leaves Susie's office to wait in the solarium for Verena, who says she's Ransome's daughter too.

'Why not?' she says aloud to the skylight, feeling suddenly giddy. Above her, the night sky is reddish pink, like the sky over a burning city, she thinks, like Atlanta in Gone with the Wind.

The lift doors open and Brendan steps out. The two policemen on guard bar his way, and then, realising who he is, let him pass. He lumbers towards Kit and catches her up in his arms.

She has been going to reprimand him for talking to reporters, but her anger is drowned in tears. When at last they subside, she pulls away, suddenly horrified at what she's done. 'I told them all about the photographs!'

'You what!' he shouts. Then, easing up a little: 'Hell, why not? They probably would have found out for themselves sooner or later. I suppose old Tooey and his buddy in there can be persuaded to keep it out of the papers. It's not as if it has much bearing on the case.'

Kit stares at him. Now that it's over, he seems maddeningly self-contained, jovial even. 'What do you mean?'

'You actually think they were fighting over you? Oh, my poor paranoid darling.' He draws her to him again, but she shoves him away.

'I'm Archer's daughter!'

'I know that, my darling.'

'You know! How do you know?'

'Your mother told me, bless her heart. Downstairs. You know, Kit, she looks terrible. I told her and Liberty to go to the hospital and wait. The lobby's mobbed with reporters, and –'

'You told Liberty Adams to go to the hospital with Mother? Why not invite the entire press corps while you're at it?'

'Easy, darling, easy. It's not as simple as that.'

'Really? Well, it seems very simple to me.'

Kit collapses into a gloomy silence. A half-hour later, Verena comes out of Susie's office looking calm and refreshed.

'Hi, guys,' she says. 'Well, I sure spilled my guts.'

'Good girl,' Brendan says to her. 'Now, ladies, shall we go to the hospital and see how your father's doing?'

At the hospital, they find the two women sitting outside the intensive-care unit. Someone has brought a chair for Kitsia, but Liberty sits on the floor at her feet, her head resting on upraised knees.

'I hope you have your tape recorder on for all this,' Kit cannot resist saying.

Liberty looks up. Her face is drawn and tear-streaked. Kit instantly regrets her remark.

Kitsia shakes her head wearily. 'Oh, Kit, for Christ's sake, stop being so bitchy and say hello to your sister.'

EPILOGUE

'EXPECTANT MOM/WRITER TRAVELS HALFWAY AROUND WORLD TO STAND AT GATES OF HELL.'

Liberty tried out the sound of the headline under her breath as she took another step back from the heat. The fire from the furnace coloured the faces of the other two women bright crimson as they stood over the trough, mesmerised by the molten bronze glowing brighter as it grew hotter. Soon it would be ready to pour. Liberty didn't know how much longer she'd be able to hold out.

Sweat trickled down her spine and between her breasts. She fanned herself with the copy of yesterday's *International Herald Tribune* Vernière-Plank had brought on board when the Ransome Enterprise DC-8 picked him up in Zurich yesterday. She pulled the light cotton shirt away from her damp skin and fanned her belly where the baby kicked against the right side of her stomach.

'A wacko pilgrimage,' Eben had called it. Maybe he was right. Although he hadn't been able to come himself (election-year insanity had struck Washington), Eben had insisted a doctor accompany her. Brendan was wrapping up location shooting in the Amazon basin. Archer was still recuperating, and Mandy would not leave him. That left only the three of them – Liberty, Kit, and Verena – to fly to Zwar and carry out the bizarre instructions of Kitsia's last will and testament.

Vernière-Plank, in a rumpled white linen suit, stood talking to the old Zwarian who ran the furnace. Liberty waved the newspaper and caught his eye, signalling for another glass of water. He went instantly. When he opened the door, she felt a cool breeze waft in from off the desert. How hot must it be in here if the desert felt cool by comparison?

She took the sweating glass from Vernière-Plank and said, 'No ice?'

'You Americans and your ice. One doesn't want too much cold in the desert.'

'Wrong!' Liberty corrected him sweetly, sipping. 'I think I'll go stand outside on the veranda and listen to the monkeys sing.'

'But the bronze is almost ready to pour,' Vernière-Plank reminded her in an urgent whisper.

'Why are we all whispering?' Liberty raised her voice. Then her eye caught the black leather bag holding the ashes and she remembered why. She ignored Vernière-Plank and ducked outside. It *was* cooler out here! The desert sun made her eyeballs ache clear to the back of her skull. She pulled on her sombrero and slid down the wall, folding herself into her own shade, peon-style.

It was so strange, being with her sisters again. Kit and Verena were used to being together. They'd worked on *Last Chnace*, which would be opening in a month and a half – when her baby was due. They were about to start a second project Kit was producing. But Liberty had been off on her own, writing. Seeing them again brought it all back – that evening a year ago in the hospital when Mandy had come out of the intensive-care unit and told her her father was asking to see her.

The way Kit and Verena – and even Kitsia – had looked at her then, she had wanted to say they had nothing to be envious of: she didn't *want* to see him now. What would she do when she saw that vital man lying there, tubes sticking out of him every which way?

'Two minutes,' the nurse prodded; she had wanted to scream. He was in a cubicle on a high bed on wheels, wearing hospital pyjamas. How had they got him out of his suit if his neck was broken? she wondered inanely. His eyes were closed. She stood at the foot of his bed staring at him, crying silently. Tears splashed on her hands and onto the green tiled floor. Was he already dead?

He lifted three fingers and she came closer, coming up the side of the bed and finally taking his hand. He brought her hand slowly up to his face, gazing at her tears as if they were something rare and precious.

'Hi!' She managed to speak.

'You know, Mandy called me this afternoon, before Rush came in ... to tell me you were Cassie's and mine.' His voice sounded surprisingly hearty. As he looked in her eyes for the first time, she saw that his eyes glittered like bright blue wheels. They'd given him morphine. He must be flying, she thought, praying he felt no pain.

He went on. 'The first time I saw you – was it only early this week? – I thought you were this exquisite doll ... and yet so smart.

Cassie would have been so proud of you!'

Liberty was just dozing off when she heard someone clear her throat.

'Are you all right, my dear?' a voice asked.

Liberty pushed the sombrero back and looked up. A figure stood silhouetted by the sun.

'What must you think of all this?' the voice asked.

Liberty shaded her eyes to make out the face. Certainly the voice seemed familiar.

'If she were alive, I'd give her a piece of my mind,' Liberty said, pulling her sombrero back down over her eyes.

'I think she knew that, somehow. She didn't want you to come, you know. She said if you came, you were a fool. And I said that *she* was the one who was the fool – the dying are always God's fools.'

Liberty struggled awkwardly to her feet; the woman finally had to give her a hand.

'Posy Crowther, I thought you'd never show up!' Liberty embraced the short stout woman in the indigo-striped djellaba.

She had run a six-month search for Posy Crowther. Both her Louisberg Square town house and the house in Provincetown had been vacant, boarded up for three decades and the taxes kept up by a family lawyer who had no idea as to her whereabouts. She'd combed the indexes of scholarly periodicals and found several articles written by 'Posy Crowther' over the past twenty years. But the articles had been submitted by mail without return address. Reading those articles, she had become acquainted with her mother as a case study in nature versus nurture. Only when she began to find articles with such titles as 'Early Childhood Education for Neglected or Orphaned Youth' did she begin to suspect the truth.

Over sixteen years had passed since Liberty had last seen her dressed in the grey-and-white habit of the Order of the Sisters of St Mary's on the River. In the loose-fitting robe, she merely looked as if she'd switched orders: from St Mary's on the River to Our Lady of the Sands of Zwar.

'Sister Bertrand!' Liberty grinned.

The other woman nodded, wiping tears from her eyes.

'So you've been here with Kitsia this past year!'

Posy nodded. 'On and off.'

'I went to St Mary's looking for you last spring ... after I'd figured it out. Mother Superior said you'd left.'

'To care for a sick friend. You see, Kitsia came up to see me last year ... after Archer's terrible accident. She'd wanted solitude for the last forty years – now she couldn't bear to be alone. She begged me to come back with her. You see, she knew she was dying.'

'If she knew, why didn't she tell us? Any one of us would have dropped what we were doing and run to her.'

'Kitsia never was one for letting other people's troubles interfere with her work. I'm sure she meant you girls to go on with your work and not mind her ... until she was gone.'

Vernière-Plank stepped out of the foundry and signalled Liberty.

She nodded to him and said to Posy, 'Showtime! Might as well get this over with before I go into early labour.'

'She'd understand, you know, if you didn't want to participate.'

'Come halfway around the world and punk out? I'll scatter my share of the ashes, don't you worry. Will you come in? I'm sure the others won't mind.'

'No, child. We've already said our good-byes, Kitsia and I. It's a beautiful statue, you know, the one you're casting right now. Her finest work! A Madonna and Child.'

Liberty went in. The other two women had just finished taking their turns emptying Kitsia's ashes into the conduit carrying the bronze from the kiln to the cast for the statue. Vernière-Plank held out the sack to her.

Liberty slipped on her asbestos glove and took the sack. Gazing into it, she saw the ashes – as fine and white as the sands of Zwar. She stood over the conduit, staring at the enormous cast of the Madonna and Child.

'This is your finest work – or so they say. But you know and I know that it's no Madonna and Child. It's the last of the Cassandra Series. Cassie Ransome holding the child she never knew. Well, Cassie' – she patted the baby in her belly – *'this one's for you, too.'*

She poured the ashes into the trough and they rose like dust, driven upward by the heat from the bronze, and dissolved in the glittering air above her head. Turning away, she bid a final farewell to her fairy godmother, who was merged with her beloved at last.

Forty-five minutes before the première of *Last Chance*, Verena was taking the main staircase two steps at a time with a peanut-butter-and-jelly sandwich in one hand and a glass of cold Quik in the other, when the telephone rang. She froze, calculating whether she'd have the time to make it up two and a half more flights to the top of the house and answer the extension by her bed, or whether she should stop being such a chicken and go answer the phone in the library. The sandwich and Quik decided it. She turned around and went back down, taking her time as she walked down the hall and pushed open the mahogany doors with her foot.

The phone sounded unnaturally loud in the dark, rugless room. She groped over boxes of books, trying not to spill chocolate milk in Rush's legacy to the Harvard Library. Verena came up short. The small Spanish desk where the phone once had sat was gone. She spied a wire, following it with her eyes through the maze of boxes. The desk must have gone up to Millbrook, along with all Mandy's best pieces. The three old wing chairs hadn't been so favoured. They sat among the cartons like old hounds who'd survived their master.

Verena finally came to the phone and took it with her to her old wing chair. She picked it up breathlessly. 'Hi!' She found herself facing a cold empty fireplace.

'Hi! I was beginning to worry. I thought I'd check up on my star.'

'Oh, hi, Kit. You don't have to check up on me, you know. Liberty's called twice this afternoon. I'll tell you what I told her. I'm fine. Just fine.'

'Fine like Brendan? Do you know he put his glasses on upside down to read his funnies this morning? And, naturally, he's refused to read anything about *Last Chance*. It's understandable if you're spooked. By the way, did you get Brendan to button you up before he left?'

Verena groped down the back of her gold gown. 'Shit! I forgot. I was so busy listening to him tell me opening nights were a cinch –'

'Are you eating something, Verena, or is your diction deteriorating?'

'I'm eating, of course,' Verena answered with her mouth full. 'You know I always pig out when I'm nervous. Two reporters have already called.'

'And?'

'I didn't embarrass you, don't worry. I put on my Hungarian accent and told them, "I don't know nothink about no Miss

Verena. I'm doink the cleanink, dat's all".' She looked for somewhere to wipe the peanut butter off her fingers.

'Good girl.'

'Good with the accents, lousy with the memory. I guess I'll just have to wear something else tonight.' She thought of wiping her fingers on her dress, but stuck her fingers in her mouth at the last moment.

'Like what?'

'Like maybe parachute pants and my black BVD V-neck? Devin Lowe says I give new dimension to the old uniform.'

'Devin would. May I remind you that you have a commitment to Timmy Taylor to wear his dress tonight? He's worked very hard to make it easy to look beautiful in – if not easy to put on.'

'That's just it, Kit. I'm sick and tired of looking beautiful. My face hurts.'

'And whose fault is that? I told you not to take those modelling jobs. How you honestly thought that having your face appear on the cover of anything with pages could help *Last Chance*...'

'You don't know for sure. Maybe it *is* helping. Maybe if you did one of your marketing surveys, they'd tell you –'

'Stop honking at me, Verena.'

'Honking?'

'You sound like a goose. You're bearing down too hard on your vocal cords. Think of them as a delicate instrument – with which you happen to make your living.'

'Jeesh, you sound like Brendan.' Verena lowered her voice to a Marsh-like growl. ' "Even a Stradivarius when sawed upon can produce the sound of a dog shitting razor blades." '

'Somehow, it sounds more quaint out of Brendan's mouth – but never mind, you need a vacation. I've already decided to shoot around you for the first four weeks. You'll go up to Millbrook and mellow out, as you'd put it.'

'I don't want to mellow out. I want to work.'

'Did it ever occur to you that you're trying to run away from reality?'

'I'm an actress. That's my job. Me and Brendan are two of a kind.'

'That's "Brendan and *I*". That's no reason why you shouldn't learn to control it early. I knew it wasn't a good idea to let you stay there alone. If Brendan hadn't insisted –'

'Look, can you blame him? I've been living over you guys' heads for a year now. I'd think you'd want to be alone once in a while.'

They'd been some family out at Clara this past year, Verena sleeping upstairs on a convertible futon with Kit and Brendan down below in Kit's bedroom. She heard them some nights when the surf below was calm: Brendan's voice vibrating Clara's windows and Kit's laugh rising like little bubbles up the spiral staircase. Only Brendan could make Kit burst into laughter that way. Suddenly Verena realised what Kit was so uptight about: this was the first time she'd been alone in a year.

'I'll be fine,' she assured Kit for the millionth time.

'Will you really?'

'Sure. I'm Sally Stable. Remember me?'

'I wish I believed that.'

'You've been talking to Liberty.'

'I have not. Where would Liberty find time to discuss your welfare?'

'Well, before the baby was born, she talked to you plenty. I can tell. About me seeing a shrink, right?'

'It isn't the worst idea in the world, you know.'

'You *have* been talking to her, and it is too the worst idea. Shrinks suck. Ask Brendan.'

'Verena, not all shrinks suck.'

'Yeah, well, how do you know when you've got a good one? Forget it. I'm an actress. I can act it all out.'

'I wish I thought that were a healthy solution.'

'I wish you'd stop wishing. I swear, the two of you!'

'Verena?' She heard muffled voices on the line. Kit got back on. 'You'll have to excuse me. Some people have just arrived. I promise I'll send someone from the office to do you up. Meanwhile, finish your snack and take some deep breaths. Do a little yoga warm-up. It will help you feel surer of your poise later tonight.'

'Poise? I'll probably trip on the carpet and fall flat on my face in front of the *Entertainment Tonight* reporter and millions of her faithful viewers.'

Kit wasn't listening. 'I'm sure you will. Good girl. Well, I'll see you soon.' Verena heard Kit kiss the phone and hang up. Verena put down the receiver slowly and sat staring at the mantelpiece, taking deep breaths, like the lady said.

Even in the dark, she knew that the mantel was empty, that the photographs in their jewelled and velvet-padded frames had been swept away to lie in storage somewhere until one of them, herself or Mandy, had the guts to bring them out, Rush and all, and look at them.

Rush and all. That was the rub. His father and mother on their wedding day in Constantinople before they boarded the ship to come to America. Her grandfather, old, white-haired Poppup, standing beside his wife, Cynthia, who looked more like his daughter, pale hair and dress blowing in the tropical breeze. Young Kitsia in a white dress and baby Archer in a sailor suit. Kitsia and Mandy arm-in-arm beside one of Kitsia's Angels in the courtyard of her house in Zwar. Kitsia and Verena on that same afternoon. Verena and Rush at the Ruba party.

The truth was that no matter where the pictures went, she and her mother – and Archer as well – would be spending the rest of their lives trying to reconcile themselves to the memory of a man who had lived among them, known their love, and still betrayed them. But had they each betrayed him as well?

'Look,' Liberty had said that afternoon outside the church where they'd gone to compose themselves during Rush's funeral service, 'for seventeen – sixteen, if you want to discount the year you ran away – *fucked-up* years, he was your father. Like it or not, he's a part of you.'

She might have been part of him, but Verena did not want to go to his funeral. Mandy had made her. Akmed's yacht had exploded two days after Rush died. It was then that they had all made an agreement to keep everything – from the vendetta to how Rush died – out of the papers. When Verena said she wanted everyone to know about Rush, Liberty told her that Dhali had kept his word. He had had his own brother killed. Even Liberty promised not to publish her story – her novel, as she now saw it – for a year and a half. All Verena had to do was to go to the funeral and carry on like Rush Alexander's bereaved daughter. She could act that part for Mandy.

But it hadn't been Mandy who had made her look at him lying in the open casket. She had made herself do that, looking out of the corner of her eye. It hadn't been hard. She'd spent most of her life looking at him out of the corner of her eye. With his perfect hands folded neatly over his dark blue lapels, in his maroon striped tie, he had looked alive to her. She'd turned to Liberty in the procession and whispered, 'I think somebody's made a terrible mistake. This man's still alive.'

They'd crammed their white gloves into their mouths to keep from laughing out loud and quickly filed up the aisle and out of the church, bursting into giggles. It had been too much: the casket lid covered with daisies, the eight beefy pallbearers who, under the terms of the will, had to be not only of Russian descent but also occupied at one time or another as bouncers. Though they all thought Mandy was crazy, she carried out Rush's specifications to the letter – through it all, never saying a word against him. Nor did she ever shed a single tear.

But outside the church, Verena's laughter finally turned to sobs; she'd broken down and cried for the first time since he died.

Later she had asked Liberty if she supposed Rush was looking up at them and laughing.

'For giving him his daisies and his hero's funeral?' Liberty said. 'You bet he's laughing. Only he's up there.' She pointed to the blue, blue sky.

'Rush in heaven? You've got to be putting me on!'

'Absolutely not,' Liberty said solemnly. 'Haven't you heard the myth of Castor and Pollux? Only Pollux was divine, but Castor won a sort of immortality because of his brother's love. Archer's love for Rush got him past the pearly gates, take my word for it.'

'A lot of us gave him that love,' Verena thought.

She clambered up to the top of a stack of boxes in his room and looked around for the last time: then she climbed back down. She paused at the door, whispering, 'I forgive you'.

As she closed the doors behind her, she met her face in the mirror, horrified. 'Did I really say I forgave him? Liberty's right, I do need to see a shrink.'

Just then the front doorbell rang. 'Gee, that was fast. You suppose they brought a straitjacket with them?' She ran to answer the door.

Jay Scott, looking chipper and handsome in a double-breasted tuxedo, black velvet bow tie, Scotch plaid trousers and spats, held out a bouquet of wild roses. Verena took them with a hoarse squeal of delight.

'They're gorgeous, Scottie! Just like the ones that grow outside of Clara. Where did you get them?'

'Where else? Talk about straitjackets, I hear this item you're wearing has forty-seven teeny-tiny pearl buttons between your shoulder blades and your tush. Good thing I have the hands of a surgeon.' He held them up and they trembled. Verena dragged him into the hall.

'You're a godsend, Scottie. I've been sitting here talking to ghosts and Kit. I'm not sure which is more depressing.'

'Ghosts! Ghosts! This is no night to entertain ghosts. I'm not Scrooge, and you, my dear, are certainly no Tiny Tim.'

He walked ahead of her into the house and turned the lights on in the parlour. 'Look at this place.' He ripped the dust sheets off the Provençal love seat. 'No wonder you're talking to ghosts. I'm sure I would too in this mausoleum. Let's liven the joint up.'

He went around uncovering all the furniture and turning on the lights.

'Now,' he said, wiggling his fingers, 'about those buttons.' While he worked, he asked her, 'Champagne on the premises, by any chance?'

'Somebody sent me a bottle of Dom this afternoon. Brendan said to watch out, it might be from Bic Crawford. But just in case it wasn't, I put it in the fridge.'

'I sent you that bottle and I'll have you know it's Dom 57. There.' He finished buttoning her and spun her around. 'You look stunning. Now, go and get your glass slippers while I pour the bubbly.'

Verena hesitated at the door. 'It feels weird not to have to be combing my hair.' She reached up and pulled a one-inch tuft.

'Your haircut looks dynamite. Don't worry. *You* can carry it off.'

'I look like a pinhead.'

'Go get your shoes and bag, pinhead.'

When Verena came back down, Jay stood at the foot of the stairs with glass raised.

'To a lovely young actress who will, I know, live up to her promise.'

Verena took a glass for herself and sipped modestly. 'I never make promises. No, seriously, it's been thanks to you. And to Brendan. And to Kit.'

'Isn't it strange the way we're all over the place this evening?' Jay asked. 'You'd think we'd all be huddled together holding hands, but we're really scattered. Kit is in the Ransome screening room on the phone with everybody and her mother – Kirk on the bridge of the *Enterprise*. Brendan's loping around like a grizzly bear looking for a tea party. And now that he doesn't drink, he's even more nervous than he used to be. And me? Well, I'm here getting slowly but surely drunk with a minor.'

'Correction,' Verena said. *'Major.'*

'I'll drink to that,' Jay emptied his glass and quickly refilled it.

After they'd drunk to everyone they could think of – Herman Miller; Kit; Brendan; Michael Sheridan, even; Liberty and Eben's new baby; Kit and Brendan and Jay's newly formed production company – Jay, looking thunderstruck, hit his forehead. 'I forgot.'

'Forgot what?'

'Devin's out in the limo waiting. I forgot to bring him in.'

'That's okay. We'll open another bottle in the limo.' She picked up the bottle and stared down its neck. 'For a half-empty bottle, it's mighty heavy.'

'We can lighten it up in a minute.'

As they rose for a final toast, Jay said, 'To who will undoubtedly be the next best actress.'

Verena started to drink, but stopped, puzzled. 'Wait a sec. *Next* best actress? Next to who? Let me at her!'

'No, silly goose. I mean next year's Best Actress at the Academy Awards presentation.'

'Oh, that thing they hold in The Dorothy Chowder Pavilion! Well, in that case, here's to the next best director, too.' She hiccuped and finished off her drink.

They set down their glasses, Jay Scott put out his arm, and Verena took it.

'Fasten your seat belt, Cinderella, it's going to be a bumpy pumpkin ride.'

'Kit? Is that you? What are you doing in here in the dark? Where are the goddamned lights?'

'Don't turn them on.' Kit spoke in a hoarse whisper.

'It's almost time, you know.' Brendan felt his way across the darkened screening room and sat down next to her. He reached out for her hand.

'It seems like a lifetime ago when we started *Last Chance*.' She stared unblinking at the white screen. 'I was just thinking about –'

'Kit,' Brendan interrupted her, 'no matter what happens tonight, I want you to remember that I love you.'

Kit fiddled with her earring, twisting it around and around.

398

'I don't know why I let them talk me into this screening. If it goes badly, it's over.'

'Jesus, Kit. You sound as nuts as Scottie. Don't you know it will be okay?'

She turned to look at him. His face was in shadows. She couldn't see him. For an instant she couldn't remember what he looked like. 'No, I don't,' she said simply.

'Miss Ransome.' It was Frank, the projectionist, on the intercom. 'Your car is downstairs waiting for you.'

Kit raised her hand towards the small projection window and waved her answer.

'Brendan?'

'Yes.'

'Radio City Music Hall! It has *six thousand* seats. We should have had a small screening first.'

'Doesn't matter. Six, six hundred, six million. It's time, Kit. You have to show the baby.'

'But it's not ready yet. If Randy would only have postponed the release date. Given us a little more time to work on the music. It isn't quite there...' Her voice trailed off with a sigh.

'You're scared.' There was wonder in Brendan's voice.

Kit stood up, hands limp at her sides. Finally she started to climb the spiral staircase. She stopped halfway up and spoke down to Brendan. 'You coming? We're already late.'

'You know I never go to screenings. I'll catch up with you later,' he mumbled.

Kit gripped the banister. It was cold and her hand wrapped easily around it.

'Don't make me go alone. Please.' She tried not to sound like she was begging.

'Can't, Kit. I just can't go.'

Kit walked up the rest of the stairs. She looked around the office. They had redone it. All the white had been scraped away like so much ice. Even the marble had been stripped from the walls. Kit stared down at the blue carpet. Maybe it covered the bloodstains. The banks and the lawyers were dismantling Ransome Enterprises. They probably preferred corporate blues and beiges. It showed discretion, even a little humility.

She walked over to the windows and leaned against the glass, looking down. Fifth Avenue was dressed for Christmas: only one week away. Kit hadn't spent Christmas in New York in over ten years. Last Christmas she had gone to Zwar to visit Kitsia. It hadn't gone particularly well. Kitsia was more obsessed than ever with her work and Kit herself was so nervous about Verena's first shooting days on *Last Chance* that she had insomnia every night and slept away most of the days in her mother's courtyard.

Archer's driver, Ali, slammed the limousine door shut. Kit sat back, grateful for the traffic jam before them. She wanted to postpone this evening for as long as possible. No one had seen the final film yet – except for Scottie and herself. Scottie thought it was a masterpiece; Kit was convinced it was a disaster. She didn't cry at the end. A real tearjerker, but she hadn't shed one tear.

'Miss Ransome...' Ali spoke up. 'Shall I take you to the side entrance of Radio City?'

Kit nodded. She spied a small arrangement of yellow bud roses sitting on the car's bar. She looked for the card. Written in a shaky hand was the message: 'Good luck tonight, Daughter. Archer'. Kit had offered to screen *Last Chance* for him and Mandy last night up at Millbrook, but Archer had declined her offer, saying, 'I'd rather read about it in the New York *Times*.' Kit had been relieved. She didn't really want Archer to come to the première. She was nervous enough.

Ali pulled the car up to the kerb. Kit looked out at the narrow gold door, a miniature of the front doors.

'Ali, take me around to the front.'

'But, Miss Ransome, there will be photographers and –'

'I know. It's okay.' Kit pulled a mirror out of her evening bag and looked at herself. Her newly cut hair hung straight to her shoulders, her black pearl earrings barely visible. She fingered the pin that decorated her low-cut neckline – a small cloisonné turtle – and snapped the compact shut.

The car door was opened by a young man in a tuxedo with white gloves. Kit stepped out onto a plush red carpet. She looked up. Enormous klieg lights mounted on flatbed trucks were throwing beams taller than the skyscrapers on Sixth Avenue.

'Is Marsh with her?' one of the photographers called out.

'Where's Brendan?' a young man in a blue windbreaker with a minicam over his shoulder asked. He pointed his camera at Kit, and another shone a spotlight on her face.

'She's alone. He must be in the next limo.'

The light was instantly turned off and the cameraman backed away.

'This way, Miss Ransome.' A studio publicist directed her towards the door; she was holding up the arrivals. The crowds standing behind stanchions were kept on the pavement by police on horseback.

'Miss Ransome, look this way, please.'

Kit turned towards the voice. It was Arnold Blatsky.

'Sorry to hear about your mother.'

Kit hesitated, not sure what to say.

'Smile.' His camera clicked. A flash crisscrossed her vision, momentarily startling her.

'Thanks.'

Kit was propelled through the doors by a famous rock singer who was desperately trying to avoid the photographers. His entourage surrounded him like offensive linemen protecting a quarterback.

Devin Lowe scrambled from behind the red velvet ropes that separated the VIPs from the ordinary guests.

'Kit, over here!'

'Oh, Devin.' Kit was relieved.

'Great crowd.' Devin was at her ear. 'About five hundred press people. Six hundred friends, cast and crew, celebs. And the rest are regular people.'

'Regular people?' Kit repeated densely.

'They'll let us know what we've got...'

'Or don't have,' Randy Sheridan finished for him. 'Hello, Kit. You look lovely.'

'Hello, Randy.' She held herself stiffly while he kissed her cheek.

Sheridan was edgy. 'God, I hope we don't bomb tonight. I think the press is really waiting for this one. We should start. It's eight-oh-five.'

'Fine. Devin, let's start.' Kit was trying not to show Randy just how close she thought he was to the truth.

'We can't start. The mayor's coming.' Devin spoke quickly, looking from one to the other. 'We should hold five or six more minutes.'

'Five minutes. No more!' Sheridan disappeared into the theatre.

'Get him!' said Devin, his eyes never leaving the lobby doors, scanning the crowd for the mayor.

Kit grabbed Devin's arm to get his attention. 'Verena arrived yet?'

'Yeah. She was being interviewed by some bitch from *Entertainment Tonight*.'

'Devin.'

'Well, what do you call someone who asks Verena what it feels like to make her debut in one of the most over-budget movies ever made?'

'She didn't.'

'I walked away after that. I wanted to hit her. Verena's probably upstairs now in the reserved section. Where's Brendan? Isn't he with you?'

'No, he's coming later,' Kit lied. 'I'd better go up.'

'I should stay here. Can you find your seat by yourself?' Devin pressed two cards into her hand.

Kit pushed through the art-deco doors and made her way towards the grand staircase. The inner lobby was crowded with people elbowing their way towards their seats, some making large circles around famous actors or TV personalities, who stood talking in small groups. In one corner of the vast lobby a news crew was interviewing people before they went into the theatre. A giant Christmas tree stood in the centre of the room. It was decorated with plaid bows, candy canes, and hundreds of white lights. The houselights blinked on and off and the audience flowed together into the theatre.

Kit stood motionless, watching the lobby empty. Such a beautiful old-fashioned movie palace. They just didn't build them this way any more. It was too impractical. *Last Chance* was as old-fashioned as the theatre; she hoped with all her heart it wasn't impractical too.

'Can I show you to your seat, madam? The show is about to start.' An usher held out her hand for Kit's tickets and clicked on her torch.

Kit stepped away from the woman, shaking her head. She looked around nervously and on an impulse started running up the steps.

At the uppermost balcony, breathless and slightly faint, she found a seat and watched as the red curtain parted to reveal a dark screen. Small white letters came on one by one spelling out: 'A Kit Ransome Production of a Jay Scott Film'. Then, in letters seemingly storeys high, came on Brendan's name. Weak, scattered applause. Kit had trouble catching her breath.

'The music's too loud,' the man next to her said to his date.

'Shh.'

Kit looked at her watch – 8:13. She didn't know how she was going to sit still for two hours. She wondered if Brendan would come at all. He had to come; she couldn't face this by herself.

Close-up on Verena's face. A slow pull-back.

'I can't hear her. What did she say?' a woman behind her asked.

Panicked that the soundtrack was badly recorded, Kit jumped up and ran out of the auditorium and down one flight of stairs. She stood on the landing, winded, talking to herself, convincing herself that the print was fine. She decided not to go back into the theatre. Tired, she looked around for somewhere to sit. She spied a telephone booth and went over and sat down. One hour and fifty minutes to go.

She dialled Information. 'Operator, what is the number of Mt Sinai Hospital?'

Kit repeated the number as she dialled. 'Liberty Adams, please.'

'Hello.'

'Liberty.'

'Hey, Kit.'

Pleased that Liberty recognised her voice, Kit relaxed a little. 'How are you? Am I calling at a bad time?'

'I'm great, Kit. How about you? Shouldn't you be at Radio City?'

'I am. But...'

'Don't tell me. You thought you'd catch up on a few calls.'

'I'm afraid to sit in there.'

'I can imagine.'

'How's your baby?'

'She's beautiful. She's funny, too.'

'I'll bet she is. How do you feel?'

'Like the luckiest woman in the world.'

'Oh, Liberty, I envy you.'

'Can't miss what you don't know, Kit. Besides, you have babies. You have your movies.'

'That's kind of what Brendan said tonight.'

'He did? Well, that just shows how smart your friends are. You know what Brendan sent me after the baby was born? A tiny... I mean teeny-tiny Christmas tree, decorated with real balls and different-coloured lights.'

'I never told her I loved her before she died.' It just came out.

Liberty switched gears smoothly, her voice gentle. 'She knew you loved her. Anyway, she wouldn't have wanted you to be concerned with what she – or anyone – thought.'

'Are you going to teach your daughter not to care what other people think?'

Kit could hear the phone drop and then a muffled sound. 'Liberty, are you all right?'

'Yeah. Sorry I dropped you, but they just brought her to me.'

Liberty nursed her newborn as the two sisters talked at length. Finally Kit calmed down.

'I'll come over and see you tomorrow, okay?'

'We can't wait, Aunt Kit. Good luck.' Liberty hung up.

Kit sat there for a long time, then looked at her watch; it was almost ten-fifteen. She wanted to see the last scene in the movie. She ran downstairs. She had to see how it looked.

Rushing into the mezzanine level, Kit saw the final scene of Judd Hines crying at his son's grave. Lacy was standing off in the distance, dry-eyed. Brendan's face slowly dissolved into blackness. In white letters across the screen it read: 'This film is dedicated to Kitsia Ransome'. Suddenly Kit missed her mother terribly. She thought back to the funeral that day in Zwar: the heat in the foundry bearing down on her, making her dizzy; the molten bronze coursing beneath her. Ashes. Was that all that was left of her mother? Her eyes filled with tears. She searched frantically for Brendan and Verena. Wasn't this where Devin told her they would be when they finally arrived?

The houselights came up very slowly. The audience was silent. Kit looked down. A couple of people walked, heads down, to the exit. Her heart thudded. No one liked the film. She sat down in one of the empty chairs, exhausted.

Then suddenly six thousand people all began to clap at once. The house filled with a deafening roar. Abruptly a spotlight was turned on the seats across from her and all eyes followed the white beam of light. The audience stood up, applauding the stars, who looked dazzling – Brendan in a traditional tuxedo and, holding his hand, Verena in the gold gown.

Kit stood up, starting to cry. She joined the applause for her actors, clapping harder and harder until her hands burned.

As Verena pulled Jay Scott up to the front, the audience went wild. Kit fumbled in her bag for a Kleenex.

'Will this do, madam?' A red silk handkerchief was waved before her.

Brendan's mouth was warm on hers. He pulled back and smiled. 'They're clapping for you, Kit. It's all for you.'

BEACHES

IRIS RAINER DART

FOR EVERY WOMAN WHO HAS EVER HAD A BEST FRIEND

Cee Cee and Roberta. Two strikingly different women who
from the moment of their first meeting are friends . . . for life.

For thirty years they shared their loves and losses, excitement
and tears, their fallings-out and ups and downs. Cee Cee becomes
a Hollywood celebrity while Roberta is content as a quiet
suburban mother.

But the day would come when their friendship came full circle,
when tragedy would tear them apart, and only a little girl's love
could bring them to the shores of peace.

0 7221 2816 9   GENERAL FICTION   £2.95

MOMENTS TO TREASURE...

FAMILY ALBUM

The major new novel by

Danielle Steel

Shipping heir Ward Thayer and screen star Faye Price
fell hopelessly in love. Within weeks they were married.
But how was Faye to choose between her Hollywood
career and motherhood? How could she decide between
fame and family? Faye's choice would not only change
her life: it would shape the lives of generations to come.

From the uncertain post-war days, through Hollywood
in the storm-torn political years and the turmoil of the
Vietnam era right up to the present ... FAMILY
ALBUM follows the Thayer dynasty through generations
of love and hope, of strife and reconciliation.

"A big lush saga in the Dallas mould ... compulsive".
Sunday Telegraph

0 7221 8305 4   **General Fiction**   **£2.95**

Don't miss Danielle Steel's other bestsellers – also available in Sphere Books:

THE PROMISE	**A PERFECT STRANGER**	**SUMMER'S END**
(based on a screenplay by Garry Michael White)	**TO LOVE AGAIN**	**REMEMBRANCE**
NOW AND FOREVER	**LOVING**	**CROSSING**
SEASON OF PASSION	**THE RING**	**THURSTON HOUSE**
GOLDEN MOMENTS	**PALOMINO**	**CHANGES**
GOING HOME	**LOVE POEMS**	**FULL CIRCLE**
ONCE IN A LIFETIME		

A selection of bestsellers from SPHERE

FICTION

BEACHES	Iris Rainer Dart	£2.95 ☐
RAINBOW SOLDIERS	Walter Winward	£3.50 ☐
FAMILY ALBUM	Danielle Steel	£2.95 ☐
SEVEN STEPS TO TREASON	Michael Hartland	£2.50 ☐

FILM AND TV TIE-IN

9$\frac{1}{2}$ WEEKS	Elizabeth McNeil	£1.95 ☐
BOON	Anthony Masters	£2.50 ☐
AUF WIEDERSEHEN PET 2	Fred Taylor	£2.75 ☐
LADY JANE	Anthony Smith	£1.95 ☐

NON-FICTION

THE FALL OF SAIGON	David Butler	£3.95 ☐
LET'S FACE IT	Christine Piff	£2.50 ☐
LIVING WITH DOGS	Sheila Hocken	£3.50 ☐
HOW TO SHAPE UP YOUR MAN		
	Catherine & Neil Mackwood	£2.95 ☐

All Sphere books are available at your local bookshop or newsagent, or can be ordered direct from the publisher. Just tick the titles you want and fill in the form below.

Name _____

Address _____

_____

Write to Sphere Books, Cash Sales Department, P.O. Box 11, Falmouth, Cornwall TR10 9EN.

Please enclose cheque or postal order to the value of the cover price plus:

UK: 55p for the first book, 22p for the second and 14p per copy for each additional book ordered to a maximum charge of £1.75.

OVERSEAS: £1.00 for the first book and 25p for each additional book.

BFPO & EIRE: 55p for the first book, 22p for the second book plus 14p per copy for the next 7 books, thereafter 8p per book.

Sphere Books reserve the right to show new retail prices on covers which may differ from those previously advertised in the text or elsewhere, and to increase postal rates in accordance with the PO.